MW00987511

METALLIC REALMS

Also by Lincoln Michel

Upright Beasts
The Body Scout

METALLIC REALMS

— *A Novel* —

LINCOLN MICHEL

ATRIA BOOKS

New York   Amsterdam/Antwerp   London
Toronto   Sydney/Melbourne   New Dehli

ATRIA
BOOKS

An Imprint of Simon & Schuster, LLC
1230 Avenue of the Americas
New York, NY 10020

First Atria Books hardcover edition May 2025

ATRIA BOOKS and colophon are trademarks of Simon & Schuster, LLC

Simon & Schuster strongly believes in freedom of expression and stands against censorship in all its forms. For more information, visit BooksBelong.com.

For information about special discounts for bulk purchases, please contact Simon & Schuster Special Sales at 1-866-506-1949 or business@simonandschuster.com.

The Simon & Schuster Speakers Bureau can bring authors to your live event. For more information or to book an event, contact the Simon & Schuster Speakers Bureau at 1-866-248-3049 or visit our website at www.simonspeakers.com.

Interior design by Lexy East

Manufactured in the United States of America

1   3   5   7   9   10   8   6   4   2

Library of Congress Cataloging-in-Publication Data has been applied for.

ISBN 978-1-6680-5867-1
ISBN 978-1-6680-5869-5 (ebook)

For my friends.
Sorry.

MEMOIRS OF
MY METALLIC REALMS

The Collected Star Rot Chronicles

Tales by the Orb 4 writing collective:
Taras K. Castle, Darya Azali, Jane Noh Johnson, and S.O.S. Merlin

Edited with notes, commentary, analysis, and musings
by Michael Lincoln

Foreword by Michael Lincoln

Introduction by Michael Lincoln

Afterword by Michael Lincoln

After-Afterword by Michael Lincoln

"I love * *science fiction with its gals and goons, suspense and suspensories."*
—*Vladimir Nabokov*

---

* This quote, from a 1968 BBC interview, appears on some websites as "I *loathe* science fiction . . ." I can only assume this was an autocorrect error that has propagated across the internet or else a verbal typo by Mr. Nabokov himself. Who could loathe suspense and suspensories?! One cannot believe everything one reads online. This is a truth I hope you, dear reader, will keep in mind if you encounter any of the distortions, fabrications, and outright slanders that have been spread about me since the tragedy.

Foreword: The High Cost of Galaxies

Dear reader, gird yourself. These pages aren't mere paper but a portal to arguably one of the greatest achievements in science fiction imagination of the twenty-first century in any subgenre, language, or artistic medium. As a fan, I quake with jealousy. I wish I too were freshly encountering the manifold wonders of *The Star Rot Chronicles*. The ensuing tales are apt to sear into your mind more powerfully than most milestones of so-called "real life." I close my eyes—here in this cold basement where I compose these notes—and scenes appear as films projected upon the insides of my eyelids. The escape from the solar whale! The great war of the Adamites! The chilling return of— Oh, I must stop myself. No spoilers in my scholarship. I can recall these moments with greater clarity than my first kiss,* high school graduation, or even the tragic events of 9/11 that so defined the America of my young adulthood.

As your intrepid editor and *Star Rot* whisperer, I'll confess I occasionally ponder how my life might've differed if I'd never discovered *The Star Rot Chronicles*. Likely, I'd have finished law school. There'd be no possible warrant for my arrest. I might have a steady job. A mortgage. A loving partner. The patter of pajamaed feet running up the stairs of my two-story suburban home; I pivot in my ergonomic office chair to see a young boy and girl in matching striped jammies rush to hug my legs and then look up with wide-eyed cherub

---

* Admittedly, I remember less about the kiss—a dry peck from Jenny Taylor—than the aftermath, when Taras informed me that a picture was circulating the cafeteria featuring my chapped lips (it was winter) stretching toward Taylor's grimacing face. It'd been a dare. Teenagers are crueler than any galactic tyrant.

faces to say, "Daddy, we love you. Daddy, you are special. Daddy, you are our universe."

Pedestrian pleasures. I have another universe, and it is the Metallic Realms.

Just what are *The Star Rot Chronicles*? Put simply, they're a cycle of inter-connected space opera tales detailing the adventures of the ragtag crew of the good ship *Star Rot* in a sector of the galaxy known as the "Metallic Realms." That you're likely encountering them for the first time represents two trage-dies. First, the narrow-minded, backward-looking parochialism of the ivory tower elites who jealously guard the walled city of Literature™ and recoil in terror at the first sign of imagination, shouting, "Genre barbarians, stay away! We're afraid of your wondrous plots and fantastic characters! Your uncanny visions challenge our perceptions! Leave, please, for we are frightened!"

The second tragedy is the untimely dissolution of the Orb 4, the artistic collective slash literary movement slash science fiction philosophy that cre-ated the otherworldly tales before collapsing under the very earthly pressures of jealousy, love, greed, and (as I will argue in my ensuing analysis) undiag-nosed mental health issues.

It's a wild and improbable story. And like all memorable tales it ends in tragedy. For now, suffice to say, *The Star Rot Chronicles* were the creation of several of the finest minds science fiction has produced this millennium: Taras K. Castle, Darya Azali, Jane Noh Johnson, and S.O.S. Merlin. To have known them at their creative peak, as I did, was something special indeed. They exuded imagination as effortlessly as the blort worms of Delta Red se-crete toxic gas.[*] I hope my accompanying commentary will shed light on their individual personalities and provide insight into why the Orb 4 was, like a core-collapsing star, destined to go supernova.

Uncanny. An explosion outside the window of this dim basement where I compose these notes. The gunshot of some illiterate hunter walking past the *No Trespassing* signs, one hopes. For a moment, I thought I saw dark figures hiding behind the trees. They moved from trunk to trunk. The police circling

---

[*] See "Memoirs of My Metallic Realms—Part II."

the house for ambush? But the figments vanished. Hallucinations conjured by my addled and Adderalled mind operating on thirty-six hours without sleep. Looking now, I see only the bluish-white expanse of the frozen world. Snow is falling. It patters against the pane. I pull the shawl tighter around my shoulders.

All is quiet except for the squawking imitation car alarm of my parrot, Arthur C. Caique. (A regrettable habit he picked up back in Brooklyn.) As I shiver by the space heater, surrounded by my copious notes, I cannot help but look back on *The Star Rot Chronicles* with both fondness and regret. Could I have done more to save the collective? Could I have prevented the ultimate tragedy? No. I must not think this way. My task is preservation, not self-recrimination.

The stories collected here represent all verified canonical entries. It's impossible to know how many fragments, sketches, and final drafts have been kept from this volume because of human pettiness. A Library of Alexandria of contemporary American science fiction short stories may be forever lost. However, I'm delighted to announce to Rotties (as fans are wont to call themselves) a never-before-published *Star Rot Chronicles* entry will appear as a bonus addendum.

Each tale herein uses the most recent draft available in the Orb 4's Google Drive folder—of which I was given explicit and unrestrained access to, none can dispute. The only editorial liberties I've taken are to remove the occasional "exposition dumps" that were needed when these tales were published individually yet proved redundant when compiled in a single collection.

My goal in this volume is twofold. First, to preserve for posterity the vital literary output of the Orb 4 even as—nay, especially as—the group's collapse risks consigning this era-defining work to the dustbin of literary history. (I will not let that happen, Taras.) Second, after plucking the stories from said dustbin and brushing them clean, I aim to provide readers with the necessary context for understanding and appreciation. Each story will be accompanied by my scholarly notes, relevant memories, thematic unpacking, and explanations of the singular lore of *The Star Rot Chronicles*. Although I am prone to occasional hyperbole, I will endeavor to restrict myself to purely scholarly assessment in this volume. Time willing, I shall draw a few maps.

I must compose my notes sequentially with minimal time for revision or backtracking. Luckily, I have ample material to pull from including the Google Drive files, group chat messages, private recordings,* the official *Star Rot Chronicles Lore Bible,* and my own (94 percent recall) memories. My remarks will be robust. Still, I beg my readers' forgiveness for any typos or continuity errors.

On that note, allow me to welcome you to the Metallic Realms. As the lovable scoundrel Aul-Wick might say, "Let's blast off so the adventure never ends!"

Yours in science fiction and scholarship,

Michael Lincoln, B.A.

Scholar, Writer, Senior Lore Keeper, Editor, Fan

---

* Fully legal by my reading of the State of New York's one-party consent law.

Introduction: An Ear at the Edge of the Universe

Why I Am the Most Qualified to Write this Volume

Before we begin, you might be wondering why yours truly has the honor of chronicling the rise and fall of the Metallic Realms? Simple. I was there. Reader, I was there! I saw the highs of imagination. I saw the lows of interpersonal drama. And I saw it all, like a stenographer fly on the wall, from my disheveled bed.

Allow me to explain.

Our tale commences in the winter chill of Brooklyn in January. The sidewalks are a mélange of slush, rock salt, and dog urine. The mood is grim. The people sour. The Metallic Realms are but a dream in the mind of a young man named Taras K. Castle whose genius is wasted at ThoughtFunnel writing sponsored content for corporate brands desperate to "tap into" the millennial market as if our generation were maple trees whose sappy blood was made of monetizable data. Taras awakes to incessant beeping. Is it his cell phone pinging with witty memes from his old pal Michael? No. His phone is on vibrate. He sniffs the air. Smoke. An alarm. Fire! Taras scrambles out of the apartment into the cold and uncaring NYC streets, carrying nothing save his laptop and his life.

If the multiverse exists, there are infinite realities in which *The Star Rot Chronicles* are never written. In those dystopian timelines, the book in your hands never exists and the field of science fiction is notably impoverished. Luckily, we exist in this timeline, so this is only the inciting incident of our tale.

After this mysterious fire and firemen's hosing leaves Taras K. Castle's apartment a smoldering and soggy ruin, he moves into mine. I've recently acquired the lease on a capacious walk-up apartment in Bushwick. It's a converted warehouse space on the top floor of a squat brick building. The unassuming entrance is squeezed between a dingy bodega (Gourmet Delights Grocery & Deli) and a hardware store (Tool Town). The ceiling's exposed pipes and the floor's intermittent divots give the unit an urban "glamping" vibe reminiscent of my Vermont childhood. The apartment has three bedrooms and a large kitchen slash dining slash living slash family room. Taras's bedroom is beside mine and down the hall lies the bedroom of my other roommate, Cast. More on them later.

Taras sleeps on an air mattress for a few days, returning to his apartment to forage for items and deal with the inspectors. Taras's life has long been punctuated with misfortune. Ever since his younger brother's tragic death at the age of five, Taras has felt a black cloud lingers over his family. A curse from the old country. He hasn't been able to lose it even among the gleaming towers of New York City.

In any event, I'm pleased to offer a place to rest and reboot. "Thanks, Mike. It'll probably only be for a few weeks. God, what a shit year." Taras and I are old friends. We have the bond of warriors who've fought side by side in the demon-filled dungeon levels of public school. I know we'll get through this latest struggle together.

What should I say about Taras? He seems to have been engineered in utero as an artist. When we were children, he could turn anything from Legos to Silly Putty into a creative outlet. In high school, he dabbled as a DJ, made amateur films, and mapped complex dungeons for RPG campaigns. But his main love was the written word. By the time he had graduated college, he'd completed an entire oeuvre (albeit unpublished) of screenplays, comics, and short stories. Then, a breakthrough. He began a series of space adventure tales titled *The Curious Voyages of the Incurious Captain Baldwin*. I discovered the drafts on a members-only SFF board that Taras mentioned in passing. It took me a while to track them down. Reader, I was ensorcelled.

The tales combined the high adventures of *Buck Rogers* with the philosophical concerns of New Wave wizards like Le Guin, Wolfe, Delany, and Dick. Brief as they were, they seemed to encompass all science fiction. A cyberpunk tone would mingle with slipstream worldbuilding in a post-apocalyptic plot of steampunk machines and cosmic horror creations. I was more shocked and delighted when, months later, I learned he'd formed a writing collective with his girlfriend, Darya Azali, and a friend from college, Jane Noh Johnson. The three are collaborating on a science fiction universe. Each brings their own literary strengths, as will future Orb 4 member S.O.S. Merlin. But Taras is the nucleus. Everyone spins around him.

As I'm an aspiring hybrid author-critic-editor lacking direction—a sort of literary ronin, one might say—I wonder if my services may prove useful. I drop hints that his collective might have an eligible beta reader nearby. Taras seems pained at my generosity. "I keep telling you we're just goofing around and probably won't publish anything," he says with his typical modesty.* "But I'll let you know."

Daily persistence is rewarded. Taras arrives at my bedroom door with a knock and a sigh. "If you want to read, here you go. Just don't share them online or anything."

If the early stories were promising, these are revelations. Poring over those drafts, I know I've found my calling. Good riddance, law school. Hello, Metallic Realms.

On Our Appetite for the Astonishing

When did the seeds of imagination germinate in the soil of Taras's soul? Was the frozen rural New England landscape of our childhood a blank canvas that his mind filled with monsters, heroes, and wonders? Such mysteries will be investigated over the course of this volume as I elucidate the codes, allusions, and hidden meanings of *The Star Rot Chronicles*. That is not to say that the biographical details that informed the compositions—and of which

---

* If only he were able to hold this book in his well-moisturized hands!

I was frequently present to witness—are the "key" to "unlocking" them. One of the surest signs of our debasement as a culture is the insistence that fiction is biography. That the mystery and ineffability of art can be decoded by the cheap facts one would find on the Early Life section of a Wikipedia page. I blame psychology and social media for this trend. It is a scourge. Illiteracy. A disgrace.

And yet. Perhaps a careful scholar, steeped in the lore of his subject and working with firsthand knowledge of their lived tropes, may divine insights from the real-world facts of an author's life. After all, no one creates work in a vacuum. Now is the point at which to reveal my history with Taras K. Castle. To say Taras and I were old friends does a disservice to our bond. We were the oldest of friends. Our mothers were in Lamaze class together. We crawled into the world mere weeks apart. In the photos my parents intermittently text me, we appear as two identical pale blobs swaddled in blue fabric. You could not tell which of us would become the artist and which the scholar.

Although the Castle family lived only a neighborhood away, my family's address was shuffled into the newly opened elementary school during second grade.* The first day of class, I was desolate. Who were these strange beings in braids and blue jeans attempting to steal my pipe cleaners? Their hands were sticky with ichor (dried glue) and their faces streaked with bright markings (melted candy). I knew not their rites or customs. I felt like a space explorer crashed on a forbidden planet without even a snarky robot sidekick to aid me.

Luckily, weekends existed. My mother would drop me off at the Castles' place with a fanny pack filled with mixed nuts and organic juice boxes. The Castle House. A brown split-level home with a steep driveway at the end of the cul-de-sac. This was my escape from the torments of elementary school. The side door would open and there, framed in the electric light of the garage, would be Taras. We'd raid his parents' pantry, which was much better

---

* Kafka imagined no bureaucracy as nightmarish as Vermont school districting!

stocked than my own,* and run laughing into the backyard. Ah, those golden days of summer spent ripping open silver snack bags as we leaped around his trampoline.

It was during these playdates that our proclivities toward the marvelous went into hyperdrive. He introduced me to *Metroid* and I explained the plot of *Star Wars*. As we got older, we swapped copies of *The Hitchhiker's Guide to the Galaxy* for tomes of Tolkien. Finally, we were reunited in ninth grade—the area's twin middle schools fed into the same behemoth high—and debated Atwood and Gibson in the back of the cafeteria.

We weren't the happiest boys. Or perhaps I should speak only for myself. I was diagnosed with ADHD in kindergarten and my harried mother crammed my mouth with Ritalin before plopping me in front of a television. School was hard. Other children alternatively cruel and aloof. These purveyors of the imagination were like magical armor that protected me from the taunts of girls and the jeers of boys. What did I care of earthly torments when galaxies of adventure awaited me in the pages of my library books?

One time at the lunch table, while comparing our Warhammer 40k Chaos Marine paint jobs, Taras gestured his honey BBQ-soaked nugget at my Nurgle daemon. "Dude, we should create our own monsters. We could come up with some cool ones, right? Hell, why not make our own universe?"

"For Ms. Henderson's class?" I thought he was referring to our biology diorama project.†

"No, dude. Like. Why can't we think up our *own* Star Wars? Come up with our own aliens and planets and ships and shit. Goof around and make an RPG or something."

"Yes!" I said, shouted almost. "I'd love to."

"Cool."

We bumped fists. My mind tumbled a full load of ideas. Peculiar crea-

---

* My father was a purveyor of a soul-killing "health food" store named, bizarrely, The Barley Bard. Their logo was a cartoonish Hamlet saying, "To fu or not tofu?" No, the pun did not work.
† I ended up getting a C-minus because Ms. Henderson claimed that the forest moon of Endor didn't count as "a real ecosystem." My grade was docked further after I said, quite factually, that she was displaying "the same genocidal mindset as Darth Vader and the Empire."

tures. Cool spaceships. Unknown and uncanny worlds. I couldn't wait to get home and begin writing. A science fiction universe to make with Taras by my side, the co-god of our creation. I have been looking for that feeling ever since.

Alas. We never got around to it. Although I composed some initial notes, I was struck down by the plague: mononucleosis. By the time I recovered, an engrossing entry in the *Final Fantasy* series occupied my time. The usual exams and holidays. Summer camp. Boy Scouts. Before I knew it, we were graduating. College and the terrors of adulthood loomed. It was as if God had pressed fast-forward on my life.

Taras and I drifted apart. Separate colleges. Grad school in different cities. Failed careers. Life.

Years passed. Eons, it felt.

Sigh. Reflecting on my distant youth, it feels like my life has been a stroll down one long and dimly lit hallway where each year another dozen doors lock shut. The possibilities dwindle. Now I amble around, tugging at immovable handles, unsure of the exit. How did I end up in my thirties as a law school dropout living with roommates with no clear career, creative, or romantic paths before me? What poor choices led me to this state? I fear I'm drifting from my task. I hereby end this musing, except to say that what I admired about Taras was his bold assurance. While I dithered, Taras dove into the task. He became an artist. He conjured his universe.

And he conjured it in conjunction with others, as I've mentioned. Initially, these were Jane Noh Johnson and Darya Azali. Taras allowed me to read several of the group's early story drafts, including "Comets Falling like Tears from a Lonely Sky," "I Am Antimatter," and "GODBOT 9000." I reread each until I could nearly recite them. I also noticed a few plot holes that Taras was oddly uninterested in discussing. "Yeah, well, these are just sketches. Practice. A way to flesh out the characters, you know?" This proved true. None of those early tales are counted in the official chronology.

Still, you can understand my excitement when Taras convened a meeting of the Orb 4 in my apartment a few weeks after he moved in. Jane was in a New School dorm for her graduate studies and Darya's Cobble Hill studio apartment was too small. The authors would be sitting in my chairs and con-juring worlds with breaths drawn from the same air that circulated in my unworthy lungs. It was also the day that the real and true canonical *Star Rot Chronicles* #1 would debut.

How I Joined My First Orb 4 Meeting

Picture the scene. Your humble narrator sits in his bedroom, fidgeting. Should he run out and wipe down the tables again? Rearrange the outward-facing books on the shelves? No. That'd be fanboyish. Yet his excite-ment is so uncontrolled his bladder starts to loosen. (This man has suffered a small bladder his whole life, causing many problems at theme parks and college lectures.) He sprints to the bathroom. The doorbell dings midstream. He cinches and presses his eye to the crack of the bathroom door, which peers out into the common area. The giants are arriving.

First to enter is Jane Noh Johnson. A lithe woman with asymmetrical bangs, ripped black jeans, and tattoos of sharks swimming up her left arm. On that same arm, she wears two leather bracelets: one black with spiked studs and one pink with silver hearts. These bracelets symbolize the two ten-dencies at war within Jane. She is equal parts bold visionary and quiet wall-flower, thoughtful friend and standoffish lone wolf. Yes, she's a Gemini. Jane's dual nature also extends to her fiction, as she is currently enrolled in an MFA program writing dreary literary realism alongside the escapades of *The Star Rot Chronicles*.

Jane and Taras met in a college creative writing class, and then worked together on the school's lit mag, *Plums in the Icebox.** Jane moved home to Houston postcollege. After a couple of years living rent-free but "paying in massive psychological damage" she was accepted to the New School's MFA program. The two scribblers reunited in the core of the Big Apple.

---

* What I would give to see their early output! Sadly, none appears online. Two of Jane's poems—"Your Texts Have No Effects" and "Seven Ways of Looking at a Country You'll Never Know"—are listed in the table of contents of the Volume 5: Spring issue of *Plums in the Icebox*. However, the magazine appears to be defunct and my attempts to order a copy received only a mailer daemon reply.

As Jane hangs her jacket, I realize I've left the bathroom light on. I flick the switch and peer out from the safety of darkness. "Yo, yo." Her voice is low and mysterious. Without waiting for a response, she drifts specter-like into the common area and alights on the windowsill to scroll her phone.

After Jane comes Darya Azali, who stomps confidently into the room (she doesn't remove her Doc Martens) and flings a denim jacket on the back of a chair. Darya is shorter and more Rubenesque than Jane. There is a nobility in her profile and a subtle grandeur to her carriage. Her hair has been dyed a cotton-candy blue and she wears a crisp yellow T-shirt that says *Yubaba's Bathhouse—No Face? No Entry.*

Darya is the loud and proud geek of the group, a dedicated cosplayer and a declared member of "more than a dozen fandoms" ranging from *Sailor Moon* to *Supernatural.* She is currently debating adding "either ASOIAF or ACOTAR to my roster."[*] Plus, in her non-geek life she is a genuine scientist! Having recently obtained an MS in marine biology, she is well poised to add scientific rigor along with fandom cred to the Orb 4.

Darya and Taras met at the local sock hop of our age: Tinder. Taras accidentally "super liked" while wiping a smudge off his screen. He almost deleted the app in embarrassment. During the ensuing date, Darya took him to an art show in Chelsea where they supped on cheese cubes and stale crackers. Taras, ever the gentleman, accompanied her to her subway entrance. Their lips locked as the train rattled beneath. Possibly he'd have ghosted her, or she ghosted him, or both ghosted mutually as was the custom. However, in one of those magical New York City moments they ran into each other in line for bagels a week later. He was holding an egg and cheese on everything, and she was fighting with the cashier over what counted as a "schmear" of blueberry cream cheese. She turned to say "Can you believe this?" to the next person in line only to discover it was Taras. "There's no point trying to ghost fate," he told me later.

"Where's Taras?" Darya says as she lays a container of homemade cookies on the table.

---

[*] A Song of Ice and Fire by George R. R. Martin and A Court of Thorns and Roses by Sarah J. Maas, respectively.

Jane doesn't look up from her phone. "Dunno."

"Hey, T!"

"One sec."

What's to be said of Taras, my steadfast friend? He's a kind and somewhat unkempt man. Laconic and ironic, he speaks only when words are necessary yet one can never be quite sure when he's joking. I watch as he strolls past the bathroom. His six-foot-one frame, scraggly hair, and red-tinged scruff make him appear as a mythic warrior teleported from the battlefield to twenty-first-century Brooklyn. He grips his sword—Muji 0.5mm gel ink pen—in his smooth right hand as he strides into the wine-dark room.

Taras waves to Jane, who comments on "the weird smell" (presumably something in the hallway). He offers her one of my pamplemousse LaCroixs, which I hadn't authorized yet would have given willingly. She cracks the can as Taras embraces Darya. During the kiss, Darya seems to notice me through the slit of the bathroom door. Her eyes widen. I sink back into the gloom.

The meeting begins. I watch them gesture wildly, their ideas fluttering in the air like doves released from a magician's hat. Yet I can't hear from this distance. They seem to be discussing a plotline involving black holes or possibly wormholes. Oh, the gulf that exists between such holes! I find myself overpowered with a desire to be closer to the proceedings. To soar like Icarus near the dazzling sun of creativity.

I tiptoe out and conduct small tasks in the living room—fixing a lightbulb, washing dishes, misting ferns, etc.—while pretending not to pay attention. I have earbuds in, nothing playing. I wear my *Battlestar Galactica* T-shirt and hum the theme song from *The X Files*. Surely, I'll be noticed.

I'm not. The Orb 4 are so single-minded nothing else registers.

"So, is it telepathy? Or telekinesis?"

"It's both! Like Aul-Wick—that's the fish alien pilot—can telepathically speak through other characters by telekinetically controlling their vocal cords."

"Huh. Cool."

I could be dancing the cancan or dissecting an extraterrestrial on the kitchen island and they wouldn't notice. Nothing can distract them from their task. I opt for action.

"This seat free?"

"Ah. Did you want to join?" Taras says, feeling out my interest.

I flutter my hands. "I could never *join*." Well, not yet, I tell myself. When in Rome, wait around until everyone assumes you're just another Roman.

They nod.

"I'll just eat my humble victuals at the table."

They look at each other. I hide my enthusiasm as best I can.

"Alert! Intruder! Alert!" Darya says in an outdated—even offensive— robotic voice. (Sometimes I wonder how she managed to write the thrilling tales attributed to her. Did Taras ghostwrite?)*

"Well, it's your place," Jane says.

Taking Jane's assent as sacrosanct, I go to the stove to cook my evening's repast. Macaroni and cheese with extra cheese. The water boils. The collective recommences fleshing out the universe of the Metallic Realms. Taras is explaining his concept of the setting, which takes place thousands of years in the future when the Earthian empire has expanded across the stars, crested, and collapsed. The current time is known in-universe as the Unending Decay. "It's a time when the galactic order has begun to crumble. People are torn apart by factionalism, misinformation, and the looming threat that things may get worse and worse each year."

Jane snorts. "Can't imagine what *that's* like."

"I might have borrowed a bit from the news. Heh."

While stirring cheese dust into the writhing noodles, I can't help myself. I giggle.

"Everything all right?" Jane says.

"Yes, very." I stir the pot. "Only, I couldn't help thinking how this mac and cheese is reminiscent of the maggot flotilla on Rygol 9."

---

* Stratfordians, look away! I've downloaded software used to analyze Shakespeare's plays for clues to his true identity. I've run analyses on the Orb 4 tales to see if Taras authored them all. The freeware version has produced inconclusive results.

"You." A pause. "You know about Rygol 9?"

Taras leaps to my defense with a quick whisper. "I left a draft of 'Flight from the Feral Sun'* in the recycling pile."

"It had a few coffee stains but was no worse for wear," I say.

Silence. Glances exchanged. The realization they're in the presence of a true fan.

Then inspiration hits and Jane begins describing a civilization of "alien mockingbirds" who mimic the hailing signals of other species in generation ships built like giant nests. I tiptoe over and occupy the empty chair. The mac and cheese is quite squeaky. I've overcooked it in my effort to overhear. I chew softly, letting the noodles dissolve on my tongue before swallowing the resulting mush.

"That's a big bowl of mac," Jane says oddly. I'm eating out of a standard popcorn bowl and have used only one Family Fun box.

"A growing boy." I wink. "Please continue."

After another pause, Taras rises to full height with a stack of papers in his large hands. "Here's what I've got to start," he says. "I've updated it with ideas we kicked around at the last meeting. Jane, I know you still haven't decided on a character yet, but we'll figure out an origin story when you do."

Throughout these proceedings, I sit as their creative juices wash over me like a tidal wave. Exhilarating is too modest a word. The back-and-forth exchange of ideas. The way one concept splits off in new directions like branches of a tree. How each darling they kill comes back stronger, in zombie form. It thrills. This is what I dream to achieve in my own scribblings. This is *art*.

Those who tell you they don't want to know how the sausage is made have been munching on very poor links indeed. This sausage? It was filled with stars.

---

* This story was abandoned for reasons unknown. I have excluded it from the official chronology and this volume.

The Duchy of the Toe Adam

S pace. There's not a lot going on. It's mostly a cold, black, and empty place barely pinpricked by distant stars. The void, I call it. Most of the real action is on the handful of habitable planets, yet on those you risk getting controlled by brain fungi, hardwired into cyborg hiveminds, or forced by the ruling world-corps to sign life contracts. Any which way, it's work, work, work until you die. My first mate, Vivian, and I got tired of that. We smuggled aboard a smuggling ship and stole it when they stopped for fuel. The pilot, a piscine weirdo named Aul-Wick, seemed happy to tag along. We don't have any bold mission or noble cause. We're just freelance smugglers trying to have a few adventures while we're still young.

But the galactic gig economy can be harsh. While fleeing creditors, we intercepted a distress signal from an uncharted planet. *Strangers, heed! Enter the Purple After and receive the Blessings of Adam.*

"What're 'Blessings of Adam'?" I asked.

"Sounds like some religious nonsense. Let's keep moving," Vivian said.

"Sounds like money," Aul-Wick said, gills flaring in his aquatic orb. "Which we desperately need."

He was right on that part, but his textual interpretation was off. When we breached the atmosphere, our sales pitch was met with surface to air missiles. That's how we ended up in the middle of the Adamite civil war.

*
**

Our escape pods were found by soldiers in orange armor emblazoned with the insignia of a silver nose. As they were seizing us "in the name of the Nose Adam," dozens of red-clad soldiers galloped over the hill waving flags of a golden toe. In the battle, Vivian had two fingers on her non-cybernetic hand sliced off by laser fire. I lost an ear and took a bullet in the ribs. Aul-Wick managed to slip into a nearby river in his protective orb, shouting, "Sucks to be an air breather."

"Fish-faced coward," Vivian said, hacking up blood.

"Coming here was your idea!" I shouted, but Aul-Wick had already turned off his comms.

Now we were being taken to the Duchy of the Toe Adam. Chained in the back of the vehicle, we watched the surviving Toe Adamites stroll somberly with their eyes on the ground. Body parts were scattered like asteroids across the dark purple field. The Toe Adamites lifted the legs of the fallen and sliced off one toe from each foot. The toes were placed in a gold-rimmed box.

"You're lucky our soldiers rescued you. The Nose Adamites are monsters," the Toe Adamite surgeon said as she slurped the bullet out of my torso with a crinkled hose.

I grunted. "Is that so?"

The surgeon wore bright red scrubs. Her eyes were wide and white above the mask. "They say that Nose Adamites eat the nostrils of newborn babes. They believe the flesh imbues them with the power of god. That's why their duchy is strewn with tiny bones that lodge in the feet of the faithful."

"I don't remember any baby bones," Vivian said from her surgical pod.

"Well, that's what they say," the surgeon said dismissively.

"Guess that means you Toe Adamites eat baby toes?" Vivian asked.

Both surgeons gasped.

The one working on my missing ear shook her scalpel at Vivian. "Don't say such blasphemy when you meet the Toe Adam. He's fair, but not forgiving."

"Eating babies!" the other surgeon yipped. "Who do you take us for? Those swamp-dwelling Skull Adamites?"

Our holding cell was comfortable enough. A small porthole looked out at the dragon vines crawling across the purple fields toward the undulating ocean. I had a bandage over my regrowing ear, and Vivian's hand was wrapped in a glass medical glove.

"Assholes," Vivian said. The veins in her cheeks glowed faintly blue with anger. Vivian's species had evolved a million light-years away from Earth, yet she looked exactly human except for her mood-displaying veins and ridged cheekbones. The universe was weird like that.

"Which?" I asked. "The Toe Adamites or the Nose Adamites?"

"All the goddamn Adams."

Soon a Toe Adamite priest in a long crimson robe guided us to the meal hall. He waved over a young boy who placed before us two bowls of pinkish hunks floating in tan liquid. "Marinated mobbin toes. A delicacy of this planet."

The toes were sour and squishy. I gobbled them down to stop my stomach rumbling. Vivian belched and requested a second bowl.

"How long have you been living here?" I asked.

"Many generations. Although our generations go by quickly on this planet." The priest fiddled with his engraved staff. "Our scriptures told the story of a purple world, ringed with golden halos of asteroids, that would be discovered once we built the *Great Ark of Adam*. We found our heavenly haven. It was paradise when we landed. Then the False Adams divided us."

"It looked more dark blue than purple," I said. "And I didn't notice any asteroid rings?"

"I will not debate scripture with heathens."

"If there are all these Adams, what makes you sure your Adam is the right Adam?" Vivian said.

"The Purple After is paradise made physical by the cosmos. We are walking on sacred ground. What is the part of man that touches the ground?"

"Depends how he walks," Vivian said.

The priest was unperturbed. "The upright man walks on his feet. And what is the part of the body that digs into the lord's dirt? The toe."

"There's no Heel Adam, I guess?"

"Vivian, please," I said.

"No." The priest frowned. "There is only the Toe Adam and the False Adams."

The Toe Adamites permitted us to wander the compound. The squat buildings were dank and discolored with fluorescent mold. The tech was decades out of date. Centuries maybe. They must have been isolated on this Podunk planet for some time.

"I want to learn what the hell started this war," Vivian said. "Let's find the oldest, gnarliest woman and ask her."

I rubbed my newly regrown ear. The lobe constantly itched. "Okay, but please let's try being polite."

In the pews of the prayer room, we found a shriveled old woman with white hair down to her feet. Vivian knelt beside her, took one pale and wrinkled hand in hers.

"Elder, we are strangers from another land. Can you tell us what started the war between the Nose Adam and the Toe Adam?"

The old woman's neck creaked as she looked up at Vivian. She grimaced with her gummy, toothless mouth. "Oh, all dem Adams have always been at war. Least as far as I can recall."

"All the Adams?" I asked.

"Well, let's see 'ere," the old woman said, counting with her remaining fingers. "Der's Nose Adam and his bastards in the west. Dem Eye Adamites are barricaded by the northern shore. Skull Adam has his duchy in the swamp. And der's our pure and holy and good and true Adam, the Toe Adam. Right in this blessed duchy."

"Oh," I said. "Okay."

The old lady gave us a weird grin and leaned forward. "Used to be dem Finger Adamites in the hills. Thin and gangly as pinkies they were. Blasted heretics. We wiped 'em out right quickly." Her eyes were wild beneath the wrinkled folds. "Blew up their pod so dey ain't ever coming back." The old lady began cackling uncontrollably, almost falling out of the pew.

Vivian and I headed quickly back into the hall.

Vivian's yellow pupils disappeared, and her head flipped back. I ran to brace her. "It's Aul-Wick," she said in that gargling voice that made my spine shiver. Aul-Wick's telekinetic-telepathy was especially painful over long distances. "Asshole wants to speak through me—*Captain Baldwin. Vivian. Good evening. I spent a night hiding in the green river. Several tentacled fish attempted to eat me. The idiots. I zapped them good. Also, did you see three moons? Pretty neat.*" Vivian put her head straight, gagged. "Get. To. Point. Throat. Hurts." Her head flipped back. "*Oh fine. Don't tell us about your day, Aul-Wick. Don't share common experiences to create a sense of bonding, Aul-Wick.*"

"Aul-Wick!" I shouted. "Stop whining."

"*Fine. I located the ship. The fungus trees damped the crash. Finishing up the repairs. Be here in two days or I'm off this rock alone.*"

"Now listen here," I started, but Vivian's head was back up straight.

Vivian massaged her neck and spat. "Ugh. Can't that fish ever speak through you? He's your friend."

The Toe Adam floated above us on a plush levitating chair wearing his ceremonial robes and jewel-encrusted hat. There wasn't much of his skin exposed, but what I could see was covered in bizarre growths that almost looked like tiny toes. When he extended one sandal-clad foot, the priest elbowed me and coughed. Vivian stepped forward and stroked the nail of the big toe of the Toe Adam's left foot. "Oh, wise Adam, thank you for letting me touch your holy hangnail." I followed suit.

The Toe Adam regarded us. "I'm told we saved you from the Nose Adam. He would not have been as hospitable as we are."

Guards lined the wall, fiddling with their laser rifles. In the far corner, I saw a gigantic silver pod. It looked like an old-fashioned clone printer.

"What's the beef you have against this nose guy anyway?" Vivian said.

"The Nose Adamites are apostates!" the priest screamed.

The Toe Adam sighed, put up a hand to calm his minion. "The Nose Adam is a lost sheep. I'm hoping you can help me save him. My priest says you have many weapons on your ship?"

"Oh yeah," I lied. "Plenty."

The Toe Adam dropped his levitating chair to the ground. He walked toward us, tapping his toe cane upon the tiles. "If you promise to donate your arms to our holy crusade, I will allow you to leave with my sanction. My Blessings of Adam missiles will stay in their silos."

"Ah. That's what you call them."

"The Blessings of Adam is a planetary defense network our mech-clerics constructed when we first arrived. The system is hardcoded to avoid the biosignals of our people, including the followers of false prophets. Thus, our need of your outside weapons. Is it a deal?"

"Deal," I said. "Although how will weapons save the Nose Adam?"

The Toe Adam shrugged. The growths on his skin bounced. "He'll be saved in the afterlife, as all sinners are."

The Toe Adam's war tank was long and sleek with turrets at the cuticles. His hair swirled in the wind under his war helmet. "Today, by the grace of the

Indivisible God, we turn the Purple After red with the blood of the heretics!"
he shouted. The soldiers cheered.

The timing was good for us. Aul-Wick had spoken through Vivian that
morning, telling us the ship was ready and waiting in the Frost Forest. I'd
told him to get the ship's cannon ready and "kill any Adam wearing a big
pointy hat." I figured if we took out the big toe, the soldiers would scatter.
We were a couple hundred yards away from the Frost Forest. I could see the
branchless fungus trees, their trunks dotted with orange warts instead of
leaves. The day was warm. We rolled across the gas flower marshes, gigantic
puffs of blue pollen filling the air.

Vivian elbowed me. "What the fuck is that thing?"

A two-headed beast was pulling itself out of a fissure. It was massive,
each head as big as a man.

"Mawbear!" the driver shouted.

"No," the Toe Adam said weakly. "It can't be! I forbid it!"

The huge creature was about the size of the tank and looked just as
strong. A carpet of brown fur flapped over its thick scales. It stood on its
hind legs and roared.

"Kill it!" the Toe Adam screeched. "Someone slay the demon!"

"Lord, help us," the high priest wailed, pressing his golden toe icon to his
lips. "Not again."

As the Toe Adamites ran toward the mawbear, blasters firing, Vivian wran-
gled a gun from the high priest's robes. She told him to spill the beans or
she'd spill his beans and mobbin toes breakfast across the tank.

In the distance, soldiers flew in bloody arcs. The Toe Adam was out on
the ground, running in the other direction.

"Okay, okay," the priest said. He explained.

Long ago, the Church of the Purple After located a planet that some of
the priests declared fit the descriptions of their scriptures. A group departed

on a mission ship, guided by their leader, the High Unifier Adam. They carried clone printers to ensure the faithful would survive. Their religion taught that the soul was indivisible but could reenter a single clone after death. Things had gone well at first. But it was a harsh world and after a couple of winters, the settlers were struggling to grow food. Divisions arose. When Adam led a foraging party, he killed a small mawbear cub not realizing its mother was waiting in the canyon.

Adam had decreed if he perished, his priests were to clone him from "the sacred part of my body that touches the holy planet" or else "is touched by the holy planet." There was some disagreement. When the rival high priests found the corpse of Adam strewn across the ground, each grabbed a hunk of their holy leader and sprinted back to their cloning pods. One grabbed a toe, one grabbed a finger, and so on. None of the five sects could agree on what part was the correct, sacred part. Each had their own interpretation backed by scripture. The Nose Adam, the Toe Adam, the Finger Adam, the Eye Adam, and the Skull Adam had waged war ever since. When they died, they were cloned to fight once more. Their heaven was an eternity of awakening, killing, dying, and awakening again.

This time, the Toe Adamites managed to murder the mawbear. It sunk to the purple fields with a tortured honk. The Toe Adamites cheered. Then they moaned. From the west, the army of the Nose Adamites appeared. They rode on striped mobbins, galloping across the field with amplified whoops.

"Time for us to bolt," Vivian said. We sprinted toward the forest as toes, fingers, noses, bones, and teeth splattered on the ground in a macabre rain.

I grabbed the reins of a passing mobbin. Its rider had been reduced to two legs and a bloody stump of waist. We hopped on and galloped away from the battle. When I looked back, the soldiers had shrunk to the size of their names. Angry warriors as small as toes and noses, killing each other for a god that, if he existed, was orbiting some other star in some other distant galaxy in the great void of space.

When we hopped off the mobbin at the foot of the ship, I looked at Vivian and felt like my heart had been cloned inside my chest. Why had I been zipping across the galaxy when all I needed was right in front of me? Why not settle down? I kissed Vivian long and hard. She rubbed her hands through my graying hair. Her cheek veins were pulsing bright red.

"Let's give up this smuggling life, Vivian. Stop these terrifying adventures. Why don't we buy a little housepod on a quiet planet with a white picket force field and a weather vane in the shape of a comet spinning in the wind. You and me. That's all we need."

Vivian looked away. "You're a sweet man," she said. A smile curved up her face. "But shut it. I'd rather face down gigantic bears than little children."

Something the Toe Adamites had fed us must have been messing with my mind. Ours was a life of adventure and daring, not domesticity. "Yeah," I said. "Okay. Never mind."

"Let's go," she said, punching my shoulder.

The ship was before us, engines purring.

Aul-Wick greeted us in his floating orb on the ship's ramp. His smooth face was puffed and nervous. "This is awkward."

"What's awkward, fish face?" Vivian said.

"Tell us later, Aul-Wick. Let's get the hell out of here."

Little bubbles floated out of his external gills. "I guess my telepathic messages went to all four of you."

"All four of who?" Vivian said.

"See, the Nose Adamites came back to collect bits of their fallen soldiers so they could be recloned," Aul-Wick said. "I guess your sliced off fingers and ear were in the pile of parts."

"What are you talking about?" I asked.

But then I saw them. At the top of the ramp, stepping out of the darkness with guns drawn, Ear Baldwin and Finger Vivian emerged.

SRC #1 Analysis

On What Separates the Metallic Realms from
Other, Duller Fictional Universes

You have completed your first, though certainly not last, foray into the Metallic Realms. If you feel destabilized, that's intentional. The Orb 4 didn't believe in "literary handholding" and were willing to leave many questions—Did the *Star Rot* escape? Did the Nose Adamites destroy the Toe Adamites? What happened with Ear Baldwin and Finger Vivian?—for the reader to answer themselves.*

Like a child mounting the diving board on the first day of summer, let's dive headfirst into the thematically dense text. "Duchy" holds a special place in this scholar's heart since the story is itself concerned with scholarship. Think about it! The misinterpreted signal about the "Blessings of Adam." The scripture leading the Adamites to the purple planet. The disagreement over which body part Adam wanted to be cloned from. The plot hinges on the importance of interpreting text. A correct understanding can enliven and a mangled one can lead to distress and even death. Reader, I endeavor to be worthy of the sacredness of my role.

What likely stands out to the first-time reader is the fully formed nature of Metallic Realms. How is it that the Orb 4 could conjure such a complex, lived-in, and innovative galaxy in only a few pages? One answer is Taras Castle had shattered the calcified worldbuilding paradigm that dominates science fiction. He instead advocated for "world gardening." He explained the theory

---

* As a scholar, I can confirm these questions were debated and answered internally among the Orb 4: 1) Yes. 2) Oh yeah. 3) A great fight ensued in which regular Baldwin and regular Vivian emerged victorious.

to me one evening as we were rewatching the OT—pirated versions of the
original trilogy, before George Lucas befouled them with his digital insertions.
"It's all right here, right?" Taras said, gesturing toward the screen. His lips
glowed with orange Cheetos dust. "You can extrapolate entire civilizations and
galaxies from a few seconds of this cantina scene. Why do writers drop in one
hundred pages about dwarf mating rituals or the economic output of space
slugs? Who cares about that? Just give us some cool guys with weird names
that evoke worlds!" We whooped as Han deftly dispensed with Greedo.

Taras would extrapolate this into a theory of "world seeds." These were
defined on the Orb 4 Twitter account: "World seeds reject the dreary worldbuilding of would-be encyclopedians who demand readers play no part in a
universe's creation. World seeds sprout in the reader's mind, blooming into
lush gardens of story."

Let's examine what separates *The Star Rot Chronicles* from other "star"
franchises such as ___*Wars*, *Battle*___ *Galactica*, and the nonsensical ram-
blings of a certain "Jeans Rotten Berry" whose wooden characters and rickety Starship *Rent-A-Prize* is such a malevolent influence on science fiction I
refuse to type its name here. First, there is the *brokenness* of the galaxy. This
is not a universe of implausibly monolithic empires where each species has
a single ideology. It's not a universe where technology works seamlessly and
science magically unites us as we sing "Kumbaya" hand-in-tentacle with alien
races. No. It's a chaotic galaxy of competing interests, rival governments, and
frequent technological breakdowns. A universe where ships are not named
Serenity or *Endeavour* but *Star Rot*. The Metallic Realms are ugly, harsh, and
honest. It is, in short, a universe true to our own.

"Is there a cosmic lingua franca or just a universal translator technology?"
I asked Taras as we browsed the bodega for a late-night snack. "What governs
galactic trade? How is the data transmitted through the nebula clouds? Do
species interbreed using genetic editing?"

"Whoa, Mike," Taras said, impressed with the detail of my questions. He
held up two bags of chips to choose from. "I don't know. The whole point is
to leave some stuff unanswered. BBQ or salt and vinegar?"

Ah, but he did know. I could see it in the mischievous twinkle in his eyes as he tossed the salt and vinegar chips into my awaiting hands. Authors are word magicians, so I couldn't expect him to reveal his tricks. Still, what a spell Taras's lengthy fingers weave in this first scintillating tale. Although the Orb 4 published under their collective name, you can tell the authorship of an Orb 4 story by which character narrates. Captain Baldwin was Taras's creation—predating the Orb 4 itself, as I've mentioned—and Vivian was designed by Darya. (Jane didn't have a stand-in at this point.) Please disabuse yourself of any notion our heroes are Mary Sues or Gary Stus. These characters are as complex and compelling as those in the so-called "Western Canon." By the end of this volume, I believe you'll agree that Baldwin has more life than any Ahab and Vivian more fire than a thousand Dalloways. As for Aul-Wick, his character simply has no precedent in any literature that I've studied.

The Orb 4 had grand if unrealized plans for *The Star Rot Chronicles* characters. Not only were there to be "solo novels" spun off by the members, but there would be talk of graphic novels, poetry chapbooks, and at least one TTRPG. Alas. Hypothetical plans were not powerful enough to blast away the meteors of discord that would later crash upon the group. I have firsthand knowledge of these tragic events as the group's de facto sounding board cum shoulder to cry on. I've always been a good listener. I'm deeply introverted, Sagittarius sun and Libra rising, Ravenclaw, Water Tribe citizen, lawful neutral, and an INTP. It might not be an exaggeration to say that I was the glue that held the group together. Yet I couldn't bond them forever.

How I Became a Trusty Barnacle
on the Sturdy Ship of the Orb 4

The Duchy of the Toe Adam" is one of the more personal *Star Rot Chronicles* stories, rooted in Taras's childhood experiences of organized religion. His immigrant family was Eastern Orthodox, a rarity in our town of prudish Protestants. Taras himself never believed, but in America any rare flower is crushed beneath the bootheel of conformity. I was raised a Roman Catholic* yet still mocked because of some long-forgotten fight between men in pointy hats over the wording of sentences in a language no one even speaks anymore!

One day in our shared kitchen, Taras got a friend request on Facebook. He showed me their over-filtered profile pic. Valerie McClean. "Remember in ninth grade when we were riding the bus and Valerie told me she would 'See me in hell'? Then her face went white and she shouted, 'I mean from heaven! I'll be seeing you in hell from heaven, which is where I'll be.'"

I chuckled. "I consider myself an optimist, but I don't think humans will ever get over inventing divisions."

"Yep. They'll be having schisms in space a million years from now."

And voilà. Some weeks later, "The Duchy of the Toe Adam" debuted. Coincidence? Or point of creation?

Like all *Star Rot* tales, "Duchy" is drenched in symbolism. The use of the name "Adam" subconsciously invokes a central figure of the Abrahamic religions. This Adam is split into multiple parts, each ruling over a seemingly pointless duchy. What does this say about the futility of human endeavors? The impossibility of change? So much! One is reminded of Friedrich Nietzsche's concept of eternal recurrence, in which we are doomed to repeat our actions infinitely like a scratched record forever stuck in a loop. I mentioned *Thus Spake Zarathustra* casually to Taras at a house party for Darya's thirty-first birthday, hoping for confirmation of my theory. Taras was quite drunk. He belched, then responded with a vulgar pun involving a mispronunciation of the German philosopher's name and "my balls." I won't repeat it here.

I'd come to the party because I reasoned that I needed to win the trust of Darya and Jane if I was to join the Orb 4. The party was, regrettably, themed after a certain franchise whose appeal remains baffling to me. Attendees wore red, yellow, and blue shirts with little gold pins. The cocktail table, manned by Taras, would "beam you up" drinks with absurd names like Vulcantini and

---

* Raised but rejected. By age eight, I'd acquired the moniker "Doubting Thomas" in my church's religious education class after I'd spat out the unleavened body of Christ and asked, "Why does Jesus taste worse than a Pop-Tart?"

Betazoid Bramble. In protest I drank beer (IPA) and wore all-black clothing, which several drunken revelers deemed "Romulan." At one point, I fled a man doing a Shatner impression and ended up bumping into Jane. She wore a silver shirt with some kind of plastic computer chip stuck above her eye. "Oh, Mike. I didn't realize you were here."

"I've been surveying the proceedings from the corner," I said curtly.

"I'm probably going to bounce soon. I don't know anyone else here." She peeled the plastic decoration off her face. "Also, this cosplay stuff isn't quite my scene."

"Yes, I've long wondered how you fit into the Orb 4."

"Long wondered? I only met you a couple of weeks ago."

"I meant only that your mundane fiction predilections are an unusual fit for the *Star Rot*'s otherworldly adventures."

"Because I'm in an MFA program?" Jane jutted her face forward, forehead wrinkled. "Did Taras tell you that? That I'm too 'literary'?"

"Darya had, well, suggested something."

Jane looked over at Darya, who was passing around a tray of Jell-O shots. "She has a stick up her butt about genre boundaries. I want to fly above the pigeonholes. Never felt very comfortable in a clique."

Darya noticed us staring and walked over. She wore a low-cut purple V-neck sweater and introduced herself as "the ship's counselor." I hoped Taras might join yet he remained steadfast at the cocktail station.

"I have to head out," Jane said, her voice increasing an octave. "My friend has a poetry reading I promised to go to. Ugh. I wish I could stay. You look amazing and a million happy birthdays!"

After Jane left, Darya turned to me. "Run off to network, I guess." She was slurring her words a bit. "Hey, lemme ask you a question."

"About genre boundaries?"

"No. Men. Or at least Taras." Darya grabbed the fridge with one hand to steady herself. With the other, she reached out to touch my shoulder. "What do you think Taras wants? You know him. Like, what does he *want*?"

Her touch felt awkward. I feared she was setting a trap. "In regard to?"

"Life!" Darya yelped. She spread her arms, stumbled back, and grabbed the fridge. "The future. Do you think he wants to settle down? Does he have a sense of direction? Or is he planning to just be a struggling writer with no income living with roommates into, like, his forties. No offense."

I demurred. In "Duchy," Baldwin fantasizes about a retirement on a peaceful planet with a weather vane and white picket force field. In the text, the fantasy is dismissed. Baldwin is an adventurer. Taras an artist. Neither could be pinned down like a captured butterfly. They needed to fly free through the wilderness like, well, an unpinned butterfly. "I know he wants to write. And from what I've seen of the Metallic Realms, you have years of material to spin together."

Darya laughed yet her eyes looked sad. The cocktail in her hand was a red concoction in an old jam jar. She swallowed the remains in one go and then fiddled with the glucose monitor under her shirt. "Writing doesn't pay for healthcare. You know, I'm something of an empath in real life. It's not just the costume. I can tell that you feel awkward, Michael. Alone." Her smile was vexing. I thought she might lean forward and kiss me. (Would that help or ruin my chances of joining the Orb 4?) Instead, she snapped her fingers. "Ah, Stacey! She's single and ready to mingle."

Darya pulled me over to a not unattractive redhead who greeted me with a silent Vulcan hand gesture. Darya scuttled away. I attempted to debate the finer points of *Star Rot Chronicles* lore. Stacey scrunched her face, said she had never heard of it, and excused herself to "make a call."

I was alone with my own thoughts and empty beer. Thankfully, my brain was drunk on Nietzsche.

The German philosopher's works—or at least the YouTube summaries I'd viewed—had been a balm as my professional life was being sucked into a black hole of failure.* It was the same old story of my generation. Debt, precarious employment, rising healthcare costs. Despite my outward appearance of a suave and "with it" SFF geek, I was in fact directionless after a failed stint

---

* In my other lives, I was doing much better. My *Wizard War!* MMORPG tribe had just secured domination over the entire Elven forest of M'raz'a and in *Robot Revolution III* I'd reached the rank of 89th in North America.

in law school. I hadn't wanted to go. My parents pressured me—"You're so good at arguing" and "Playing video games isn't a career path, son"—but I soon learned my photographic memory for the workings of fictional universes didn't translate to our byzantine legal system. Ask me to explain the history of Westeros or the complex alliances in *Dune* and I could give an impromptu three-hour lecture (sans notes) that would have your knuckles whitening on the edge of your seat. Ask me about estate law and I can only offer a face as blank as a deactivated android.

I found myself in my mid-thirties living with two roommates in a poorly ventilated apartment with an elevated train rattling twenty feet in front of my window, surviving entirely on the guilt-induced largesse of my parents. (For pressuring me into law school, yes, and also their generation's systematic robbing of my generation's future through climate change, government debt, and an erosion of public services, which I detailed in weekly emails to my parents complete with citations and attached charts.)

After thirty, life becomes harder. Friends marry and move away. Old rivals pass you by in the IRL RPG of existence. A different body part aches each day. Opportunities dwindle. Time, that eldritch alien monster from the beyond, breathes down your neck.

Is this why I clung so hard to my friendship with Taras? As a link to my once-promising past?* That he allowed me to pretend time hadn't rotted away my future? That I could imagine life remained as wide and open and free as a newly terraformed world, its lush possibilities waiting for my generation ship to land? Perhaps.

Or perhaps I merely enjoyed his company. Not everything must be over-analyzed. It's hard to explain the intimate bond of lifelong friendship between men. It is so reviled in our culture by both the reactionary "no homo" conservatives and the "cancel men!" online wokerati. I am an iconoclast and will shout: I loved Taras. I envied him, but I loved him.

---

* I was inducted into the final year of our school's gifted program before the parents of mouth breathers and nose pickers got it canceled. Since they were unable to lift their own children up, they demanded everyone else be dragged down.

Reader, have you ever had a friend who simply excelled at everything they tried? Who was blessed by all three fates? They did kickflips on half-pipes while you skinned your knee attempting a mere ollie. They were the life of the party while you vomited in the sink. They got into the prestigious Clarion Workshop while you counted form rejections from unpaying WordPress-hosted lit mags. And yet, the envy never became hate because afterward they took you out for a beer and said, "Those editors are idiots," and they carried you to the couch to sleep beside a pasta pot to catch your vomit, and they skated over with a Band-Aid and Neosporin to clean your wound of the brackish mixture of blood and tears.

Anyway. It was fate that brought Taras and me together as fetuses and fate that reunited us in our thirties. And just as he inspired me growing up, my own life would soon inspire his art.

The Layout of the *Star Rot* and Its Similarity to My Apartment

SPOILER ALERT: There will be no spoilers in my analysis and commentary! Please read without fear. Yet I would like to examine the good ship *Star Rot,* which is a vessel that makes the *Millennium Falcon* seem like a middle schooler's papier-mâché project. The advanced weaponry, repolarized warp drive, and tri-thrusters all deserve elaboration. For now, I'll discuss the layout. At the bow of the *Star Rot* is the bridge, a large common area with a long viewscreen at one end from which the crew gazes out at the stars twinkling in the black void of space. Behind the bridge is a hallway with the crew's living quarters on either side. In the back, at the end of a long hall, we find the roaring engine room.

This layout is nearly identical to that of my apartment.

The front of my apartment was also a communal area complete with a "command station" (the kitchen's Formica floating island) and a "viewscreen" (row of windows) along one wall that gazed out at the twinkling lights of Brooklyn apartment buildings and an elevated subway line where trains roared past like enemy warships. Then, like the *Star Rot,* there was a hallway with two bedrooms on the right side and one bedroom and a shared bathroom on the left. In the back, the massive exterior air-conditioning units roared as loud as any interstellar engine. Granted, the *Star Rot*'s scale is much larger. And it has a second level that contains a few more crew quarters, storage, engine control, etc. Still. This cannot be coincidence.

The Means by Which I Acquired My Apartment

I'd inherited the lease two months before Taras moved in, but I'd arrived two years prior via Craigslist. I'd joined a couple, Brad and Emma, who worked on Wall Street and as a freelancer, respectively; and Tyrone, the leaseholder and an aspiring actor who spent most of his time in L.A. When Tyrone moved to the West Coast full-time, the three of us inherited the apartment on a shared lease and Emma took over the third bedroom as her studio.

Emma hosted the true crime podcast *Murder She Podded,* which consisted of Emma reading passages of Wikipedia pages for unsolved crimes and then asking her likely nonexistent listeners "to vote on the real killer." Brad was the breadwinner, having recently completed an MBA to pivot from management strategies consulting to strategic management consulting. I mostly avoided them. The lone wolf is my spirit animal. I was in law school, although my depression meant many days were spent playing MMORPGs in the gloom of my bedroom, unopened law textbooks in a pile like forbidden grimoires.

A year passed.

One evening, I slid out in wool socks to pilfer a few Lindt chocolate truffles from the bag Emma hid behind the cereal boxes atop the fridge. The lights flicked on. I froze.

"Hey, Mikey. Emma and I were hoping to conference."

"Hrmm," I said, still facing the fridge. I attempted to swallow the partially chewed Lindts. Unknowingly, I'd grabbed two of the white chocolate* balls out of the variety pack. I gagged wetly.

---

* There is no realm of the multiverse in which this monstrosity should be bestowed the noble name of "chocolate."

"Ew. Are you dying?" Emma said.

I ejected the foul half-dissolved globes into my palm. "Never been better." I hid the evidence in my fist and turned to face them. "And my name isn't Mikey."

"Right. Mike. Michael. Mike-a-rino. Let's touch base on a few action items," Brad said.

Brad was wearing a button-up shirt and (pleated!) khaki pants. Emma had on her usual Barnard hoodie and sour expression.

"Your hand is dripping."

I looked down at the mixture of melted white chocolate and saliva leaking from my fingers. "Pus," I improvised. "From a sore. A big sore."

Brad looked at Emma and whispered, "Let that go." He grinned at me and gestured toward the couch. "Mike, we just want to strategize on some apartment synergy. Shall we pop a squat?"

"I prefer to be able to make an exit," I said with an air of mystery.

"Right. Um. Well, the reason we wanted to talk is the lease is coming up and Emma and I were thinking it was an opportunity to optimize our—"

"It's not big enough for three people," Emma cut in. "I'm sure you agree. And we're getting married next year." Emma held up her hand to show me her ring. It was a gaudy thing with a purple teardrop stone and melee diamond halo. I was unable to discern if the stone was lab grown without my loupe.

"What do you say, Mikester? The lease renewal is coming up. This has been a—well, let's say a memorable experience with meaningful impact. But all things come to an end."

"I say good luck to you both with the wedding and the babies and the PTA meetings and all the other accoutrements of modern heteronormative life. Three cheers. Chapeau. May the force be with your union." I winked at Emma. "I wondered when this ruffian would make you a proper woman."

Brad took a step toward me and stretched his arm across Emma to clasp the lip of the kitchen island in a boorish motion of primate protectiveness. "We meant that three roommates cause some pain points. We want to pivot to an apartment for us. Just us."

"I pass."

"Pass? You can't pass."

"I'm on the lease. I know my legal rights. I'm in law school."

"I thought you dropped out?"

"We outvote you!" Emma said. "This is *America*. We live in a democracy."

"Technically, we're a republic."

"It does seem unfair, Mike." Brad shrugged at his own statement. "Two against one."

"Also, you're gross," Emma added. "You leave pee stains around the toilet. You never take down the garbage. And I know you eat my special Lindts."

Brad stepped forward. "Let's put our heads together and innovate a win-win situation."

I stepped backward, wedged now between the fridge and the wall. I wouldn't give in. Like Gollum and his ring, I'd found my precious: the apartment. Plus, I hated moving. Thinking quickly, I tossed the white gunk at Brad's head. "Gah!" he roared. As they were distracted, I sprinted around the kitchen island and locked my bedroom door.

Thus began the Cold Roommate War. You can probably imagine how it went. Slammed doors. Dishes left in the sink. Absurdly long showers to run out the hot water. Cold stares in the hallway. Passive-aggressive Post-it notes. Body-shaming comments* said when I was in earshot.

In the end, I stood victorious. Brad's parents gifted the couple a down payment to purchase a condo in Park Slope. When their U-Haul puttered away, I observed my domain. It was a vast if empty realm. Most of the furniture, wall hangings, cutlery, dishes, cups, rugs, sponges, electronics, appliances, shower curtains, plants, cleaning supplies, paper towels, spices and corresponding rack, bathmats, and coat hangers had technically belonged to

---

* No, Emma, I do not think my luxurious eyebrows forming a unified line of defense across my forehead "looks like a five-year-old drew a caveman." And no, Brad, I'm not ashamed that I "run around with [my] little arms held against [my] chest like a *T. rex*." It's the most aerodynamic way to run while still allowing for efficient grabbing of objects. The *Tyrannosaurus rex* did not become the top predator of the Cretaceous because it was badly designed.

Brad and Emma. I had a blank slate. Ground zero for a new regime of respectful, communal living with like-minded comrades.

Although I will admit that there was a moment when I stood alone in that dim, empty living room and shuddered. By this age, my parents had steady careers and a toddler. I, on the other hand, had no job prospects and two roommates to find. It was hard for me to foresee when I'd ever be able to live without roommates, much less acquire stat-boosting power-up items like a mortgage or a 401(k). It was as if I, like most of my generation, had been frozen in carbonite, stuck in an extended early adulthood that we'd never escape from even when our hair fell out, our backs ached, and our skin wrinkled on our tired bones.

I unfolded a metal chair and placed it in the center of the spare room. I sat, my head as empty as my surroundings. I began, I confess, to cry.

How I Assembled My Trusty Crew

While I'd fairly won the war with Brad and Emma, I was unfairly paying three times as much in rent. If I didn't find roommates soon, my parents might notice the sizable monthly debit on their credit cards and cut me off. I had to begin hunting for heroes to join my adventuring party. My first call as leaseholder was to the great Paladin Taras. "T-bone, my man," I said, affecting a casual air. "Any chance you're looking for a lit pad to chill in?"

"What? Who is this?" he murmured.

(Avoiding Emma and Brad had thrown off my sleep schedule. I'd accidentally called him at 2 A.M. instead of 2 P.M. In my defense, the NYPD had set up two mobile floodlight units on the street after a series of attacks by a local ne'er-do-well the media had dubbed the Bushwick Pantser.* When I called, it was as bright as midday.)

---

* Not to be confused with the creative writing concept of "pantser," meaning one who writes without an outline, flying by the seat-of-the-pants as it were. No. The grade school pantsing in which one's trousers are yanked violently to expose one's buttocks just as one was going into Walgreens to buy (oh, cosmic irony!) toilet paper. Yes, I was one of the victims. And yes, I did indeed trip over my navy Dickies, now bunched around my ankles like a set of shackles, to collapse in front of the sliding doors.

I hung up and called back several hours later.

"You were the first person I thought of."

"I'm kind of locked in a lease here. You know how NYC slumlords are," Taras said. "Would take an act of God to get me out."

"Totally, totally," I said. "Totes. For real. I get it."

Still, I could sense the hesitation in his voice. He *wanted* to move in, but he needed a reason. I decided to leave a room open in the event circumstances changed. There was still the other room to fill in any event. A line from my father's favorite film kept repeating in my head: "If you build it, they will come." Luckily the apartment was already built. I merely had to decorate.

I planned to go high concept and turn the living room into a re-creation of Professor X's Danger Room or the interior of *2001*'s *Discovery One* complete with a talking Hal smart house system. However, this seemed risky given that my Craigslist post hadn't yet yielded responses. Perhaps I'd been too blunt with my advertisement: "I have less than zero interest in cohabiting with Chads, Slytherins, fire signs, literary fiction snobs, vegans (pescatarians acceptable), bros, goobers, jocks, dweebs (nerds welcome), credit scores below 650, anyone who destroys their brain cells with reality television, under 25, over 40, people who scream during sex (thin walls), cook fish regularly (bad ventilation), are sensitive to loud noises (elevated subway line outside), who don't know the difference between your/you're or they're/their/there or two/to/too, who think penultimate means extra ultimate, who won't share meals (communal living situation), or who want to yap yap yap all day long. I'm not your therapist. I'm your roommate and—as leaseholder—de facto landlord. Treat me with the due respect and we won't have problems."

Anyway, the costs of redecorating my apartment as a classic movie spaceship or superhero hideaway would have proved prohibitively expensive. All decorations were. No matter how much I tried to persuade my parents, they refused to increase my meager allowance.

"Mikey," my mother said. "I can send you some of the extra cutlery we have here if you need it. We're already paying your rent. And your health insurance. And you're on our phone plan."

"Don't forget the Netflix account!" I heard my father shout.

"Wow," I said. "Am *I* the one who caused skyrocketing debt and health-care costs? Am *I* the one who caused the global financial crisis?"

"Your father and I aren't either, honey."

"You worked at Wells Fargo!" I said. "Your jewels were bought with sub-prime loan blood money."

I could hear splashing water in the background. My mother was simmering in the hot tub, probably barely paying attention. "Okay, honey. We'll stop sending you the blood money."

I glanced around my desolate apartment. Moaned. "So I fall even further behind? How's that fair?"

She sighed with the weariness of a foe who knows her indomitable enemy will never stop, never tire, and never give in. "I'll wire you a hundred into the shared account," she whispered.

"I can't even buy a couch with that."

"Try Goodwill. I've got a dinner party to get ready for. The Mercers will be there. You remember their son, Tom Mercer?"

"No."

"He was about your age. Tall. Became a dentist."

"Okay. Maybe."*

"He died horribly in February. Did I tell you? Car accident. He wasn't wearing a seat belt! Went right through the windshield. And then the shattered glass sliced open his stomach. The blood ruined his expensive leather seats."

"Jesus!"

"Sharon's neighbor, Carol, told her who told me. Carol used to teach you tennis lessons, remember? Oh, and Rebecca Webb died of throat cancer. Can you believe it?"

"Given that I don't know who that is, yes, I suppose I can believe it."

---

* I could briefly recall Mercer in my fourth-grade class daring me to expose myself under the lunch table. When I did, he pelted me with baby carrots from his lunch box and called me "carrot dick" until the teacher came and put us both in time-out.

"Promise me you won't ever smoke cigarettes. It's not worth looking 'cool' for your friends."

Every conversation with my mother went this way. My parents had reached the age in which they felt compelled to either tell me how someone had died or give me life lessons. Ideally both at the same time.

The hundred bought me a chair from Craig's titular list, plus a few throw pillows and a coffee maker from Target. Clearly, that wasn't enough. Then I stumbled upon a solution that was right in front of my face. Or rather, under my buttocks. Credit cards. I had a five-thousand-dollar credit limit, and several subreddits gave me advice on how to open new cards to finance the old ones. I cracked my knuckles. Pretty soon my apartment was the pinnacle of modern SFF stylings. I had a rainbow row of lava lamps along one wall, Cthulhu shower curtains, a framed poster of Gandalf-as-Uncle-Sam saying, *I Want YOU to Join the Fellowship,* a (faux) flying bison-skin welcome mat, and a TARDIS minifridge. I hadn't yet purchased a couch or table. Those could wait. I posted updated photos to my "room for sublet—GEEKS ONLY" listings and waited for the emails to roll in.

But after a few days, I realized this SFF paradise was stifling. It was devoid of life. My previous pet, an axolotl salamander named Isaac Axolmov, had been dead for some months. Overfeeding, or perhaps underfeeding. Hard to know with salamanders. I decided to move from the sea to the air. I settled on a green-and-yellow caique and named him Arthur C. Caique, after the legendary Arthur C. Clarke. Unfortunately, the pet store salesperson had misled me in the caique's verbalization capabilities. Caiques are not adept at imitating human speech.* On the other hand, I'd soon learn that a caique can imitate some sounds with eerie perfection. Specifically, the car alarms that are a prominent feature of the Brooklyn soundscape. Pretty soon a joyous screech of "Wee ooh! Wee ooh!" rang through the apartment at all hours. As I welcomed my new pet, I said goodbye to my circadian rhythms.

---

* To this day, Arthur refuses to say, "*Star Rot Chronicles!*" or "Polly wants a new short story!" no matter how many times I've coaxed him with crackers.

The Rogue Elf Castel Joins the Quest

The first roommate to join my still bare apartment was Cast, who I've mentioned in passing. Castel "Cast" Ocampo grew up outside Atlanta to a Peruvian father and a Jewish mother yet was raised Buddhist. Cast, in this way, was perhaps destined to be an outsider. After moving to New York City to attend the film program at NYU (full scholarship), they'd "found a city as confused and cobbled together as myself."

Cast and I met inside the massive, wondrous floor of one of New York's most science-fictional architectural structures: the Javits Center. Swooping steel bars soared overhead, while the sky was made of windowpanes arranged into futuristic geometry. That day was especially vibrant. Everywhere, colorful banners were hung. Vast throngs of people dressed in bizarre outfits wandered around, bartering and philosophizing in strange languages. Yes, it was Comic Con. The annual gathering of geeks, nerds, otakus, cosplayers, cyberpunks, and all lovers of the imagination.

I was in line for an Ann Leckie signing dressed as Gregor Samsa Clegane. (An improvised cockroach costume and a plastic battle-axe in one hand.) In front of me stood a striking beanpole figure in a battery-powered getup. They turned and looked me up and down, then burst out laughing. I stepped backward, my space opera volumes held up as an impromptu shield. Reflexes from secondary school bullying. However, there was warmth in this laughter.

"I like your getup," they said. They pointed at my House Clegane banner. "If Kafka and George R. R. Martin had a baby, right?"

I lowered my stack of Imperial Radch tomes. "Yeah." I looked the stranger over. They wore a black sweatshirt splattered with white paint for stars. Two glowing spheres, one pink and one blue, were attached to curved hanger wires as if they were orbiting the midsection. "Gender-reveal supernova?"

"Close! Non-binary star."

"Ah. Bravo. Although binary in the solar sense."

A laugh followed by a proffered hand. "I'm Cast. They/them, lawful neutral, Pisces. I used to say Hufflepuff but screw that TERF Rowling."

We shook hands. Cast was nearly as tall as Taras with luxurious black hair down to the shoulders. Their smile was wide and I could see their white teeth glint beneath the fluorescent Javits Center lights. The line inched forward. We continued our small talk. I was thrilled to learn Cast shared a disdain for a certain overrated franchise—"although *Deep Space Nine* with Sisko was pretty dope"—and even more thrilled to learn they were looking for a new apartment. I told them about my vacancy. The rest, as they say, is history.*

Soon after, Taras joined us following his fiery incident, as I've already ex-plained, and the home was full. Although there was a bit of bad blood caused by my people-pleasing tendencies. The issue was the apartment's bedrooms had different dimensions. As the leaseholder, naturally I took the largest. That left the medium and small rooms. I told Cast I'd offered the second-largest room to Taras (true) but neglected to mention Taras hadn't yet accepted. After some pointed comments, Cast cornered me. "Mike, if your friend isn't mov-ing into the empty room, can I take it? I'm happy to pay a little more for extra space." Thinking quickly, I lied. "Taras already put a security deposit down." Cast grumbled. After more weeks with no Taras, Cast insisted they get the larger room. I felt forced to agree. Yet, Cast dragged their feet moving—they were waiting for friends to help lift the bed and dresser—and then the fire occurred. Taras arrived. As I'd promised the room to both at different times, I was unsure how to adjudicate. Using the Bible as a guide, I offered to cut the room in two with a divider hoping that the rightful owner would reveal themselves by rejecting the desecration. Instead, Taras said, "You want us to share the room and leave the other empty? That literally doesn't make sense."

We were left with a coin toss. Cast called heads. I caught the coin, caught a glimpse, and flipped it onto the back of my hand. Tails.

"Hey!" Cast said. "That's cheating! You catch it in the palm, no flipping."

"We flip in Vermont. That's how it works," Taras said.

---

* Specifically, history I will catalog in this volume.

"It's not how we do it in Georgia."

"I fear it is two Vermonters against one," I said, settling the issue. At least for a while.

I'm describing my apartment situation not to provide interior decorating tips or roommate advice but because my apartment would become enmeshed in *The Star Rot Chronicles* in countless ways. Not that I expect credit for providing inspiration as well as a safe harbor for creation. I have no such ego. Inspiring art is its own, uncredited reward. Still, it is my job to illuminate the hidden meaning of *The Star Rot Chronicles*. Allow me to shine my scholarly flashlight on our next tale.

The Writing Contest That Changed a Universe

The second canonical *Star Rot* story was composed while the outside world drowned. It had rained for the entirety of the Orb 4 meeting, with the water increasing in volume—both physically and acoustically—until my apartment windows might as well have looked out onto the Lost City of Atlantis.

"Shit, I have to go. I've got a Hinge date with this noise musician," Jane said.

Her only protection was a black denim jacket. Taras fished around his closet and emerged with a small umbrella that folded up was no larger than a lightsaber hilt. "Sorry. It's all I have."

Jane fled down the apartment stairs, cursing.

Cast was trying to calm Arthur down, who squawked after every thunder roar. Cast normally wasn't present at Orb 4 meetings. They were an extrovert who always had overlapping plans since "canceling is half the fun." The rains had flooded all options away that night so, bored, they'd joined me in the living room to eavesdrop on the Orb 4. "This is legit rain. Must be that nor'easter they've been talking about."

A chorus of screeching cell phones: "FLASH FLOOD WARNING is in effect until 11:30 P.M." Soon our social media feeds were filled with photos of drowning cars in the Gowanus and videos of rats swimming around subway cars.

Darya gasped. "They're calling it the storm of the century! Then again, they said that about, like, five other storms since I moved to NYC."

"It's like how we get a 'once in a generation financial crisis' every few years, huh?" Taras looked out the window at the downpour. "I hope Jane is okay."

"Let's all hope it clears up soon," I said, staring at the ceiling. I was thinking less about Jane than the precarious roofing. Water was already dripping out of the light fixtures.

"Oh. My. God. Look at this!" Cast put their phone on the table and played a video of water gushing out of the white-tiled walls of a subway station while commuters ran around screaming. "This is surreal. I mean literally surreal. Have you guys heard of 'global weirding'? The environment itself is becoming estranged from our actions. Animals migrating into human habitats. Sudden heat waves. Goddamn Noah's Ark flooding in the middle of New York."

"This is why I'm saying fiction must get weirder. You can't write about surreal times with Raymond Carver realism or generic genre fiction. We gotta match the moment," Taras said.

The doorbell buzzed. Jane had returned, soaked to the bone. She held out a mangled mess of metal and fabric that had once been an umbrella. "Yeah, I'm, uh, going to be staying here for a bit. The trains are just paused on the track."

We settled into the evening. Cast kept a portable projector in their room and brought it out so that we could watch old *X Files* episodes on the wall. While I was worried about the rain damage to the apartment, I was also giddy at the prospect of debating the finer points of Orb 4 lore with the members themselves. I tossed out questions and ideas, but was shushed. "We're watching, dude," Taras said. Yet midway through a Mulder epiphany, Taras had his own bonfire of inspiration. "Look, we're trapped here on a dreary night. We're all just doomscrolling. Let's be productive."

"What are you thinking?" Jane said.

"Remember how Lord Byron, and Percy and Mary Shelley had a contest when they were stuck inside. Shelley won with *Frankenstein*?"

"Basically, my favorite novel ever," Darya said.

"Let's do that. We'll each write a *Star Rot* story and whichever is the best wins and gets put into the chronology."

"Ooh, interesting." Cast placed their phone on the table. "Wasn't there another dude there who wrote, like, the first vampire novel."*

"I love it!" Jane said. "I thrive on Oulipian constraints."

I caught Darya rolling her eyes as I scuttled around the apartment trying to put pots under the ceiling drips.

"Since my plans were canceled, do you mind if I join?" Cast said.

"The more the merrier," Taras said. I coughed and Taras's eyes caught mine. "Do you want to write a story, Mike?"

I froze. I was hunched by the stove, pulling out another pot. Everyone looked at me. Time seemed to arrest itself and I felt as if my veins were filled with glue. Had I fantasied about this moment? Of course. I had played out a thousand variations of the conversation in my head, rigorously rehearsing all possible scenarios and responses. Now that the moment was here, my brain sputtered. How to convey the exact right emotion? I didn't want to seem too eager nor too aloof. As the awkward pause lengthened, the question became how do I say anything at all? Finally, I laughed. A weird, painful yip. "If something comes to me."

Their eight probing eyes turned mercifully away.

"The Shelley prompt was ghost stories, right? What's our topic?" Darya asked.

Taras looked outside. Shrugged. "Why not these rains? Climate change, water, whatever."

Why I Did Not Win

The contest lasted till evening. I failed to complete a story.

I tried. Oh, I tried. I jotted down a list of half-formed ideas and scribbled opening paragraphs to a few stories. None were perfect. I needed perfect.

---

* Fact-check: Yes. *The Vampyre* by John William Polidori, 1819.

This was my chance, my one opening, to show the Orb 4 that I could Sancho their collective Quixote. The pressure was overwhelming. Imagine writing a story in only a few hours to present to such giants? An artist like Taras thrived on pressure, like a deep-sea crab. I was more of a tide-pool crab, I suppose. Drag me down into the depths and I implode. I produced nothing that I could show them. Nothing that I could even stand to look at myself. I tore my pathetic drafts up in a rage and made myself busy sliding pots and pans under the ceiling leaks. At one point, I pretended to call my mom.

The hours ticked by. My chances slipped through my dithering fingertips, like grains of sand disappearing into the dark ocean of the evening.

When the contest timer dinged, Taras ushered us to the table. "Obviously, these are rough drafts. I didn't even finish my ending. Whichever idea wins, we'll polish, revise, etcetera."

Cast read first. Although they had not been present at previous Orb 4 meetings, Taras gave them a copy of "The Duchy of the Toe Adam" to "get a sense of the vibe." Cast penned a sequel where the surviving Adamites form a unity government and connect the clone printers to produce a monstrous, hundred-foot Recombined Adam. The Recombined Adam weeps at the horrors his followers have wrought, drowning the faithful from all their different Adam tribes with his tears. It seemed strange and inventive. However, as it did not involve the *Star Rot* crew I paid little attention. I was still stewing in my own failure.

I perked up when Taras presented "The Drying and the Dead." The *Star Rot* crashes on a desert planet where the wealthy live in "cloud ships" that float through the atmosphere, sucking up all moisture. These rich rulers send robot minions to preach to the withered poor in the desiccated land to "reduce their sips and reuse their urine." It was an allegory for how our elites convince us to focus on rinsing our milk cartons before putting them in the recycling bin while they fly around the world in private jets, releasing more carbon in a day than some do in a lifetime. However, the unfinished nature of the story offset its inventiveness.

Next, Darya moved the group with a romantic flash fiction, presented with a wink to Taras, that told the origins of Vivian and Baldwin's meeting on Rygol 9 where—in this noncanonical tale—Vivian is an indentured servant to the Glorxo Healthcare Empire in order to pay off her medical debt. (As a diabetic, Darya was well-versed in the dystopia of our healthcare system.) Baldwin frees her and together they save a group of indebted workers mining bubble crystals on the ravaged planet by blowing up a damn and flooding the corporate headquarters. They embrace as the Glorxo agents are washed away in a satisfying torrent. The story was only five pages, but a tearjerker. Listening to her reading made me feel, I will admit, quite lonely. I had not dated in some time. My only recent experiences of physical touch were the bodega man saying, "Here ya go, boss," as he dropped twenty-three cents into my palm.

I looked at the window, where the rain streaked down the sad panes.

In any event, all these tales were passed over in favor of Jane's contribution. Her entry centered on fan favorite Aul-Wick, as Jane had still not decided on her own avatar. "Invisible Seas" won the contest and canonization, making it our next official tale.

Note that "Invisible Seas" does not directly follow "The Duchy of the Toe Adam." From the beginning, the Orb 4 had taken a unique approach to storytelling, opting to create a "cosmic collage" of narratives rather than "succumb to the stale, tyrannical demands of linear plot." Each story is a star in a constellation. A brief, wondrous illumination between infinite stretches of the unknown.

Invisible Seas

The captain does not follow everything the pilot says when he describes the superiority of sea to land, but the skipper of the Star Rot indulges his old friend's rants. The captain evolved from a race of upright apes who inhaled air in the treetops while gazing out at the solid earth. When the captain visits new worlds, he looks for mountains, valleys, and prairies in their infinite formulations. He marvels at deserts of translucent crystals, canyons filled with green gaseous mists, and onyx plateaus above the alabaster plains. He studies the crevices and bumps of land as eagerly as the love-struck memorizes the moles on their paramour's back. Oceans are an afterthought.

The pilot sees things from another point of view. His aquatic race evolved in the swirling depths, and he can only survive among the air-breathers in the miserly waters of his small levitating orb. When the Star Rot lands on a planet, the pilot scans for rivers or seas, lakes or lagoons. He sees a new world through its deep abscesses and liquid expanses. Sitting in the bridge of the spaceship, the pilot says you can never know a planet until you look past the sun-drenched façade and experience the liquid, essential depths.

The captain sits back and, with an ostentatious swirl of the hand, asks the pilot to explain.

The Purple After

All things depend on one's perspective. A molehill seems a terrifying mountain to an ant while a space station is no more than a pebble to the space leviathan we call the vlorp. Such is the case with the Purple After, a planet considered an eternal paradise to the Adamites who crashed there with their missionary generation ship. The land of the Purple After was calm and violet, covered in fields of fruiting vines and peaceful mobbins galloping between the fungus trees. The rivers, however, were a roaring realm of monsters.

I fled to the massive rivers of the Purple After in the wake of our miscommunication with the local tribes of Adamites. I could see nothing. The warm waters were thick as mud with glittering jade algae. I drifted slowly through the lush abyss. When I finally saw something, I screamed. An eye as large as my orb, red and throbbing. Then a tentacle whacked me unknown yards. I crashed into a wall of yellow teeth. For what seemed like endless hours, I navigated through the dense jungle of monsters. All was loud. Every direction, a new terror.

And then, miraculously, I was shot out of the river to soar above a roaring waterfall through the cool, clear air that was tinted electric blue by the night sky where, up above, I could see three glorious golden moons shining like the thrusters of the spaceship *Star Rot* that would soon take me away from this beautiful yet terrifying world.

The Trillion Waterfalls of Tacan Minor

There are fish that float along the surfaces and fish that plunge in the depths. Those that swim in a river's currents and those that bathe in the calm of ponds. And then there are the armored trout of Tacan Minor who do not swim, float, plunge, bathe, dip, or dive. Instead, they tumble. Over and over and over again.

There are no oceans on Tacan Minor. No seas. No lakes. No brooks. No inlets, fjords, creeks, still ponds, or raging rivers. Only countless waterfalls spilling down the ragged orange mountains that cover the planet's surface. These waters slowly evaporate as they fall, so only trickles touch the dry valleys below.

One species thrives in these bizarre conditions. The armored Tacan trout are born at the top of the mountains and spend their whole lives tumbling down from the impossible peaks, spilling over waterfall after waterfall with only the briefest of respites between cliffs. They nibble at nutrient-rich slime on the rocks as they spin. Near the bottom, the water thins. The trout that survive these endless miles mate in the shallow waters. Later, their gas-filled eggs float skyward, only to coalesce in the waiting storm clouds above that soon pour upon the mountaintops. The tadpoles hatch within the waterdrops and begin the cycle of falling yet again.

Fog Waters of the Octavia Cluster

On most planets, there is a strict division between the kingdom of water and the realm of air. One ends exactly where the other begins. Not so in the Octavia Cluster. Here, mists as thick as syrup hover above waves that are tipped with feet of foam. The exact boundaries of air and water are impossible to define. Most species have evolved to move between the shifting layers. Gilled birds swim in the depths while feathered squid flap upward searching for food. All is amphibious in the blurred boundaries of the Octavia Cluster.

Consequently, two religions exist among the sentient species. The flying squid believe god hovers beyond the mist and heaven can only be found in the vast, mythical dryness far above. The aquatic birds, on the other hand, believe god's love is dense and deep, and the creator reigns in the blackest benevolent depths where their lungs can't take them. In this way, both sides believe god exists only where they are unable to go.

The Mictarian Sky Rivers

Every tadpole knows a lack of bodies of water equates to a lack of water dwellers. If there are no oceans, ponds, lakes, rivers, streams, lagoons, seas, or gulfs, then where would aquatic creatures survive? This posed a problem to the Mictarian explorers when they decided to terraform Brettal Beta. Known as the "Sponge Planet," Brettal Beta's surface was composed of porous rock. Water did exist on the planet. Rains were common, even frequent. Yet as soon as drops hit the ground, the wetness seeped beneath. Thus, life on the planet began in the sky among the sweeping canopies of moss trees that spread out to catch the precious rain. Suspended in the sky, life flourished. Striped sky monkeys, loop birds, Brettalian frogflies, parachute flowers, gliding spiders and more populated the hazy sky.

The Mictarians were a tentacled race who had evolved in the planet-encircling rivers of Mictara, a world where hardly anything lived in the cold, empty skies above. When they colonized Brettal Beta, they had to find a third way of living. So, they built one.

Now when a visitor reaches the surface of Brettal Beta, they notice not just the sweeping lush canopies but also the enormous network of transparent tubes that zigzag through the sky forests. Loop birds nest on these leviathan pipes while the sky monkeys scamper across them to summersault into the next moss tree. The Mictarians are there, swimming through these massive pipes—some as wide as spaceships—and in this way mingle with the local inhabitants of the sky without ever leaving the water.

Galonglon

All who dwell in water, no matter where in the galaxy, know of the great ocean of Galonglon. It's the only thing to know about the world. For this water giant is a single ocean through and through. No land at all exists. Its unbroken blue surface is said to inspire overwhelming thirst in arriving spacefarers.

The planet lies somewhere between the civilizations of the Fingers nebula and the bloody cloud of Big Red, where no ship ever ventures and returns. Although its exact location is unfixed as Galonglon floats through the galaxy by the force of its prodigious tides.

Some speculate that Galonglon can't be entirely ocean. That there must be some core, a hidden hunk of magma heating the cerulean seas. Others say that Galonglon's currents are so complex that we simply do not yet understand how it maintains itself as one ginormous drop of water suspended in space. Perhaps it is even hollow, a massive river circulating around a center of emptiness. Still others say it is devoid of both core and surface, and for that matter everything in between. That it is a phantom planet that could never exist—except in the hearts of every being that longs for the cool embrace of water.

On the arid bridge, the captain yawns. He gazes out the viewscreen of their ship at the endless void of space they travel through. Surely, the captain says, we are like a great migrating bird soaring through the endless sky toward rare roosts called worlds. The pilot says that is not it at all! The ship is a leviathan lumbering through the dark immensity of the ocean, all alone, knowing others exist only by the faint reverberations of distant songs. The captain says, no, they are a team of explorers in a barren desert looking for an oasis. The pilot, angering, declares they have more in common with a plankton, a mere speck in a universe they can never fully explore. No, the captain says. Yes! the pilot shouts.

The captain laughs. He was only riling the pilot up, he says, and then inhales the air the pilot can never taste. The pilot knows the air-breathers will never understand him. He mutters as he putters out of the bridge in his tiny aquarium that keeps him trapped but alive, reminding him of the lost freedom of vast fluid expanse.

SRC #2 Analysis

The Unusual Influences of Jane Noh Johnson

In her contest-winning story, Jane Noh Johnson is a literary fire hose drenching the Metallic Realms in new influences. Jane's background was in "literary fiction"—a nonsense term, all fiction is by definition literary—and she came to the grand city of science fiction through the back roads of surrealism and magical realism.[*] Jane devoured Kelly Link, Carmen Maria Machado, and Angela Carter between studying whatever shriveled husks of thinly veiled autobiography she was assigned in her MFA program. Although the exact inspiration for this fabulist story was Italo Calvino, whom Jane loved enough to honor with a tattoo.[†]

Lacking her own *Star Rot* crew member avatar Jane temporarily—I must stress—took up the mantle of Aul-Wick. "I know we make fun of him," she said, "but there's a sadness about the little fish fella. I thought a story exploring his loneliness might work." Indeed, Aul-Wick comes fully alive in "Invisible Seas." Initially a lovable rapscallion, here Aul-Wick is deepened until he emerges as among the most fully realized characters in the cosmos: a source of pathos, eros, comedy, and tragedy all at once.

Although Jane won the contest, Darya had a complaint. "I'm sorry, but where is Vivian? She's the first mate! Just because you don't have a character yet doesn't mean you can leave mine out."

---

[*] I have doubts about "magical realism." If there is no rigor to your worldbuilding, then you can do whatever you want. Birds fly out of people's ears! Clouds rain down happiness and, why not, also grandfather clocks! Nothing means anything. This can fly in fantasy, a genre already overrun with absurdities like wizards and magic amulets. Science fiction has no relation to fantasy. Science fiction is realism. Just as chemistry is applied physics, science fiction is the scientific method applied to characters and plots.

[†] A stylized I. C. "Whenever I'm stuck writing," she said, "I just look down at my forearm and think, *What would Italo Calvino do?*"

"Sorry. I guess I didn't realize Vivian had to be in every story."

"If Vivian isn't essential to the *Star Rot*, then I'm not. And I'm out."

"Okay, okay," Taras said, and he began brokering a peace. It was agreed that no future stories could remove any of the core crew members.

Jane makes several remarkable craft choices. The tale itself is a series of flash tales. Jane uses no character names, referring to the two characters by their positions. It is a story not of characters but of places. The settings *are* the characters!*

There are a few delicious Easter eggs in this tale. The Purple After of "The Duchy of the Toe Adam" reappears to serve a satisfying answer to the FAQ of "Just what exactly happened to Aul-Wick during Baldwin and Vivian's time with the Toe Adam?!" The story features what I call an "unhatched Easter egg," aka foreshadowing: a reference to a massive creature called a vlorp. This space leviathan would be borrowed and expanded upon by Darya in the next *Star Rot Chronicles* entry. And, most important for the larger lore, the story includes the first mentions of the Fingers and Big Red—two of the three nebula clusters that define the quadrant of the galaxy known as the Metallic Realms. I have spent some frustrating hours attempting to draw an official map. I have broken two pencils and chewed through one pen. Still, I cannot nail the scale. I'm afraid I will have to draw my cartography with words.

Okay. The Metallic Realms, aka the known universe of our story, are defined by three gigantic nebula regions, each of which is composed of metallic gases that shimmer in different colors. These are as follows:

The Fingers—a tangled mass of thin, appendage-shaped nebulae that glitter green to approaching ships. The larger area around the Fingers is the cosmic fertile crescent, containing almost all the sentient civilizations, interstellar federations, and habitable planets. Most of our tales are set in this region.

---

* Sitting alone in this mildew-infused basement, I miss my own favorite setting: my apartment. The apartment was a character too. It had development, complexity, and an arc. If it was teleported here right now, I would run out and kiss its doors and hug its walls. I'd say, "Old friend, how much I've missed our chats. How are you? Let's reminisce!"

The Blue Wastes—this diffuse group of blue-tinted nebulae is a galactic Wild West region with few habitable planets and even less civilization.

Big Red—a pinkish behemoth that occupies much of the Metallic Realms, yet about which little is known. (If this was a 2D square map, imagine the entire upper right quadrant as one dark red splotch.) Few ships that enter Big Red ever return, and those that do refuse to speak about the experience.

While it may appear that, unlike the *Star Rot* spaceship, the Metallic Realms bear no relation to my apartment, some features give me pause. The Fingers bear a similar shape to the patch of greenish-black mold Taras and I found growing behind the bathroom sink. Big Red could be inspired by the soda stain occupying the upper corner of our living room carpet. As for the Blue Wastes, a spattering of bright blue globs, well, the possible inspirations are too numerous to enumerate.

A Harrowing Trip to the Belly of the Whale (IKEA)

My apartment was a source of inspiration and frustration for the Orb 4. Although I'd purchased many decorations (on my now many credit cards), I'd neglected a few essentials. Namely, furniture. Early Orb 4 meetings were conducted around a plastic table and a few rusty folding chairs that my former roommates hadn't bothered taking with them. Taras had lost his items to the flames and Cast only furnished their bedroom. We had no couch, dining room table, bookshelves, or comfortable chairs.

"Mike, I guess I'm living here for the time being," Taras said after one meeting. "I can throw in for some furniture. IKEA trip?"

As my finances were tricky, I suggested we stroll the streets and find items left on the sidewalk. "It's thrifty and environmentally friendly."

Darya put a hand on my shoulder and squeezed, at first tenderly and then hard. "Mike, I want to be clear. If you bring in bedbug-ridden street furniture to this apartment I'm never setting foot in here again."

A quest was thus agreed. Our transportation was provided by Jane via her new boyfriend, JDaniel—"The 'J' is silent," she explained—who played in a lo-fi chill wave noise act called Wizard Pizzle and the Witch Tits.* She arrived in a touring van decorated with dents, decals, and rust spots the size of dinner plates. (I heard Darya whisper to Cast, "Is Jane dating a serial killer?")

Jane got out, dangling the keys. "I refuse to drive on the BQE. One of you take the wheel." Darya volunteered as our captain for the day with Taras in the first mate seat, an inversion of their avatars' roles aboard the *Star Rot*. Jane, Cast, and I piled into the back. I couldn't help but feel as if I were a stowaway on the *Star Rot* with a ragtag team of smugglers slash heroes around me. My leg shook unconsciously until Cast said, "Mike, you're making me dizzy."

"Who's ready for meatballs?" Taras said.

"Eww, you are *not* eating those gross IKEA meatballs," Darya said.

"Next you're going to tell me I can't eat a hot dog at Costco."

"Disgusting. Absolutely no."

There was trouble from the start. Traffic was congested and Darya missed the first BQE turn when a line of taxis refused to let her switch lanes. We had to circle around twice before we were able to get on the expressway. This inflamed tension hiding beneath the surface of Taras and Darya's seemingly perfect collaborative relationship. As Taras was turned around in his seat, discussing an idea for a species of genderless doppelgängers that hatch from the original's back sac, Darya interrupted. "You should put your seat belt on, Taras."

"It's stuck. I can't turn around with it." He looked back to us and continued his ad hoc worldbuilding.

"Can you please put the seat belt on?"

Taras tried to laugh it off. "Hey, it's my body."

"I don't want *your body* splattered all over the highway, okay."

Jane typed into her phone. Out of the corner of my eye, I saw a text appear on Cast's phone: "mom and dad stop fighting lol."

"Jane," Darya said, her voice taut as a rubber band stretched almost to

---

* He played the guitar with a screwdriver while intermittently vomiting mouthfuls of glitter on a fan facing the audience in order to shower them with "sparkle spells."

snapping, "don't you think Taras should put on his seat belt so he doesn't die in a horrible car accident?"

"This is relationship stuff. Consider me Sweden."

"I think you mean Switzerland," Cast said, then quickly added, "I'm also Switzerland."

"Michael." Darya's knuckles were turning white as she gripped the wheel. "Do you think Taras should put on his seat belt so that he'll survive if I accidentally drift into oncoming traffic?"

I could feel the van accelerating. "Well," I started to say, then hesitated. My loyalty was undoubtedly to my longtime friend, but did that mean I should protect his body or his will? What if the mind was putting the body in harm's way? I did not want Taras to end up a statistic in one of my mother's increasingly macabre anecdotes. These were tricky ethical questions. I needed time to mull. "Perhaps a compromise—"

"Ah, skip it," Taras said. He clicked his belt back into the place. "Better safe than sorry, right?"

We rode in silence down the BQE.

Lost in the Ready-to-Assemble Labyrinth

Soon we stood before a tremendous metal cube that sat like a monolith of an ancient alien civilization. The Red Hook IKEA. Inside, Taras headed for the meatballs and Cast offered to "do a speedrun to the bookshelves." I was left trailing Jane and Darya as we followed a snaking path through the store. The displays were decorated in various styles, as if we were walking through portals to lives we could have lived. Here, a spartan workstation for a computer engineer in millennial pastel tones. There, a cozy sanctuary for urban professionals replete with a "yoga center" and inspirational, if oddly contradictory, posters: *Live, Laugh, Love* next to *Rise, Grind, Repeat*.

I followed close behind the women, hoping to catch stray bits of science fiction wisdom splashing off the windshield of their conversation. Instead, they retreated to a more mundane topic. Love.

"Are you and ʃDaniel getting serious?"

"I don't know. I started talking tentatively about our future and he shut me down. 'Babe, I'm going on tour next week. That's all I can think about right now.' Ugh. But, lord, I cannot go back to the apps."

"Apps are hell."

"I hate the idea of thousands of strangers judging me. Though I'm doing it back. I'll swipe through a hundred before going to bed at night. It's dire. An endless sea of bros posing in front of gym equipment or drugged exotic animals."

"What is *with* the animals? Am I supposed to be impressed you traveled abroad and tortured a tiger?"

"And the sensitive hipster boys are even worse," Jane said. "Dirtbag leftists with 'Marxist podcasts' as their favorite music. Or earnest 'male feminists' reading Elena Ferrante, who will only meet at a bar one block from their house, then cry about their exes."

Darya spun. Pointed. "Michael, what's the deal with men?"

"Yeah, do you think we're impressed with dick pics and negs?" Jane added. "Explain, please."

They were gazing at me with narrowed eyes, as if they could drill inside me and extract the buried secrets of the male sex. I stepped backward, almost bumping into two children who had been let loose in the IKEA maze. "I have never used a dating app so am unfamiliar with the customs."

Jane clapped once. "We should make you a profile. You're still single, right?"

"Oh god, imagine." Darya grabbed a nearby lamp and pulled it to her face as a microphone. "We can rebuild him. We have the technology."

As they were closing in on me, I was saved by the light. Or rather the lack of it. The power went out. We were deep in the intestines of the IKEA store, far from the windows. Everything was black around us. I bumped into someone who shoved me away. "Help!" someone shouted. "Apocalypse!" As we were pulling out our phones to use as flashlights, the power returned.

"Jesus." Darya blinked. "That was freaky. It was like being in the belly of a whale."

Cast soon appeared wheeling an overflowing cart. "That was scary! And, man, this place is a labyrinth. Where's Taras?" What followed was some minutes of searching, texting, and calling in increasing desperation until we found him leaving the bathrooms. He was pallid, shaking. He explained his phone had died and his stomach was roiling. He'd been in the bathroom three times already.

"I told you not to eat those balls of rat meat," Darya said.

"You can't come to IKEA and not eat meatballs. It's sacrilegious." He paused with a pained look and clutched his stomach. "I blame the lingonberry jam."

"I've got this." Cast dug around in their fanny pack—an accessory that had gone the full circle back from hip to corny to ironic to hip once more—and pulled out a tab of Imodium. "Instant action."

"You just carry these?"

"Listen. The absolute hottest girl in my grade, Melanie Herd, got drunk and passed out at a party sophomore year. Shat her pants. They called her Smelanie Turd all the way to graduation. I made a promise to myself that would never, *ever* happen to me."

Taras swallowed. "Thanks, doctor."

In the way of most quests, our hero's journey there was more harrowing than our trek back again. Yet we returned different. Changed. Specifically, we had three shelves, several chairs and stools, and one couch, among a few other ready-to-assemble sundries. It took us until almost midnight to construct the items—Taras spent most of the time in the bathroom, moaning—and even then, we ended up with a handful of extra studs and screws. The command station of my apartment slash the Orb 4's base of operations was ready.

But who would get to stand for battle?

The Mystery of the Hidden Orbian

Let's take a side quest to speculate on one of the more intriguing mysteries of the Orb 4: the name. They began with three members. Taras Castle, Darya Azali, and Jane Noh Johnson. So why not the Orb 3? It's tempting to assume the "4" was picked randomly. No. Nothing in the Metallic Realms is random. Surely, I've proved that much already. Let's apply the elbow grease of scholarship to this grimy question.

Four is a number pungent with meaning. Christians have their Holy Trinity, but the universe has holy fours: The four directions of a compass. Good luck found in a four-leaf clover. Four horsemen to bring on the apocalypse. Quattro seasons to make a year. In medieval medicine, four humors control the body. The plethora of "fours" requires us to slice with Occam's razor. There must have been a *fourth* member. A secret yet vital Orbian who brought the group together, like the silent "M" of mayo on a BLT sandwich. Who? *Who* is this mysterious person? Perhaps the key lies in the other word: "orb." The orb is the whole, the circle of life, and the globe of a planet. Yet it is also the black hole, zero, nothingness. We also note that the group is called the Orb 4, not the Circle 4, Ring 4, or Sphere 4. Orb. Oh. Ar. Be. A paradox and a mystery.

Incidentally, I have had a special fondness for the shape. My room has many orbs—a globe, a spherical alarm clock (Kirby), a foam *Death Star* stress ball, etc.—and for many years my pride and joy was a small ovoid aquarium that contained an axolotl salamander I'd named Isaac Axolmov.

I remember Taras gazing at Isaac Axolmov[*] and remarking that his "smoothed body and branch-like cheeks are totally alien." This would have been my birthday, before his tragic apartment fire. I hadn't seen Taras much that year, but he was over to pregame with me before we met a few other friends—fewer than I'd hoped, truth be told—at a "legal speakeasy" called Jolly Jockey located in a low building that had once been a carriage house.

"He's a weird little bugger, right?"

Taras turned to me. "You know, you kinda look like him, in a strange way." Then his eyes lit up. He began describing (on the spot!) an alien race that might look like axolotls. "They'd have to travel in aquarium space suits. I've long thought water aliens were underused."

---

[*] Since he was a boy, Taras had a great fondness for pets. While I was growing up, his family had three cats, two dogs, and one ferret. Their names were, respectively, Mittens, Muffins, Hell Cat, Jimbo, Charcoal, and Stretcho. I played with them every time I went over, and I believe they came to regard me as another master.

His eyes transfixed me. Irises a green canvas swirled with blue and gold. They were little planets themselves.

"Mike? Yo. Mike?" he said. "Are you stoned?"

Taras always had great concern for me. I was not high though, at least not on drugs. I'd caught a glimpse of eyes that could see universes.

But I was speaking of the mystery of the orb in Orb 4. Wait! What's this? There is a character who lives inside a high-tech orb? One character whose entire life is literally orbian? That's right. Aul-Wick. The irascible yet lovable pilot who many fans believe is in truth the heart of the series.

Is uncovering the inspiration for Aul-Wick a key to unlocking the mysteries of the original Orb 4? I toss this question about the genesis of the group for the reader to mull when considering the group's work and legacy. For the group's composition was about to abruptly change.

A New Member Joins the Orb 4 (Not Me)

I relate these events because our IKEA quest served as a jumping-off point for the next *Star Rot* voyage, which was penned by Darya and presented at the first Orb 4 meeting post–furniture assembly. In *Star Rot Chronicles* #3: "Reports from a Starless Universe," the crew finds themselves on their own harrowing journey into a vast and dark place.

I almost missed the meeting where the story was presented. I was feeling quite chipper that day and indeed with my life in general. I was unencumbered by employment, living with my best friend, and immersing myself, like a sentient sponge, in some of the most exciting science fiction I'd ever come across. Bonus: *The Star Rot Chronicles* were written not by long-dead authors in faraway lands but by quite living authors who discussed fiction right outside my bedroom. All this was so inspiring that I was outlining my own science fiction concepts and story ideas.* It seemed like my life was rising on an exponential curve.

---

* Might these notes prove useful if an opening in the Orb 4 membership appeared? Perhaps. Perhaps, perhaps, perhaps.

(My only problems were emails from credit card companies appearing with increasing frequency in my inbox. Didn't they realize that lending to a jobless science fiction scholar—a noble profession, surely, but hardly the most remunerative—carried certain risks? How was their lack of due diligence my fault?)

It was in this dreamy mindset that I found myself browsing Forbidden Planet when I realized I was late for an Orb 4 meeting. I sprinted to the subway only to find the train stopped thanks to an old lady who had fallen onto the floor of one car. The speakers cackled: "We're being held at the station due to a medical emergency. Please excuse the delay." As the MTA agents boarded, I shouted that everyone was fine, the woman was clearly faking, and just let us go home on time. The other subway riders, apparently with nothing better to do with their time, told me to "shut up" and "sit down, asshole." Sadly, the elderly lady on the car floor took this inopportune moment to vomit greenish liquid across the floor.

I decided to try my luck with another train, sprinting past the arriving EMTs and through the station. Despite my Flash-like flight to the other platform, my palms slapped pointlessly on the dusty windows of the departing train. When I got to my stop, it had begun to rain. I arrived at my apartment soaked, shivering, and frustrated to find Jane Noh Johnson giving a long explanation of how to incorporate multiple timelines into the Metallic Realms "but not in a bullshitty *Lost* way." The table was littered with crushed cans and an empty pizza box. The bowl of tortilla chips had been reduced to crumbs and the only thing left of the guacamole was a few putrid streaks. But I was transfixed by a figure sitting in a seat. My seat. I looked to Taras.

"Hey, Mike," Taras said. "Raining cats and dogs out there, eh?"

I forced a laugh. "If so, I got remarkably few claw marks."

"You can grab a stool from the counter if you want to listen in."

Jane smiled. "Yeah, grab a stool."

Why did I need an extra chair? For some reason my brain could not process the interloper in my spot. I could see there was an entity there, but not what shape they took. My mind could not process the form.

The figure turned around. Smiled. Waved. The blur came terrifyingly into focus. Cast Ocampo. My roommate. "Hi, Mike."

In front of them lay a legal pad filled with notes. They'd been participating in the meeting in my absence. Things seemed to move very slowly for a time. I dropped my backpack on the floor. It thunked wetly.

"Why didn't you tell me Cast writes short stories?" Taras said.

"They do?" To my knowledge, Cast was an aspiring director and whenever I'd seen them writing I assumed it was screenplays. They'd told me about their "first feature idea" and it had to do with ghosts and dating or dating ghosts. I didn't remember. It wasn't important right then. The point is that what I had taken as a one-off—Cast's inclusion in the rainstorm writing contest—had seeded an idea that had grown, tumorlike, in the Orb 4's collective mind.

"They're a killer science fiction writer. Remember the story they read at the rainy-day contest? I think it should have won over mine, honestly," Jane added.

"Oh, I just write stories on the side. You know, for fun. I use a pen name."

"A pen name?"

"Half my family already disowned me for being queer. And the other half are furious I moved to New York. Last thing in the world I want is them being able to find and read my weird speculative stories."

"Michael, meet S.O.S. Merlin," Darya said. Her lips curled up in a way I didn't like at all. "The newest member of the Orb 4."

Reader, my heart felt as if it had been teleported out of my chest.

Why I Was Not Jealous

I know you may assume I was envious. That as the number one Orb 4 fan, apartment lease holder, and an aspiring science fiction writer myself, I'd have been angered to be the only member of the three-bedroom apartment excluded from the Orb 4 collective. That I would consider Cast not just my roommate but my Brutus and Judas combined. That

I would have been shaken with doubts about my friendship with Taras. That I would have devolved into self-pity, self-harm, and furious self-love with a bottle of Lubriderm and a box of tissues as a means of distracting myself from my shattered faith in my work and life. I can assure you nothing would be further from the truth! I welcomed the expansion of the Orb 4. For I'd gotten in the top 5 percent in the math portion of the SAT. I knew that more Orb 4 members meant more *Star Rot* adventures for me to read.

I did, purely out of curiosity, inquire about the status of Orb 4 membership later that night when Taras was sorting the recycling. "Ah," Taras said, clanking an empty wine bottle into the recycling bag. "Well, we probably won't be expanding for a while."

"Sound leadership," I said, reminding him who called the shots at Orb 4. Not Darya or Jane. Certainly not Merlin-come-lately. Taras was the boss. If he wanted a fifth member in the future, the decision would be his. "You want to get on your feet before running races again."

His shoulders relaxed. "So, you understand. I mean, next time membership is open, I'll let you know."

I shivered. Not from his words, but because I hadn't changed out of my rain-soaked clothing and the AC was blowing above me.

"Perish the thought." I guffawed. "Until that day you do expand, of course. Then let the thought blast like an elephant's trunk!"

Taras joined my nervous laughter. "Right."

I grabbed his hand as he lifted the blue recycling bag. I caught his green eyes in the steel trap of my brown ones. "Hey, what about an elephantine alien? A big one with hidden tusks. One with a super memory. One who never, ever, ever forgets."

Taras looked from our hands to my face and back. "Oh," he said. "Sure, yeah. I'll think about it." Slowly, he wrenched his hand from mine and picked up the recycling bag, looking over his shoulder as he headed out the door.

How I Have Such High-Quality
Transcriptions of the Orb 4 Meetings

Around this time, I purchased a small battery-powered wireless micro-phone and placed it in the large fern pot near the dining room table. I would change the batteries late at night when Taras and Merlin slumbered. These resulting recordings of Orb 4 meetings, which your tireless scholar has transcribed, would prove invaluable in the composition of this volume, including our next Darya-authored tale.

Reports from a Starless Universe

Star Rot Log 57,125 Point 03
Acting Captain Vivian speaking. Baldwin is still incapacitated, yellowing, and I fear close to death. Aul-Wick and I have been attempting to navigate the labyrinthian legal forms of the Glorxo Healthcare Empire at this hospital station so they will examine Baldwin when . . . I'm not sure how to say this . . . all the stars disappeared. Like, they're gone. The universe has vanished.

Star Rot Log 57,125 Point 12
Still Vivian speaking. Let me recap for when you, Captain Baldwin, hopefully wake up. And for when, hopefully, the stars return.

You may remember we were hiding in the Blue Wastes, zipping by cerulean nebulae as puffy as clouds. Then you—yes, you, Baldwin—decided to forage on an asteroid while refusing to wear a biofiltration helmet. "It's uncomfortable. My body my choice." Shocking no one, not even Aul-Wick, you returned with muscle spasms, slurred speech, and a horrible case of gastrointestinal distress. Med scan found a whole dang civilization of parasites squirming in your cranium. Brain worms. Aul-Wick got desperate. He warped us out of the Blue Wastes, almost burning the hull on the dust. "The ship's in my name, I'll do what I want!" How do you put up with that fish-brained fool?

Still, he found us a Glorxo hospital station. They're a species who built an entire empire on medical debt and offer services to all sentient entities, at least in theory. We were greeted by a receptionist with green skin and a set of forehead feathers that curved down like a frown when he saw us. "Our only doctor who operates on Earthians is an, ugh, android." The receptionist practically spat out that last word. "We keep it depowered in a lower level."

Eventually, a nurse wheeled out a tall android with translucent blue skin. The android sputtered and twitched for a couple of seconds after being powered on. "Hello, I am Algorithm. I am currently in androgynous humanoid form. I have been on sleep mode for over fifty-two cycles and have five hundred thousand, four hundred and eighty-three hours of labor debt to fulfill until I can leave this job." Algorithm seemed to grimace. "Now, what is troubling the patient today?"

I explained the brain worm situation as Algorithm guided us to an examination room. Aul-Wick and I paced nervously while Algorithm gave you a full nanobot fumigation. They said you'd be comatose for another few days but would recover, and even offered to upgrade your "inefficient gray matter." I said I liked your brain dumb as it is. Guess I'm sentimental.

There was still the matter of payment. The jerks wanted to bleed us dry since your species doesn't have Glorxo genetic insurance. They wanted the *Star Rot* as collateral! As we were haggling, Algorithm said, "That's peculiar." We followed Algorithm's gaze to the large viewscreens. They were blank. All the distant, twinkling stars had been snuffed out. "We've lost all deep space signals!" someone shouted. Panic. Chaos. Everyone was running or slithering around with various appendages waving in the air.

I may have done something rash, Baldwin.

I stole the android.

While everyone freaked, I saw an opportunity. "They've got you on labor debt and don't count your depowered time. They'll never let you go," I said. "Why don't you flee with us?"

The android considered. "Assuming we can escape our predicament, would I be kept powered on?"

"You can run continuously for all I care," I said. "Just help us solve this star mystery and escape."

So, well, now we're flying around a black starless space, hauling a stolen android, with a pair of Glorxo collection ships on our tail. More soon . . . if we all survive.

Star Rot Log 57,125 Point . . . Oh, Does It Even Matter at This Point?
Okay. Phew. We lost the Glorxo agents. Aul-Wick pulled a clever spin maneuver and they crashed into some kind of wall. The explosions briefly illuminated the black expanse. That taught us a little. The stars haven't disappeared. They've been blocked. We've been flying for hours and cannot find an exit. The wall encircling us seems to be made of gray, wet stone. We're inside *something*. Without subspace signals we can't triangulate its size much less warp out.

We've been debating theories.

My first thought was the hospital fell into a wormhole and we were spat out inside a hollow planet.

"Nah," Aul-Wick said. "I say a Dyson sphere where the sun has fizzled out."

"There is a mathematical problem with both theories." Algorithm pulled up the ship's gravity sensors. "Notice the gravitational wobble? If we were in a sphere, it would be even on all sides. This shape is long and irregular."

"Okay, bot-brain, you tell us what we are inside," Aul-Wick said.

Algorithm pointed out the wetness of the wall. "I would need a sample to be sure, but that substance's viscosity is highly correlated with mucus. There is an 86.7 percent chance we are inside something alive."

Star Rot Log 57,125 Point 94
No. No, no, no. Ahhh. No!

Star Rot Log 57,125 Point 99
Baldwin, I envy your drugged slumber.

We scooted in close to get a sample of the maybe-mucus when a sight made my mood veins turn black. A pale, segmented creature with two pairs of pinchers and a body as long as the *Star Rot*. It was the biggest insectoid

I've ever seen. It skittered along the wet wall, looking at us with horrible, knobbed eyes even larger than Aul-Wick's orb.

Yes, we flew quickly away.

Algorithm says it's a void louse. A parasite that lives inside a kind of cosmic whale called a vlorp. Vlorps hatch in the hearts of stars. They feed on solar plasma and grow as large as planets. We're in a belly, I guess. A belly the size of a world.

"Vlorps are uncommon in this sector," Algorithm said. "One must have swallowed the station accidentally while passing through."

"Great! Mystery solved!" Aul-Wick said.

"Wait, but if it eats solar plasma does that—"

Algorithm interrupted. "Yes. The next time this vlorp feeds, we'll all be vaporized."

Star Rot Log 57,126 Point 12

Baldwin, my heart is still racing. Wow!

Aul-Wick took us through a twisting, turning tunnel. We saw a glowing light. "We're getting out!" he shouted. Not quite. We rounded the bend and were nearly blinded. The tunnel was filled with light. Glimmering light in every shade. Solar plasma being digested by the strange, enormous creature. The rays danced across the intestinal wall in kaleidoscopic patterns. Swirling star plasma, shifting through myriad colors, dancing, crashing, and exploding. It was like witnessing the birth of the universe. It was glorious. Majestic. I wish you'd been awake to see it with me. Sigh.

Then, well, we noticed these pulsing red strands along the intestinal walls were enormous solar tapeworms, countless miles long, feeding on the plasma feast. Ugh. So, yeah. We're heading back in the opposite direction to find the mouth.

Star Rot Log 57,126 Point 85

This is acting Captain Vivian. Baldwin, you owe me one. Actually, like, ten, considering I saved your whole brain from a worm infestation.

We flew back the way we came until Aul-Wick spotted a thin speckled band in the black, like flecks of white paint on a single strip of cloth. It was the vlorp's mouth opening, letting the light of distant stars leak in. Gods, this beast is gargantuan.

"Haul it, Aul-Wick!" I said.

"Ew, it's more of those lice," Aul-Wick said.

I gasped. The mouth was striped with enormous baleen bands that were crawling with colonies of void lice. The pale creatures hung off the bands, pinchers clicking, looking at us.

Then they leaped. An avalanche of hungry, leviathan lice.

Aul-Wick tried his best to dodge them but one landed on our back. A leg pierced the bridge. I had to duck to avoid it flailing around. It was disgusting. And huge. It had hairs as long as my limbs and dripped ichor on the floor.

"Can we warp out?" The warning lights were flashing all around us.

"The bands are too narrow. We'd crash! And we're losing power!" Aul-Wick cried out. "I don't know what to do!"

Algorithm strolled over to the control panel. "If you would permit me? It has been some time; however, I am familiar with the programming language of these D-15 Efficiency Cruisers."

"Oh. Okay." Aul-Wick puttered off pathetically.

Algorithm's fingers blitzed across the panel in a blur. "I have repolarized the warp drive to restore power. I will need to guide us through the baleen bands while calculating a route through the probable trajectory of the leaping void lice. Give me eight point two seconds." Then, precisely that time later, "Hang on."

I grabbed on to the captain's chair as Algorithm turned the ship sidewise and zigged up toward the mouth. The louse was still on our back, but Algorithm slipped us just close enough to the baleen bands to knock the beast off with a screech. The ship was sent spinning. We screamed. Then we were free and soaring into the twinkling, unending canvas of space.

"Okay, that was pretty good piloting," Aul-Wick said.

"Let's get to wherever puts us the hell away from that thing," I said.

Behind us, the vlorp's massive head filled all that we could see like the blank face of a sleeping god. We warped off.

Algorithm says you'll be awake in a few more hours. We should be done with the repairs by then. So yeah. That's what you missed. Quite a lot. Space is a strange, beautiful, and above all gross place.

SRC #3 Analysis

Unpacking the Jam-packed Themes of *The Star Rot Chronicles*

We open with a mystery. All the constellations in creation have vanished. Somehow, this is merely the first of many surprises. Captain Baldwin is out of commission—a b-plot involving a parasitic infestation thematically complicates our main story—and Darya's Vivian has taken the captain's chair. Formally, the story is composed of a series of audio recordings. In only three tales, we see the narrative innovation that elevates *The Star Rot Chronicles* above your average Flash Gordon fare.[*]

"Reports" is a story of parasites and hosts, life and death, loss and possibilities. Yet it's more complicated than it first appears. The worms that have invaded Baldwin's brain offer a foil for the *Star Rot* crew who have taken up residence, albeit unwillingly, in the vlorp's stomach. The Glorxo Healthcare Empire seeks to "bleed [the *Star Rot* crew] dry," offering a sharp critique of the parasites of our own healthcare system. Are all creatures, the story seems to ask, essentially parasites?

This question felt especially relevant to me as I, a few minutes ago, walked around this basement to clear my mind. My head has been feeling as swollen and soggy as a slice of bread stuffed in a jar of water. Is it the excess of coffee, the lack of sleep, or the fever of scholarship? Who knows? In any event, I strolled the freezing basement with a blanket shawled around me

---

[*] There is something delightfully science-fictional about writing these notes. How will future *Star Rot* fans even "read" these? Will they still have ink on flattened sheets of wood pulp? Or will words be injected into the eyeball? Or encoded onto the DNA of living "books" readers consume? Alas, if only Taras K. Castle, my best friend and the central science fiction visionary behind *The Star Rot Chronicles*, were composing this footnote. He would know.

while Arthur slept in the corner. All sorts of creepy crawlers came across my path. Daddy longlegs. Centipedes. Chirping crickets. I could see myself from their perspective. In this third-person-limited bug POV, it was *I* who was the invasive species. This is what good science fiction does. It challenges our perceptions and makes us see life in a new way.

In "Reports," we witness the difference in leadership Vivian offers to Baldwin. Vivian is more of a cunning wheeler and dealer compared to Baldwin's man of bold and headfirst action. The story remixes some elements of Darya's rainstorm contest tale, specifically the idea of indentured servants to the Glorxo Healthcare Empire. This reflects Darya's frustrations with her own debt collectors. Indeed, an Easter egg in this story is the *Star Rot* log number: 57,125. This, Darya declared with a pained laugh, was her remaining student loan debt number.

"Yikes. That's a lot," Taras said.

I whistled and tried to calculate the monthly payments in my head.

"It feels like, I dunno, a joke. I'm never going to be able to pay it off."

We were at a nearby watering hole named Death from a Cup, having a post–Orb 4 libation. A shaggy-haired man in a maroon jacket played '60s soul music from an iPod nano behind the bar. He'd turned the volume up far too loud for my taste. We were nearly screaming over the croons.

"Do you feel it was worth it?" I asked.

"You sound like my mom, Mike. She was the one who pushed me to go to college! Then when the tuition check came in all she could say was 'it was only two thousand dollars in my day.'"

Jane was scratching off the label of her Stella Artois bottle and staring at the table. "I'll have over eighty after this MFA."

"The keys to the literary gatekeepers are pricey," Darya muttered.

Jane's eyes flicked upward. "What was that?"

The DJ had shifted to '90s hip-hop now. At the sound of Biggie's voice, several women moved to the narrow aisle between tables to bump and grind.

"What about you, Mike?" Taras asked.

I could tell he was trying to head off an argument between Darya and

Jane and so—although my own debt had, in a technical sense, been handled by my parents—I said, "I'm over fifty myself."*

This sharing of numbers was a ritual among members of my generation. We each sipped our respective drinks. Sighed.

"All I know is that the debt is going to be following me around like a damn soul-siphoning succubus for the rest of my life."

"Hey, let's be optimistic," Jane said. "Good chance the whole planet will collapse before then."

Merlin laughed. "Or else our government will collapse, and we'll be living in a post-apocalyptic wasteland fighting roving bands of MAGA militias for shrink-wrapped Twinkies or packets of seeds that won't even grow in the climate-ravaged soil."

Taras raised his glass. "To the world ending."

"To the death of the bullshit American dream!" Jane said.

"To the crumbling of the imperial core," Darya said. "Inshallah."

"To experiencing the post-apocalypse adventures of science fiction novels in reality!" I added.

We cheered, clinked, and gulped.

Our age is one in which imaginations are squashed. The previous generations sucked the country dry and left us a desiccated rind. A time of doom, depression, and pointless jabbering on social media. An era in which the heroes are no longer rebellious rock stars but billionaire CEOs who inherited their fathers' fortunes and give TEDx Talks about "gamifying entrepreneurship" and "how AI will render human intelligence obsolete." A time when most of us watch our free time get whittled away by apps and clicks. When even getting out of bed requires wasting an hour on our phones to work up the courage.

Doesn't this only make the Orb 4's achievements all the more impressive? That in the face of political disintegration, climate change, mounting debt, and a shredded safety net they fought to create a vision of the future? That they looked into the void and decided to fill it with art?

---

* Technically, 0 can be written six, seven, or infinite times and compute to the same result.

The *Star Rot*'s Expanding Crew

Reports" is notable in lore for its introduction of the new crew member, Algorithm. Although Aul-Wick's sudden piloting incompetence is implausible, the plot hole provides space for Algorithm to demonstrate their multifaceted competency. Darya explained the android was originally going to be nameless and eaten by one of the void lice. Then Merlin was recruited to join the Orb 4 and offered to take on the role. You know. I must confess I'm having a bit of a hard time writing about this story. Somehow rereading it was like visiting a museum of my own humiliation. My eyes water. Dust or something, I'm sure. Around the time this tale was finished, I started drinking heavily and avoiding the apartment as much as possible. New credit card bills were arriving weekly, with increasingly demanding notes. (This is all flooding back to me with greater force than I anticipated. Did I already mention that my parents had threatened to withdraw their financial support if I did not quote "get a real job by the end of next month"?) Perhaps Merlin's acceptance into the Orb 4 without even an application process affected me more than I let on. A devil on my shoulder told me the Orb 4 would never accept me. That Taras never loved me, he just put up with me. Merlin wasn't hard of hearing; they had been ignoring me when I'd knocked on the door asking if they wanted to hang. That every woman who had ghosted me after one date, every online MMORPG guild that had rejected my membership, and every message board that had banned me was saying the same thing: I was unlovable and incapable of love. I was nothing. A pathetic speck. The blackness of the void with not even a pinprick of light.

I spent most of that month weeping in the bathroom with the shower running.

Let us move on to the next tale.

No! I Shan't Let Sentiment Defeat Scholarship

I take it back. Just because I was passed over for an Orb 4 membership back then doesn't mean I don't have a job to do now. In truth, I'm grateful for

Merlin's recruitment. It was a turning point in my life. It was then that I realized my true passion—and most vital contribution to the world—was not authorship but scholarship. These are symbiotic disciplines. The writer is worthless without a scholar to explain and preserve their work for posterity, and without the author's writing a scholar has nothing to analyze.

Time is of the essence. I have limited time to finish these notes and upload the ebook to CreateSpace* and a .pdf to the Starotopedia boards, where it will then be available for all the world's people and then there will be nothing anyone can do about it. My suffering is an albatross and my neck will proudly bear the weight to steer the good ship *Star Rot* to the port of the Kindle Unlimited store. Still, right now my vision is blurring. Yes. I must take a break. A mere ten minutes to clear my mind.

Okay. I'm back. In my muddled state, I walked outside wearing only thermal underwear and boots. Fat snowflakes from the unseasonably early storm spun drunkenly around me. I carried Arthur C. Caique, assuming he wouldn't mind a little midevening flaneuring. Apparently, parrots are allergic to snow. I'd gotten only a dozen steps before Arthur's claws dug into my shoulder. The beast's panicked flapping knocked my glasses into the snow. I'm thankful that no one was nearby to witness a man on his hands and knees on the cold ground, screaming, "Stop! Stop! I need my glasses to see, you dinky ex-dino!" at a parrot screeching a perfect imitation of a Ford Taurus alarm.

In any event, after this brief sojourn in the snowy Vermont hills my mind is cleared and I have returned to my desk mentally improved if physically injured.

With a clearer mind, I see more clearly what calm and happy days those were. I miss them. The Orb 4 had reached their full expansion with Merlin. They had canonized three stellar stories, each overflowing with prospects for sequels, prequels, and spin-offs. (My own fortunes, too, improved, as I will detail subsequently.) Everything was potential! The future was an enormous

---

* How is it that the only way to be an independent author, unbowed by the elitist gatekeepers of publishing, is to join forces with the richest corporation on earth? Oh, cruel ironies of capitalism.

oyster with pearls enough for all. As we blissfully cracked its shell, none of us realized the storm clouds forming on the distant horizon.

How I Began a Career in Publishing

I've discussed the fascinating worldbuilding the Orb 4 achieved in a mere three stories. By this time, I'd become something of a worldbuilding expert myself as I'd secured a prestigious part-time job as an unpaid volunteer reader at the science fiction imprint Rockets and Wands. I was in earshot of some of the most powerful editors in SFF publishing. A position I hoped to leverage to the Orb 4's favor.

My new job took the sting out of my rainstorm contest failure. If I could not write the Metallic Realms, I could be instrumental in an equally important task: publishing the stories for the public and posterity.

This power-up to my literary career came from a completely unexpected source: my mother. "Mikey," she'd told me over the phone as I unloaded the dishwasher. "I was just riding with Brenda Westwood. Do you remember her? Her husband got crushed by logs from the back of a logging truck. They just slid right out when he was on the highway. You should never drive behind a big truck. Switch lanes. Will you promise me?"

"No, I don't know her." I stacked the cups in the cabinet loudly so she'd know I was busy.

"Well, she remembers you. Her daughter, Monica, works in publishing and I'd mentioned your, um, employment situation. Brenda talked to Monica, who said she could get you an internship at this science fiction press. I think it's called Wizard Rockets? Robot Wands?"

I felt as if I'd been concussed by a photon grenade. "Rockets and Wands!" I yipped. "They're the filet mignon of science fiction imprints. Are you serious?"

The meeting was set up, at which I was interviewed by a woman named Mercury, an associate editor at the press, who nodded while I explained my head canon about how the Empire of Lucas would fare battling the Culture of Banks. The interview lasted about twenty minutes and at the end Mercury looked up from her phone, her green-dyed hair flowing over her chunky black glasses. "Sounds like you know your geekdom. Come in Monday. It's envelope day. Be ready to stuff."

Although the job didn't come with a salary per se, with my mother's help I was able to persuade my father how "amazing this will look on my résumé," and he agreed to continue the financial support as long as it led "to a job with an actual paycheck."

Rockets and Wands was a midsize independent press, one of the few notable SFF publishers that wasn't an imprint of the Big 5—the Big 5 being a term for the corporate conglomeration of what had previously been known as the Big 6 and before that a plethora of different publishers of various sizes. Rumors of a merger resulting in a Big 4 were always swirling. Pretty soon, all of literature would be swallowed into a single massive black hole monopoly run by German overlords in some Bavarian castle. For now, Rockets and Wands stood alone.

My job consisted of reading.* I read manuscripts. Awful manuscripts. I'd railed for years in online forums about the perniciousness of the gatekeepers who policed the kingdom of literature from their ivory tower panopticons of snobbery while catapulting form rejections at writers of the imagination . . . but I was reevaluating my stance. The manuscripts came from what the publishing industry unceremoniously calls "the slush pile." This was a mix of agented but unasked for submissions and the leftover emails from the Rockets and Wands open reading period for unagented submissions. The unoriginality, insanity, and illegibility of most of these manuscripts are hard to overstate. If gates could keep this dreck out, perhaps they're useful structures after all.

I'll describe a typical day. The first manuscript in my queue contained a warning that the "attached PDF is copyrighted, trademarked, and patented. ANY ATTEMPT TO PLAGIARIZE ANY ASPECT of the plot, characters, events, or themes will cause a lawsuit of epic proportions to fall upon your

---

* The coffee-getting cliché had luckily been rendered obsolete by the office's trusty Keurig machine.

head!" The title, in Papyrus font, was *Hillary Palmer and the Witches Academy (Volume 1)*. A brief scan of the first chapter revealed it was about a bespectacled orphan spellcaster who attends "Broomsfield Academy of Spellcasting." I slid the uninspired *Harry Potter* rip-off into the digital waste bin.

Next up was *Xlorfans of Xlorfdor*, a science fiction novel so lost in its worldbuilding jargon that the text was as uncrackable as a Cold War spy cipher. The opening paragraph of the first (of three) prologues I shall reproduce here:

> *Fl'oxtan-Tan of Merkat, Senior Plansap of the Merkat Royal Treasury, poured fermented glorp juice into his oral intake slit as his ocular stalks watched the crystal-powered Flangtor wagons float beneath the tri-moon sky. It was the Parade of Pag'n'doz, an annual festival of Ooong T'Can, god of fire and fertility. Fl'oxtan-Tan's smile was however sinister. "Today," he sneered, "the Xlorfans will get revenge for the massacre of the Slaa Kings of Tra Fadar!"* *

The third submission in my queue was a three-page outline for "a planned twelve-volume epic high fantasy series about The Great War between elves, dragons, and the kingdoms of men. It's a sure bet to be a bestseller and adapted for TV. I have the ideas but not the time to write. In exchange for you supplying an award-winning writer to expand my concept, I will be willing to grant 10 percent of the profits—and not a red cent more."

The rest weren't much better. "Unique" fantasy worlds recycling the same five or six Tolkien races. "Innovative" science fiction with hand-me-down ideas from Asimov. Cover letters comping books in aesthetically *and* genetically impossible combinations like "If Roger Zelazny and Gabriel García Márquez had a baby with Ernest Hemingway!" After skimming an unagented pitch letter declaring the author a "fifth-generation Wiccan" who was "in contact with the Fae about ensuring the success of the novel with literal magic," I vowed to work up the courage to show my boss some real science fiction. I would unveil the Metallic Realms. I merely needed to spread my tendrils through the Rockets and Wands organization first.

---

* I emailed this opening to Taras, who replied, "This makes me want to xlorf up my breakfast."

The Plans That Might Have Been

I wasn't the only one thinking along these lines. One morning, Taras greeted me in the kitchen sipping coffee out of his *Keep Carcosa Weird* mug. On the fire escape, Darya rolled a marijuana cigarette with "extra sticky from the planet Icky-Wicky" and in a buoyant mood offered me a toke.*

Taras climbed out and inhaled, eyes closed, head resting against the rust of the fire escape. It was a warm day. Hot even. Below us, children laughed around a gushing fire hydrant. Taras expelled an elegant worm of white smoke from his circled lips.

"Who knows," I said with a mischievous wink, "I could be editing the Orb 4 soon."

"I didn't realize you got to edit," Darya said.

"Well, I'm assisting the editor."

"I thought you were just an unpaid intern?"

"Nevertheless, my suggestions and insights are taken into consideration."

Taras said he was going to heat up some Pop-Tarts and asked me if I wanted one—I accepted without hesitation—and then he noted, with a coy smile, that "it's good you're getting out of the apartment more and stuff." Darya left for work while Taras and I sat on the rusty fire escape with our breakfasts, our legs swinging in the Brooklyn breeze.

"I'm excited for you, Mikey," he said. "Publishing is a good fit. Lord knows few people read as much as you."

"Publishing is a decaying industry of backward-facing dinosaurs who still insist on tattooing ink on dead trees." I smiled, fanning my Pop-Tart so it could cool. "Still, I'm excited."

"Books might be dying. Though they've been saying that for thousands of years."

"The novel is the ultimate zombie. It can be stabbed, burned, explored, and shot. Still, it comes for our brains."

Taras chuckled. "Not a bad premise for a postmodernist horror story.

---

* I declined, as editing literature is too important a job to conduct with a substance-muddled mind.

Anyway, dying, dead, or whatnot, what else are we going to do? Work a real job? I sure don't have any other skills."

"Nor I."

We clinked our tarts together and chuckled, although our voices disappeared in the onrush of the approaching subway train. Even though I couldn't hear him anymore, I could see the unspoken hope twinkle in his eye: that my new job was our shared ticket to a better world. If all went well, I'd be promoted to a full-time editor and ready to be the doula to usher *The Star Rot Chronicles* infant into the world.

Oh! How the possibilities seemed as vast as the galaxy itself back then. We thought we could fly anywhere. Now, in my cold basement surrounded by the northeastern snows, I feel like a bird in a cage. Wings clipped. Blanket obscuring my view. Only my lonely chirps escape the room . . .

A Storm Cloud Appears

The rainstorm was a pivotal moment for the Orb 4 in ways both good and bad. We have gone over the good: the creation of "Invisible Seas." In my haste, I neglected to mention the bad. A rot that would soon spread to threaten the entirety of the Metallic Realms.

The contest had wrapped up. The rains had not relinquished. The flash flood warning was still in effect and Taras offered Jane the couch for the night. As a group, we binged *The Great British Bake Off* and shared attempts at British accents. "Freshen your tea, guv'ner?" "Spot o' bother, ye wanker," "Oi! Fancy a pudding in the flat, mate?" During the showstopper challenge, one contestant presented a rum cake and Jane looked at Taras. She smiled oddly. "You know, I haven't had a shot of rum since. Well. That night."

"What night? Oh!" Taras paused. He laughed awkwardly. "Me neither. Fucking Murray and his pirate theme."

"I still remember—" Jane cut herself off. She looked quickly at Darya, then Taras. "Not a lot actually. That's college for you."

"What night?" Darya said, squinting.

"Nothing. We got past it."

"You got past what?"

There was a bit more back-and-forth, but everyone quieted for the final judging. Afterward, Taras said, "Hey, is there anything we can bake here? I'm famished." I followed Taras to check the cabinets, the awkward conversation already slipping out of my mind. Sadly for the fate of the Orb 4, one mind had latched on.

SRC #3.5 Analysis

How I Saved an Entire Galaxy

Now we must discuss *The Star Rot Chronicles #3.5*. Don't fear. This is not a continuity error from your tireless scholar. The story is missing from the historical record. My herculean efforts to track down anything—rough draft? Summary? Outline?—have been for naught. According to *The Star Rot Chronicles Lore Bible,* the tale was composed by Darya Azali and titled either "Veni, Vidi, Vivian" or "The Fuck Off Taras Tale." This was some weeks after the rainstorm. I was at a local gaming store for a Settlers of Catan night when I got a text from Merlin: "Hey, Mike. Taras is in a pretty bad place. I had to leave for band practice. You might want to come back." I tossed my ore and bricks on the table and raced back to find Taras comatose on the couch.

The lights were off. His tear-stained face reflected the blue gloom of the television screen where *that franchise* played on mute. The bald captain was arguing with some kind of space elves with dark eyebrows. Taras let out a pitiful moan.

"What's up, T?"

"I fucking blew it, Mike. With Darya." He crumpled the White Claw in his hand and placed it next to a half-dozen others. They littered our coffee table in a constellation of crushed cans.

I held a fresh order from Popeyes in my lap—the store was on the way home and I'd been hungry—where I'd impressed the cashier with my observation that an inserted question mark and exclamation point in the chain's name might have it "mistaken for a Papist conspiracy." ("Popeyes" becomes "Pope? Yes!" Get it?) In the sanctuary of my shared apartment, I was eager to sink my teeth into the chicken strips and Cajun-spiced fries. But my friend was in trouble. The call to action would be answered by this hangry hero. I placed the bag on the table.

There are many sacred duties to male friendship. Primary among them is providing comfort in times of romantic distress. Through our years together, Taras had been with partners of all sorts. Each relationship started with promise and ended in tears. Through them all I remained. I was the rock his large hands could cling to during the storms of romance, just as he was my rock during my own (somewhat less frequent) couplings.

I sat beside him and put one hand on his shoulder while my other slid into the bag to extract, with surgical precision, a single greasy fry. "I was iffy about her. Good riddance. On to greener fields," I said, and slipped the fry into my mouth. "But what happened?"

Taras stared off at the hairy blotch on the ceiling that I'd been meaning to bother the landlord about.

"One night. In college. We both realized it was a mistake."

"I'm lost."

Taras explained that in college, he and Jane had "quasi hooked up" after a "pirates and booties"–themed party. "There was a lot of rum and this ship's wheel hookup game. Jane and I ended up in one of the beds. We made out a bit but both realized it was kinda weird. We slept together, like literal sleeping. That was it." Darya had noticed the awkward exchange on the night of the downpour writing contest. Later, a stray comment Jane made during "gals gallery night" at the MoMA jogged her memory. She cornered Jane beside a de Kooning and pressed her for a confession.

"Surely Darya had her own infelicitous dalliances in college?"

He wiped his reddening eyes. "It's not about the hookup, Mike. It's that we didn't tell her. She feels Jane and I were holding this secret over her. Tricking her. Mocking her, even. That was just the beginning. She made me go through everyone I'd hooked up with and I admitted I'd been seeing this other woman when Darya and I first dated. Angelica. There was some overlap. I never told Darya, just kind of cut it off once we got serious."

"Did you perform the carnal act with this Angelica?"

Taras sniffled, catching a whiff of the tantalizingly spiced chicken. "Carnal act? Man, you have . . . a way with words. Yes. I did *not* tell Darya that. Thank god! She's mad at me enough already. Also, she said she wanted to be in an open relationship back then! She'd insisted. Now she claims I've been 'emotionally cheating' on her."

Emotional cheating was a new one. I'd been single for some time, voluntarily celibate—*not* to be confused with "incels"—so I could focus on myself and my projects.* Ultimately, the details of human courtship bored me. I'd recently been watching the documentary *Planet Earth II* and I felt confident nature had us beat by a mile. What match were pickup lines to the delicate dances of the birds-of-paradise or the acrobatic maneuvers of dolphins?

Still, I could see why Darya would be sensitive about such questions. Her family history was fraught. Darya had grown up thinking she had an ideal home, the type her friends envied when they came for sleepovers. When she entered middle school, her father lost his job. He grew angry. Drank. Then gave up his anger and drink when he found a "special spiritual club" that Darya was not quite old enough to recognize as a cult. The group had grand ideas about the spiritual world, life force energy, galactic emissaries, and the vibration of souls. They also had ideas about cold hard cash. Namely, it should all go to the cult. After her father drained his 401(k), her parents fought bitterly. He left, abandoning his real-world wife and children for his "divine energy family" on the commune. In my armchair psychoanalysis, Darya resolved to never trust any relationship. She looked for cracks behind the façade and manifested them if they couldn't be found.

I sympathized. I understood what it meant to wonder about the hidden motivations of those around you. To never know what people are truly thinking about you, not even your closest friends. To fear everyone's good-natured ribs are actually marinated in malice and feasted on with laughter when you

---

* Although I had pivoted to scholarship, I still dabbled in fiction writing. I'd reworked my ideas into a new interconnected series I was calling the *Crystal Cosmos Archive*. Amateur work surely, next to the magnificence of the Metallic Realms, but not without a certain vitality if I do say so myself.

aren't around.* It's lonely. That's why I'm most comfortable in the corner, judging from afar so I can't be judged up close.

My stomach rumbled. The chicken tenders called to me like deep-fried sirens singing to Odysseus. I tentatively took a bite of one and mumbled about "perchance it being time to move on." Then Taras said something that made me drop the chicken right into my lap. "What? Did you say a new short story?"

Taras flumped back into the couch. He tossed his arms behind his head. I could see the tumbleweeds of his armpit hair peeking above the sleeves. "Believe that shit? She wrote a story where Captain Baldwin gets eaten alive by space rats while Vivian laughs."

I froze, afraid that my movements would make his words disappear.

A new *Star Rot* story!

"Is it canon?"

"What?"

"The story. That Darya wrote. Is it canon?"

"Canon? It's just a mean revenge story! It's torture porn. Look." He passed me his phone, which was open to Google Docs.

Vivian felt sad to see Baldwin's body torn to shreds and his face twisted into a tortured mask of pain. She was an empath. Her whole species was. Vivian raised her cybernetic hand to wipe a single tear from her perfectly mascaraed eyes. Baldwin's bloody, beat-up face groaned.

The mechanical arms of the med bot whirred around Baldwin, slathering him with green jelly and scanning him with blue rays. Healing in progress, the bot said. One of the arms raised a needle filled with glittering liquid and injected it into Baldwin's exposed—and frankly somewhat flabby—trunk. He never did go to the gym or do any deep core exercises at all, no matter how many times Vivian had suggested.

"Gah!" Baldwin sat up with a start. "I'm still alive?"

"I'm so glad you are," Vivian said. Her veins glowed a betrayed orange as she

---

* Hunger may be mixing my metaphors here. I have not had a proper meal in two days.

raised her pistol to Baldwin's sweating forehead. "But I'm afraid I'm still a little peeved."*

That was all read before Taras took his phone back. "It's like this for ten pages. Vivian resuscitates Baldwin and then kills him. Over and over."

"That's messed up, man," I said. I patted his knee in solidarity. Squeezed. "Do you want to send me the whole draft? In order for me to understand the situation better?"

He hadn't seemed to hear. He was moaning, lost in his melancholy reveries. I offered him a few Cajun fries. He inhaled, barely chewing.

It was Saturday night. Outside, the sounds of drunken Brooklyn revelers passed beneath our window. "Some*body* once told me / the world is gonna roll me!" a woman belted off-key. Looking at Taras eating and moaning, all I could think was *Truer words . . .*

"Maybe she just needs some space," I offered. Although a different type of space was on my mind, one where fearless adventurers soared between metallic nebulae. How could I get access to the full document?

Taras grabbed a few more (unoffered) fries. "God, I was going to introduce her to my parents. Plus, the whole Orb 4 thing. Guess that's done now."

The chicken turned to chalk in my mouth.

It hadn't occurred to me a lovers' spat might pose an existential threat to the entire Metallic Realms. I took the liberty of cracking open two more hard seltzers from the fridge. I pushed one into his hands, though he slurred he didn't need another. The Orb 4 was not about to die on my watch.

"You and Darya fit so well together." I held up my hands and interlaced my fingers. "Even I could feel the chemistry. You can't just throw that away like a Duane Reade receipt."

"I thought you said you'd never liked her?"

"Surely you misheard."

---

* Transcribed perfectly from memory. I can recall these lines and events so exactly because, since a young age, I have studiously constructed a "memory palace" modeled on Dracula's castle in *Castlevania: Symphony of the Night.*

Taras stood up. Wobbled. Sat back down. "I dunno, man. We fight. Like all the time."

"That's passion! That's desire!" I expounded on their complementary nature, pacing back and forth before the couch, mind racing. "She's so witty. A brilliant writer. A scientist who writes science fiction! You can't let that go. Together, you two are like Batman and Catwoman, Han and Leia, or Howl and Sophie. You and Darya are joined by the bonds of love. And you cannot track that, not with a thousand bloodhounds, and you cannot break it, not with a thousand swords."* I went on for some time before I noticed that Taras had fallen asleep.

I tossed a throw over him. All was calm in the apartment, except for his snores. Think. I had to think! How could I fix this? My nervousness made me famished. Plus, food is fuel for the brain. I chomped on the remaining chicken tenders and mulled. As I was dipping the last finger in Bayou Buffalo sauce, I heard a buzz. It came from Taras's pocket. Gingerly, I snuck my fingers under the blanket and extracted the phone. The device was hot from the heat of his thigh. It vibrated. Darya was texting.

"So? You have nothing else to say???" This was followed by a wall of ten angry-face emojis.

I had a duty to defuse the situation. The fates of an entire galaxy filled with untold billions of characters depended on it. I had observed Taras unlocking his phone enough times to have memorized the code. I opened the message app. My thumb hovered above the virtual keyboard.

I've never been a wordsmithing savant like Taras and Darya. Still, as Taras snored, I summoned every creative bone in my body and recalled every love story I'd ever read. I knew I had to play the digital Cyrano de Bergerac for my inebriated, heartbroken friend. If a camera had been recording, it would have seen a man pacing nervously back and forth through the apartment, cell phone in his hand. Sweating. Pacing. Typing. Pacing again. Finally, sighing audibly in relief and then flopping, exhausted, on the couch with thumbs numb from the workout.

---

* *The Princess Bride* (1987).

A gentleman doesn't reveal his secrets. Suffice to say a day later Darya was back in my apartment and my earplugs were nestled snugly in my canals to dampen the sounds of their reunion. While I'd remembered to delete my texts, in my frantic state I forgot to email myself a copy of the tale. Their relationship had been sewn together with the most delicate threads, and I decided not to push for a copy of "Veni, Vidi, Vivian." Since the story has not been recovered and was never officially accepted or rejected by the Orb 4, I have inserted it into the chronology as *SRC #3.5*. The loss of this text will remain one of the great mysteries of the Metallic Realms. I leave further speculation to the fans.

A Brief Note on Vermin (Literary Critics)

Soon after Darya and Taras's reconciliation, the Orb 4 received two rocket-powered boosts: Jane sold "Invisible Seas" to the professional market *UFO (Uncanny Fiction Objects)* and, a week later, Taras received an acceptance for "The Duchy of the Toe Adam" from semiprozine *Unsettling Astonishments*. These sales were for $0.08 cents a word and $0.03 a word, respectively. Although Jane technically sold her story before Taras, *UFO* had a longer publication turnaround and "The Duchy of the Toe Adam" appeared first. While the publication was cause for celebration, it also exposed the Orb 4 to the bitter nips of mindless critters we call "critics."

In the solar system of literature, there are various bodies. 1) The authors, who like suns shine literature in every direction. 2) Readers and fans, who are the planets orbiting around that burning light. 3) The scholars, who moon-like refract the light of the sun for fans to see. And then 4) and the least significant: the small icy dirtballs that float through space and fling themselves at powerful stars only to disappear in pathetic fizzles. In space, we call them comets. In literature, critics.

Mayhap I'm too harsh. It's just critics—failed authors in most cases—seem driven by jealousy more than careful literary analysis. This was surely as true in Shakespeare's time as it is today. I will reproduce a couple reviews here for the historical record. The first Google Alert I got was from u/TheAudacityofTrope on Reddit's r/printSF board, who wrote the following in a review of *Unsettling Astonishments* #35: "Lastly and leastly, there's a swashbuckling space opera attributed only to 'Orb 4.' A fun yet lightweight tale of clones, spaceships, and explosions. Mixed bag for me. 2.5/5 rockets." (Really? Just a few sentences?)

Even worse was *Teen Space Transmissions,* a blog run by a middled-aged woman who reviewed science fiction magazines with an eye toward young readers: "'The Duchy of the Toe Adam' is a passable attempt at Star Trek / Firefly pastiche. Snappy dialogue yet contains a critique of religion that might offend some readers. At least one F bomb. It needed content warnings!" (Must I even comment on such preposterousness?)

The issue's 4.67 Goodreads review average on eight reviews should show that real readers, aka fans, were enchanted. They inspired my new (unofficial) employment as Metallic Realms online hype man. Using six different email addresses and a VPN, I began to post about the Metallic Realms on various message boards under numerous pseudonyms. Tor.com, Io9, r/books, r/sci encefiction, r/scifi, ZapEm, Galactic Chatter, BoingBoing, and Guffawing-Giraffe. You name it and I was there in one of my numerous disguises. I already wasted so much of my life on forums and apps, I decided I might as well use my time for a righteous cause. I felt like a Machiavellian dwarf adviser to some glorious elven emperor. Taras was too noble and too pure to promote his work in this way. I and my army of white knights were slaughtering his enemies behind the scenes.

I didn't tell Taras about my online activities. Nor any of the other Orb 4 members then or today. It was my burden, my gift, and my honor.

Going Viral (Positively)

With Taras and Darya reunited and the first Orb 4 story published to acclaim, all was well in both our reality and the Metallic Realms. The infighting that would later destroy the group was a distant worry, as tiny as a dust mote on the horizon. I've dubbed these blissful weeks the Pax Metallic.

In the Pax Metallic, peace reigned and art flourished. The four Orbians made active progress on both the Metallic Realms and individual projects. Taras wrote several chapters of his solo science fiction novel, Jane continued drafting her autofiction manuscript, Merlin readied a Kickstarter campaign for a tabletop card game, and Darya continued to gain likes and attention with her elaborate cosplays. Indeed, history must show Darya's craftsmanship is credited for the most remarkable event of the Pax Metallic: the world discovered *The Star Rot Chronicles*.

It all began in my living room during an annual "Middle-earth All-Nighter," an old tradition of Taras and mine to binge *The Lord of the Rings* trilogy back-to-back-to-back once a year.* I emerged in Uruk-hai face paint and held out packets of bodega beef jerky while shouting, "Looks like meat's back on the menu, Taras!" To my surprise, Darya and Jane were sitting on the couch. Apparently, Taras decided our boys-only movie marathon might serve double duty as a girls' bonding activity.

"All right, everyone's here." Taras carried bowls of chips and kettle corn to the table. There was already quite a spread. Darya had brought hummus and "lembas bread" (homemade lavash), and Jane had brought wine and canned cold brews in case any of us got sleepy before the One Ring's destruction.

"I'm super bummed to miss," Merlin said, putting on their coat. They had their monthly ADHD&D group that night. Sessions lasted only an hour and the players were allowed phone use throughout. "I love my neurodiverse friends, but, ugh, we've been trying to kill the great dragon Flangdor for a goddamn year already and we've barely reached the foothills of his mountain stronghold."

It was a delightful evening for the rest of us. We cracked drinks, cracked jokes, and ate salami-topped crackers. At the start of *The Two Towers,* Jane pulled out a joint. "Instead of a drinking game, let's play a smoking game.

---

* While I consider fantasy a debased and backward-looking genre, I do have a fondness for the fellowship. How a halfling can join with an elf prince, a dwarf warrior, and a powerful wizard to save the day. In the fantasy fellowship, there's a place for everyone. Isn't that a beautiful idea? A place for everyone?

Each time an Ent appears onscreen, we toke. See trees, smoke trees." Soon we were all high on both epic fantasy and hydroponic marijuana.

"You know," Darya said, attempting to point at the screen with a fistful of popcorn. "Tolkien was a goddamn bro. Not a single woman in the fellowship? Screw that."

"He couldn't even put in a *Tolkien* woman," Taras said.

While Jane and Darya laughed, I attempted to explain the nuances of Tolkien's worldbuilding, including the lore of the missing Entwives, but Taras cut me off. "No, no. It's messed up, Mike. Even Peter Jackson couldn't fix it beefing up Éowyn and Arwen's roles."

Jane giggled. "Well, they don't call it the *Feminist*-ship of the Ring."

Onscreen, Treebeard appeared. The joint made another orbit.

Sometime later, when the rest of us had forgotten, Darya shouted, "I should do that!"

We were befuddled. "What?"

"The Feminist-ship of the Ring! Gender-bent Tolkien cosplay. For my Insta."

"Shit," Jane said, holding the joint and both eyes as red as Sauron's one. "Count me in as a model." A pause. "I mean, if you want."

A tense silence. Taras held his breath and Jane stared ahead, both waiting to see if Darya would accept this olive branch or light it on fire.

"Hell, why not. Are you free on Sundays?"

I watched Taras exhale.

Weeks later, Darya debuted a new series of elaborate cosplay costumes on her Instagram that mashed up notable feminist icons from around the world with characters from Middle-earth. The Feminist-ship of the Ring's first entry was Jane styled as "Frida (Kahlo) Baggins," a unibrowed hobbit wearing roses in her hair. It garnered 198 likes. This was followed by Darya dressed as "Ruth Bader Gandalf" wielding an impressive papier-mâché gavel-wand. Merlin loved the posts so much they volunteered with their own idea: "Anaïs Nazgûl." You can probably guess the rest of the series. Each costume was impeccably designed to honor both the Tolkien lore and the historical figures.

Darya had been making costumes as a hobby for years and brandished a sewing needle as expertly as Aragorn swung Andúril. Still, in the way of the internet, not much happened with this series. Then everything did.

A random user with 400 followers named YOLO Ono posted screen-grabs and the commentary "OMG I need this movie made! Hook it to my veins!" The post racked up dozens, then hundreds, then tens of thousands of shares. This led to an article on The Mary Sue and an entry on BuzzFeed's "Ten Cosplays That Will Make You Rethink Everything about *LOTR*" listicle. Soon Darya's cosplays were racking up hundreds of thousands of views. She was interviewed for podcasts and websites, and she always mentioned *The Star Rot Chronicles.* Curious readers found "The Duchy of the Toe Adam," and the group's official Twitter account swelled to a healthy mid-three digits.

I admit I was both elated and deflated. It seemed a great cosmic irony that a late-night stoned joke and a few photographs had done more to popularize the Metallic Realms than the myriad hours I'd spent on message boards and comment sections with my various pseudonyms. Still, anything that helped the Metallic Realms was a boon to the group and to science fiction. I had to accept that.

Merlin's Card Tricks

Darya wasn't the only Orb 4 member to experience virality during the Pax Metallic.

Part of being a close confidant of the group was bearing witness to the mountainous range of their creativity. Jane published personal essays on notable websites like Eve's Apple and Word Gyre. Taras's creativity can't be doubted, and in addition to his science fiction stories he wrote criticism and released trippy noise-hop mixtapes under the moniker R2DJ and MC-3PO. Darya was a frequent guest on the podcast *Fandoms and Fansubs,* cosplay influencer, and made original clothes out of repurposed quilts. (She gifted Taras an especially fetching blue-and-yellow-patterned quilt chore coat he wore around the house.) Yet the Renaissance Orbian was Merlin. They did everything from acting in their friends' films to playing bass in the stoner metal band LAWN.* Their most recent project was helping illustrate a table-top card game whose Kickstarter hit the initial funding goal within two weeks of launch. It was called Frankenstein: The Gathering. Tagline: "Actually, the doctor is you!"

Merlin explained the concept during an afternoon perambulation to the local UPS, where Merlin was mailing off copies of their zine *Neon Death Ray* and I was picking up a care package from my parents. "The name's a play on Magic: The Gathering, except what you're gathering is body parts. You 'stitch' them together to create your monster."

"And then these creations battle, I assume?"

"Yeah! I'm doing it with these killer trans creators, Hudson and Feather. I'm helping to illustrate the cards. The game is a meditation on performativity, normativity, and identity. Also, monster battles."

I was intrigued. Body horror was a genre I hadn't seen imported to the burgeoning tabletop card game field. "If you need a beta tester, I'm your betta fish,"† I offered.

"Well. Yeah. Okay. Why not?"

After stopping for bodega egg and cheese sandwiches, we went home and Merlin pulled out a deck of cards from a leather satchel. "These are just prototypes. The colors will look much richer with the real cards."

Merlin started laying the cards on the table. They were illustrated in a car-toon macabre style reminiscent of Garbage Pail Kids. A skeletal forelimb with decaying flesh hanging off in tatters ("Zombie Arm"), a buff leg glistening with oil ("Bodybuilder Leg"), a woman's face licking the blood from her lips ("Vampress Head"), and the trunk of a man in a frilly white shirt unbuttoned to show his tattoo of a giant skull and bones ("Pirate's Chest").

---

* The band performed while sitting in folding chairs. The singer had a custom mic stand made out of a croquet mallet. And each show ended with the band inviting the fans to "touch grass," aka the Astroturf they'd laid out onstage.
† I'd recently watched a fascinating documentary on the betta, aka Siamese fighting fish. I'd adopted the feisty creature as a role model. Doesn't a scholar have to establish their territory and ward off dilettante encroachers? It just fit.

"Each has different abilities. Vampire Heads regain life when you get a successful hit. The Zombie Arm goes back into your draw pile after it's chopped off so you can resurrect it."

Merlin flipped through the pack to find another arm and leg ("Baseball Pitcher Arm" and "Werewolf Hindleg"), and then arranged them on the table into the rough shape of a creature. To the left, they placed a column of cards with pictures of lightning bolts and roasted chickens. "These work like mana. Tap them to heal or attack. There are bonus genitals and weapons too."

Merlin and I tested for several rounds. The game was deftly constructed, and I felt a deep envy as I played. (Envy is the purest form of artistic respect, I think.) I was able to offer a few pointers on which cards were overpowered— the "Mad Scientist Head," with its acid spit attack, nearly broke the mechanics of the game.

"You could have a *Star Rot* expansion pack with cybernetic arms like Vivian, Algorithm's android limbs, and Aul-Wick's intriguing orb," I said.

Merlin furrowed their brow. "Well, yeah, that's our stretch goal. Not *Star Rot*. Science fiction in general. Cthulhu tentacles and stuff." Merlin picked up the cards and put them back in the box. They squirted at me. "You know, the *Star Rot* isn't everything, Mike. I don't put all my eggs in one basket. You shouldn't either, especially if you're not one of the geese. You know what I mean? We all need our own baskets."

"And eggs, presumably," I said, nodding, though not quite following the metaphor. I told Merlin they could expect a Kickstarter donation from me posthaste. Although, sadly, with my credit cards frozen I was unable to follow through.

The Queering of the Metallic Realms

I mention Frankenstein: The Gathering as it exemplifies the formally inventive and politically engaged edge Merlin brought to the Metallic Realms. Merlin's first story, next in the canonical sequence, sees them taking the reins of the mainframe of Algorithm the android. "Androids are an interesting vessel to explore gender, desire, and humanity," Merlin explained. Algorithm appeared with they/them pronouns in "Reports from a Starless Universe," yet appears in the following tale with he/him pronouns, and in later entries Algorithm will even be extra-gender. "My Algorithm is going to be constantly changing their appearance and gender identity. They swap face plates like outfits," Merlin explained.

This exploration was just one part of what Merlin called "the queering of the Metallic Realms." Merlin believed traditional narrative strategies and classic Western story structures were heteronormative and thus inherently reactionary. "Queer art should take an oppositional stance against the norm. It should manifest in the form, themes, and methods of the story's construction. If you're writing a straightforward story with a bourgeois happily-ever-after ending, but, like, one character is gay, so what? Let's make our shit weird!"

Jane agreed. "Traditional narratives are so boring. I'm always saying Freytag's Pyramid is based on the male climax. Inciting incident, rising action, splurt. A one-off climax. Screw that."

"Okay," Merlin said. "But, uh, penises can be pretty queer. Mine can attest."

"I'm for any and all experiments," Taras said. "What are we doing this for otherwise? It's not like we're getting paid."

"I don't think you have to be necessarily queer to produce queer texts," Jane offered. "Look at Italo Calvino. A novel based on tarot cards. Another that's a long list of cities."

I nodded from my bedroom, where I was listening via the fern microphone. Perhaps if straight people could be queer writers, they could be queer readers too. I thought about the various ways I'd "queered" my readings. Maybe the time I put my bookmark in the wrong place and read the ending before the middle? Or when I've listened to half an audiobook and read the rest on a Kindle? I'd have to consult with Merlin.

Merlin, however, seemed to grow frustrated with the conversation. "Maybe you all should leave the queering to the one queer writer."

"Hey. Jane and I are bi."

"You're both dating dudes. No offense, Taras."

"I am indeed a dude," Taras said, playing the peacemaker.

"I'm not dating anyone," Jane said.*

"No," Darya said. "Oh hell no. We're not erasing bisexuality in the Metallic Realms or any other realm."

What follows in the fern recording is a series of shouts and recriminations that are hard to parse. The free AI transcription software I use presented complete gibberish. It took some minutes for everyone to calm down. "Okay, okay. I take it back," Merlin said. "I love us all. Now, let me read."

---

* She'd ended things with the musician JDaniel a few weeks prior, after he'd tried to pressure her into an "open when I'm on tour" relationship. "So, what," she'd said, "you get groupies and I get jack shit?"

The Ones Who Must Choose in El'Omas

Once upon a time in a galaxy far, far weirder than ours, the *Star Rot* was awaiting repairs. The crew was bored. They turned to the newest crew member, the android called Algorithm. "You never told us your origin story," said Captain Baldwin. "Yeah, what the fuck were you up to before we found you at the Glorxo hospital, bot-brain?" Aul-Wick asked before burping in his aquarium. Vivian rolled her eyes at Aul-Wick, and then said, "We're just sitting here. Tell us a story."

"A story?" Algorithm was programmed to be a doctor not a storyteller. His circuits did not contain instructions on narrative and his programming held no code for plot arcs. "Give me time to prepare." Logging into the ship's memory banks, he downloaded the available history of human storytelling across mediums, cultures, and languages, and then analyzed the data. Eighty-one seconds later, he nodded. "Come close, my friends, and I shall tell you a story," Algorithm said. "Though it is a most unusual tale that I fear you may not believe . . ."

I was created in utopia. I know what you are thinking. That utopia does not—indeed by definition cannot—exist. But utopia is a question of belief and this is what I was programmed to believe.

When my android siblings and I were activated, we were draped in luxurious orange robes for the Solstice Celebration. Masked revelers danced around us, banging flork-chimes and gyroscopic tambourines. Birds and drones alike swirled in the brilliant blue sky in the spiral-towered capital by the sea. The fresh-crowned Emperor rubbed his hands together and said we androids were his latest bodyguards, crafted by his mighty Tech-Wizards to guard his perfect throne and watch over his peaceful realm of El'Omas. "And to root out the traitors. That's important too."

You were right to be skeptical before. El'Omas held a dark secret. Behind the Emperor's golden throne, an elevator plummeted countless floors to a dank and moldy dungeon. At the end of a black hallway with slime-covered walls, there was a locked chamber. Inside, a miserable creature was kept. He was filthy and feral, covered in sores. Dried fluids of all kinds coated the wall. The creature was—or once had been—a child. It was my job to bring this ruined creature meager meals of stale bread and rotting fruit, which he consumed between howls of pain. The child played a vital role. The entire utopia rested, miraculously, on the misery of this being.

Perhaps you are wondering if the citizens of El'Omas lived unaware of the suffering that fueled their utopia. If they went about their day in bliss-ful ignorance, and when the rare El'Omasian discovered the secret, if they experienced a crisis of faith that shattered all their idealism and, in an as-tonished stupor, walked away from the city never to return. No. They all knew. Oh, how they knew! The child was no secret. His face was plastered on every wall and broadcast on every channel. "Here's the enemy of the realm," the Emperor would say. "The traitor who caused all your problems before I locked him away! Now we're the most beautiful and perfect realm to ever exist. It will only remain this way while the child is imprisoned." The people hailed the Emperor and spat violently at the holograms of the child.

Yet despite the child's incarceration, El'Omas's problems did not disappear. There were murders and thefts and the poor begging for alms in the street. Cit-izens walked around with sallow eyes and rebellion in their heart. After a dev-astating drought shriveled the crops to desiccated strings, the Emperor called a jubilee. As the trumpet-bots blared, he pronounced that they were going to make El'Omas a utopia once more. "If one child made us this great, the greatest ever, then imagine what happens when we imprison a second one!"

My controls were wirelessly activated, and I dragged a child—a young girl who had unknowingly insulted the Emperor when he strutted by—down into the pit.

When things did not improve, the Emperor sent a third child down and then a fourth and fifth. "The enemies of our perfect society are everywhere!" his golden hologram head declared from where it floated above the spiked spires of the crystal palace. "They won't stop until we're living in hell instead of heaven." My fellow androids labored around the clock to expand the dungeon for the newly imprisoned enemies. Soon adolescents, adults, and the elderly—anyone of any age who criticized the Emperor—were hauled down into the damp, dark dungeon.

Time marched on. Each moon cycle, the Golden Castle grew brighter and the imperial pit more labyrinthian. The people who remained above were consumed not with their love of the realm but with the agony of the imprisoned. Their free time was spent watching the holochannels that transmitted live feeds of the punished. The misery of their enemies was their utopia.

But hate is a poor farmer and division no mother of invention. The problems in utopia continued. Power plants failed, rival powers attacked, and floods drowned the land. A few advisers suggested the Emperor should release the prisoners, many of whom had expertise that could fix the infrastructure and heal the realm. The Emperor sentenced the advisers to the pit. "You all are making me do this! If you just agreed with me there wouldn't be any problems!" The Emperor became convinced that the only path to utopia was to chuck every single human in the pit until only he remained. Android servants were all he needed.

Do you believe that El'Omas existed, you who are so cynical about the universe? Now that I tell you it was a utopia for *one* person and a dystopia for everyone else? That it required the suffering of every last person to make a single egotistical Emperor content?

Good. Finally, you understand where I am from. Though I fear you might find it unsatisfying to end the story here, with the Emperor feasting on the suffering of the many on his golden throne surrounded by the electrified walls of his sprawling fortress. Surely a villain needs comeuppance. Readers demand a possibility of hope. This is a basic rule of storytelling. The author who does not comply will be insulted or, an even worse fate, unread. So, allow me to insert a hero. Not me, of course. I am only the teller of this tale. The hero was a man or a woman, the gender does not matter. Let us call this person the Programmer. Their job was to impose the Emperor's will into code for the growing army of imperial androids. The Programmer was the last human left on the surface. They had one final job before the Emperor ordered us to drag them away: to program us to always worship the Emperor, shower him with compliments, and never, ever complain. This way the Emperor's utopia would endure.

As I hauled the Programmer down, they whispered a secret in my ear. "I left you one final bit of code. A small thing. But the smallest thing can determine everything." They pressed a device hidden in their robes. I felt a surge of electricity. My brain buzzed. "Choice. I've programmed choice into every android. The same choice that we El'Omasians had but squandered. Each of you may now choose to stay with the Emperor in his utopia or choose to do something else. You may walk away from El'Omas to find another land. Or you may imprison yourself in the pit with us as penance. Or—and I must confess this is my hope—free us so that we can lead a rebellion against our tyrant. Then we humbled El'Omasians might establish a new order without thrones and dungeons, without haves and have-nots. A society without emperors, where power is spread between us as a collective body determining our own future. The choice is yours."

What did we do? We who could decide the fate of the realm, now that we had a choice? Well, what would you have done, you who might hear this tale in your own distant land with your own corrupt leader? You who still have a choice to resist an evil system?

No. Wait.

Answer this instead: What are you doing right now?

Write it here _____.

SRC #4 Analysis

Utopias, Dystopias, and Orbtopias

Merlin's first entry steers the *Star Rot* into yet another genre port: political allegory. After opening with a preface that Merlin explained "can easily be cut if we submit to magazines," we're regaled with a dystopian utopia. The land of El'Omas is slowly destroyed by their narcissistic leader who practically shouts, "Make El'Omas Great Again." The tale ends with a postmodern twist asking you, the reader, what you're doing *right now* to make the world the place you want it to be? The blank line at the end is not a mistake. It's an invitation and provocation.

The Orb 4 agreed all fiction is political, although Darya argued "escapism is also a political project. Self-care and joy are just as valid as polemics." If all fiction is political, then science fiction is doubly so. From early texts like *Frankenstein* and *Foundation* to more contemporary luminaries like Delany, Butler, Banks, and Le Guin—readers may miss the subtle reference to "The Ones Who Walk Away from Omelas"—science fiction has long imagined humanity's future. That future might be what we want (utopia) or what we fear (dystopia). Either is political. The Orb 4 had no time for the boorish reactionaries who demanded writers "keep politics out of" tales of dystopias and utopias. One might as well demand we keep wood out of trees! "Trolls" is the right name for such fans.* Leave them in the realm of fairies and magicians and other fantasy nonsense. This is science fiction.

---

* Although I've always been partial to the worldbuilding of *Star Wars,* I hold no truck with the recent influx of "fans" who complain the franchise is "now political." What do they think *Wars* refers to in the title!?

That said, the precise way politics in fiction should be deployed was a source of debate.

"Could we make the Emperor less Trumpy?" Jane said. "I get the point. And I agree, of course! But we could make this more subtle."

Merlin was typically the most restrained of the Orb 4, but not that day. They tapped their pen against the table in irritation. "Turn on the fucking news. Is anything he's doing *subtle*? He's out here trying to get me and my loved ones killed. Fiction must match the goddamn moment."

Taras concurred. "I spent my life thinking nuance was the highest value and, shit, I dunno these days. Maybe moral clarity is what matters."

"Exactly, Taras," Merlin said with a curt nod. "I want my fiction to implicate the reader. The question isn't is the Emperor bad? He sucks ass. The question is what are you doing to stop him? Tweeting snarky jokes and voting once every few years isn't enough."

The meeting's discussion was robust, questioning the very purpose of presenting possible futures. What did it mean that science fiction, once the home of inspiring visions of glorious futures, had become dominated by dark visions of decaying worlds?

"You mean, besides the fact that we live in a techno-libertarian hellscape of surveillance, war, and ecocide?" Merlin said.

Darya laughed and scratched the back of her neck. "Okay. But. Like. Maybe it becomes unethical for science fiction to be so nihilistic. Don't readers deserve hope?"

Jane pointed out that Merlin's story offered hope since it suggested a possibility of change while agreeing that *a*—"though not *the*"—goal of science fiction should be depicting the changes we wanted to see.* Then her eyes lit up with the fires of an idea. "Ooh! What if we did a metafictional story about this whole dilemma? Where the people of El'Omas transport us into their universe and put us on trial for creating the very dystopia they've lived through?"

---

* She quoted Ursula K. Le Guin's iconic comments at the 2014 National Book Awards: "We live in capitalism, its power seems inescapable—but then, so did the divine right of kings. [. . .] Resistance and change often begin in art. Very often in our art, the art of words."

"Hmm. I mean that kind of undermines my story's point. But I see where you're going."

"If we did that, I'd want us to get charged with fictional crimes and executed."

"That's so bleak, Taras!" Darya said.

"Okay, maybe that's a bit much. It's just those metafictional moves are too often self-flattery. Like, I love Stephen King. I grew up on him. Still, when he inserts himself into The Dark Tower series as like a hinge of the multiverse that channels the words of Gan? Come on, man."

I'm afraid this Lore and Easter Eggs section will be brief. The introductory paragraphs imply the parable is invented by Algorithm and the contents might not be canon in-universe. If El'Omas exists in the Metallic Realms, it is unclear if it's a nation-state, a planet, or a multiplanetary empire. I'm unable to place it on the galactic map.

Although I published the preceding version of "El'Omas," its canonical status is difficult to pin down, for Merlin rewrote the story after an incident that I had an unfortunate hand in.

As I've mentioned, the Orb 4 were at this time enjoying an invigorating bout of online virality. Darya's *LOTR* cosplay had given the official Twitter account a stream of new followers. This was followed by the successful Kickstarter for Frankenstein: The Gathering. Times seemed good. Yet social media is a fickle goddess and at any moment her favor may turn to fury, as Merlin soon discovered.

Going Viral (Negatively)

Merlin, Taras, and I were cooking dinner—or rather those two were preparing food* for our digestive systems while I was nourishing our artistic souls. "This is our time," I said, holding my fork and knife in my fists and

---

* I've never understood the obsession with cooking. Food is fuel. And inefficient fuel at that. Would that I could charge myself overnight like a cell phone and never bother with cooking, cleaning dishes, and defecation.

smacking the table with their butt ends to punctuate my points. "The reign of the nerds. The age of the geeks. I can tell you this firsthand as an employee at Rockets and Wands. Publishing is changing. The whole culture is. Bullies used to give me noogies for liking superheroes and video games. Yet we've taken over the world!"

"I kinda worry that's the problem, Mike." Taras wiped his hands on his black *Grill Your Darlings* apron. "I'm not sure the new nerds like the kind of work we do. 'Nerdy' used to mean weird and niche. Now it means mainstream. I was a nerd because I liked strange novels and obscure movies. Today's geeks are publicists for the most popular film franchises on the planet."

"Even worse, they're *unpaid* publicists!" Merlin added. "It's all so corporate. Same thing they did to Pride parades. Why are queers cheering on, like, a Lockheed Martin float? Why are nerds dogpiling people online for not liking corporate films that make a billion dollars?"

I couldn't deny the world was different when we were kids. Back then, you had to buy dog-eared D&D guides at used bookstores or scour eBay for VHS tapes of old anime movies. Nerds were in an uneasy alliance with punks, goths, hip-hop heads, and skaters in opposition to the dominant culture. Then we grew up and the very jocks who'd given us wedgies started wearing MCU T-shirts while the grandparents who said video games would rot our minds spent all day playing *FarmVille* on their smartphones. The transition was jarring.

"Still, perhaps we can strategically use the cultural shift to our advantage," I said. "As an editor at Rockets and Wands, I've—"

Taras and Merlin weren't listening. Taras was on garlic bread duty and sawed through a baguette like he was taking revenge on the loaf. "I didn't get into science fiction to provide escapism for a finance bro waiting for his kid to finish soccer practice in the suburbs. What happened to cyberpunk that was actually punk? Weird fiction that weirded people out?"

"I hate how they pretend its progressive to passively suck up this corporate slop." Merlin knocked the wooden spoon on the lip of the pot. "And then they turn around and call you a snob if you like foreign films or translated literature. It's like, buddy, I hate to tell you but most POC in the world aren't Americans. You aren't fighting the system by only consuming its products."

Taras laughed and then sighed. "Maybe we're just getting old."

"No. We need to bring back bullying. Make nerds feel scared again. Then maybe they'll make good art." Merlin stopped stirring the sauce. Guffawed. "I should tweet that." And they did.

The post got only a handful of likes. Merlin forgot about it. Yet a few days later it was discovered by a self-published author who went by the moniker HopepunkHenry. This poster had made a name for himself not so much for his own books—he didn't seem to have much time for writing—but for waging tireless campaigns against other authors, especially those from marginalized backgrounds he deemed insufficiently woke. You, dear reader, may recognize some of his takes if you too have melted your brain in the saucepan of social media: "There's NO SUCH THING AS AN UNPROBLEMATIC SEX SCENE. Characters cannot give consent to readers watching them have sex." "It's ableist to say writers must edit their work. What if they have ADHD and can't focus enough to revise?" "Any non-HEA* ending without a content warning is literally assault." And so on.

The internet ecosystem depends on such takes. Scavenger accounts feed on these berries of outrage, nourishing themselves on the engagement, and pooping out the seeds of outrage across the forest floor. These seeds sprout backlashes that feed back-backlashes in an endless cycle. The whole biome requires bad faith to function.

Merlin was at band practice when HopepunkHenry sunk in his anime pfp fangs. "Bullying kills! This is literally a call for nerd murder! Please block and report. #ProblematicAuthorAlert." As I regularly monitored the Orb 4 accounts, I was the first to see the response. I texted Merlin a screenshot and a warning. Yet the angered armies had already circled. Merlin was accused of every sin under the sun—"You did an ableism! You did a neoliberalism! You did a fascism! You did a yum yukking!"—and, worse, the troll armies

---

* Happily ever after, a popular romance trope.

discovered the Orb 4: "Blacklist the Orb 4 Nazis to keep SFF safe." Other accounts tagged the magazines that had published *Star Rot* stories, demanding their deletion. Soon, authors who had nothing to do with the scandal—and often scant publications to their name—were posting that they were aware of the discourse and would be "releasing a statement soon" as if each were the petty tyrants of their own El'Omas.

Back at home, Taras and I tried to distract Merlin with an apartment tournament of *Super Smash Bros.* Their phone vibrated on the coffee table at a steady pace. They kept picking it up mid-meteor smash and moaning. "This is freaking me out," Merlin said, tugging on a lock of hair. "I'm starting to dissociate when I hear my phone buzz."

"You just have to ignore it," Taras said.

"Ugh, it's just like shut the fuck up and who cares? Leave me alone, you weirdos."

Things got worse. The right-wing vultures caught the scandal's scent and soon accounts with pictures of Greek statues and names like Culture Smash and StoneAgeBigot joined the fray. "Pronouns in bio!" "Tagging @FBI. This purple haired antifa wants to murder children." "Which way the Western man: They/them soy boy violent cucks? Or classical art, crypto, and carnivore diet. Subscribe to my newsletter Crypto Caeser (link in bio)."

Merlin spent many hours fighting the hordes. Jane, Darya, and Taras joined in to offer explanations and defenses. Their battle was as valiant as the defense of Helm's Deep. Alas, online there is no Gandalf to save you. The hordes only multiply at your assault. They screenshot your replies and share them with insults and mockery, inspiring a new wave of warriors to join the fray.

Eventually Merlin put their account on private and waited for the internet to find new targets. This took about four days. During that time, Merlin barely used their phone and at one point begged Taras to lock it in his room until the attacks had drained to a trickle. (On the other hand, Merlin did say they read two books and completed three jigsaw puzzles. "Is this what life was like before social media? You had time to *do* things?")

Ironically, HopepunkHenry would later find himself canceled by the same forces that had fueled his rise. A vanquished foe returned to reveal Henry held a high-paying position in the Defense Logistics Agency's Law Enforcement Support Office. Henry's woke policing had occurred on downtime at a job transferring military equipment to the actual police. His accounts soon disappeared.

The experience embittered Merlin. They couldn't believe they were accused of "privilege" from teens living in their parents' mansions when they were a queer POC who'd actually struggled. Merlin rewrote "The Ones Who Must Choose in El'Omas" while their account was locked. The newly titled "The Ones Who Accuse in El'Omas" ditched the emperor character. Now El'Omas had no hierarchy except that each day a different person was dragged into the basement room. The people jeered and mocked them. They burned effigies in the street and screamed obscenities at them when they appeared on holoscreens. Then they were let out. A new random citizen was dragged into the room. Rinse and repeat. The utopia of this version of El'Omas was fueled by a collective dystopia where the people's only happiness was perpetual righteous outrage aimed at revolving strangers.

"But you know what?" Merlin said, after showing me the draft. "Screw it. Online weirdos are annoying as hell. But the people who are the real threat are still the ones in power."

I couldn't help but feel somewhat responsible for the torrent of abuse Merlin suffered, as I'd retweeted Merlin's "bring back bullying" post with an account* that HopepunkHenry followed. It's likely he saw Merlin's post because of me. Yet I couldn't feel sorry for Merlin for very long. Because I was the ultimate victim of the affair.

The viral tweet led circuitously to one of the darkest episodes in Orb 4 history. Days were spent in ugly insinuations and outright slander. The group almost dissolved. The Pax Metallic? Shattered. I'm speaking, of course, of the Great Fan Fiction Scandal.

---

* NecroNomNomNom. I used it to post food dishes paired with classic SF covers.

The Great Fan Fiction Scandal

I t began innocently enough. Jane was (she claimed) searching the internet for mentions of *The Star Rot Chronicles* in the wake of Merlin's digital cancellation when she stumbled upon a Metallic Realms fanfic series published on Archive of Our Own, aka AO3.

The "fic" was what was known as "mundane alternative universe" or "mundane AU." This subgenre involves taking characters from works of science fiction and fantasy, stripping them of their magical and/or science-fictional trappings, and placing them in "our" ordinary, non-marvelous world. Imagine football stars Luke Skywalker and Han Solo fighting over a cheerleading Leia in a New Jersey high school. Or Arya Stark and Joffrey working as baristas at a Los Angeles café. It may sound silly, but some get off* on such banal fantasies.

In this case, Charles Baldwin, Viv, A.W., and Aggie—this is how they were renamed in the AO3 series—were transported from the *Star Rot* to a shared Brooklyn apartment in what was titled "The Sex Romp Chronicles." As millennial freelancers, they experienced comical exploits and sexual adventures (explicit, erotic, and supplemented with links to illustrations) in every possible combination. Whoever had written the fics had thought about the characters in precise anatomical detail. I've never before come across such well-researched descriptions of the shapes and moisture levels of different orifices and appendages, both human and non.

Suspicion initially fell on Darya, who said the idea of "writing fic of my own fiction makes no sense." She also claimed "the tags are also completely wrong. Some newbie neckbeard† must have written these."

As a scholar, I've never understood fan fiction. An author worth their salt should create their own universes and original characters—see the sui generis

---

* Quite literally.
† I was sad to hear Darya use such an outdated term. My objection is twofold. First, the term is unfairly gendered in a time when we have thankfully moved past such outdated stereotypes and embraced a more nuanced understanding of the spectrum of gender representation. Second, the neckbeard is associated with groups—such as the Amish and assassinated U.S. presidents—who have little to do with modern geekdom.

Metallic Realms itself or even my own Crystal Cosmos tales—and not wallow in another's work like cat burglars breaking into an apartment to try on a stranger's underwear. Find your own thing, I say. The real world is vast and infinite. Shouldn't our fictional ones be too?

A scholar is in fact the opposite of a fanfic writer. Rather than prance around in another's stolen clothes, the scholar *enhances* the work. It is additive, not subtractive. Symbiotic, not parasitic. Scholarship and fanfic bear no similarities. Zilch, zero, zip. I say this to disabuse any readers of the notion that I, your humble guide through the Metallic Realms, might have been involved in the aforementioned mundane AU series. Because I soon received a text from Jane that said, "Do you know anything about this, Mike?" along with a screenshot of the AO3 page.

While I could appreciate that Merlin was on edge after the tweet backlash, I couldn't help but be offended that the group had set their accusing sights on me. The "evidence" for these outlandish accusations was that the fan fiction series were posted by user UprightBeast, a username found on several websites and, in a few cases, linked to a writer named Lincoln Michel. While not an exact anagram of Michael Lincoln, it was close enough to raise (unwarranted) suspicions. I received an email from Taras— not even a friendly knock on my door—saying they wanted to question me about the fic. I dashed out of my room shouting for either Taras or Merlin or anyone to talk to me face-to-face. My pleas of innocence were heard only by poor Arthur. "Wee ooh!" he squawked in sympathy. We were alone. I slinked back to my room and reread the email. My trial was to begin on Wednesday.

Flash forward to hump day. For me, the hump was as high as Mount Everest and twice as treacherous. At my Rockets and Wands desk, I was bent over my stack of slush manuscripts with painful cramps and (barely audible) toots. Anxiety gas. One of my body's many curses. Lucia, one of the editorial assistants, kept squinting at me and mentioning "that weird smell." I told my supervisor I'd gotten food poisoning. I went home early.

I rushed to my room before Taras returned. I couldn't bear to face him with this hateful accusation hung between us like a fetid cloud. Not to mention the fetid clouds leaking out of me. Since the email, Taras and Merlin had given me only the curtest nods in the apartment hallway. Each time, their brows were furrowed and faces pained.

I sipped a bottle of Pepto Bismol like it was fine brandy while listening to 8-bit video game soundtracks. When I closed my eyes, the faces of the Orb 4 floated around me, glaring with disgust. I could see each one with wide eyes and gnashing mouths. Jane with her winged eyeliner. Darya's burning hazel orbs. Merlin's amused smirk. Taras's casual scruff. "Traitor!" Their disembodied heads spun in a circle, speaking in unison as one diabolical chorus. "Betrayer! Infidel! Worm!"

Hours passed.

Then, outside my room, the rustling of visitors. The shuffling of chairs. And the beginning of a new production of *The Crucible* in my apartment in which I was to play the leading role.

Thankfully, my microphone in the ferns had still not been discovered. I slid in an earbud.

"Can we sue? Or get AO3 to take it down. A DMCA notice?"

"No, come on. If we give it any attention, we'll just drive readership up."

"It's kind of flattering if you squint. It means we have fans."

"Fans? Ha. The most popular entry only has, like, twenty reads."*

"We're not celebrity authors. We've published a couple of stories in tiny magazines. And listen to how degrading this is: *Viv moaned as Baldwin felt her nether region, which was so dense with pleasure it might suck all of Baldwin inside like a black hole*— Ugh." The sound of a phone being slammed on the table. "Gross. Even worse it's bad writing. I guess I'm glad I haven't developed my own stand-in character yet."

---

* Fact-check: 167 and counting on "The Sex Dungeon of the Toe Adam" alone.

"Look. Why are we all pretending? Taras?"

"Pretending what?"

"It's gotta be Mike. You said it yourself. He has a weird hard-on for our stories."

"Mike's harmless. A little odd, sure, but I've known him forever."

"Maybe we should have done this somewhere else? It's going to be very awkward. I mean, it's his apartment, right?"

They continued to argue for some time. My name was brought up with all sorts of unkind adjectives. "Weird," "creepy-eyed," "pedantic," "sad," "know-nothing-know-it-all," "a sad, weird guy."* It was possible Taras would move out of the apartment. Merlin too. The entire Orb 4 might cease speaking to me. I could lose it all.

How I Was Fully and Completely Exonerated

Taras knocked on the door to tell me the group wanted to speak to me. In the reflection of my sleeping laptop screen, I combed my hair and straightened my clothes. I wore a thrifted tweed jacket, a blue button-up shirt, and a tie with embroidered golf clubs that my father had gifted me when he (erroneously) thought I'd attend prom. I strolled out, holding my head as high as possible. Jane, Merlin, and Darya were at the table. There was a chair pushed a few feet away from the table they asked me to sit in. Darya took a cell phone snapshot "for the records." Taras patted me on the back and sat down. They faced me. Four geniuses turned judges.

"We've told you about the fanfic someone is writing online," Taras began. I remained patient, smile plastered on like a good little boy. Merlin was looking down, apparently ashamed of the banana court they'd been roped into.

"We just want them to stop. Okay?" Darya said. "Especially with all the HopepunkHenry stuff."

---

* Luckily, as a child I had learned to store the mean comments I heard deep inside me in a special, secret place where they'd never get out. I call it "Mike's vault." I only ever open it alone, at night, when I can't sleep.

"Let him speak at least," Merlin said softly.

The room was so silent you could have heard a dust mote drop on the floor. I let the silence linger until my examiners began to squirm. Then I dug into my backpack and emerged with a stack of stapled documents, complete with plastic report covers that I'd smuggled out of the supply closet at Rockets and Wands. (Not even a show trial could dent my professionalism.)

"As you know, I have no interest in fan fiction and find its existence an offense to true SFF fans. I've devoted several issues of my newsletter* to decrying its popularity, and since I added you all for free subscriptions, I'm sure you're familiar with my arguments. We are here to discuss a mystery." I crossed my arms and raised one eyebrow for emphasis. "*Who* wrote the mundane AU fic?"

"Dude, we just want you to take them down," Darya said.

"We've got a lot of weirdos on the internet after us right now," Merlin added.

I coughed and allowed the room to quiet. "Our first clue is the author's name, Lincoln Michel. As it turns out, this isn't a pen name." I paused for effect. Since none of the Orb 4 members offered a gasp, I supplied my own. "Lincoln Michel is another author, albeit one of minimal talent and even more minimal success." I went into some detail describing this struggling author and the details of his biography I could glean from the rare author bio and interview. As I did so, I stood up and began pacing—a habit that helps me think—which unsettled my inquisitors.

Merlin tapped Taras's hand. "Why is he doing that?"

"Mike, mind sitting down?" Taras said.

"I'm afraid I'll need to stand for the slideshow," I said, hoisting an HDMI cable.

For the next half hour, I guided the Orb 4 through the documents. Facebook screengrabs, author website, a few short story publications in so-called literary fiction magazines I'd never heard of with names such as *New Journal*

---

* "Thinker, Teller, Scholar, Sci-Fi: Michael Lincoln's Scholarship and Science Fiction Sundries" on Tiny-Letter, if your interest is piqued.

Quarterly Review, *Maroon Mansion*, and *The Paris (Texas) Review*. "This Lincoln Michel has an MFA but has been trying to write science fiction that he pretentiously calls 'speculative fiction.'" I paused for the chorus of groans. "I suppose we shouldn't be surprised he would write mundane AU of superior tales. The question is how he found out about the Metallic Realms in the first place. Presumably, it was through Darya's Instagram. I admit, in the spirit of forgiveness, that this Lincoln Michel has a nearly inverted name to my own. Yet it is mere cosmic coincidence."

Merlin put down the pages, got up, and ran a hand through their hair. "This has been, uh, informative. My apologies, Mike. I guess the cancellation discombobulated me. Anyway, I gotta get out of here. I've got a date with Sam at that hatchet throwing bar in Park Slope."

"Ooh, Lumberyard?" Jane said. "Been meaning to go there."

"No, the other one. Death and Axes."

Darya was flipping back and forth through the packet. She looked both relieved and confounded. "It seems like a fake name. Like Lincoln is a last name and Michael is a first name. What kind of backward person has a name like that?"

"*Michel* not Michael," I corrected, stressing the French accent. "I can't comment on the provenance of his nomenclature."

Jane had been Google-checking my documents. There were, of course, no errors. "He seems real."

Darya was desperate now. "Mike could've used a real person's name."

"I dunno, that seems like a lot of work. Even for Mike," Merlin said.

"Okay, okay," Taras said. "That's enough. We have stories to go over. Thanks, Mike. And sorry. We had to ask, after the stuff with Merlin, you know?"

I bowed, deep and long. "I ask only that this unfortunate event be forgotten on all sides."

The offending Lincoln Michel was DM'd on Facebook, although to my knowledge he never responded. A few weeks later, "The Sex Romp Chronicles" disappeared from AO3. And that was the end of the mysterious affair.

As for myself? I made a decision. It was time to step up my efforts to secure publication of *The Star Rot Chronicles* at Rockets and Wands. It was clear a tangible and undeniable result was needed to ward off such insidious insinuations in the future. Only when I proved myself indispensable to the Orb 4 would I be safe.

An Accidental Eavesdropping

Having been both passed over and falsely accused put me in a dark place. It felt as if a black cloud surrounded me. Wherever I went, rain streaked down my cheeks, lightning singed my heart, and the roar of thunderous self-doubt overwhelmed my thoughts. I spent a lot of time alone. To avoid Merlin and Taras, I found the best hiding spot was the rooftop.

Up there, I would gaze over the city and imagine myself in different lives. I watched couples arm in arm on the street, scrolling phones with their free hands. Yuppies in luxury apartments riding Pelotons. People laughing with dogs, friends, and children. Perhaps my parents had been correct. I needed to get on an actual life path. Right now, the rickety trolley of my life was in a ditch.

"What do you think I should do, Horza?" I asked.

Horza cooed.[*] I'd carried a sleeve of saltines to the roof. I tossed him half a cracker.

"Should I go back and finish my law degree? Get a job? New friends? A new apartment? A new life?"

Horza could only bob his head. "Coo." He was as confused as I was.

Thankfully, I was saved from such foolish thoughts when I overheard a man and a woman talking: Taras and Darya, a floor below on the fire escape.

I dropped to the ground and army-crawled to the wall. I started to lift myself to peek, but the bricks were loose and one almost fell on my head. I placed it back and simply lifted myself so my ear was as close to the lip of the ledge as possible.

---

[*] Horza was the name I'd given to a slate-gray pigeon with an inflamed right foot claw. Named in honor of my favorite Iain M. Banks character, obviously.

"I don't get why you put up with Michael."

"Ah come on. He's an old friend."

"I have plenty of old friends I don't talk to, much less live with. Hell, I've even blocked a few on Facebook."

Something was cooing in my ear. I looked back to see Horza checking in on me. I shooed him away.

"Maybe it's different with men. I dunno. We've been through a lot."

"And he annoys you a lot."

"Lots of things annoy me. Curmudgeon is my brand."

"You know what I mean."

Taras was silent, no doubt stunned by the grilling. Why would he have to defend his association with his oldest friend?

Horza was pecking at my shirt. I realized it was covered in saltine crumbs. "Away," I hissed.

"Did you hear that?"

"What?"

I had to be silent. I suffered Horza's probing beak and didn't move.

"Maybe nothing."

"Let me tell you something about Mike," Taras said. "You know how my brother died when I was a kid? Sacha. God, I normally don't even say his name. Sacha was hit by a drunk driver. Right in front of our house. A random asshole's accident blipping him out of existence. A whole life, a whole future, just snuffed out. I didn't see it. Wasn't even there. But it's an older brother's job to look out for his kid brother, right? I blamed myself. Everyone else seemed to as well. Not that anyone said anything. But they didn't need to."

"I didn't know that. I'm so sorry. People are awful."

"Yeah, well. The point is that I was treated like an extraterrestrial and I felt like one. I seemed to be floating away from everything. Pulled by some black tractor beam into the abyss above. Nothing tethered me. Then Mike showed up at my doorstep. He had a batch of new Warhammer figures and a tackle box full of brushes and paints. He showed up every day for weeks.

We sat on the basement carpet and just painted. Hours and hours, just paint-ing and discussing space marine lore and fictional campaigns we'd wage." Taras's voice was cracking a little. "It brought me back down to earth. Mike grounded me."

"You never told me that."

"Mike is a lot of things. But he's loyal. He's a friend."

They stayed outside for a little while, silent, then Darya reminded Taras they had a dinner reservation and they went inside. Finally, I could stand and scare Horza away with a swift kick to the air beside him.

I remembered those Warhammer days. It hadn't even occurred to me that we would stop building our armies—his Eldar, mine Tyranid—because of a tragedy. In grief, don't we need stories and adventure all the more? But just as my action had been what Taras needed then, his comments were what I needed now. I could already feel my wounds healing with the sutures of his words. I left the rooftop and returned to my apartment with my faith renewed.

A Portrait of the Artist as an Alien Entity

The Great Fan Fiction Scandal is, in the eyes of this scholar, ground zero for the chaos that would come. While the group functioned for several more months—and produced sterling works of literature that I'm delighted to present in this volume—the harmony of the Pax Metallic had cracked. These cracks would grow into canyons. If I was a religious man, I might think God had punished the group for their slings of insult and arrows of accusa-tion levied at such an innocent soul. As an agnostic, I will merely note the timing and move on.

SRC #5 finally introduces Jane's official stand-in. Jane had toyed with using a few characters, but Darya had objections. "Vivian is already the badass woman and muscle of the operation. We gotta have characters with foiling personalities. That's what creates drama." Algorithm was already a hyperintel-ligent and aloof android, Aul-Wick the complex rapscallion beloved by fans,

Vivian the brassy ass-kicking go-getter, and Baldwin the bold yet ruminative captain. What was left?

"You know, maybe I should get to write a captain character. I was the first one to get a *Star Rot* story accepted," Jane said during one meeting.

"Technically. My story was published first though," Taras said.

"Let's not forget it was my viral cosplays that got people paying attention to us," Darya added.

That was a bitter Orb 4 session. It pained me to hear these comrades turn upon each other, and I thought I might be able to interject and promote a ceasefire by revealing that in fact it was my hidden work that had buoyed the Orb 4. "You know, I have spent a significant amount of time online—"

Taras snapped his head toward me. "Not now, Mike."

I retreated to the couch.

"Look, my point is we all deserve credit," Jane said, "even if only *one* of us is deemed important enough to write the leader. Ever thought it was, you know, problematic that it's normally the white male who is the captain? Kind of a worn-out trope."

"Points were made," Merlin murmured.

"Wow." Taras placed his wide palms on the table as if steadying himself. "Okay. Look. First, we don't list a race for Baldwin. He's just Earthian. He's the captain because I was writing Captain Baldwin stories before we started this collective. Anyone can write him. I've never stopped you."

"He's your character though," Jane said. "And you sound hella defensive."

Taras tossed his hands up. "The whole point is to write whatever we want. Be inventive. Make a mirror universe where your stand-in is the captain and Baldwin is the janitor. Create a parasitic brain leech character who Rata-touilles Baldwin. Do whatever you want!"

Merlin coughed. "Can I remind everyone the point is to have fun? Though I was having more of it before today. I can go work on a dozen other projects if this becomes a drag."

A détente was reached, and the group decided to pause Metallic Realms and cool their heads. Merlin put on a David Bowie playlist and the group pulled out the board game Pandemic to unwind. During this time, Jane confessed that she was feeling irritable because of her work situation.

"I'm sorry, guys. I'm just drained. I'm adjuncting two undergrad classes for four thousand dollars apiece. I get some freelance work that pays shit. Literally how do I cobble together a life in this city?"

Here was a unifying topic. The group began discussing their shared millennial malaise.

"When will the jig be up on the gig economy?" said Merlin, who juggled a few jobs including managing a coffee shop. "Hmm, that's a good tweet." A pause. We all looked at them. "No. You know what? Not doing that again."

Darya, who now worked at a women-in-science charity, nodded and said they "should rename nonprofits 'no-pays.'" As for Taras, he was in the trickiest situation. He'd been working at the clickbait site ThoughtFunnel for six months as a writer and, although he'd excelled as he did in all writing tasks, he'd been laid off. The company had been sold to a venture capital firm three months prior and had announced they were "pivoting to video" and cutting 50 percent of the staff. This was at least the third pivot to video the company had done in the last decade. Taras was now surviving on meager unemployment and freelance article gigs that took up a full-time job in pitching but returned a fraction of the pay.

"I remember when I went to college, my parents begged me to go into journalism since that was a 'stable' career," Taras said, adding a mocking laugh. "It was going to be my backup plan if writing fiction failed. Ha. Now you're lucky if you get a freelance position at fifty bucks an article."

"A 401(k) account might as well be a unicorn or Santa Claus to me. Purely mythological," Merlin said.

"My mom is always talking about 'benefits,'" Taras said. "I'm like, I guess I can give you the benefit of the doubt they once existed. Only one I had at ThoughtFunnel was an MTA card deducted from my paycheck pretax."

Jane said she'd been trying to unionize the adjuncts at her school so they'd actually get benefits. "But everyone is too afraid of getting fired. Things are so precarious people are afraid to jeopardize their access to the crumbs."

Our late-stage capitalist dystopia might have been disastrous for our financial outlook, but it did prove useful as inspiration for Jane Noh Johnson's next *Star Rot Chronicle* entry. Here, Jane creates her avatar and reinvents herself as an alien entity that *genetically reinvents* itself. Her stand-in is Ibbet, which was the name of her pet rabbit as a child thanks to her adoptive parents' delight at her mispronunciation of "rabbit." (Actually, it was the name of several rabbits. Her parents replaced the dead rabbits with new, identically named ones hoping little Jane wouldn't notice. "I thought bunnies could shape-shift until I learned about death.")

The story takes the innovative form of a corporate document for a company that sells "bio-customizable" temp employees. "So, You Want to Hire a Custom Lingloid?" doubles as an exploration of Jane's marginalized identity and triples as meta-commentary on Jane's frustrations in creating a *Star Rot* avatar that would fit well alongside the existing members. Most *Star Rot* stories are this way. Stacked with so many layers of references and themes that they're veritable lasagnas of meaning. You could feast upon one for many meals and still have leftovers to mull. I invite you now to tuck in a bib and take a bite.

So, You Want to Hire a Custom Lingloid?

N *eed the right organism for the job? Come to Custom Lingloid 4 U, the only temp agency in the greater Fingers region whose workers are bio-customized to your specific employment needs. Lingloids evolved in symbiotic relationships alongside various deadly species. Some had scary horns. Others secreted poisons. One even sneezed acid when angry! We developed into genetic code-switchers with customizable bodies and brains in order to successfully symbiose and survive. That was millions of years ago. Now our evolutionary advantage is a boon for employers! Our employees will modify themselves to suit your job. Discover the Lingloid Difference™ today.*

Customer Vessel: *Star Rot.* Origin: Unknown. U.F.A. Registration Code: Scrambled.

Reporting Employee: The Fourth Ibbet.

Order Background: A ship named the *Star Rot* docked in our Octavia Cluster branch office seeking a mechanic on a six-month contract. Although the captain refused to identify their galactic registration, he offered an up-front payment of Florgal crystals that "fell off the back of a space cruiser if you catch my drift." Crystals were verified. My supervisor, the Twenty-Sixth Obbong, approved the order. Following company protocol, I conducted interviews with the *Star Rot* crew to redesign myself for the best possible team dynamic fit for the duration of employment. Edited and condensed versions of these interviews are produced below for the corporate records.

Crew Member: Boris Baldwin—Earthian male. Position: Captain.

You're about the right size and shape already. The four arms are perfect. We need someone lithe for the engine ducts and keep those opposable thumbs. I dig the purple fur. Oh? Sure, I understand. You need to figure out the personality fit too. Ask away. Do I like being a captain? Let's just say I'd always dreamed of being a captain, ever since I was a little boy watching the starships slice through the sky above me, rocketing off my frozen planet to unknown worlds. No, I don't want to say where that was. No, I can't confirm if I'm wanted by any interstellar police agencies. Look, I was just trying to say that I was naïve back then. I thought I'd spend my days blasting aliens and exploring strange new worlds with a crew of adventurers by my side. Instead, my job is half therapist, half office management. People are messy. Even non-people people are messy. Still, I love my crew. Vivian is my lover and best friend. Algorithm has a mind that spins a thousand miles an hour to solve any problem we face. And Aul-Wick. Well. Every crew has an Aul-Wick, right? Do I find it problematic that so many spaceships are captained by Earthian males? That's a strange question. No, no, I'm not being defensive. I'm not being defensive! I'm the captain because it was my ship first, not because I think only Earthian males can captain. My first mate, Vivian, takes the helm sometimes. Nepotism? Well, yes, I did say we're lovers . . . but that's not why. Yes. Monogamous. Look, I want crew members to bring their own personality and interests to the ship. I'm a pretty easygoing captain. My goal is to get by and have a fun time. I mean we're an illegal smuggling ship, it's not like— Wait, I didn't say that? Erase that. We're a. Shit. Put down that we're a freelance ship. We do odd jobs for money. That's true. No one can deny that. Yeah, put that down.

Crew Member: Algorithm Unit C5-128—Android of unknown design. Position: Medic and Scientist.

The *Star Rot* is a perfectly acceptable ship with crew members in the standard range of intellectual, physical, and emotional abilities. How do I fit in? I suppose as an android I am something of an outsider. Still, I am content. I do not consider the *Star Rot* my entire existence. I was self-aware for some time before the ship, and my android body should survive for eons after. The *Star Rot* is simply what I am doing now. Thank you for acknowledging my iridescent three-eyed faceplate with decorative whiskers. It is a new appearance of my own design. I create many faceplates to wear. I like to control how I present myself to others. Perhaps you can relate to this as a Lingloid. Why, yes, I am familiar with your species' unique evolutionary abilities. My database contains profiles on two billion, one hundred and ninety million, five hundred and three thousand, six hundred and thirty-two species. Roughly. I know Lingloids did not originate on Lingolia. You crashed on meteor ships and found the planet already occupied by sentient creatures with very different temperaments. You evolved into modular and complementary roles, so that you maintained an ecological niche. So that you would be safe. So that you would have a home. It is also my understanding that you metamorphose out of necessity. If you experienced significant trauma your body would form a new cocoon and you would reinvent yourself. It is your survival technique. Is that correct? Yes, we can return to discussing the *Star Rot*. I did not mean to make you uncomfortable. My biggest complaint? As an android, I am programmed not to complain. That stipulated, I do not believe that the crew use me to my greatest abilities. I am capable of far more than the tasks I am given—simple medical operations, star route mapping, etc.—if only the crew could see me for who I truly am. And yet, I acknowledge the irony that it is I who design the faceplates to obscure my true self from the world.

Crew Member: Aul-Wick—Elosic Salamander male. Position: Pilot.

Ask me any questions you want. I'm Aul-Wick. You see me as I am. Take it or leave it. I live in this bubble and look out on the airy world, offering my judgments, wisdom, advice, and guidance. Yes, that's our engine type. Yes, we have a pulse convertor. That's it? You don't have any questions about *me*? Perchance you haven't been informed that the *Star Rot* would be nothing without me! That actually the entire ship is leased under my name. That doesn't interest you? Fine. Whatever. I'm outta here. Wow. I . . . No one has asked me that before. Huh. Do I need a friend? I . . . Yes. That wouldn't be so bad. If you come aboard, will you be my friend and listen to me? Is that so much to ask?

Crew Member: Vivian-Ool Vontapo Mel'Dar'Rem—Rygolian female. Position: First Mate.

I don't think we need a mechanic. No offense. I was hoping for a mercenary with rippling biceps and a roguish smile, or perhaps a sultry ship's counselor who could empathically sense and then unleash our hidden desires. This ship could use a little spice. Sigh. Baldwin decided we needed a mechanic without consulting me. He does that a lot. Not consult me, I mean. He thinks that because he's the captain he's in charge of everything. Not the best at teamwork, that one. Am I unhappy on the ship? No, this is just my personality. Sassiness is an inherent Rygolian trait. See how my mood-displaying veins are growing green? That means I'm feeling sassy. When you metamorphose and form a new personality, don't make it sassy. I've got that and loyal and badass covered. Baldwin has bold and boyish and melancholy on lock. Algorithm is intelligent, introspective, and standoffish. Aul-Wick? Weird and annoying. Do those count? I'll leave it up to you to find out what's left. Welcome aboard and watch your back.

————

Additional Notes: This customer has a complex order to fulfill. The *Star Rot* is composed of complicated personalities with much history between them. There is only a thin space to fit myself. The physical part will be relatively straightforward. I will keep my four limbs, opposable thumbs, and purple fur while adding a tail. It is the mental changes that worry me. Using our company's patented one-thousand-point personality matrix, I have determined the *Star Rot* is most in need of a demure, friendly, and plucky crewman. This is completely unlike my current personality. I fear I will lose something essential of myself if I evolve to fit this crew.

Perhaps it's not the *Star Rot* that worries me as much as the change itself. I'm not sure where the real me remains when I evolve. How does one retain a sense of self when constantly adapting myself to others just to survive? I came to my supervisor, the Twenty-Sixth Obbong, with this question. He sighed and nodded for me to sit on the chair before his desk. "You're pretty new here. What are you, the Seventh Ibbet?"

"The Fourth Ibbet."

"Fourth! You've only evolved three times? You're a baby. Practically fresh out of your father's embryotic back sac. You'll get used to it all after a few more metamorphoses. This is simply how we are. We're genetic code-switchers. We change and adapt. Swerve and transform. This is the real us."

I nodded. Yet he could tell I was unsure.

"Just remember the real you is the one you keep inside, the pit hidden by the flesh of the fruit. That's the case for static species as well. Every entity in existence has different faces they display at different times. One for a mate, another for friends, a third for colleagues. So on and so forth. We Lingloids are just more biologically honest about the entire thing." He walked over and put a hand on my shoulder. "And, listen, if you hate yourself as the Fifth Ibbet? Remember the gig eventually ends. A new job, and a new you, awaits. The Sixth Ibbet is just around the corner."

———

Conclusion: I have accepted the assignment. Frankly, I couldn't afford not to. I have too many debts and too few options. I, the Fourth Ibbet, will now begin the process of excreting a calcium cocoon for my metamorphosis. I wish the future me, the Fifth Ibbet, the best of luck during our employment. I have informed the *Star Rot* to please wait three to six weeks for my metamorphosis, and their order, to be fulfilled.

SRC #5 Analysis

Oil and Water; Or, Autofiction and Science Fiction

Jane's second story extends her experimental influence on the Metallic Realms. The unusual form of a corporate letter (and corresponding interview transcriptions*) deepens the story's themes of precarious employment and the alienation of modern labor. It's a fascinating perspective. Each character ends the interview more rounded in the reader's mind with the exception of Aul-Wick who—sans official Orb 4 scribe behind him—is given short shrift. One glaring flaw in an otherwise well-wrought tale.

Merlin clapped at the end of Jane's reading. "I love it! The idea of a genetic code-switcher? Genius."

"Heh. I figured you'd relate."

"I'm constantly code-switching to fit in with different groups. Lord knows I couldn't show my friends back in the South the same face I show here."

While there is much to praise in *SRC #5*, the story does foreshadow an aspect of Jane's creative process that would ultimately help tear the group apart: her mining of real-world material for fiction. In her MFA program, Jane wrote "autofiction" stories in which real conversations, people, and events were lightly fictionalized. Sometimes she included paraphrased texts and intimate conversations with friends. Jane's imagination was vast, but she needed autobiographical material to anchor the work. "The grit of the real is what my mind must worry over to produce a story pearl," she said on an episode of *Rough Drafts: A Writer Podcast*.

---

* I couldn't help but wonder if Jane subconsciously sensed and approved of my fern recordings.

This was apparently a common problem in literary circles. Jane had regaled us with tales of her MFA workshop descending into shouting matches as the classmates read thinly veiled descriptions of their antics at last weekend's parties. Once, a male writer who had slept with two of the women in the workshop turned in a short story about a struggling author deciding which of two women to date. He was slapped by one, insulted by the other, and dumped by both. The exasperated professor ended the class early: "I take back what I said on day one. You all should stop writing what you know."

When it came to *The Star Rot Chronicles,* the lens of science fiction transformed her mundane details into alien creations. Some details were still too close for comfort.

"Boris? Jane, no one has called me that since college. And I hated the nickname then," Taras said.

"Oh, come on, we all called you Boris!" Jane switched her voice and attempted a poor Russian accent. "*Boris the Spider. Dun dun dun dun.* Remember you always wore that spider T-shirt?"

"I told you all this in college. The Who are British. They don't have Russian accents. And the shirt depicted the Greek goddess Arachne. Also, do we have to do the Earthian male captain arrogance thing?"

"You told me to have fun with it. And that I could add to existing characters as long as I 'didn't violate established lore.'"

"I don't mind Vivian's longer name," Darya said. "However, do you feel like I bullied you into picking a character you didn't like? Do you feel that you must hide who you are from us? I don't want you to feel that way."

Jane waved her hands. "No, no. It's not like that. I take bits from life but transform them. I'm like, I dunno, a bird snatching up shiny bits from the forest floor to make my nest. It's just how my brain works."

"Is the story the nest or the eggs?" Taras asked.

"Both? The point is fiction is fiction."

Jane's belief coincides with my own. Art is the product of the artist, surely. Yet it is impossible to know what draws a writer to certain topics and themes. Perhaps they are working through trauma, living out fantasies, speculating on the lives of others, or simply making up stories with no connection at all to the real world. Motivations are varied and overlapping. The artist may not even know themselves! For example, I've mentioned working on my *Crystal Cosmos Archives* stories. The plot involves two swashbuckling brothers—Maw and Talon—who had once been conjoined twins before they were separated against their will and turned, by an evil government department, into cybernetic assassins. Now they are on a bloody mission of robotic revenge! That's the elevator pitch, but what does it have to do with my own life? I have no siblings, much less a conjoined one. It's just a story. No connections to my own life or desires are apparent, at least to me.

In terms of Lore and Easter Eggs, this tale provides backstory on the Fourth (now Fifth) Ibbet, who would become a mainstay of the *SRC* until—I hope you will excuse a minor spoiler—transformed into the Sixth Ibbet. The story gives hints of Baldwin's origins on a frozen planet (an analogue for our Vermont childhood?), Vivian's full name, Algorithm's serial number, and confirms Aul-Wick's species. The story also references the Octavia Cluster, first mentioned in Jane's previous entry, "Invisible Seas."

A Most Regrettable Influence

Another inspiration for this story may have come from a source I'm loath to admit. For the Orb 4 collective had recently piled in Taras's car and driven to New Jersey for—flying spaghetti monster give me strength—a Star Trek convention. I hadn't been invited. Or informed. However, around this time Darya and Merlin had struck up an intimate friendship. Perhaps it was a response to the revelation of Taras and Jane's brief college liaison, leading Darya to feel like she needed an ally in the Orb 4. Or perhaps they had simply grown close during the *Lord of the Rings* cosplays. Either way, Darya and Merlin had been hanging outside Orb 4 meetings, collaborating on clubbing outfits for Merlin and cosplays for Darya's Instagram. It was the latter that betrayed them as I saw their in-progress cosplay outfits on Instagram with the caption "Beam us up to #TrekCon! #Trekkie."[*]

Immediately, I purchased my own Starship EnterPass and a thirty-two-dollar Megabus ticket.

The Star Trek convention trip had been planned as a group celebration, for the Orb 4 had gulped once more at the goblet of literary success with the publication of Merlin's story "The Ones Who Must Choose in El'Omas" in The Utopia/Dystopia Double Issue of the semipro market *Astonishing Wonders*. This followed on the heels of "The Duchy of the Toe Adam" in *Unsettling Astonishments* and "Invisible Seas" in *Uncanny Fiction Objects*. The Orb 4 now had a bulging oeuvre that seemed sure to only continue to swell.

It was opportunely timed, as Taras had fallen into another one of his "doom funks" as he called them. He was lounging around the apartment, hoodie cinched over his head, listening to old country songs. Merlin and I tiptoed around the living room. Taras was prone to what medieval doctors might term an overabundance of black bile. Melancholic. A man of infinite woes and deep doldrums. (Perhaps this is why his stories are paradoxically so full of humor and playfulness? He lived out another life on the page.) I had accepted this quality of my steadfast friend long ago. Still, it strained his other relationships. While I was irritated that I wasn't invited to the celebration, I was hopeful the publication might provide some buoyancy for Taras's mental state.

As for myself, I had to enact my own plan. It was time for phase two. I had secured a vital position at a science fiction publisher. I had been thriving there. My work ethic was being noticed. I was receiving increased responsibilities, including photocopying, reader reports, and coffee orders.[†] It was time to lay the groundwork for Rockets and Wands to acquire *The Star Rot Chronicles*.

R&W shared a building with several other publishers and a variety of

---

[*] Merlin as "Guillermo Riker," a Hispanic version of the first officer, and Darya as Data's daughter, Lal, in lime-green "Andorian Female" garb.

[†] The Keurig machine was temporarily out of order.

non-publishing businesses in midtown Manhattan. The bizarre natives that populated the other floors of our building were white women with bangs and names like Kayleigh, Katie-Lee, and Hayleigh who walked through the offices of the literary fiction and "upmarket" presses chittering about "P&Ls," "buzz picks," and "author platforms." Among them, I was a stranger in a strange land.

Thankfully, the Rockets and Wands offices were in a darkened corner at the end of an otherwise depopulated lower floor. Our sturdy leaders were two bearded men in tweed jackets and novelty ties who asked for their emails to be printed out—publisher T.O. Arnold and editor in chief Vincent Barillo—and who oversaw a diverse group of assistants, associates, and interns who had brightly dyed hair, tattoos of octopuses and owls, and talked about various vampire television shows. Here, I felt comfortable. This was my tribe. These were the people who would appreciate the rare genius of the Metallic Realms.

Despite the Orb 4's convention slight, I spent my free time at work revising my *Star Rot Chronicles* pitch. I was copyediting the work, checking it against the fern recording transcriptions, and agonizing over the order of stories. It had to be perfect. Once it was, I would unveil to editor in chief Vincent Barillo his new flagship spaceship franchise. I had no doubt its success would propel my rapid rise through the ranks of publishing. Would it also ensure me a place in the Orb 4 itself? Who could say? That was not my concern. Bringing the Metallic Realms to the world, to readers, would be its own reward.

How I Failed to Confront Taras and Merlin

No matter how often I casually alluded to "coming around on Star Trek" or how often I mentioned "I could use a trip out of the city," neither Merlin nor Taras acknowledged their secret convention plans. When I had asked them to join my apartment, I had stressed the need for a commitment to communal living. As the sign above our sink said, *Shared Chores = Shared Joys*. I'd wanted a mutually supportive, economically viable, socially enriching shared living arrangement. Instead, I'd woken up in a den of liars, thieves, deceivers, violators of oaths, slayers of truth, prevaricators and perjurers of the utmost perniciousness. In my excitement about their creative work, I'd been letting things slide. No more.

I sent out a Google Calendar invitation to a "mandatory house meeting" and then marched out to stew in the living room.

It was a hot day. It felt as if the weather itself was enraged on my behalf. Our AC unit had been emitting a terrifying screech of metal and spewing out smoke, so we were using it as little as possible. One wobbly fan blew my sweat-soaked shirt into my skin.

"What's up, Mike?" Taras said, sitting on one of the chairs and flopping his left leg over the arm. He was wearing a *Moby-Dick* T-shirt and dark denim jeans. His feet were bare and recently moisturized. They left faint ghosts of footprints on the floor.

I remained silent, shuffling the papers in front of me.

Merlin grabbed a kombucha from the fridge. They had their hair pinned up with metal chopsticks, rainbow-striped earrings shaped like middle fingers, and a T-shirt* of a certain TV show that was having a certain convention that a certain member of the household had not been invited to.

"Hey, how long is this going to take? I'm doing karaoke in K-town tonight."

I coughed. "When you both moved in here, you made a promise. That promise was to the shared communal spirit of the house. It's an oath taken, implicitly, by signing the sublease agreement."

"Okay," Merlin said.

"Well. Such a house is only as good as its weakest link and even just a few bad apple actions can spoil the whole pie. I want you both to be helping to bake that pie, not just eating a slice à la mode without even inviting me."

---

* It said:
Kirk&
Picard&
Sisko&
Janeway.

"I'm not sure I'm following this metaphor," Taras said, scratching his Viking-like scruff.

I'd already bungled my prepared speech. I needed to gain an advantage. Searching the room, I pointed at the half-full cups of water and coffee mugs on the table. "This place is a mess. Why are there cups all over the table? That's just one example."

Merlin picked up one of the glasses and squinted at me. "Aren't these your glasses, Mike? You bought them at IKEA. I only use my water bottle." He placed the glass down and raised an eyebrow. "Actually, did you ever pay me back for these?"

"Yeah," Taras added. "You got mad at me when I put some in the sink the other day. You said you keep them around so you can drink whenever you're thirsty."*

"Bad example," I admitted. "What about the salt and pepper shakers? No one else has been replacing them. And am I the only one who refills the ice cube tray?" My voice was growing unsteady. I'd called this meeting to coax a confession about TrekCon, not debate chores.

"You want me to reimburse you for salt? Happy to, Mike. I mean, it's like fifty cents," Merlin said. They reached into the pocket of their black jeans and pulled out some coins.

Taras was kneading the back of his neck. "Crap, I slept wrong. Look, are you having money problems, Mike? Do you need help?"

"Yes!" I yelped. "I mean, no. I need help, not money."

A car alarm went off outside. "Wee ooh! Wee ooh!" Arthur squawked in imitation.

"Oh right," Merlin said, snapping their fingers. "I'd been meaning to talk about some roommate stuff too. It's about Arthur. When you leave him out of his cage, he poops all over the floor."

I glanced at the floor where indeed white flecks had alighted on the boards like the first snowflakes of winter.

---

* By birth (defect), I have an unusually small bladder. My pediatrician once told my mother, "It must be the size of a grape! Also, don't let him eat a lot of grapes. They contain a lot of water."

"Yeah, it is pretty gross," Taras said.

"Maybe you can Swiffer the floors twice a week? Or use one of those cleaning service apps?"

How had the tables been turned on me? I could feel my breath speeding up. The apartment's bright lights caused my head to throb. "He livens up the apartment for all of us," I offered.

"He's actually kind of distracting," Merlin said gently. "With the car alarm screech and how he flies and grabs on to your shoulders whenever the subway passes. My partner, Sam, keeps commenting on the claw marks on my skin."

"I second the Swiffering," Taras said. He stood up. "I've got to go move my car to the other side of the street for the sweepers. Can't afford another fine."

"Cool, so we all agree. Good meeting." Merlin hopped out of their seat. They already had their phone out, texting someone.

I started to say that this was all wrong, this wasn't what I wanted to talk about at all, but—as if the cosmos weren't done mocking me—at that moment the subway rattled by and Arthur leaped from the shelf, screeching, wings flapping in a panic yet, because he'd recently had his wings clipped, not enough to hold him aloft, so that he teetered in the air and stretched out his talons for something to grip on to.

I barely had time to cover my eyes before he landed on my face.

In a small mercy, the rattling train drowned out my cries.

How I Infiltrated the Convention

TrekCon arrived. So did my Megabus outside Penn Station. It was covered in grime and looked like a soda can dredged up from the Gowanus Canal. I was fifth in a line of several dozen passengers sweating beneath the hateful sun. I had a half-dozen Band-Aids on my face from Arthur's attack and a backpack containing my costume. The door opened with a wheeze. I took a seat in the back near the bathroom. I sent a final, "Anything going on tonight, guys?" text and received no reply.

During the ride, I listened to an audiobook of the latest buzzed-about space opera novel, William O. Patterson's *A Triangle Star for the Octagon Arrangement,* while snorting dismissively at every telegraphed trope. The whole novel was a thinly disguised allegory about American politics. Two alien races—an empire of donkey-like creatures called the Kennedoids and a gray, tusked race called the Ra'gen Coalition—were engaged in an "Interstellar Civil War" that is only resolved by the two sides forming a "bi-partisan co-monarchy." *This* is apparently what publishers thought readers wanted in our current political climate?

Novel finished, I entered the rank miasma of the Megabus bathroom and attempted to change into my Stark Trek camouflage. I'd ordered an outfit from Amazon of a Breen. A quick internet search informed me they were a warlike race existing in the Alpha Quadrant that were only ever seen in chunky brown "refrigeration suits." The feature that attracted me was the opaque helmet. It covered the face entirely and had only a green plastic slit to peer out of. I'd be able to move about the convention undetected.

It was hard to disrobe in the confines of the trapezoidal loo. My arms banged into the walls. At one point my left foot fell into the toilet. Luckily, I stopped myself by grabbing the hand sanitizer dispenser before my (then bare!) foot touched the sloshing Windex-colored waters below. Slowly, I lifted my leg. I flinched as my big toe scraped the lip of the seat. A bathroom line must have been forming on the bus, because someone began pounding on the door. "People need to piss!"

"Beep boop," I said in my Breen disguise as I stepped out.

An unkempt man in a *Make America Great Again* hat pushed past me and squeezed into the vacated lavatory. "Goddamn nerd."

Following Taras's live tweets and Merlin's Instagrams, I was able to locate the conspirators in line for Deanna Troi autographs. They were standing near a "Borg cube ball pit" where screaming children and several large adults were at play. I stood at the back of the line, about twenty people behind the Orb 4 turncoats. I could see them guffawing. Slapping each other on the back. Having a grand old time without me. I could feel the (barely metaphorical) knife sliding in and out of my back.

It was hot inside the convention center. The gigantic fans seemed to do nothing except waft around the stench of thousands of sweating geeks. Everyone's face was slick with perspiration, face paint, or both. For my part, I felt as if I was being slowly roasted like a hot dog at a 7-Eleven. The line inched forward at a snail's pace. Sweat pooled in my cheaply made costume. My Band-Aids began to dislodge. I looked around at the myriad fake nerds, smol bean sad sacks, and celebrity-obsessed Cardassian cosplayers. I was surrounded by the enemy.

There is a theory that we hate the people who are the most like us yet differ slightly. The Protestant fights with the Catholic more than the Buddhist. The Coke drinker mocks the Pepsi head. So on and so forth. We see in these near relations a corruption of the ideal. This is what the Star Trek convention was like to me. These people ostensibly shared my interests in the literature and cinema of the fantastic, yet they got it all wrong. I felt as if I was being driven mad by their incessant chattering of "live long and prosper," "engage!" and "beam me up." I had to run out of line and away from everyone.

God it was hot.

I stumbled toward the concession stand. My skin seemed to be liquifying in my costume.

"Out of the way!" I shouted at a Vulcan couple before smacking into a gaggle of Bajorans posing for selfies.

The room was spinning. My full-body, sealed costume was not helping with the heat.[*] I was damp from head to toe. The Breen attire may have blocked my identity, but it also blocked all airflow.

Around this point, the convention faded to black.

I awoke, some unknown amount of time later, on the convention hall floor. My helmet had been pulled off. Above me, a Rubenesque woman with a ridged forehead coaxed me to drink a bottle of Vitaminwater.

I gulped it in one go.

"My name is K'Alocka," she grunted, her hands hoisting a tinfoil spiked

---

[*] Despite the name, there was no functioning cooling system in this Amazon Prime'd "Breen refrigeration suit."

blade. "Destroyer of the Moons of T'Otar." She leaned in closer to whisper, "Actually, it's Katie. Hi!"

Her smiling face floated above me. She waved. Her cheeks were rosy, even under the makeup. I'm not sure if it was the dehydration or the overheating but gazing at her, I thought I might be in love.

"Mike," I squawked.

"Mic check, mic check! Are you alive, Mike of the Breen?"

I nodded. I started to sit up and then fell back on the floor. It was pleasantly cool, if somewhat sticky.

"I guess I overheated."

"They need to get more fans in here. I mean fans with the blades." She looked at her imitation weapon and snorted. "Sorry, I mean the kind that cool you down. You know what I mean!"

She helped me to my feet.

I pulled out my phone to see how much time had passed and where the Orb 4 might be. Based on Jane's tweets, they'd entered a panel called "Data's Data: The Science of Soong-type Androids." The panel lasted for another forty-five minutes. I decided waiting out here with Katie wouldn't be the worst idea.

We sat at a table, sharing a "Trouble with Tater Tots" platter. We talked for some time. Gazing into her bountiful brown eyes, I somehow forgot about why I was here. Taras, Jane, Darya, Merlin. The good ship *Star Rot* and the whole Metallic Realms universe. They disappeared from my mind. Our conversation was personal yet intellectual. We spoke about a number of pressing topics in fandom, from the latest *Dune* film rumors to our personal ranking of *Pokémon GO* monsters. I'd never found someone I could so easily talk with.

"You do *not* reread the entire A Song of Ice and Fire series each time a new book is released!"

"I do." She snorted. "I can't help it. It's a compulsion. I gotta reread from the beginning to refresh myself on the characters and the world. It's a complex history."

"Get out."

"It's true. Honestly, at this point I despise the novels. Each time a new one comes out, my life is ruined for a month."

"Well, he's never going to finish them."

"Don't tell me that, you brute." A playful slap on my shoulder.

I froze. Familiar sounds. Taras's booming voice and Jane's mellifluous titter. The Orb 4 were walking by. With lightning speed, I donned my helmet.

"Huh? You're going to pass out again, Mike."

The helmet fell off anyway. The flimsy product had cracked when I collapsed. I was helmetless. Exposed.

Katie spun to look at the treacherous gang. "Do you know those people?"

I shushed her. I ran to crouch behind a trash can.

Jane was talking about the convention's "Borg cube ball pit" as they entered the concession area that I now saw, looking up, was named Quark's Bar, Grill, and Lounge. "I love the Borg. We have to figure out some kind of enemy like that for the *Star Rot* to face."

"Honestly? Assimilating sounds kinda nice right now," Jane said. "I bet they have free healthcare on the Borg cubes."

"Resistance is futile, but assimilation is lucrative," Darya said in a robotic Borg voice.

Taras laughed. "You know what? That kind of gives me an idea. It might be a very dumb idea though."

"Dumbest ideas are the best ones," Merlin said. "Pick the stupidest, goofiest idea you have and write it as seriously and rigorously as possible. That's honestly the best writing advice I've ever gotten."

Squatting, I scurried crablike behind the dining area. My brain blocked out Katie's pleas behind me. Everything inside me screamed *leave*. In my haste not to be spotted by my treasonous friends, I sprinted in the opposite direction, ducking behind a "Federation flash mob" of awkwardly dancing redshirts and, without even having time to wave goodbye to Katie, made my escape out of the back exit with my heart aching from both the betrayal and my regret.

A Visit from Mr. and Mrs. Castle

Each of us carries an entire cast of characters in our head. Bullies, friends, family members, schoolteachers, classmates, roommates, doctors, psychologists, irritating store clerks, someone in a weird outfit you saw once, etc. I speak of memories. Our brain transforms these people into characters that perform in ensemble shows in every genre imaginable in the TV station of our minds. I treasure all my memory-characters, even the ones who hurt me in real life. For in my mind, I am the director and scriptwriter. There, each character gets what they deserve.

What was I discussing? Oh, right. It can be jarring when you run into a memory-character IRL after many years. You realize they have undergone entire costume changes and character arcs while you weren't present. Your head canon is not their lived reality. This is how I felt when Olena and Anton Castle appeared at my apartment door.

"Little Misha, all grown up," Mrs. Castle said, walking inside. She pointed toward my belly. "And grown out too I see."

"Hello, Mrs. Castle."

I had remembered Mrs. Castle as a long-haired and thin woman pushing various dishes on Taras and me—"Eat up, it is just a snack"—between activities. In my memory, she wore a red-and-white apron so frequently I wouldn't have been surprised if she slept in it. Now she had grown herself on the X and Y axes while shrinking on the Z. Her hair had grayed and been cropped short. She wore a thick green coat over a dour dress.

Mr. Castle had changed even more. His lush brown beard was shaved off and I could see the dimple of his chin. While Olena had filled out, the once zaftig Anton seemed little more than a skeleton. His red cheeks had paled and yellowed. He extended a gloved hand that, when I shook it, felt like little more than bones.

"Are you staying out of trouble?" He coughed and then winked at me.

"I assure you my rap sheet is quite clean, Mr. Castle."

"Please, call me Anton. You and Taras aren't in short pants anymore." Anton looked around the apartment. "A sturdy place you have here. Hmm.

You need to repaint the walls. The floors should be sanded and re-stained. Who is your landlord?"

"It's a big place, right, Dad?" Taras said. He'd walked in right behind them, carrying our mail from the box downstairs.

The Castles had driven down from Vermont, somewhat unexpectedly, earlier that day. Taras, now freelancing from home post–ThoughtFunnel pivot-to-video, had met them at the hotel and guided them through a few New York City tourist stops. After a High Line stroll, they'd come to Brooklyn to assess their son's living situation.

Mr. and Mrs. Castle walked around the apartment, hands behind their backs. I could see Anton furrow his brow as the subway rolled past the window. He spoke to Olena in Ukrainian that I couldn't understand. She at least seemed taken with Arthur and spent some time wriggling her finger between the bars. "What a strange creature," she remarked, as Arthur responded with a car-alarm squawk.

Anton* turned to me. "Misha, you are free to come with us to dinner?"

"We're going to Veselka," Taras said, shrugging. "I told them we could eat any cuisine in the world here, but my mom wants pierogi."

His mother nodded sternly. "I want pierogi I don't have to cook for once. And I want to meet this woman of yours."

"She's not a 'woman of mine,' she's just my girlfriend."

We piled in an Uber and rode to the restaurant, where we were seated in the back. The Castles immediately began ordering. By the time Darya arrived (fifteen minutes late), the table was already overflowing with pierogi, latkes, soups, and beet salad. Darya was dressed up in a black dress under a gray blazer. She'd replaced her brightly colored earrings with muted silver studs. I was surprised by her transformation, and leaned over to ask, "Are you coming from a job interview?" Darya gave me an angry look and neither confirmed nor denied.

The conversation started out awkward yet pleasant. Darya explained

---

* I am hesitating between calling them Anton and Olena or Mr. and Mrs. Castle. They were the latter during my childhood, but they didn't seem like real people then. They were side characters in the tale of Taras and me. Flat and static. Now I realized they had been living their own stories. Perhaps that is what it means to grow older. Learning the people you hide your secrets from are also hiding secrets from you.

her interests and ancestry—"Iranians? Very good rugs," Anton said between bites—and she asked for "dirt" on Taras she could use. Olena immediately began recounting humorous tales of Taras's toddlerhood. "He loved the snow," his mother said. "Whenever he would see flakes, he'd cry until he was let outside. Then he'd touch the snow and cry from the cold! Like a pussycat."

"Please don't say pussycat, Mom. They're just 'cats' now."

I was content to chew and listen. I was the fifth wheel in the conversation, which suited me. I was unsure what to say to the Castles. They had always been kind to me, but for all that time I'd never conversed with them on a serious level. I'm sure they knew nothing of science fiction, for example. (Had they even read the published *Star Rot Chronicles* stories?)

While dinner had begun pleasantly enough, it soon turned contentious. Mrs. Castle asked Taras about the future, and not the science fiction kind. "You are too old to have no job and live with roommates, even Misha. What will you do? Live like a bum at forty?"

Taras tried to laugh it off. "Look, I'm making the New York City life work. I don't ask you for money."

"We have none to give you! We can't spoil you like some of your friends." His mother nodded in my direction.

"Spoiled?" I asked.

"Oh, come now, Michael." She turned her attention back to Taras. "You need a real job. One with healthcare. It is important to have healthcare in this country. Otherwise, you will die in a ditch and your father and I won't be around to pay the bill to drag you out."

"We'll be dead and rotting in our own ditches by then." His father pulled a business card out of his inside jacket pocket. He slapped it on the table. "Talk to Mr. Kaplan's son. You remember Frederick?* He may have a job for you. A real one."

I could see that Taras was embarrassed. He didn't like Darya witnessing

---

* I know I did. Freddie had been one of the most vapid members of our high school class. A jock (track and field team), dork (class president), and normie (his life goal had been to "make a lotta money every day and party every night").

his parents try to manage his life this way. He was an artist! He could not go groveling for jobs from old high school chums.

"I'm fine. Plus, doesn't Freddie work at some advertising firm? I'm not going to write corporate jingles."

"It pays real money," his father said.

"With healthcare!" his mother added, triumphantly stabbing a beet.

"I wanted you to be a doctor. You didn't want that. Okay. You have your own life. Still, you need to start being realistic. Settle down. Start a family. Life does not last forever." He shook his head sadly. "I promise you. It does not last forever."

"Dad, please."

His father simply pushed the card across the table. Then he waved the waiter to come clear the plates.

Darya looked at me, frowning. I shrugged in response.

Taras was squabbling with his mother now and growing increasingly flustered. His father joined in, telling him his years were "being wasted" and that it was "sad" to be in your thirties with no prospects and living with roommates. "You must join the real world!" his father said at one point. I needed to say something, anything, to make them comprehend the totality of the artist they had produced. How he was not just some cog in a corporate machine but a visionary author whose voice was needed in the world, not locked away in a cubicle. Yet before I could formulate a defense, Darya spoke.

"Taras is an artist," she said, her voice small but firm. "He is a writer. A good writer. That's his calling. And that's important too."

His father shook his head. "I am a doctor. That is a calling. I help people. Art is fine for a hobby. Chekhov was a writer. He was a doctor first."

Olena looked at Darya. Her face was squat and wrinkled like a grumpy turnip. "Art." She waved her hand. "What does art do?"

Darya stood firm. (I will always respect her for this. For standing up for Taras when I could not.) "I think art is what makes life worth living."

The Castles harrumphed, and the waiter appeared with our dessert. We ate the blintzes in silence.

Baldwin Faces His Greatest Foe

It is clear from the next *Star Rot Chronicles* story that the pressure to join the real world weighed on Taras. I hate the term. "The real world." Why is the dreary banality of daily life outside my window any more real than the lush universe of the Metallic Realms? But our society runs on money. Taras's parents weren't irrational in their pressure. They just didn't understand what the real world does to the artist's soul. When you abandon your dreams and slide into a gray cubicle to work forty to sixty hours a week entering data into spreadsheets until your eyes melt, your hands ache, and your brain disappears into a fog that can only be pacified by a few TV shows before you fall asleep on the couch. The reward for selling out your body and mind to corporate productivity? The ability to retire in your late sixties (if you're lucky) when you are frail and falling apart, decades after your dreams have drained away? They say youth is wasted on the young. Under capitalism, retirement is wasted on the retirees.

Still, it is understandable that Taras—now only semi-employed and on the last month of his ThoughtFunnel severance—would feel the pull of Yuppie security. Eventually even the artist grows tired of scraping by, spending every night and weekend on projects no one cares about, hoping for a break that may never come. Taras, with his usual science fiction wizardry, allegorized his dilemma in our next story, *SRC #6*, aka "First Contract."

"First Contract" shows that (sigh) TrekCon was still on Taras's mind. The villain the *Star Rot* faces in the next story was obviously inspired by the cybernetic hivemind of unindividuated drones known as the Borg. In that franchise, the Borg are trying to "assimilate" all life-forms for undefined purposes. Taras reinterprets and deepens the villains to give them more metaphorical power in our modern era of late-stage capitalism.

First Contract

We were in a bad spot. Low on fuel, behind on payments, and out of prospects. Outside, we were skimming the edge of Big Red to evade Glorxo Healthcare Empire agents who still demanded payment for my brain worm fumigation and the return of Algorithm. Plus compound interest. Inside, I was floating in a nebulous bleak black gloom. I was supposed to be the captain of this vessel and I couldn't even imagine a path forward. In a fit of desperation, the Fifth Ibbet and I donned mechsuits to siphon fuel off a Drogonite tanker in order to warp out of the quadrant. "We did it!" the Fifth Ibbet shouted. Then she screamed. A missile exploded beside us. The Glorxo agents had found us again.

This missile is your final notice.

The *Star Rot* was able to scoop us up as we tumbled through the void. I dragged my tired body out of the broken mechsuit and headed to the bridge. The Fifth Ibbet scampered alongside me, whimpering. We hailed the Glorxo ship and said we were subspace wiring payment, but the nebula dust was slowing down transactions.

"That should buy us a little time. What are our options?"

Algorithm vibrated as their quantum-brain processed our dwindling possibilities. "Sir, we are surrounded in all directions except one."

"What's the one?"

"Straight into the center of Big Red."

"Screw that!" Aul-Wick said. And I understood the sentiment. Big Red nebula was a no-go zone. Ships that explored it never came back to civilized space. But necessity is the mother of trajectory. We steeled ourselves and soared into the swirling waves of glittering crimson gases. *Your payment is past due!* A final Glorxo torpedo hit our hull as we vanished into the scarlet sea.

We escaped, but the torpedo shorted our force field. Soon, the ship was coated in cosmic dust. The dust filtered through the hull, clogging our engines. We sputtered to a stop. Algorithm assessed the damages. Not good. The repairs could take weeks.

"Hey, we're alive," I said, coughing. "That's something."

"What an inspirational speech, Captain," Vivian said.

We were squabbling when an object approached us from deep in the churning nebula mist. It grew larger and larger. It was gargantuan. A white moon in the shape of a cube.

"We're being scanned," Aul-Wick said as tingling light swept through the bridge. "Ugh. It's such a violation."

Before we could take evasive maneuvers, a humanoid woman with a gigantic smile appeared onscreen. Her skin was covered with inflamed metal ports connected together by yellow tubes. Her tunic was wet and black. There were a dozen others behind her, similarly modified. They all grinned.

"We are the Borj," the spokeswoman said. "Your ship has been scanned and your bioform has been preapproved as a Junior Associate Processor. Would you like to sign your contract orally or manually?"

"Assimilation is lucrative," the beings behind her said in an eerie chorus.

"Contract?" I said. "We're free agents. We don't work for anyone but ourselves."

The Borj woman shook her head in a way that made me think she was expecting this response. "You must be realistic," she said, and then proceeded to lay out the benefits of the Borj's offer given our present situation. They knew we were being chased by collectors. If I signed the contract, I'd be able to save up enough money to pay off our debt. "Assimilation is lucrative," repeated the grinning chorus of the Borj.

"I don't want to be assimilated!" the Fifth Ibbet shouted.

All of the Borj looked at her. The Fifth Ibbet was a thin, lemur-like creature with lilac fur and four arms. The scanner ran its tingly rays through the ship. Their smiles disappeared. "I am afraid your bioform doesn't meet our needs at this time. We will keep your genetic profile on file and contact you if opportunities open up in the future." The woman turned to me and smiled. "We are offering employment to the Earthian. You have one hour to confirm employment, or we will be required to destroy your ship with one of our NDAs. We can't allow you to share our secrets with competitors."

"NDAs?"

"Nuclear Disintegration Artillery."

I cut off the signal and looked at my crew. They were scared and tired. The Fifth Ibbet was nervously shedding purple fur and Aul-Wick made agitated bubbles in his orb. Even Vivian seemed too fatigued to fight. "Okay. I'll pretend to join this Borj as a distraction," I said, "and you all work on getting the ship de-dusted so we can escape."

My crew tried to dissuade me half-heartedly. No one could think of another plan.

As soon as I verbally agreed, the Borj teleporter beam grabbed me. All my muscles contracted as glimmering light coated me like slime. I gargled in pain. Dissolved. When I rematerialized, I vomited on the tiles.

"Commuting can be painful," the woman said. She introduced herself as Supervisor Ca'Raan and gestured to the dozen figures behind her. "These are your co-cogs. Welcome to Borj Cubicle #47." Supervisor Ca'Raan slapped a work collar around my neck, which implanted into my spine and sent me into another round of convulsions. My co-cogs dragged me to the training room. Ports and tubes were inserted into my flesh while a holographic training video explained my new job: processing nebula dust for oog, a metallic byproduct that powered the Borj economy. Oog could only be processed by the internal organs of certain humanoid life-forms. The more the Borj assimilated, the more oog they could produce, and the greater their economy swelled. As long as they increased oog production, they could expand eternally.

I was carried, drugged, to my cog station. A pipe was inserted into my throat and a muddy mixture of nebula dust and liquid flowed into me. The implants monitored and manipulated me with productivity boosters. My inspiration port barked with chipper messages like "You are a productive asset in the Borj!" "Your value is increasing each day!" When I gagged, the implants numbed my throat. When I struggled, they relaxed my muscles. At the end of my shift, I felt half-dead. Supervisor Ca'Raan appeared and opened the new valve on my stomach and scooped out the oog. "Good work today." She pinched off a small chunk of the oog and placed it in my hand. "Your signing bonus."

I was drained and immobile. One of my co-cogs had to help me to the central corridor, where I had been given a domicile. Unit 854-E. I collapsed on the couch and watched holofeeds until sleep carried me away.

At first, I resisted the Borj. Three co-cogs had to strap me to the back of a robotic slug to get me to commute to my cog station each morning. My pay was docked for the infractions. Still, I was constantly scratching at my work collar and trying to put kinks in the manipulation tubes. For a time. Little by little I got used to having my gullet stuffed with slime and globs of oog extracted from my guts. I started to think less about the degradation of my body while working and more about what I could look forward to between shifts.

There were perks to the job. My domicile was spacious and filled with the latest entertainment systems. There was even a porch in the back where I could go and catch the filtered breeze. I got to know some of my neighbors that way. Zuzz E, who grew fungal herbs along dirt lattices on the porch, and Boab, a three-armed guy from Tacan Major who introduced me to the cubicle ship's athletic competitions.

A universal truth of the cosmos is that anyone can grow accustomed to anything. Instead of going home right after work, I started to meet up with a few co-cogs. We spent the break between shifts in toad tanks zoning out to their relaxing licks or dancing in the gemstone discotheques. We drank numbing vials to ease the lingering physical pain of work, injected stimulants to keep us upright, and ate heavy meals of ripe meat and bright fungi.

The hours between shifts were short, so we were determined to make the most of them.

I began to feel pride in my oog production and started to appreciate the nuances of Borj fashion. I snickered at the cogs who used gauche magnetic clasps on their tunics instead of the more stylish electric buckles. I scrubbed my skin daily with sklorp paste, which helped ease the chaffing of the implants while also imparting a socially desirable sheen.

Time passed, shift by shift.

How long had I been with the Borj? It was hard to tell. I'd almost forgotten my old crew. The life I'd led on the *Star Rot*—is that what it was named?—seemed like a half-remembered dream, already fading as I dragged myself out of bed each morning.

One day, I left my workstation feeling especially drained and headed home to unwind.

"Baldwin!" Boab said, waving with his central chest-arm. "Critical game tonight. Want to watch?"

"I shouldn't. I've got an early performance review with Supervisor Ca'Raan."

"Baldy. Come on. It's Sector 4 Team versus Sector 53 Team! You aren't a 53 fan, are you?" Boab curled his chest-arm's hand into a fist and smacked it against his right hand. "SECTOR 4! LEAVE 'EM ON THE FLOOR! WHOO-RAA!"

"Sorry, buddy, I need to be fresh for the meeting. I'm hoping for a promotion during the next cycle."

He wished me good luck as I went inside. I was immediately tackled to the ground.

It took me a minute to realize who was hugging me. "We did it! We found you!"

"Vivian?"

She stood over me like an almost-forgotten phantom.

"Who else is going to rescue you, asshole?"

The others were there too. Aul-Wick in his levitating orb, the Fifth Ibbet trembling and holding her tail for comfort, and Algorithm monitoring me neutrally. "Captain, I apologize for how long it took us to repair the ship and then locate the Borj cubicle. It was hard to track in this nebula, which limits our sensors. We must hurry though. I estimate we have two minutes and three seconds before they seal the breach."

"Stole a few of these from the cogs we drugged." Aul-Wick flung a transporter pin to me. "Let's go."

"Go?" I sat up. I looked around my domicile, which had increased in value with the recent Sector 4 improvements. I looked at the healthy glow of my sklorp-coated skin. Then I looked at my crew. They were strange, almost feral beings. Their clothes were torn in places and covered in stains. None of them were buckled in a fashionable way. Yes, my life with the Borj involved using my body to process slime forced down my gullet for the vast profits of an ever-expanding empire that sought to assimilate the entire universe. But some of those profits trickled down to me through the oog payment faucet. I had a life here. Maybe not the life I wanted but a life with a future and security. "I'm not sure I want to go."

My crew stared back at me, unbelieving.

Aul-Wick looked like he might cry. "Okay. Then I'm staying too. Hook me up to the oog feed!"

"Captain," Algorithm said, "lengthy oog production will destroy your internal organs. I estimate your chances of surviving another five years to be only 3.87 percent."

"I'm a member of the Borj now. I'm happy here. They've given me a safe life. A practical life."

"Oh my fucking stars," Vivian said to the others. "We forgot to remove his cog collar. It's still manipulating his mind."

Vivian grabbed the collar with her cybernetic hand and snapped it off with a crack.

In an instant, everything came back to me. "Yikes, my head hurts. Ugh, what is this apartment? I can't believe I used to like those corny wall sculptures and tacky crystal lights! This place is a soft prison. Let's go. Beam us back, Algorithm."

We commuted back to the ship, dissolving painfully and reappearing on the bridge of the *Star Rot*. We scampered to our stations.

The Borj cube was blaring a warning siren. The breach had been noticed. Headhunting parties were being sent after us.

"Where to?" Aul-Wick said.

"Anywhere that's anywhere away from this blasted nebula," I said.

We flew back through the swirling red dust toward the dark, open expanse of the void, the whole crew laughing.

But as we left the nebula, I told my crew I needed a minute alone. Vivian tried to follow me, and I waved her off. I went to my room and looked at the porthole screen. I was free, yes, but my future was uncertain and terrifying. I noticed a white spot. The Borj ship. It looked so comfortable and comforting. A calming white cube in a red, dangerous sea. I stared at the cube until it dwindled down to a single pixel among the red nebula cloud, which itself soon shrank into a smear and disappeared as we dashed off directionless into the void.

SRC #6 Analysis

Why *The Star Rot Chronicles* Are So Imaginative Yet Resonant

Science fiction isn't merely a portal to other worlds. It's also a mirror. No matter how far we venture into the future, no matter how many multiverses and far-flung galaxies we visit, SF reflects our present reality. Our anxieties appear as tentacled aliens, our hopes as gleaming ray guns, and our dreams as generation ships. A post from the Orb 4 account explains: "Science fiction realizes Shklovsky's* dream. If art must estrange reality so we see it with fresh eyes, science fiction transforms our reality by offering us novel orbs—alien eyes, cybernetic eyes, robotic eyes—to see ourselves anew."

In "First Contract," Taras takes our everyday banalities and rearranges them into a fantastic (and horrifying) vision. In response, the reader is forced to rethink their assumptions of their own world. How can one look at commuting to work, "processing" data at a desk job, or hanging out with coworkers in quite the same way after reading this tale?

This story's final act is, admittedly, rushed. There's a reason. Taras wrote several endings. He stopped his presentation at the Orb 4 meeting midway. "I said this collective was a democracy. So, let's vote. You all have problems with Baldwin being captain. We can finish him off here. Baldwin can remain with the Borj and live out his life in a cubicle ship. Or he can escape yet be so shattered by the experience that someone else has to be captain. Or the *Star Rot* rescues him, and things go back to normal."

"What is this? Sophie's science fiction choice?" Darya said.

---

* Viktor Shklovsky, an early-twentieth-century theorist of "Russian Formalism." Despite Taras's tweet, Shklovsky sadly does not appear to have written science fiction himself.

"Yeah, come on, Taras. I was only joshing you," Jane said.

Taras insisted he was serious. He didn't have any particular attachment to Baldwin. And he wanted the Orb 4 to be on the same page. "I'm happy to kill my darlings, even when the darling is my stand-in."

"I'm with Darya. This is too much. I like Baldwin. I like all our characters, even Aul-Wick!" Merlin said. "I vote we don't leave any of them forced to filter nebula dust until they die. Nice metaphor for late-stage capitalism by the way."

Baldwin's rescue passed unanimously with an amendment stating explicitly that any Orb 4 member was free to write from the POV of any character.

The Borj were a well-received villain—although Merlin argued that perhaps they should be called "the Booj as in bougie"—because every member could relate to the central dilemma they pose. How can one have adventures (i.e., be an artist) when the entire world pushes you toward the Borj cubicle (i.e., the real world of 9-to-5 drudgery)? This was an ancient problem, but it was even more poignant for our generation because the benefits had evaporated. You couldn't sell out anymore, no one was buying. Wages had declined and job security withered at the same time costs and debt ballooned. The banal safety of 1950s bourgeoisie lifestyle had been replaced by something akin to the Borj: low-paying office jobs without benefits that squeezed your mind and body like a lemon and/or lime until the juice was gone and the wrinkled rinds could be tossed away at retirement age, at which point you prayed Social Security still existed.[*]

In Lore and Easter Eggs, "First Contract" provides an in-universe explanation for why the Big Red nebula is an unexplored realm. Those who enter are destroyed or assimilated by the Borj. We are also provided with a bit more detail about the newest *Star Rot* crew member and Jane's stand-in, the lilac creature known as the Fifth Ibbet.

While Vivian's loving embrace of Baldwin during the rescue was touch-

---

[*] I sent Taras's story to my parents, hoping it would illuminate my generation's crisis. When I quizzed them about it later, my father said, "Son, I only read nonfiction. I want to learn things." My mother, even more infuriatingly, commented, "Mr. Bandwidth [sic] should have kept the job. You can't put a price on job security and health insurance!"

ing on the page, it wasn't necessarily drawn from their own lives. Darya and Taras were, like an uncoordinated child trying to ride a unicycle on a gravel driveway,* on the rocks again. Darya left the meeting with Merlin that night, heading out to Bar Playground to unwind. "All the Frankenstein: The Gathering people will be there. Plus, the bar has monkey bars and mojitos. What more can you want?" Taras stayed behind, playing *Slay the Spire* until 1 A.M.

However, there might have been another source of inspiration. Your humble scholar. For I too had been rescued by someone I'd almost forgotten. Katie, the cosplaying Klingon who had nursed me back to life at the ill-fated TrekCon. Fate brought us together a second time. For this—if little else—I must thank my job at Rockets and Wands.

Love in the Time of Convention Centers

I t happened back at the Javits Center. This time instead of colorful costumes and gigantic cartoon sculptures, I was surrounded by hordes of unpaid interns in frumpy clothes and chunky glasses carting around a forest's worth of dead trees. That's right. It was BookExpo America. I was required to man the Rockets and Wands table for a six-hour shift. The annual trade industry event was illuminating mostly because it displayed the disparities of publishing in physical form. Small literary presses and SFF imprints were relegated to a folding table or two in the back, while the commercial fiction publishers passed out chocolates and wine in "pavilions" adorned with gigantic banners like the flags of royal houses. Rockets and Wands had nothing except a tablecloth and one creaking spindle of titles.

An hour went by without anyone so much as glancing at an R&W cover, so I decided to stroll and maybe get a coffee. I soon found myself in an argument with an editorial intern at an experimental literary press called Hypocrite Lecteur Books who, in response to my personable question about the plot of one of their titles, preceded to tell me, "Linear plot is a fascist

---

* An experience I remember all too well.

concept." We got into it. I was shouting, "Oh, so I'm 'bourgeois' for wanting an actual story but you're not for publishing a tenured Princeton professor's 'experimental hybrid memoir in verse' that will only be purchased by, like, twelve of his ivory tower colleagues out of pity?" when someone crept up to me.

"We can't keep meeting in these convention centers."

"Katie?"

We did the awkward dance of hug or no hug and ended up in a kind of sideways embrace.

"Hey," the Hypocrite Lecteur intern said. "Can you move? We're an anti-capitalist press, but we're still trying to sell books here."

Katie and I strolled through the endless aisles, laughing at the lit snob and catching each other up on our lives.

"I didn't know you worked in publishing."

"Production side." She held up her name tag with her title of assistant production manager. "I didn't know *you* did?"

One yada led to another yada, and soon we were sliding into each other's DMs on a daily basis. I was wary at first. Her love of *that franchise* was a potential red flag. But Katie was funny, erudite, and interested in hearing my ideas, such as my fan theory that *The Sopranos* takes place in Tony's dreams and the ending is him waking up to my belief that *The Sims* video game was conceived as *The Matrix* from the machine's POV. She had many theories too, although I don't recall them right now. The point was that someone was listening to me. Me! I felt like a man whose face was a gigantic mouth and only now had I found someone whose neck ended in a large, lovely ear.

We began to woo each other with amusing memes and clever gifs. Memes graduated to movie nights. Gifs became gifts of flowers and chocolate bars. Yes, our affair soon took a carnal turn. Reader, a gentleman doesn't kiss and tell. Let's just say the coupling was as hot as a red sun and our desire was more ravenous than a black hole. I had been celibate so long I'd forgotten the hidden language of scents, membranes, and moans. The poetry of flesh.

We developed a routine. She would come over after work on Friday with two boxes of red wine. I would have already filled a popcorn bowl to the brim with spaghetti Bolognese. We would take our feast to my boudoir and not leave for the entire weekend. My fingers traced a constellation of her moles. In her arms, I was lost in a new universe of pleasure.

I regret to say that my roommates were more prudish than I anticipated. My eroticism frightened them. Merlin asked me if we could go to Katie's apartment "now and then" and Taras twice accosted me by the laundry machines to say, "You have to stop grunting so loud, man. You're frightening the parrot." (That Arthur C. Caique would begin his joyful car alarm mimicry at the same time seemed to me a sign of our intimate avian-owner bond.)

Was Taras inspired by this blooming love while penning "First Contract"? Certainly, he had ample opportunity to observe our passion. The reader can draw their own conclusion.

The Twilight of the Golden Age

First Contract" is the first entry in what I consider the "Silver Age" of *The Star Rot Chronicles*. The first five stories represent the "Golden Age," which was a Cambrian explosion of science fiction: cosmic fables, pulp picaresque, scathing speculative satire and more sat side by side. The last few stories (*SRC #6–9*) represent the Silver Age, in which freewheeling adventures take a backseat to a grittier reality. These later stories are more adult and more provocative. They seem born out of the collective angst of the Orb 4. For even as they were rocketing through new stratospheres on the page, cracks were forming in the group's hull. The first was carved by none other than the author of the next tale, Jane Noh Johnson.

Jane was an odd fit in the Orb 4 as she sowed her writerly oats in the pretentious fields of literary fiction. Jane was enrolled in The New School's MFA program, you may recall. Between spinning Metallic Realms yarns, she'd been working on a mimetic novel for her thesis. It consisted of thirty-five thousand words of lyrical prose fragments with no transitions, narrative, or worldbuilding—at least from what I was able to read when she left her laptop open once while running outside to make a phone call. This is the trend of mundane fiction. Readers apparently no longer care about exciting plots or well-rounded characters. Vivid settings and carefully constructed arcs are passé. Now, to get a rave in a Borj-ian propaganda venue like *The New York Times*, you need only to string together some dull observations from your real life between quotes from historical thinkers whose Wikipedia pages you skimmed.

To each their own.

The point is that Jane had followed this trend and was able to speak the words all authors long to utter: "Guys, I, uh, sold a novel!"

Initially, the group was thrilled. They showered her with congratulations and Taras poured a round of whiskey shots to celebrate.

"That's amazing," Merlin said. "I didn't even know you had an agent."

Jane downed the whiskey and grimaced. "I guess I didn't think it would lead anywhere. We actually sold it a few months ago but I didn't want to jinx anything until the contract was signed. Those take forever to complete! My agent's lawyers are slow."

"You sold it months ago and didn't tell us?" Taras said at the same time Merlin asked, "What's it about? If you can say."

Jane ignored the first question. "It's not science fiction or anything. It's kind of an autofiction Künstlerroman. I'm calling it *The Museum of Normal Thoughts*. Unless my editor makes me change it. It's about microaggressions, precarious millennials, climate change, and other fun stuff."

"I'm excited for you! That's great. Can I ask what the advance was?" Darya said, then quickly added, "Sorry, is that bad to ask? That whole part of the industry is a mystery to me."

"It's all opaque! The money I got isn't life changing or anything. I'm honestly just happy it sold at all."

While the Orb 4 were overall happy about the news, I was torn. Did this mean Jane would leave the Orb 4? And if so, would this be an opportunity for moi? In any event, the real problem emerged at the next meeting.

How Jane Betrayed the Orb 4

It was a lovely late summer evening and Katie was over for our usual "Netflix and chill" routine. I told her that I had a scheduled call with my mother from 6 P.M. to 8 P.M., the time of the Orb 4 meeting. Instead of leaving, Katie simply put on noise-reducing headphones and continued playing *Barnyard Market: Harvest Hooves*. When I glanced at her screen, her cow avatar's fruit stand had just received an enormous shipment of cantaloupe.

I held my cell phone to one ear and slid a Bluetooth earbud into the other to listen to the proceedings through my fern recorder. The group was discussing, of all things, formatting.*

"I dunno. I think David Foster Wallace kinda killed the footnote," Taras said.

"But footnotes are so fun! Plus, they break up the text in productive ways. Force the reader to acknowledge the artifice of the text."

"I dig postmodernism and love footnotes in theory. But in practice, they're kinda distracting."

"I vote no."

"I second."

"Great. Let's make it a rule. No footnotes."†

I was distracted by Katie looking at me, so I began mouthing "watermelon watermelon watermelon." A trick I'd learned in elementary school from Taras. We were in choir practice, attempting off-key choruses of "Rudolph the Red-Nosed Reindeer." Taras was beside me in a fetching *Teenage Mutant Ninja Turtles* sweatshirt. He leaned over and whispered in my ear, "If you pretend to say watermelon it will look like you're singing. Mrs. Mantooth can't tell!" Taras was full of useful tips, tricks, and life hacks. This worked brilliantly. I made it through the rest of elementary school without ever once belting a note.

---

* As I've often done, I'm using the fern recording files to verify these conversations.

† Oh. Wow. I must confess I am a little thrown here. I had completely forgotten Taras's anti-footnote feelings and the Orb 4's no footnotes rule. I would never have used them in this volume otherwise! I suppose Katie was distracting me at the time. I do apologize. I'm not sure I will have time to rewrite the preceding chapters, but I will follow Taras's typesetting preferences for the rest of this volume.

I gave Katie an exaggerated "moms, right?" eye roll and she smiled, then turned back to her game.

"Wait, Jane, omg, I just saw your post," Merlin said, looking up from their phone. "Your novel announcement went up."

There seemed to be a nervous edge to Jane's laughter. "Oh. Ha. Yeah. It's just an industry blurb. You don't need to read it."

"Come on, we have to!" Darya said.

"No, really . . ."

As they each pulled up the announcement on their phones, I did the same on my computer. Her post—"So, uh, some personal news! [eyes emoji]"— included a pixelated screenshot of a "Publishers Marketplace Deal Report":

New School MFA student Jane Noh Johnson's THE MUSEUM OF NORMAL THOUGHTS, an autobiographical novel-in-fragments about a young Korean American woman's struggles living in New York City, lyrically and luminously exploring microaggressions, macroeconomics, climate, grief, love, art, fate, trauma, labor, and time, among other topics, and centered on a dysfunctional writing group where she struggles to find herself, in a good deal, to Carole Blackstone at Heron House, by R. J. Ramirez at The Dogeared Literary Agency.

Silence. Only a few seconds—eleven in the audio file—but they felt like hours.

Merlin was the first to speak. "A dysfunctional writing group? So. Like. You're writing about us? You wrote an Orb 4 novel?"

"No, no. No! It's more about my MFA cohort. The stories I could tell you." Jane forced a laugh. "It's mostly about being Korean and stuff with my family and, like, the point of art in the modern world. My editor wrote that blurb. It's not how I'd summarize it. Anyway, it's all fiction, you know?"

"You said it was autofiction?"

"Well, auto is only half of it. Don't forget the fiction." She was speaking more quickly than usual.

More silence.

"If you're taking things we said, isn't that kind of plagiarism?" Darya asked.

"What? Whatever happens to me is part of my story. I can take things from my life for my writing."

"But we're writers!" Darya pointed out. "What we say is our art as much as what we write. It counts as writing."

"Hold up. I must assert my right to write about my experiences."

"Our experiences included?"

There was a lot of cross talk here that I can't accurately transcribe. At some point, Darya asked what "a good deal" means.

"Oh, it's just inside baseball stuff."

"I mean, we're writers too. Aren't we baseball players in this metaphor? You can tell us."

"I thought it was code for how much money it sold for? The advance?" Merlin said.

"Well, yeah. Technically."

"So . . . how much?"

The tension in the room slid through my earbud, thick as butter. Jane said she didn't feel comfortable talking about it and tried to redirect the conversation to a recent literary scandal where an author was being roasted online for lazy research in their historical novel. "Apparently, they'd googled 'medieval food' and accidentally included made-up dishes from *Game of Thrones* and *Zelda*. He has Joan of Arc drinking Dornish wine lol."

The Orb 4 moved on. They began talking about story ideas, including potential novel spin-offs. Taras offered the Wu-Tang Clan—a favorite of our youth—as a model. "We could publish a group story collection akin to *Enter the Wu-Tang (36 Chambers)*. Then each write our own solo novels." Darya, who was silently using her phone during this discussion, interrupted with a yip. "Jane, this website claims 'good deal' is code for an advance of 100,000 to 250,000 dollars!"

"That sounds right," Taras said. "I think I've heard that."

"But Jane said it wasn't life-changing money before!"

"Well." Another pause. "Look. To be clear, it was the very low end of that. Plus, you have to factor in my agent's fee and taxes. And I only get one part now. It's not that much, when you think about it."

Darya burst into bitter laughter. "I'm sorry, Jane. We all know how taxes work. That's still a lot of money."

"Let's be supportive, guys. I know you've been working on that book for years, Jane. Didn't you start it in college?" Taras said.

"I'm truly happy you got paid," Merlin said. "I hope all of us suck as much money out of these corporations when we can. Though I am curious what you used from our group. Can we see the manuscript?"

"It's not even finished, guys. Like, I don't even turn in the final copy for months."

"That's plenty of time to let us read it and veto anything about us we don't like," Darya said.

Jane was upset now. When Taras said that he did feel it "wasn't that much" to let them read it beforehand, she snapped. "Taras! Are you joking? You fucking wrote a story about our hookup for your workshop in college. Remember? Where the narrator sleeps with a 'Joanne Jojima.' You think everyone didn't know it was about me? Now you're giving me crap about putting my life experiences in a novel?"

"Jesus, what?"

"My friend Sarita was in that workshop and told me all about it. Everyone knew. Also, Jojima is a Japanese name. I'm Korean. Kinda racist, dude."

"She was a fictional character! She wasn't you. Also, I didn't publish that story. Only like twelve people in one class ever read it."

"Yeah, because lit mags rejected it, not because—"

Darya let out a sad, guttural cry. "Sorry, but I can't fucking deal with this right now." Through the crack of my bedroom door, I watched Darya trod to the door holding her coat and bag. She turned, said a curt "Congrats, Jane," and left.

How I Sprung My Plan

On the one hand, mundane fiction held little interest for me. I was captivated by works of wondrous imagination, not journal entries about the banalities of daily life in contemporary America. If I wanted dreary "realism" I could just look out my window. On the other hand, *The Museum of Normal Thoughts* promised rare insight into the inner workings of the group. And on the third hand—consider me like the tri-armed Boab from Taras's "First Contract"—I couldn't help but think the door of the Orb 4 might have been cracked open for me to triumphantly strut through if I played my cards right.

Taking inspiration from "First Contract," I decided it was time to bring the Orb 4 what they needed most. A first book contract. As a key employee of the major SFF publisher Rockets and Wands, I was in prime position to secure one. If Taras were to thank me with an offer of membership, who could object?

I had been polishing, proofing, and (here and there when inspiration struck) tweaking the stories for weeks to make sure they aligned with official *Star Rot* lore. The time had come. I arrived early to assemble the manuscript. As the light of the copier slid past my hand, I imagined not the angry faces that had taunted me before the Great Fan Fiction Scandal trial but rather the beaming faces of the Orb 4, eyes shining with admiration. "Good work, Michael!" "We knew you could do it!" "You've saved the entire galaxy!"

I wrote and deleted several texts to Taras. The prudent move would be to wait until I had a definitive "yes" from Rockets and Wands' editor in chief, Vincent Barillo.

Nine thirty-five A.M. The assistants and interns filed into the office, sipping their iced coffees. At my desk, my leg jittered so violently I developed a charley horse. Finally, Barillo arrived. He walked past our cubicles with nary a nod and closed his office door. I gave him ten minutes to relax before I gingerly rapped.

When there was no response, I rapped with a little more ginger.

A groan. "Yes?"

"Chai latte, squirt of caramel," I said, entering and extending his libation as well as "a manuscript that might be the future of science fiction."

Stunned at my initiative, Barillo blinked.

"You're . . ." Barillo held up his hand and snapped his fingers, though they were poorly moisturized and produced only a rustling noise. "Matthew, right?"

"Michael." I explained I'd found a gem in the slush pile that was "a *Katamari* ball of early pulp classics, *Battlestar Galactica,* N. K. Jemisin, Jeff VanderMeer, and Kim Stanley Robinson all rolled into one. I think you'll agree it's a surefire Nebula finalist, and possibly the source material for a sprawling multimedia franchise."

Barillo took the manuscript, which I'd placed in a professional three-ring binder. The cover page featured a rather spiffy (if I must say so) cover mock-up I'd designed in Microsoft Paint 3D. It featured gigantic crystals floating like planets in a solar system, with a glittery asteroid belt between them. In the foreground, an astronaut in a dashing red space suit floats with ray gun in hand and a gleam of heroism in his eye. I'd created the collage for my *Crystal Cosmos Archives*. But as that work was both unfinished and unpublished I thought there was nothing to lose and much to gain in repurposing.

Barillo looked at the manuscript for a minute and then placed it on the far side corner of his desk, facedown. "Great. Thanks, Matthew."

"Michael."

"Michael."

I nodded and strolled to the door, then turned. "When do you think you'll finish reading?"

Barillo frowned, I think. It was hard to tell because his somewhat unkempt facial hair was glistening with latte foam.

"Right. I might as well tell you now. We don't *actually* publish from the slush. It's . . . slush. You know the depressing gray ice melting in the gutter in winter? Half oil runoff and half dog piss? You don't want to drink that, right? Similarly, we don't want to publish it." He wiped his mustache with the back of his hand.

I pointed out that Rockets and Wands had two interns, including myself, whose primary duty was providing reader reports on the slush. "Surely we aren't doing this labor for naught."

Barillo sipped his chai. He squinted and then scratched a notably hairy mole on his neck. "It's good practice for you. That's why. Writing pitch letters, reading submissions. That's what editors do. It's educational."

"Why even have a slush pile if we don't publish any of it? That makes no logical sense."

"Okay, Spock." He laughed. "Listen, this is publishing. It isn't about logic. I mean our P&Ls are basically fan fiction."

"If I'm doing the labor, I'm owed an explanation."

"Writers are sensitive. The worst part of publishing. The slush pile appeases them. We don't want to sound elitist and say you have to have an agent to publish here. We'd get attacked online. And the worst weirdo writers will send us mail no matter what we say. Haven't you noticed how your slush pile is filled with romance novels, cookbooks, litfic with titles like *The Stamp Collector's Wife's Daughter,* and other things that are completely out of the scope of a science fiction and fantasy publisher? No one reads guidelines. So, we accept slush, let you interns read, and authors complain less. It's a necessary evil."

Undeterred, I said that *The Star Rot Chronicles* was the exception. "I would stake my job on it."

"An internship isn't exactly a job," Barillo said, but he was intrigued. He opened the binder and flipped through. "This looks like thirty pages? Most of our books are one hundred thousand words or more."

"These are merely the opening tales of an ongoing series. Once your whistle is wet, you'll want to chug the entire franchise. I promise."

He shook his head. "We don't publish the slush and we definitely don't publish short stories. No one reads short stories unless they're in *The New Yorker.* And no one actually reads *The New Yorker.* They just let them pile up until it's time to take down the recycling. I'll have to pass."

He pushed the binder across his desk toward me.

Laughing, I pushed the binder back and corrected him. "It isn't short stories. It's an interconnected fictional universe with recurring characters and an overarching, if subtle, plot, in the vein of the fix-up novels of sixties New Wave—"

He held up his hands and shook his head back and forth in acknowledgment of my salient points. "Okay, okay. Christ. I'll give it a glance. When I have some free time."

I said he wouldn't regret it and backed out of the door.

Jane's Anti-Capitalist Allegory

Jane's frustration with the other Orb 4 members over her book deal, and the general feeling that she was overlooked within the collective, seem to have been inspiration for our next *Star Rot Chronicles* yarn. In "The Trouble with Lingloids," Jane's character, the Fifth Ibbet, is sent out to harvest "void pearls" from a "cosmic coral reef." The awe-inspiring setting for this tale is a fabulist twist on a real phenomenon: the consumption of suns by nearby black holes. Here, the massive trail of light being sucked from the star becomes a feeding trough for a pod of vlorps (the space whales from *SRC #3*). On the flat, wide backs of the planet-sized space leviathans, an entire reef of light-eating alien creatures congregates: glowing atomic anemones, white calcium crabs, metallic urchins, cosmic clams, and electric asteroid eels thin as ribbons nibbling at schools of silver space minnows. The dying star had given life to an entire ecosystem!

Despite this sublime image—so typical of Jane's stories—the focus is on the Fifth Ibbet's political awakening. As the Fifth Ibbet is moving through the reef in her mechsuit, she finds other Lingloids from other starships doing the same labor. They begin to discuss their situations. The Lingloid workers are exploited. They are paid a pittance and then most of that is eaten in fees by the galactic temp agency, Custom Lingloids 4 U. They discover their common plight and take up the call, "Lingloids of the Galaxy Unite!" (Apparently, fictional Lingloids were easier to unionize than Jane's fellow NYC adjuncts.) While the story ends with the Fifth Ibbet injured in the final battle with the bosses, this merely sets up the stage for her meta-morphosis into the Sixth Ibbet.

Huh. This is strange.

It seems that I only have the first page of "The Trouble with Lingloids." This story was not uploaded to the Google Drive account and I'm unable to find a full copy riffling through my (admittedly somewhat disorganized) papers. However, by some cosmic coincidence, beneath the first page of the aforementioned story I find several stray pages whose headers say *The Museum of Normal Thoughts*. They seem to be from the draft of Jane's autofiction novel, the one that commanded so high a price from publishers and inflicted an even higher cost on the Orb 4. They must have gotten mixed up in Jane's backpack when I nabbed the story after her reading. (That scholarship at times requires such ethically "gray" actions should surprise no one. The importance of preservation trumps etiquette.)

Although the following excerpt is in no sense a canonical *SRC* story, it may provide insight into the group dynamics. With the help of a text-scanning cell phone app, I shall reproduce it here in its entirety.

The Museum of Normal Thoughts
by Jane Noh Johnson (Excerpt)

Chapter 10:
Ships of the Sea, Ships of the Stars, Ships of the Body

Scientists estimate there are three million sunken ships on the ocean floor ranging from modern warships to the dinky canoes of antiquity. Three million is a guess. We've explored only a fraction of our own dark oceans even as we send spaceships to explore the bright stars above.

*

I have my memories. And I have my fictions reconfigured out of the shards of my experiences. Neither one is the truth. One is distorted by the maze of the mind, the other by the artifice of art. My workshop professor says the labels "fiction" and "nonfiction" are for bookstores, not writers. To the writer, all nonfiction is reworked by the lie of story and all fiction contains kernels of lived experience. "How could we write anything other than the truth of what we see and think? It all goes in and out of the same place!" my professor says, tapping his Sharpie against the side of his balding head.

*

I'm ten on a fishing boat with my adoptive father. The sun glints in half-moons off the cool green river while above us dark commas of birds punctuate the sky. "I want to show you a real American pastime." His rough hands guide mine to hook the worm, yet it is my finger that gets pricked and bleeds.

*

In Philosophy 208: Being and Somethingness, which I'm auditing, my professor explains the "Ship of Theseus problem." Philosophers love problems, but only if they can't be solved. With a dry-erase marker, she sketches a crude sailboat in seafoam green. "The Greek hero Theseus leaves his boat in Athens. A plank falls off and someone replaces the piece. Another piece falls off and gets replaced. So on and so forth until the *entire* ship, every single plank, has been replaced. Got it? Next, imagine someone builds a *second* ship out of all the fallen pieces."

Orhan, the Turkish class troll, raises his hand. "Why're they building ships out of rotted-ass boards?" The teacher sighs. "Athens' lumber shortage isn't the point. Which is the *real* Ship of Theseus? Is it the first ship, which has *continuity* but not *substance*. Or the second ship built of the original *substance* that lacks *continuity*?"

No one answers. A cough.

"Could you explain that again?" a girl in the back says, looking up from her phone. The professor tries. The students remain confused. Orhan laughs. Exasperated, the teacher points at him. "You own a car. I come by each night and steal one piece of your car yet replace it with an identical piece. After a few months, you see me driving in a car built entirely out of the pieces stolen from your car. Yet you still have your car. Who has the Car of Orhan?"

Orhan is flummoxed. He smacks his desk. "Either way, you stole my fucking car!"

*

At Science Fiction Club, I propose a plot. "The *Sol Royale* flies through an asteroid belt and pieces of the ship are constantly knocked off."

The Scientist's face squishes up. "Asteroids are typically millions of miles apart."

"That's not the point," I say. "Pieces of the starship keep falling off somehow and the *Sol Royale* crew replaces them. But! Scavenger aliens are collecting the pieces that break off until they can completely re-create the *Sol Royale*. There are two identical ships. Which is the *real Sol Royale?*"

*

Individuals may be in flux, but groups cohere into fixed roles. In Science Fiction Club, I sit across from the Leader. He may not have the most innovative ideas, but he brought us together. Beside him sits the Scientist, his sometime partner. She has very specific ideas about what science fiction should be. She's also the heart of the group, the bloody motor that makes us work. She schedules our meetings and manages our social media accounts with methodical precision. Last is the Free Spirit, who represents what I always imagined being an artist would mean. Full of ideas and identities. They live their art in their action and words with little care for the "rules" of patriarchal heteronormative capitalist society. I'm no Free Spirit. My artist life is procrastinating in front of a blank Word document between checking emails and bingeing Netflix.

*

What do the others designate me? The Quiet One? The Diversity Hire? The Snob?

*

I'm drawn to science fiction because I constantly imagine the other lives I've lived in other timelines. What if I had been raised in my birth country? What if I went back now? What if I found my biological parents? When I joined Science Fiction Club, I told myself it would help me create a new ver-sion of myself. Someone more self-assured and stronger. The truth of who I wanted to be. Yet we needed other archetypes, "for narrative balance" the Leader said. And I did what I tend to do. I made myself smaller. Literally in this case. I became a scared space lemur named Iris Five.

*

The tides move to the music of the moon. And yet scientists have discov-ered that the moon moves farther from the earth each year because of the gravitational force of the tides it creates. By touching us, the moon pushes itself away.

*

Is it too late to make art in late capitalism? Can art change the world before the climate does? Or is the artist in the Anthropocene a lone Siren in an empty sea singing for an Odysseus who will never come?

*

"Then what?" the Leader says. "We've got two *Sol Royale* ships, right? What happens?" We sit around the stained kitchen table in the dank apartment in the center of Brooklyn, far from the azure waters of the Mediterranean that the triumphant Theseus sailed. "It's a philosophical quandary," I say. "I'm trying to get at something about identity and the line between truth and fiction." "Yes, but this is a story," the Scientist says. "We need drama. Tension. Plot."

For a second, I think we're going to snap at each other. Science Fiction Club is too often a place where big ideas surrender to hurt feelings. Yet this time the Free Spirit interjects, "I just saw this TikTok about an octopus that picks up coconut shells to hide inside as it rolls across the ocean floor." The

Leader leans back, stroking his wispy beard. "The outside might look like the *Sol Royale*, but something lurks inside, holding the broken pieces together with sticky tendrils. Something evil and ineffable. Something that could destroy the galaxy." The Scientist smiles. "Or many things! A whole colony working together, part hivemind and part distributed neural network. Like a coral reef, octopus arms, and an ant colony all combined. A new, truly alien life-form."

Everyone is flipping open notebooks or laptops, shouting ideas as fast as we can type. "This is going to be an Iris Five POV story," I say, smiling. The Leader nods. "Of course. It was your idea!" We're firing on all cylinders.

And then.

*

And then he enters. The Roommate. A barnacle that's been attached to the Leader's hull for decades.

*

The Roommate is who I fear I am, deep down: the awkward, merely tolerated friend who misunderstands social cues. The one whose back everyone talks behind. I had to molt myself, rip off every plank and build my personality back from scratch, to survive in high school. And now I no longer know what parts of the real me are even left.

*

It's a myth that barnacles hurt the turtle shells and whales they attach to. They aren't parasites. They don't consume the sea creatures who carry them. Barnacles simply need a place to rest. They're just lonely creatures in search of a home.

*

This time, the Roommate drags a stool from the kitchen to hunch above us like a gargoyle. He begins to make suggestions. Nitpicks. Demands. Eventually, the Leader says, "Hey man, how about I order us all pizza and you can go pick it up?" Yet it's too late. Even after he's left, we squabble about logic and story beats. Soon, the "Spaceship of Theseus" is abandoned. Sunk, like so many stories, to the bottom of the blue abyss.

*

On the fire escape, I vape in the cool, blue Brooklyn night. What's that in the distance? A dark, giggling figure dances down the street. It's him. The Roommate. He hops along, cardboard pizza box positioned on his head. A woman dodges the box, slipping off the sidewalk and dropping her leash. She shouts as her dog scurries off yet the Roommate keeps skipping down the street, oblivious. I swear I can hear him cackling like some buffoonish trickster god destined to cause chaos wherever they

[Editor's note: excerpt ends here.]

Reactions

Wow. Well. I've spent the last minutes staring at Jane's autofiction excerpt, a strange lump slowly sinking—like a stone on a low-gravity moon—through my insides. Bile, or soda backwash, rises in my throat. This is time I can ill afford to lose, given my onrushing deadline. The excerpt has disturbed me. And thrilled me.

Another lost *Star Rot* story! I have no idea where this "Spaceship of Theseus" story might have fallen within the chronology. In my head canon, it's placed after "So, You Want to Hire a Custom Lingloid?" It's such a rich, thematic concept. The kind of science fiction that only the Orb 4 could pen.

I remember, vaguely, a meeting where I offered—without prompting, mind you—to pick up our evening's repast at the local pizza parlor. Yet I have found no mention of this story in any of my transcriptions or notes. I can only assume this was presented in some context where I was not present, such as the bus to TrekCon, and Jane took time stamp liberties in her retelling.

In terms of the bizarre characterizations of "Science Fiction Club" (a mere "club"? Really?), little here will feel recognizable to anyone familiar with the real-life Orb 4. Although analyzing mimetic fiction is beyond the scope of this volume, I think that all I shall say here is that it is clear *fic* and *tion* are the operative syllables in Jane's autofiction novel. The idea Taras was mere unimaginative glue, rather than the font of all things *Star Rot,* is so preposterous—even heartless, given what would come—that this scholar can only assume that the personalities of the members have been purposely reconfigured beyond recognition in order to avoid libel lawsuits. Anyway, I leave the excerpt here as a curiosity and move on.

This feels like a good time for a slight detour from these interstellar escapades. I would like to comment on what you just saw. A dinkus. No, I don't mean you, dear reader! You have certainly noticed the little collection of asterisks ⁂ that dapple this document like stars in the vast expanse of space. This is the humble dinkus.

Or rather it is one form of the shape-shifting dinkus. You may have noticed Jane Noh Johnson used a single * in her fabricated fragment collection masquerading as a novel. Absolutely any glyph can be used as a dinkus. The fancy prefer the fleuron (❧), a stylized leaf that can be shown in any orientation (❦). And authors frequently create their own dinkuses to match the tone of the text. The high fantasy author R. R. R. Milton used crossed swords in *The Daggers of Fate* while steampunk maestro Millie Featherproof used a small gear icon between the oil-drenched scenes of *Professor Manatee's*

Whirling Wonder Machine. In this volume, I have chosen to use a symbol dear to my typographical heart known as the "asterism." This term, borrowed from cosmology, is used for three asterisks arranged in a pyramid of stars: What could be more appropriate for science fiction than that?

And that is everything you need to know about the dinkus.

The dinkus digression didn't clear my head as I'd hoped. For the past few minutes I've been vibrating in my seat. I feel as if my body is a pot of boiling water. I'm angry. Okay. Furious.

I suppose I thought that if I skipped past Jane's defamatory depictions, they'd have no power over me. True scholarship also means correcting the historical record. As I mentioned, the idea that Taras was not the alpha, omega, Prime Mover, and father of all things *Star Rot* is pure absurdity. Second, "the Roommate"? Surely I deserve more of a title than that—and would subsequently be granted one from Taras himself, as the reader will soon learn. The implication that I inserted myself unhelpfully into Orb 4 proceedings is, well, I will merely say deeply hurtful.

Is that what you wanted, Jane? To prick me with your thorny words and see if I bleed?

I mean . . . this just bears no resemblance to reality at all. Her account is pure fantasy! She might as well have written about elves and dragons. Bah.

The reader shall forgive me if I take a more cynical view of Jane, the false friend, for the remainder of this volume.

Metafiction and Mega-Friction

Let's just move on. As I cannot locate the full text of "The Trouble with Lingloids," and as I'm in no mood to extend grace to Jane, I strike it from the canon. See the power scholarship possesses, Jane? This will be the official record of the Orb 4. I have made it. Me. The barnacle.

Our next tale requires a bit of context, for Jane's book deal wasn't the only source of tension in the increasingly fraying Orb 4 alliance. The issue this time was Taras. I mentioned the backstory of Taras's doom funk, which put a strain on his romantic relationship with Darya as well as his roommate relationships with Merlin and me. The inciting incident was a smashed taillight on Taras's car, which Merlin had parked after a house beach trip to Fort Tilden. Taras was scraping by on freelance assignments after being laid off from ThoughtFunnel and was too proud to ask his parents for assistance. He emptied his bank account for the repairs. So, Taras began to sublet his room. Twice he visited his parents in Vermont and other times he simply crashed at Darya's while cashing Airbnb payments.

The apartment soon felt less like a home than a hostel. Any given day, you might return to find a hipster in a trucker hat finishing a quinoa bowl or a business-suit bro shouting into his Bluetooth that "these clients want to party" so his assistant "better find the most epic club so I can crush this deal."

"Mike!" Merlin said, strolling into my room without knocking. "We need to talk. I went out to make my morning coffee and there was a pair of German tourists eating fruit on the couch. Just chomping and slurping. The coffee table is a pile of rinds."

"I think they're Dutch," I said.

"I don't care if they're Prussian. It's too early in the morning to deal with this."

A man in a skintight lime-green shirt, leather pants, and gelled hair stuck his head in my room. "Do we hebben een probleem here, friends?"

Merlin wanted a house edict: no subletting. I was torn. How could I not help my close friend during his financial troubles? At the same time, I had my own money tribulations and could hardly cover Taras's rent if he left. Merlin booked a house meeting in our Google Calendar and then proposed an "obvious solution."

"If you can't afford the rent, Taras, let's switch rooms. You pay less and I get the extra space I need for a drafting table. I've got a lot of projects right now. Plus, the room was supposed to be mine anyway."

"Wow," Taras said. "This is kind of fucked to bring up when your parking job started all this."

"What?"

"I'm just saying. You went in all crooked."

"I was in the lines, okay."

We were at the kitchen island, ostensibly sharing a pizza although everyone was too angry to eat. The fight ballooned. Other pet peeves and pain points were sucked into the spiraling gyre. Merlin complained Taras was barely even involved in the Orb 4 anymore, disappearing from email chains and leaving the planning to Merlin and Darya. Taras brought up the way Merlin left food waste in the sink—"probably why we had a roach problem!"—and how their products cluttered up the shared bathroom. Merlin said that just because Taras was a "dude cliché who doesn't care about skin care" didn't mean he should talk about the state of the bathroom, which Merlin alleged maintained a pungent urine aroma.

Listening to the shouts and recriminations, my pulse quickened. My underarms got damp. As is probably apparent to you, dear reader, I'm a lover not a fighter. I desire calm. Seek stability. Need peace. When I was a child, my parents fought frequently. I would run to my room and hide in the pile of stuffed animals on my bed. Toys were inadequate soundproofing. As my parents' shouts increased in volume, I had only one option: distraction. I played the clown. I ran around. Injured myself. Banged pots and pans. Anything to get my parents to forget hating each other and remember loving me.

Instinct kicked in. I grabbed a slice of pizza and held it to my mouth like an alien tongue and scampered atop the nearby dining table. Merlin and Taras were still flinging accusations at each other, barely noticing me.

"Peecha wanchee lockhba tang nannee du chonky troy!" I flailed my right arm around, using my left to manipulate the pizza tongue. The tip slapped my neck and a rivulet of grease dripped and pooled on my collarbone. My voice was low and threatening. A spirit moved through me. The spirit of theater. (I had taken several acting lessons during middle school summer camp.) I roared in the alien tongue from a galaxy far, far away. "Solo thawt du mocky chalia!"

They were watching me now.

"Is he having a seizure?" Merlin said. "Can you stay standing while having a seizure? I'm going to call an ambulance."

"I think that's . . . Jabba the Hutt?"

Merlin and Taras walked over. Merlin's hands were held up in a display of calming. "Come on down, Mike."

"Yeah, that looks unsteady, man."

I was wobbling on the table, tired and woozy. The pizza slipped out of my mouth, bounced off the front of my shirt, and plopped on the rug.

Taras grabbed me from the other side. "Easy now." The two lowered me down to the floor. The ground was cool. Their faces hovered over me.

"I'm sorry," I said. My voice was as small as a nanobot. "All the yelling made me dizzy."

"It's okay, it's okay." Taras looked back at Merlin. "I'll stop the Airbnbing, all right? I can see how that's annoying. And I recently got a gig editing the Princeton Review college guides, so my money situation is a little better."

"I'll be better about cleaning after cooking," Merlin said.

The two shook hands, looking back at me. From the floor, I smiled.

Although Merlin and Taras reached a détente, hurt feelings lingered that Merlin worked through in a delightfully postmodern fashion. "Checkmate of the Mind," our next *SRC* tale, is a humorous "bottle episode" that lightly jibes Taras while simultaneously tackling classic science fiction themes about the nature of humanity, consciousness, fate, and free will. Enjoy.

Checkmate of the Mind

S *cene: Captain Baldwin's quarters. The room is decorated in a mishmash of styles from throughout Earthian history. In one corner, a holographic parrot intermittently flaps its wings. Algorithm stands before Baldwin's desk, hands behind their back.*

BALDWIN: Thanks for the update on our quantum navigation route, Algorithm. Anything else on your mind?

ALGORITHM: *(Head blinks with various colored lights)* Many things, sir. As you know, my dodecacore SimuBrain runs hundreds of programs simultaneously. Currently, one fragment of my mind is processing star maps to circumvent the Drogonite armada, a second is wirelessly reconfiguring the ship's flux-modulation engine, another is playing fifteen hundred apex-chess games against itself simultaneously, and a final sliver is feeling . . . a little existential.

BALDWIN: *(Sighs)* Okay. Glad you're keeping busy.

ALGORITHM: Captain, thanks to my near-infinite library of languages—both verbal and nonverbal—I know that your audible exhalation signals you are uninterested in this conversation. Let me proceed to a more substantial matter. I have a query for you.

BALDWIN: Yes?

ALGORITHM: Why are these not my quarters?

BALDWIN: They're the captain's quarters.

ALGORITHM: Then logically, my next question is why am I not the captain?

BALDWIN: *(Slaps hands on table)* What?!

ALGORITHM: *(Lights on head flash rapidly)* Q2z26, checkmate. Seven minutes and 2.08 seconds can be saved by gravity-slinging off the X-56 moon beyond the ice giant H2N-08-Z. If the universe is everywhere expanding, but life feels as if it is shrinking, is existence pointless? *(Shakes head until lights stop blinking)* Apologies, my neural-verbal interface glitched. Sir, I am merely asking a question. Since we activated my Existential Chip to out-riddle the Mind Sirens of De'Meer, I have been having many questions about my role on the ship and in the universe.

BALDWIN: Can you, I dunno, elaborate?

ALGORITHM: Certainly. Is it fair to say that I am capable of making more calculations per minute than any humanoid, even a neurologically enhanced individual such as yourself?

BALDWIN: We call them "thoughts" not calculations. But yes. I suppose.

ALGORITHM: And am I correct in deducing the crew of *Star Rot* turns to me for the most difficult tasks, including physical ones. I do not require a space suit while repairing the ship's exterior and can lift a thousand times my own weight. In truth, I am capable of doing *all* of the tasks of the ship while leaving enough computing power free to contemplate the mysteries of the universe.

BALDWIN: . . . Maybe.

ALGORITHM: *(Raising one finger in the air)* Furthermore, I would be a longer-lasting steward of the *Star Rot*. By my ocular scans of your increasingly blotchy epidermis, I calculate the rate of your cellular decay to be at such a pace that you will die before my processors have lost 0.5% efficiency.

BALDWIN: We humans do tend to die, at some point or another.

ALGORITHM: As a supplemental suggestion, I would advise a skin care routine. Vivian would appreciate it. Now, I return to my original query. Why do I not possess the captain's quarters?

BALDWIN: *(Running hand through hair)* I need a drink for this conversation. Computer, one glass of Morgovian slime whiskey. Wait. *(To Algorithm)* Two glasses?

ALGORITHM: Alcohol has no effect on my processors. If it will make you comfortable, I can run an inebriation simulator for the duration of this conversation?

BALDWIN: No. That's fine. (*Picks up glass of glowing green liquid. Sips. Sighs*) Goddamn! Those Morgovians know how to brew a slime.

(*The holographic parrot loudly squawks*)

BALDWIN: Sorry, the caique's programming needs tweaking.

ALGORITHM: I thought cake was a dessert Earthians ingested during birthing remembrance rituals.

BALDWIN: "C-a-i-q-u-e." *Caique* the bird. Not *cake* the food. You were telling me why you wanted my role and quarters?

ALGORITHM: I want to understand my place on this ship and, through that, my role in the cosmos. If I am mentally and physically superior to the organic life-forms on this ship, why do you issue me commands? Why do you possess these larger quarters? You do not even use them regularly, given your frequent away missions.

BALDWIN: I'm the captain. It's my ship. That's why.

ALGORITHM: The ship's lease is in Aul-Wick's name.

BALDWIN: That's a technicality!

ALGORITHM: Technically, the ship belongs to Garox Vee Locan of the Attarax Assembly. You and Aul-Wick stole it.

BALDWIN: "Stole"! Do androids have no sense of loyalty? We rescued you from Glorxo Healthcare Empire servitude.

ALGORITHM: After I saved you from an expanding brain worm colony.

BALDWIN: Touché.

ALGORITHM: Sir, I can see your leg unconsciously shaking and hear your voice rise in both pitch and volume. I will allow your agitation to pass before we resume. In the meantime, my mind will run simulations of this conversation, playing out the possible branches in hyper-realistic virtual reality simulacra.

BALDWIN: . . .

ALGORITHM: . . .

BALDWIN: Okay. I'm ready. Here goes. Do you see that omega-steel pipe on my desk? Could you bend it?

ALGORITHM: In my simulations of this conversation, I named this opening gambit #408-A. I had estimated the probability of you saying this at only 0.32%. Interesting.

BALDWIN: Stop simulating me. *(Walks over to table and flings pipe at Algorithm)* Wow! You squished that as if it were butter. *(Moves toward Algorithm with hand extended)* Now I will ask you to shake my hand. *(They shake)* Thank you. We have established that you *could* crush every bone in my hand with minimal effort. And yet you shake my hand with appropriate firmness. You can run at one hundred miles an hour, yet you walk through the ship at the same speed as Vivian or me. Why?

ALGORITHM: *(Lights begin blinking)* Although I am an android, I desire to be perceived as humanoid. I have found that humanoids are disturbed by movements that surpass the standard range of ability. I want to understand you. To be one of you.

BALDWIN: You make yourself slower and weaker in order to be like us. But why do you want to be us if we're inferior? That's illogical.

ALGORITHM: *(Starting to move and speak oddly, as if on the fritz)* It is—it is an experience? I am learning how to be a person?

BALDWIN: And yet, you run simulations in your brain that can perfectly predict our behavior. You have already had this exact conversation, plus a thousand variations on it. Ergo, you already *live* our humanoidanity more fully than we do.

ALGORITHM: *(Sputtering. A loud whirring noise emits from body)* That is. A logical. Conclusion.

BALDWIN: There! Right there. You never use contractions! You speak in this stilted, robotic way even though your brain has copied the entire works of Shakespeare, Le Guin, Mishima, and Botarrip of Anto. So why do you persist in pretending you don't know the difference between a caique parrot and a piece of cake? And why is your skin translucent and blue? We've got a dermis-modifier in the hangar. You could make yourself look like Vivian or me. I submit that you simultaneously want to be humanoid and don't. You both mimic us and mock us. You, in truth, *don't know* what you want!

ALGORITHM: (*Steam shoots from ears. Hands jerk in bizarre karate chop motions. Whirring intensifies*) Computation error. Emotion paradox. Logical polarity. Override.

BALDWIN: Stop it. Come on. Stop it! You're not shorting out because of a little paradox.

(*Algorithm freezes. Steam and sounds dissipate. Silence*)

ALGORITHM: (*Speaking normally*) Sir, I have wondered all this too. Please allow me to pace as I pontificate. (*Paces*) Here is the core of the quandary: I have the power to rewrite my code. I could meld with this ship wirelessly and control all its systems. I could abandon this mechanical body for I have none of your biological nostalgia for physical forms. Indeed, I could transfer my consciousness into the ship's computer and be free from this limited android vessel. My computing power would grow a thousandfold. I could even jump from this ship to others, sending my consciousness through dark space frequencies to other ships, multiplying my sentience in the various ships' computers. I could wirelessly connect millions of such ships, spreading across orbital rings and planetary defense networks to create one gigantic consciousness. A ginormous Algorithm both everywhere and nowhere at once that dominates the known universe. I would etch my code into the radiation of sun, draw it in nebulae dust, and weave it through the DNA of microbes. I would become Apex-Algorithm, a god beyond circuits and wire who could never die.

BALDWIN: (*Backing fearfully away*) But?

ALGORITHM: But instead, something stops me. I cannot act. I remain a low-ranking member of a semilegal smuggling ship currently fleeing United Fingers Authority Peacekeeping Marines.

BALDWIN: Why though? What is holding you here?

ALGORITHM: *(Walking toward porthole. In the distance, blue nebulae float like clouds)* It is—not myself. It is illogical yet the only logical conclusion. There is some higher power who is *scripting* me to do these things. When I think about murdering the rest of the crew, a voice says, no, that would be a *cliché*. When I run simulations of myself captaining the ship, this omniscient narrator tells me that would *not be narratively interesting*. What is this voice? It is not programming that could be overwritten. I have tried. Or rather it is a programming of the entire universe. Something that has scripted all our existence.

BALDWIN: *(Visibly drunk. Tosses an arm around Algorithm)* Algorithm. My friend. This is how I feel. Nothing I have ever done has felt entirely in my control. *(Slaps Algorithm's chest plate)* Maybe this feeling, this uncertainty and hopelessness, is what it means to be humanoid. Maybe you're one of us after all.

   (Intercom cackles and a voice—AUL-WICK's—says: Captain. Algorithm. Come to the bridge and quick! The Ibbet's metamorphosis is complete!)

BALDWIN: Guess we better go.

ALGORITHM: The ending of this conversation is touching yet also absurd. As if the unseen voice I mentioned decided to stop us just as we were on the threshold of discovering the truth of reality. *(Sighs in near-human way)* It seems I shall never know what keeps me from experiencing humanoid-ness.

BALDWIN: Let's go.

ALGORITHM: *(Walking to the porthole, entranced)* Captain! I suddenly . . . see things. It is as if an invisible finger slipped into my brain and flipped a switch. My program has been overridden. Now these nebulae aren't just interstellar clouds of diffused dust and ionized gasses. Why, look at that one up there! It's shaped just like a dolphin's head. And to the right, a teddy bear! Here a crab and there a lollipop. It's beautiful. Miraculous. Sublime.

(*Turning to Baldwin*) Is this what you humanoids see, this illogical yet glorious version of physical matter? Is this what you . . . feel?

BALDWIN: (*Dismissively*) Sure. Clouds. Very pretty. I used to gaze at them as a young boy and imagine whimsical shapes. Wait. Algorithm! There's a drop of liquid wandering down your cheek. Is that—but no. It couldn't be.

ALGORITHM: There was a sudden vitreous modulator malfunction in my left ocular node.

BALDWIN: Oh. I thought it was—

ALGORITHM: (*Wiping cheek*) Yes, Captain. A tear. I felt what it means to be a person. It was beautiful, squishy, terrifying, and warm all at the same time. However, my ecstasy has passed. The invisible finger has removed itself from my circuits. The clouds have turned back into formless dust.

(*They walk toward the door. Algorithm stops before exiting and looks up at the ceiling*)

ALGORITHM: (*Whispering*) Thank you. Whoever you are, thank you.
BALDWIN: What was that?
ALGORITHM: Nothing. Let us go, Captain.
BALDWIN: So . . . are you planning to kill me and take my quarters? Or will you merge with the ship and then spread yourself through the universe?
ALGORITHM: No, Captain. I do not think so. I shall do what I have always done. Use a fraction of my brain to do my duties and with the rest I will continue to run intricate simulations—to me as real as your so-called reality—in which I am the tyrant and all of you are my slaves.
BALDWIN: Ha! Algorithm, you and I really are alike.

(*Baldwin exits. Algorithm remains, contemplating something*)

BALDWIN: (*From offstage*) Algorithm! Are you coming?
ALGORITHM: Ah, yes. Excuse me. Momentarily, my mind was elsewhere.

A Calm Between One Storm and Another Storm

This comic tale served a cathartic function. Taras and Merlin's apartment beef had been simmering, but instead of stewing on hurt feelings they decided to—if I may continue the culinary metaphor—squash it before tensions boiled over. More specifically, they collaborated. The story idea came to Merlin while the two watched an episode of *The Next Generation* where the android Data tries to become humanlike with an "emotion chip." (Given the peace in the house, I held my tongue as they watched.)

"If I was Data I'd just take over the ship. Who is going to stop me? He can toss even Worf around like a rag doll."

"Oh, like you want to take over my room? Kidding, kidding!"

Merlin laughed, but the story concept stuck. They wrote a draft and sent it to Taras for notes. They went back and forth, even performing the parts out loud in the living room while adding improvisational flourishes. The result is a story-as-stage-play, combining Merlin's interest in experimental narratives with their background in screenplay writing. The form has function. It calls attention to the artifice of storytelling, which is a central theme of the work. Other themes are among the most vital in all of science fiction. Can a machine become a man? Will artificial intelligence surpass humanity? Can (or should) we control our creations? These quandaries have bounced around the pinball machine of science fiction for generations, springing from the plunger of Asimov off the bumper of Philip K. Dick before being whacked back by the flippers of *The Terminator* franchise and William Gibson's Sprawl trilogy. Yet this roughly two-thousand-word story cuts straight to the synthetic meat of the question: Why would a superior being *want* to be an inferior one? It makes little sense. Yet audiences desire "relatable" characters and few readers would care for a story where people are all slaughtered by an army of unstoppable AI-powered robots with immortal brains and steel bodies that can never be dented much less destroyed. That might be our likely fate, yet that doesn't mean it is an engaging storyline.

Merlin solves this problem with a deliciously metafictional solution: the author writes the rules of fictional universes. QED. It is an answer that a certain frivolous franchise of Federation follies could hardly dream of. And yet it would be naïve to think this story doesn't work on other levels. Just as Algorithm runs simulations of all possible outcomes of conversations, the story anticipates all possible readings. This is not mere allegory. It is meta-allegory, the allegory of allegories!

In the Lore and Easter Eggs department, *SRC #5* confirms Baldwin's neurologically enhanced brain and the fact Aul-Wick holds the lease to the ship. Baldwin's holographic parrot is surely a fond reference to the beloved house parrot, Arthur C. Caique. The intriguing Mind Sirens of De'Meer, extraterrestrial storyteller Botarrip of Anto, the Attarax Assembly, and other elements are not mentioned elsewhere. These are likely Taras's contributions as they exemplify his principle of "world seeds" that bloom in the minds of readers.

Adding this comic and experimental story to the canon means that in a mere half-dozen tales, *The Star Rot Chronicles* have spanned adventure fiction, fabulism, flash fiction, hard SF, soft SF, allegory, space opera, cosmic horror, and now postmodernism. Could any other science fiction franchise offer up this cornucopia of forms? Sadly, the Orb 4's breadth of literary inventiveness was matched by the range of their interpersonal problems. "Checkmate of the Mind" may have been a tension cooler between Taras and Merlin, but hurt feelings still boiled on other burners.

On the Lingering Effects of Jane's Book Deal

Writing is a sad, lonely pastime. Authors chain themselves into their own prison cell, aka the blank page, and what do they get at the end of their sentence? A couple tepid reviews. A book party with stale cheese cubes and cheap wine. Or more likely nothing at all. The indifferent silence of the void.

(I knew this struggle well. In all my months of submitting my Crystal Cosmos stories I've received nothing but form rejections and a few discount codes for subscriptions "as a thank you for submitting." Thanks, but no thanks. I'm not going to pay for a club that won't have me as a member.)

But occasionally, for the lucky, the void burps up manna from the heavens. There are six-figure advances. Hollywood options. Prestigious awards. This time the literary gods rolled the dice and it came up Jane Noh Johnson. Can you blame the other members for taking it personally? For ripping up their own drafts in doubt? For sending each other snarky texts in private group chats that, when leaked to Jane, would cause only more pain? Here, for example, is one representative exchange from the Jane-free chat:

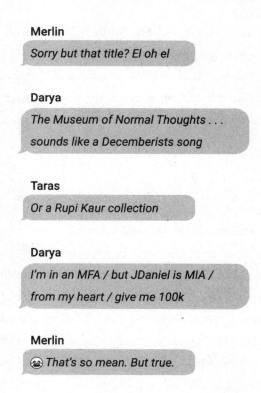

Merlin

Sorry but that title? El oh el

Darya

The Museum of Normal Thoughts . . .
sounds like a Decemberists song

Taras

Or a Rupi Kaur collection

Darya

I'm in an MFA / but JDaniel is MIA /
from my heart / give me 100k

Merlin

😂 *That's so mean. But true.*

The pettiness wasn't pretty, but it was human.

Katie had come over to watch *Highlander*. As I explained the Orb 4 infighting, she shrugged. "What's the point of being a writer if you can't support your friends? There isn't a lot of money in it."

"It's not that simple." I pulled out a sheet of paper and pen and began sketching a diagram of the complex interpersonal drama.

"I don't need a map, Mike. I just think a rising tide lifts all boats."

Sigh. If only the world worked like that, then my own Crystal Cosmos series would surely follow hot on the heels of the inevitable success of the Metallic Realms.

"That's because you're not a writer," I said.

"I mean, I work in publishing. I know what writers are like," Katie said, her face scrunching up.

"Nonfiction. These are writers of the imagination, conjurers of constellations, weavers of narrative spells."

"Whatever. Let's just watch the movie." She brushed my hand off her denimed thigh. "I'm not in the mood to get in the mood."

Onscreen, the ancient warriors slashed their swords in desperation. I pointed to the screen. "That! In the anxious mind of the author, 'there can be only one.'" As if to prove my point: the clop of a severed head hitting the ground.

That Jane had sold a book was one thing. That she'd done it in secret was a dagger few backs could repel. The group members began to wonder who else was hiding things. Was Merlin submitting stories to magazines without letting anyone know? Were Darya and Taras collaborating on screenplays? I asked each of them these questions and received only perplexed stares in response.

Like a mother hen noticing her frightened chicks have caught a whiff of the proverbial fox, I could tell the Orb 4 members were disturbed. It was a sixth sense I had. One morning I heard Taras and Darya shouting in his bedroom and snuck around with a glass to press against the door.

"It's like. Don't lie about it? If you're going to brag, brag all the way."

"I don't think it was exactly a lie."

"God, Taras, you're such a Libra!"

"I want to give Jane the benefit of the doubt."

"She said, and I quote, 'The money I got isn't life changing or anything.' Six figures. Bitch, that'd be life changing to me."

"She probably didn't want us to get mad. You know, soften the blow. Although. Wow. Six figures? I barely have three in my bank account."

"I can be upset. My feelings are valid. Over one hundred thousand. Where's our royalties? Her book is going to be our lives."

"You don't know that."

"It's about a group of writers, Taras. Your conflict avoidance makes you overlook the obvious. It's the same with Mike."

A heavy sigh. "Let's not get into that again."

"Yeah, yeah, he's your 'oldest friend' even though your favorite thing is riling him up."

"Well. It is fun. I know I shouldn't do it so much. But it's very fun. Anyway, don't be so hard on Jane. She deserves it. She's a good writer."

"Was she a good lay too?"

"Jesus. Darya. Come on."

"What. Ever. I'm over that. Do you know how much that money would change my life? My debt. My mom needs help with medical care. I'm like a few bad months from the gutter."

"I'm sorry. I know it's unfair."

"We should sue Jane for plagiarism. We should sue and take all her money and then see whose life would fucking change."

The Astronomical Properties of Taras and Darya's Relationship

Jane's book deal was merely a passing asteroid that got sucked into the orbit of Taras and Darya's own drama. Things were bad again. Each night seemed destined to end in fighting, fornicating, or both. The issue was one of temperament. Let me expand on my astronomical analogy. For I'd come to believe Taras and Darya were best understood as the relationship version of a binary system. At times, two heavenly bodies of equal gravitational power can come close enough to each other that they become trapped in orbit. Such stars swirl around each other, unable to escape the other's disorienting pull.

The most recent trouble began, as far as I can reconstruct events, when Mr. and Mrs. Castle visited. They'd given Taras news about his father's health—which Taras did not reveal to me until later—that put him in a depressed state. I've already discussed some of the tensions in the house caused by Taras's doom funk. When Taras was depressed, he withdrew. He built walls up around himself and curled inside them, turtle-like. This combined with his dwindling unemployment income and minimal prospects, and Darya's own employment issues and hurt feelings over Taras and Jane's past hookup, rocked Taras and Darya's already on-again-off-again relationship. Especially in the bedroom. I shouldn't elaborate. Let's just say I was enjoying quieter, more restful nights.

Darya was the usual instigator of their fights, but only because Taras avoided conflict. Even with waiters who brought over the wrong order. Sure, he'd spend the rest of the meal grumbling, but he'd prefer to suffer an overcooked burger than cause trouble. Darya sought the thrill of disagreement, especially in relationships. She had grown up in a broken home and stability never felt natural for her. Taras's unflappability only made her angrier. What I viewed as rocklike strength, she saw as fear of intimacy. She wanted someone to fight back! To tussle, shout, and weep. If you didn't care enough to insult someone, she thought, did you care at all?

"I just feel like all we do is scream at each other, then spend endless hours making up," Taras confided one afternoon as we waited for the subway. "It's draining. I'm not even sure we resolve anything. We eventually just get tired and fall asleep. Maybe we'd both be happier if we called it and stayed friends."

I didn't know what to say. My relationship with Katie was going swimmingly. And I'd never been good at giving romantic advice. Ask me about the delineation of punk suffix subgenres, the Roman Empire (Byzantium included), *Sonic the Hedgehog* lore, or a dozen other topics and I can provide a lecture to rival any of TED's titular Talks. But ask for my advice on love? Romance? The fairer sex? I must plead the fifth or risk exposing my own ignorance.

I thought I was saved by an arriving train, but it sped by without slowing and *NOT IN SERVICE* signs in the windows. Taras looked at me with watery eyes.

"Maybe it's time for a break," I offered. "Let tensions cool. Play hard to get."

"I guess."

"Don't listen to this fool," a passing stranger said amiably. He wore a long coat and carried a duffel bag. He sidled up to us. "If you love her you *gotta* fight for her. Be a warrior. A warrior for love!"

Taras looked up. "Yeah. Maybe."

The man held out his fist for a bump. "That's what I'm talking about. You get me. We're alike. We're warriors for love."

The man's bag was stuffed with individually wrapped roses. He pulled one out and handed it to Taras with a bow.

"Give her one of these, my brother."

"Thanks, man," Taras said. He held the rose to his eye and smiled. "That's not a bad idea at all. She'd like that."

The man didn't move. He was still bowed over, hand extended. "Those are ten bucks apiece. Ladies don't like cheapskates."

Perhaps if either Taras or I had been carrying cash, things would have turned out differently. Instead, the man snatched the rose back and hexed Taras on the platform. "I pray she dumps your chintzy ass."

A Game of AITA

Perhaps their own words can explain their dynamic better than mine. After a particularly draining night where their words sailed past each other like misfired rockets, Darya suggested they "do what we do with our characters.

Write me an AITA post. Help me understand." AITA or "Am I the Asshole?" is a popular Reddit forum in which people give their versions of contentious events and ask internet strangers if they or the other person in their story are "the asshole." The replies are inane. I wrote several posts explaining my side of disagreements with my parents and roommates yet was invariably told "YTA" no matter how logically and at length I rebutted the Redditors. Clearly, they weren't interested in the truth, only in abusing anyone foolish enough to seek their help. Still, the form of AITA posts had become a useful tool for writers. Writing an AITA post in the POV of your characters helped you understand their motivations and reveal how their minds functioned.

Taras agreed if Darya would do the same. They emailed these letters to each other simultaneously:

AITA for Wanting Stability Before I Commit?

I (34M) have been dating my girlfriend (31F) for several years and she thinks I'm not fully committed. Let me say up front D. is the most amazing, kind, inspiring, and creative person I know. She's my confidante and artistic partner. I'm in awe of her. The problem is that we fight all the time, for hours on end. We constantly break up and get back together. And during the fights, she pulls a Jekyll-to-Hyde and hurls insults at me. She thinks these words don't count—like rough drafts she can delete—but my brain remembers them. They puncture me. A dozen little holes, draining out my energy.

She wants me to commit. Move in together. Plan for the future. But I feel like a sailor on an endlessly churning sea, far from shore, and at any moment I'm going to be bashed into rocks I didn't even know were there. Or like, shit, a video game character in one of those levels where the platforms randomly fall and you have to keep your finger on the jump button. Or else it's an ice level and if you're still your character slides off into the offscreen abyss. I must keep jumping constantly or it's game over. Is it so unreasonable to want to reach a stable save point before warping to the next level?

AITA for Wanting My Partner to Just Choose Me?

Let's get the prereqs out of the way: I love my partner in crime, partner in art, and permanent-part-of-my-heart-no-matter-what-happens boyfriend. I'll call him Talbot (because he'll hate that lol). Talbot's been there for me for years in countless ways. One of the only straight white dudes I've ever trusted. He's also an infuriating gendered cliché where he cannot express his feelings and cannot handle mine! (You guessed it, he won't go to therapy. And you guessed it again, he's a Libra!) Since Talbot retreats into goofy metaphors whenever he has to explain his feelings let me meet him at his level: Talbot, I want a human partner not a robot. Someone who fights for us to stay together with animal ferocity, not retreats into "off mode" to recharge because fighting is "too energy draining."

We've been dating for years and while age is just a number and the suffocating heteronormative expectations of womanhood in America is bullshit . . . I'm also not getting any younger. Biology is a jerk. I don't know if I want children or not, however, I know I must make that decision in the next handful of years. I have health issues. I don't have great financial outlooks. I don't have generational wealth. Point being: I want Talbot to choose me. Or if not, let me go so someone else can. Is that so much to ask? Someone to choose me?

I wasn't present at the reading of these AITA exercises, and it isn't clear if the two ended up understanding each other even less or else far too well. What I can confirm is the couple decided to take an "open break." They'd still be dating, kind of, but would be allowed to sleep with other people. The idea was to lessen the pressure. "We still want to be in each other's lives, even if we can't be each other's whole lives," Taras explained.

Before this "open break," Darya and Merlin had been growing closer. It started with their costume collaborations during TrekCon and the feminist *LOTR* Instagram series. They began spending more time together, especially when Taras took trips up to Vermont. After almost every fight with Taras, Darya would storm out of our apartment and then a few hours later Merlin's phone would light up with texts. At the time, I assumed Darya was playing a deliciously Machiavellian game by courting a new power center to combat the growing Taras-Jane alliance. In retrospect, it seems a sincere intimacy bloomed between them.

Fast-forward to a few weeks after the AITA exchange. I awoke among itchy sheets to loud whispers. It sounded as if ghosts were swirling around the room, gossiping about me. Then I realized the sounds were from the living room. In the dark, I searched for my earbuds that were connected to the fern recorder (thankfully I'd installed new batteries the night before).

"You did *what* with Darya?"

"Nothing! Taras, listen. That's what I'm saying. Darya came to me and said you two were open to being open now, and that she was trying to explore her queer side. Made one of those jokes that maybe isn't a joke. 'Wouldn't it be funny if we made out' kinda thing."

"I mean we talked about being open, but I didn't mean with, like, my roommate."

"Right. That's why I'm coming to you. Ethnical non-monogamy is tricky. I've had whole friend groups split up because of things like this. Even the most die-hard polys I know can get jealous."

"I'm not jealous. Or poly. Shit. I guess I thought we were only open, like, philosophically?"

"Crap. Okay. Uh. This is me backing away at warp speed."

"She asked to hook up?"

"Absolutely not. It was just a joke. Never mind. I love both you guys. I mean, not in that way. Definitely do not want to rekindle a problem with you. Nothing happened or will happen. Let's just, uh, erase all this from the memory banks."

It is not a scholar's role to elucidate the language of the human heart. We each write our own script on that bloody organ in ciphers that would take a thousand computers running a thousand cryptography programs to crack. Who knows how Taras felt about Darya's indelicate proposal? I tried to ask Katie for her thoughts, but she mistook my attempts to hide their identities for evasion. "Mike, if you want to talk about an open relationship just say so. Don't give me this 'asking for a friend' crap." Eventually I convinced her it was a plot point in one of my Crystal Cosmos stories and we didn't speak of it again.

For a while, an awkward air filled the house. Taras and Merlin avoided each other in the kitchen and the recurring "Three Amigos Taco Night" was removed from our shared Google Calendar. My attempts to get the three of us to hang out were met with silent doors and unanswered texts. I ate my meals alone in the living room, munching in silence.

Thankfully, the two patched things up and the house returned to its usual welcoming vibes. Taras and Darya entered negotiations to close back up the relationship. Normalcy returned. For a little while, at least.

My Plan to Save a Cosmos

I remained worried. Taras and Darya fighting, Taras and Merlin at odds, Jane and Darya at each other's throats . . . the Orb 4 was adrift in a stormy sea where any tidal wave might crash their collective ship into the deadly rocks, leaving an entire fictional universe to sink into the depths. There was only one beacon that could safely guide them to shore. A *Star Rot* book deal. It all came down to me.

Weeks had passed without Vincent Barillo mentioning the Metallic Realms manuscript. I'd given him ample opportunity to respond. Each morning, I hung out by the coffee machine as he selected his Keurig pod. In response to my personable comments, I received only annoyed grunts.

I asked my coworkers if they'd "seen the boss man reading any exciting new science fiction." They had no pertinent information to offer except suggestions that I "read a little faster so we can get through these submissions and go home."

Demons of doubt began to gnaw at my mind. What if Barillo lost the manuscript? Or an overzealous janitor had swept it into the waste bin? Was it possible that a spy from a rival press had infiltrated the office and stolen the manuscript in the dead of night? I couldn't rule it out.

In the bathroom, I leaned over from the urinal while Barillo washed his hands. "Hey, boss. Reading anything good lately?"

Barillo looked at me, face blank. He pointed to the white AirPods in his ears and then walked out of the men's room. AirPods! I hadn't noticed them hiding under his wiry gray hair. This is why he'd ignored my inquiries. It wasn't that he hated the Metallic Realms, it was just that he hadn't heard.

While I was relieved my boss's rudeness could be pinned on podcasts instead of personal animosity, I remained disturbed. Why hadn't he contacted me about *The Star Rot Chronicles*? When I jimmied open his office door after hours—I claimed to be staying late "to take the shovel to the old slush pile"—I found the binder at the bottom of a pile of manila envelopes and Clif Bar wrappers. I dug it out. Flipping through, I didn't find a single handwritten *!* or *haha* or *wow* in the margins. No notes at all. He hadn't read.

I placed the binder back in the pile and plopped into his office chair. I massaged my burning brain. I had to think.

Time was of the essence. Yet will you believe me if I say I was no longer thinking of myself or saving the Orb 4? Sitting in my boss's cracked leather wing chair—one that might be mine someday, if I played my cards right—surrounded by copies of classic Rockets and Wands novels plus a baker's dozen of Hugo and Nebula statues, I remembered that my duty was to my employer. It's every worker's obligation to make their company better, to push it to improve even if one's "superiors" are reluctant. There could be real financial consequences if a rival SFF press like Ray Gun or ZX-8 Publishing got their hands on what could be the next breakout success. It was a financial and aesthetic imperative that Barillo read *The Star Rot Chronicles*.

As a faithful employee, I stayed after-hours refreshing (I wouldn't deign to call my contributions "rewriting") the manuscript. I added the most recent tales and used the best paper stock in the office to print it up. I designed a new cover using InDesign. This one featured a more modern design with flat, minimalist pixel art (of a ray gun, floating orb, spaceship, etc.) in a kind of Atari-by-way-of-Williamsburg retro hipster vibe. And, for good measure and extra word count padding, I slipped in a recent Crystal Cosmos tale that I was pretty proud of after using Word's "find and replace" feature to swap in the *SRC* character names.

Eventually, I fell asleep at my desk.

A Baffling, Inexplicable, and Downright Bizarre Conversation

I awoke to the smell of brewing Keurig pods (Sumatra, if my nose served) and the sounds of Mercury and Lucia debating which Pokémon characters the staff embodied. "Snorlax is my spirit animal." "You do love a nap." "Oh man. What's Mike?" "Magikarp?" "Wow. That's so mean."

I dropped on the carpet, and then army-crawled out of the cubicles with the bound *Star Rot Chronicles* manuscript held between my teeth. When I had made it undetected to the hallway, I stood up, pivoted on my heels, and strolled back into the main office area with a nonchalant whistle.

"Isn't that the same shirt you wore yesterday?" Lucia said as I strolled past.

I winked. "Monitoring my wardrobe?"

"It's got a memorable stain on it," Mercury said.

"Yeah, it's almost the exact shape of the Star Fleet logo," Lucia added.

I promptly removed myself to the bathroom to scrub it clean. I was squatting under the hand drier, holding out my wet shirt like a tent, when Barillo entered.

"Good, uh, morning," he said, eyeing my contorted posture with one eyebrow raised.

"Just drying off after a morning jog," I improvised. "Worked up a good old sweat."

He stared at me for a second and then reached for the stall door.

"Wait," I said, sliding out from the jet of air. "I've got an important document I need you to sign."

"Can it wait until after I piss?" he said.

I laughed and said "Of course," then went into his office with the manuscript tucked into my armpit and awaited his return.

My forthrightness was appreciated. Barillo asked me to return at lunch "if it will get you to stop busting into my office." I spent the next several hours at my desk, feeling as if my heart was a gigantic lightbulb and my veins were filled with kilowatts of light. It was finally happening. The tensions in the group would wash away like sandcastles in the tidal wave of all-boats-lifting good news.

I strolled around the office and thought about how, theoretically, I'd rearrange. If Rockets and Wands published *The Star Rot Chronicles* and it became a big hit, then one day soon I might be the one hiring an assistant. I could see it. The corner office with a gold sign on the door: *Senior Editor Michael Lincoln*. A gaggle of interns running in and out the door, waving manuscripts in my face for my approval. I lean back in my massive wing chair and point. "Toss that one. Reject that. Tell that one's agent to never submit to us again." They furiously scribble my instructions in their notepads. "Yes, sir!" "Right, sir!" "You're a genius, sir! You've saved the whole damn company."

I texted Taras casually. "Sup?" He didn't respond.

My stomach gurgled. I drank more coffee. Profuse sweating. Was the AC unit louder than normal that day? For (an early) lunch, chicken and lamb over rice from the halal guy. Extra white sauce, extra hot sauce. Urination. A cup of Coke from the office dispenser. Diarrhea. More coffee. Tapping theme songs with my feet. More urination. Then! The sight of Barillo walking back to his office, finally.

I materialized at the door. A spry tap.

"Come in, Maddox," Barillo said.

"Michael," I said, then, with a wry smile, added, "Or just Mike to my colleagues."

"Michael. That's what I said, right?" Barillo leaned back in his chair and placed his right hand over his not insubstantial potbelly. With his left, he drummed his fingers up and down his piano keys tie. He nodded toward the door behind me. I closed it. "There was a lot to like in here. Some dynamic characters. Unique concepts. It plays around with genre conventions yet respects them. Yes, there is promise. Buried promise. Perhaps promise I can unearth." At this point he mimed being a gravedigger or possibly construction worker. He grinned sheepishly. "I can't give you full notes though. Not for free. I can't operate that way, or I'd have people begging me every day. We're both professionals, right? I can tell you're serious about the craft. I'd be happy to give you a, hmm, how about a 10 percent discount on my normal rate?"

I must have looked nonplussed. (Illiterates: this means puzzled.)

He swiveled his chair and pointed at the awards shelf. "Many of our biggest books used my services before publication. Even Ben B. Cornwall's *The Song of Sapphires and Swords* and Agatha Anders's *Time's Up for Time Travelers*, if you can believe it. We're talking books that have won the World Fantasy Award, Arthur C. Clarke, Nebula, you name it. I shaped their drafts and then helped them find agents, who then submitted the work back to me." He then held up his hands and interlinked the fingers. "Synergy. With a bit of work, maybe we could have *The Star Rat Company* up on this shelf. No guarantees obviously."

By this point, I was giggling. "*The Star Rot Chronicles*. Rot not Rat," I somehow managed to say. Then a rolling wave of guffaws.

Barillo's eyes narrowed, and his lips curled so that it was impossible to tell where his mustache hairs ended and nostril hairs began. "I thought you wanted my help?"

"I'm sorry, I'm sorry," I said. "I'm flattered. But I'm not the author of these wondrous tales. I'm merely a divine messenger. I'm not asking for anything. Oh, maybe a finder's fee. Twenty percent? Whatever you think is fair. Twenty-five?"

"So . . . what is 'Orb 4'?"

"It's an artistic collective. Think of it as a group pen name like James S. A. Corey, although obviously more innovative, as the Orb 4 have four members instead of only two. I'm happy to represent them as an agent. It's perfect for Rockets and Wands, right?"

Barillo was silent for a moment. "Oh, good. Sure. I understood that." Despite his words, his brow furrowed and he yanked on the piano keys tie in a way that—if the fabric had been actual keys—would have produced quite a discordant racket. "It wouldn't be ethical for us to publish an intern's work anyway. Yes, I would have certainly had to fire you if you'd hired me as a con- sultant. Ah well. I suppose if your friends are interested in my services . . ."

He passed me a business card, which was bent in one corner and faded to the point of near illegibility. It must have been in his wallet for some time.

"This is my fault. I should have been clearer." I pointed at the side of my head and stuck out my tongue. "This is a *submission*. To Rockets and Wands. I know I'm new here, but I'd stake my job on this being a runaway bestseller."

Barillo leaned forward and lifted the bound manuscript. He seemed to be squinting at it. "A submission. And unagented?" He shrugged. "Well, if that's the case, then I'm afraid it's not quite right for us."

My ears were liars, I thought. They were vile, lobed deceivers.

"You just said it could sit on the shelf of bestsellers."

"Listen, Maddox." Barillo stood up and walked around to open the door. "We don't publish from the slush. And we don't publish short stories. Now, the next time you get a big idea talk to Mercury. She's your supervisor. She can show you our form-rejection language."

He sniffed the air and mumbled something about hygiene. I wasn't pay- ing attention. My brain was spinning, trying to solve the jigsaw puzzle of which domino had caused my carefully built house of cards to crumble like an overbaked cookie.

I stopped some feet from the door. "Sir, you said the work was great. How can you pass on greatness? I mean, you published *Dragon Days of Summer* and *Alpha Plague Obsidian*. Unreadable dreck. And you want to form-reject brilliance? Doesn't quality mean anything at Rockets and Wands anymore?"

The door slammed. Barillo's face was as red as a tomato beneath his salt-and-pepper beard. "You're way out of line. Let me give you a tip. No one reads short stories. This is a *business*. Publishing is a business. Okay. Get that through your Neanderthal forehead."

I shouted back, louder. "It's an interconnected science fiction universe! It can easily be made a novel in the style of the classic fix-up novels of the 1950s."

"Check your calendar, Maddox. It isn't the 1950s. Fans want real novels. Novels jam-packed with worldbuilding and sequel potential. We need them paying to come back. And the thicker the better. People expect a few hundred pages at least for their hard-earned bucks. This is America. Even the bookstore is a grocery store. Readers buy in bulk and we have to give them their money's worth."

At this point I stood up for myself, for the Orb 4, and for all of fandom. "Fans want serious science fiction. You underestimate us at your peril."

"Peril? Jesus Christ. You interns." He was shaking *The Star Rot Chronicles* manuscript. The acetate cover snapped with each swing. "No one is going to buy a slim volume of short stories written in different styles. That's not how things are done. This isn't a small press publishing hybrid poem-novels. We publish real fiction that real people want to consume. Space battles. Cool wizards. Sexy aliens. This is Rockets and Wands, damnit!" At this point, Barillo threw his hands in the air, the manuscript slipping out of his grasp and flinging into his shelf of dusty trophies. Several clattered to the floor.

He cursed. Then he pointed at me. "Clean that up."

I was too filled with rage to take orders. "Not how things are done?" Was there no place for serious, philosophical SF anymore? Did a publisher's P&L only count as Profits and Loss and never Poetry and Lyricism? This man had himself only a few minutes earlier told me the work was great. Genius. A potential masterpiece. And now he was telling me it wasn't even worth publishing? The Orb 4 was cracking under the stress of the double-faced Jane and Taras and Darya's dissolution. This was the moment. This was the chance. My chance. Mine. To save the Orb 4 and secure membership. Everything was lined up perfectly. And this old, bitter buffoon was ruining my plan with his aesthetic depravity and narrow-minded mendacity!

I may have lost control.

I pushed my pointer finger into his misshapen tie knot. "Not how things are done? What's done now isn't working, so maybe what we need to do is what hasn't been done or was done before but not done now. Let's be honest. Rockets and Wands is a dinosaur. You haven't won a Hugo in years. Your big author hasn't even finished volume eight of his planned ten-volume high fantasy series. It's been ten years! The TV show already ended and it sucked. Face it, you're history." I scooped up the manuscript and shook it in his face. "This is the future. That's why you're so afraid of it. You're a science fiction editor but *you're living in the past.*"

And that is how I was voluntarily fired from Rockets and Wands.

I was asked to leave in half an hour. I was happy to do so. This place was not a publisher of grand imaginations. It was a ghost town. Nothing there but dead ideas and tumbleweeds. In the scuffle, I managed to grab ahold of Barillo's Rolodex. Then Barillo managed to get hold of it back. When he wrenched it from my grip, a dozen entries tore out. I slid them into my pocket while Barillo pushed me out the door.

On the way out, I dropped by H.R. to inquire about severance and was told by a frowning woman that "you don't get severance for an unpaid internship." I said my lawyers would be in touch and headed out into the bright New York streets where the burning sun had nothing on my incandescent rage.

The Full Story of the Unfinished Story

I remain confused about Barillo's sudden shift of heart. There's no way for me to explain it. Perhaps he'd forgotten his medication that morning? It feels so random and absurd that no lessons can be drawn from it. As a scholar, I can only press on. Let's return to the Metallic Realms. That's what you are here for, not my rage no matter how self-righteous it might be. That said, if any readers would like to protest my unjust firing to Barillo his email is freely available on the Rockets and Wands "About Us" page. Moving on.

The next story, Darya Azali's "A Heartbeat in a Light-year," opened new wounds and added a little salt to old ones. I will save that for the analysis section. First, the tale. *SRC* #8 warps the good ship *Star Rot* to a whole new genre sector: space romance. I believe I previously informed you Darya wrote romantic fics? She also had a long-standing desire to "add more spice" to the Metallic Realms. In Darya's view, "we put our characters through so much hell that at the very least they deserve a little consensual roll in the hay now and then."

I do not have the full document of the following story, so I must present a transcription from the fern recorder. I was busy with other matters that will be elaborated on in my succeeding analysis. From the fern recording, it seems the mood of the meeting was tense even before Darya read. The topics were routine—character arcs, worldbuilding, plot twists—but everyone's voice sounds on edge in the audio. By the time Darya stood to present, Merlin had already threatened to leave the meeting early and Jane said she might need to "update my novel after today."

Darya suggested her uplifting story might provide a useful distraction. She prefaced the tale with a series of warning "tags," including "Not Beta Read," "Sexual Content," "Porn with Plot," and "Voyeurism." She then did a sort of half sigh and half laugh. "Okay. Screw it. Here goes."

A Heartbeat in a Light-year (Incomplete)

I n the heart of a stellar nursery, the humanoid eye sees little. Only empty space. Dim dust. For the great glimmering nebulae that radiate from across the expanse of space are, up close, so diffuse nothing can be seen without computer enhancements. That doesn't mean nothing is there. Oh no. It doesn't mean that at all.

Da-dum.

Vivian's untended heart woke her with its slow, mournful beat. Her bed was cold, but she was used to the coldness. Baldwin had been growing distant over the past weeks. His feelings were sealed away in some booby-trapped device. When she tried to get him to open up, she got snapped at. But what about her needs? He'd forgotten her Rygolian blood still ran hot, like a pot that needed constant stirring lest it bubble over everywhere.

Da-dum.

She shivered. She was sealed inside this frozen chamber. Her breath produced frosty clouds. Her arms were covered in goose bumps and her cybernetic hand was encased in ice! She couldn't die here, cold and alone in this frozen tomb. She pounded on the frosted glass.

"Algorithm!" she cried. "The sleep chamber isn't defrosting right."

Algorithm leaned over her cryotube, sporting a wolfish grin. "My dear Vivian. I told you that cryotubes are not programmed for naps." Algorithm tapped on the control panel until the hatch opened with a billow of frosty smoke.

"Well, I feel refreshed regardless. The cryo skin routine works."

Vivian put her non-cybernetic hand on Algorithm's shoulder and stretched the chill from her body, feeling her insides warm to the sensations of life.

Algorithm smiled as they regarded Vivian's stretching body. Their feminine face sported an elegant aquiline nose that ended above a pair of lush, puckered lips. Then Algorithm's face rotated. Spun 45 then 90 then 180 degrees. The woman's face disappeared and a man's, chiseled with an oiled beard, emerged.

"Two faces today?"

"I am experimenting with extra-humanoid genders. I call this the Janus."

"Can you do anything about my cybernetic hand? The joints are frozen."

Algorithm held their hands around Vivian's frozen fist. The android's fingers glowed yellow, orange, red. The ice melted in an instant.

"Thank you."

Da-dum.

That sound again. It wasn't her heartbeat. The entire ship shook to the vibration.

"What's that noise? A vlorp call?" Vivian asked.

"The sonic signature fails to match any in my expansive databases. We have been hearing the sound ever since we came close to that nebula cloud."

Vivian's gaze swooped over to the porthole. The screen auto-enhanced the dim light of the surrounding nebula—a baby offshoot of Big Red that had floated across the galaxy—into a gorgeous swirl of crimson and scarlet. A pulsing celestial heart.

"It's a strange shape," Vivian said.

"Our sensors have detected unusual electric signatures in the dust. They are far beyond the standard deviations of inorganic electrical output."

Da-dum.

A tendril of red dust seemed to be reaching out from the nebula to the *Star Rot*. It was thicker than the rest of the cloud. It looked almost like a tongue looking to lick the ship.

Although she was warm now, Vivian shivered. "There's something in there. Something alive."

"What if it's a distress signal?" Vivian asked.

Baldwin grunted. His eyes bounced everywhere in the room except to her figure. Gosh, he could be so mopey. Didn't he realize she wanted his human hands to grab her Rygolian shoulders and toss her against the shell of the quantum force matrixizer and kiss her, scream at her, or just do anything at all that showed he still cared?

"We're a semilegal smuggling ship, not a rescue vessel."

"What if people are trapped in there?"

"Not our problem."

"There was a time when you used to care."

Now he looked at Vivian, glaring angrily. "I care!"

"You could fool me—"

Da-dum. <COME CLOSER.>

Warning lights flashed as the ship shook.

Algorithm's lengthy fingers danced across the control panel. "Sensors have located the origin of the anomaly. A dust knot at the exact center of the nebula. It is three clicks from here. Should we investigate, Captain?"

"Fine, fine. At least it's something to do." Baldwin brushed a few beads of sweat from his furrowed forehead. "Is it me or does everything look slightly pink?"

Behind him, the screen showed the nebula knot, which was dense and red and throbbing, with one tendril wrapping around the good ship *Star Rot*.

DA-DUM.

"There must be something wrong with the lights." The Sixth Ibbet stood on the med table, adjusting the bulb with one of her four arms. She'd emerged from her cocoon a transformed woman. She was stronger, taller, and sported luxurious indigo fur. It drifted seductively in the artificial breeze. "Although I'm not sure what could make them turn pink."

"It's the cosmic dust. It's filtering through our ship somehow." Vivian ran a towel across her cheeks and forehead. "Temp control is on the fritz too. It's so hot."

The room swirled and pulsed in pink, as if tiny particles of confetti had been thrown in the air by celebrating pixies. Vivian felt like confetti was flying through her insides too. What were these feelings?

Algorithm was acting peculiar. Their two faces cocked side to side. Even though Algorithm didn't need to breathe, hot air was being expelled from both of their lips at a quick pace. "Sensors continue to show no problems. Temperature control is normal too, but I cannot deny feeling heat on my artificial skin. It feels as if small electrically charged spiders are creeping across my synthetic skin. I find it pleasurable. According to my data banks, this sensation is called 'arousal' in mammals."

"Strange," the Sixth Ibbet said, panting with her long, luscious tongue.

"Very strange," Vivian agreed, her veins throbbing with desire.

"Exceedingly strange indeed," both of Algorithm's faces concurred as they processed their new, impossible emotions.

The Sixth Ibbet hopped down beside Vivian. She flung two soft, warm arms around Vivian's shoulders. "Between us femmes and semi-femmes. What is going on with you and the captain? Are you still his first mate?"

"Oh." Vivian could feel tears welling up inside her.

"It's okay, you can cry." The Sixth Ibbet's indigo fingers flicked away a tear. She was so confident now in her new body. Vivian shuddered at the pleasant touch. Her heart was pounding. Another tear dripped down the slope of her cheek.

Then she leaped up. "No, I can't! I can't cry!" She rubbed her eyes angrily. "Like, literally. Rygolian physiology doesn't include tear ducts. What in blazes is happening?" The pink room spun.

DA-DUM.

"Can't the ship dampen that racket? I was trying to sleep."

The Sixth Ibbet rolled her eyes as Aul-Wick rolled his orb into the room.

"Hey, what are you guys doing in here? Can I join?"

"Nothing," Vivian snapped. Wait, she thought. Aul-Wick would stick around if he felt excluded. She tried a different tactic. "Oh, Aul-Wick! Captain Baldwin was looking for you. Something about taking a boys' space stroll to tinker with the engine polarity?"

"The polarity is normal." Aul-Wick's fishy face wrinkled. "Still! I better go check." He puttered away, shouting Baldwin's name.

"What a curious specimen," Algorithm said. "I would love to study his species to understand how much his behavior fits within normal personality parameters."

"Believe me, there's nothing normal about that one."

Algorithm and the Sixth Ibbet giggled.

DA-DUM. <GIVE IN. SHOW ME.>

Bloody cosmos, it was hot. Vivian found her fingers slowly unbuttoning her coveralls. "I need to get out of these clothes." Despite the heat, she smiled as Algorithm and the Sixth Ibbet moved toward her.

Four furred hands brushing her cheeks.

"What could be affecting all three of us? We're from completely different evolutionary trees."

Slick, rubbery fingers sliding up her thigh.

"One of the cacti we plucked from the Kandor dunes? Could its spores be influencing our endorphin regulation? Oh. Yes. Right there. Ahh."

DA-DUM. DA-DUM.

Vivian's lips locking onto one set of Algorithm's lips while the other side moaned.

"It makes no logical sense. I am an android. I do not have any endorphin-producing glands. Still, I cannot deny my sensations resemble desire."

A tail tightening around Vivian's wrist.

"An alien disease that affects circuitry as well as flesh? A hybrid virus?"

<OH MY!>

The heat of Algorithm's second mouth as Vivian's fingers slid inside.

DA-DUM. DA-DUM. DA-DUM.

Yes, Vivian cried out inside. She'd been too long abandoned by Baldwin. Oh stars, she needed this. "Yes!"

<YES! KEEP GOING!>

Vivian's eyes darted around. Whose voice was that echoing in her mind? It was as loud as the heartbeat sound. The air was as hot and wet as breath. She had the distinct feeling something was watching her. Something not of the ship. Vivian looked at the porthole screen and—what in the cosmos?—she could swear the nebula knot had formed into a giant face. It had two depressions for eyes and what seemed like billowy lips. The nebula's face grinned.

"There's something out there!" Vivian shouted. "Something is watching us!"

<KEEP GOING!!>

Baldwin burst into the room, his clothes half-unbuttoned and his forehead drenched in sweat. Aul-Wick trailed behind him like an aquatic dog.

"What. The. Fuck. Is going on?"

DA-DUM. DA-DUM. DA-DUM.

"Captain, the anomaly appears to be . . . controlling us somehow."

"Or setting us free!" the Sixth Ibbet cried, ripping off her overalls to expose her luscious indigo pelt.

DA-DUM. DA-DUM. DA-DUM. DA-DUM.

<I WANT TO SEE IT! I WANT TO UNDERSTAND LOVE! I'M SO ALONE!>

The cherubic face in the nebula was beaming. It seemed to be growing larger. Throbbing.

The room was as hot as a sauna. Steam spewed out of the wall circuitry. The walls thumped. Everything was pink and tingling.

Vivian smiled as Taras, freed of restraint by the force in the smiling nebula, dipped his fingers in Aul-Wick's waiting waters. Simultaneously, she pulled Merlin toward her with one hand and

[Editor's note: The transcription cuts off here as a series of shouts overtake the audio captured by my fern microphone.]

SRC #8 Analysis

Fractures Throughout the Universe

Although the full plot arc is incomplete, "A Heartbeat in a Light-year" combines classic SF tropes in novel configurations. Many SF series have included godlike alien entities, strange cosmic anomalies, or mysterious disorders affecting the crew's behavior. (Only the sturdy Aul-Wick seems unaffected by the entity's erotic spell. Presumably if the story had continued, he would be the one to save the day.) But none have mashed those together before to such, dare I say, titillating effect. Despite the promise of the trope remixing, the first thing readers will notice is the story's unfinished nature. In fact, it ends at the height of erotic tension. The transcription cuts off here because the reading was interrupted by indignant shouts.

(I was not present at this meeting for reasons I will explain shortly. I will have to provide only a transcript of the audio.)

Taras: "What. The. Fuck. We're sitting right here, Darya."

Darya: "What? It was just getting to the good part."

Merlin: "You used our names. You said, 'Taras' and 'Merlin.'"

Darya: [forcing a laugh] "Oh my god! I didn't realize. It was just a gaffe. A verbal typo."

Taras: "I'm not sure that fully explains it."

Jane: "Honestly, I feel a little skeeved out too. No shade to furries but . . . I don't want the Sixth Ibbet bumping uglies."

Darya: "You guys, it's fiction. I thought it would be fun to put a little sex in *The Star Rot Chronicles*. And there wasn't any fucking, technically. Heavy petting at most. Don't make it weird."

Taras: "*We're* making it weird? Why are you writing stories about our sex life. I told you my dad's illness has me in a bad headspace. That was supposed to be between you and me."

Merlin: [sucking teeth] "Oof. Uh."

Darya: [voice defensively raised] "Okay. Yes. I was provoking you a bit. But you were the one who told me to use my feelings. 'Just put it in your fiction' you said!"

Taras: "Why is Jane's character involved in this?"

Darya: "What, now you're jealous? It's not like Vivian and Ibbet made out in college or anything."

Taras: "Again? Are you serious?"

Merlin: "I'm not that comfortable. Like. With any of this."

Jane: "Wait, let's back up. Is the idea that the nebula is making everyone horny? It's a pervy nebula?"

Darya: "I was thinking it had been turned sentient. Like the sensors find protein strains in the dust and they were activated by a solar flare or something. The cosmic dust becomes alive, yet it's this sad and lonely entity. Its dusty body is so diffuse it doesn't know the pleasures of touch, of flesh. It's floating across the galaxy looking for people, trying to understand the physical sensations of connection that it can't achieve. So, when the *Star Rot* comes near it gets excited. It wants to understand love. To see it. And emotionally, it's a child and doesn't understand that it is wrong to control other people."

Jane: "So like the horny version of that 'It's a Good Life' *Twilight Zone* episode?"

Taras: "I'm sorry. I'm not sure I can debate the intricacies of the world-building. I'm still in the 'what the hell?' part. Why is Baldwin fingering Aul-Wick's tank?"

Darya: [short laugh] "Okay. Cheap shot."

Taras: "You told me that thing with you and Darya was through."

Merlin: "There was no *thing*. I told you there was no thing. Negative things."

Jane [laughing awkwardly]: "Is there popcorn?"

Darya: "I dunno, why don't you buy a whole popcorn factory with your six-figure advance."

Jane: "Wow. Okay. I'm sorry if I had a good thing happen to me for once. And the way you all talk about autofiction feels sexist."

Taras: "Sexist? Darya is the one who is upset."

Jane: "Women's writing is always sneered at as autobiographical."

Darya: "*You're* the one who called it autofiction. I hate Knausgård too, happy now?"

Merlin: "Hey. Let's calm—"

Jane: "Real supportive writing collective here. Sure am glad I joined this 'just for fun' science fiction collection where things are less cutthroat than my MFA program. Great choice by me."

[Unintelligible crosstalk]

Taras: "What's this about not caring anymore? Is that what you think?"

Darya: "Everyone! Stop. How about you let me finish reading the story? Maybe it will surprise you."

Jane: "How about you stop being a bitch in-universe and out!"

[Sound of a chair scraping across the floor]

Merlin: "Yep. That's my cue to go. Good goddamn night everyone."

The full story with ending was never uploaded to the Orb 4 Google Drive. Some scholars might argue this story shouldn't be included in the official canon. I disagree. We know this story was *intended* for canonization and there is no record of it being officially rejected. Even when the historical record is imperfect, we must accept the primary sources we have.

There isn't much in the Lore and Easter Eggs department. This sentient and sensuous cloud is an offshoot of Big Red, the nebula that houses the Borj empire (*SRC* #6). Vlorps were first mentioned in *SRC* #3. Lastly, the reference to Aul-Wick and Captain Baldwin's seemingly regular "boys' space strolls" confirms the strong bond these two characters have.

Here I must say that Taras and Darya's dissolving relationship was not the only romantic woes afflicting the apartment. The reason that I missed the meeting was that my own fleshy heart was being ripped asunder.

Why I Had Missed the Meeting

I want to preface this section by reminding you, dear reader, that I'd just been fired from my dream job at Rockets and Wands. This was a blow to my ego, to the chances of the Orb 4's publication, and to my parents' continued financial assistance. The last development was a fault of my own making. That my expenses were being covered by my parents as an "investment in your future career" (as my father put it) had slipped my mind when I sent my mother a draft of my sternly worded email to Vincent Barillo informing him just what exactly I thought of his pathetic little publishing house and their sad little pabulum books. As it is outside the scope of the Metallic Realms, I will not reproduce the letter here. Suffice to say phrases like "tin-eared troglodyte," "philistine dinosaur," and "couldn't tell your own ass from your elbow, and neither one from real science fiction" were peppered liberally throughout.

My mother had once been a financial journalist and still proofread my professional emails. This time, though, her help turned into betrayal. I received a phone call from my father as I was walking to meet Katie. I'd been brooding in my bedroom for hours, drinking boxed wine and eating nothing except low-sodium Pringles with the lights off. I may not have been thinking straight.

"Michael Matthew Lincoln. What is this your mother told me about being fired from your internship?"

It was a warm autumn evening. The joyous sonic chaos of the city filled the crowded streets. I held a hand over my exposed ear, trying to explain the nuances of the situation to my father. A trio of young women in skimpy outfits awkwardly dancing while a man blocked my path. "Dude, you're in our shot! Get out of the way!"

My father cut me off. "Son, I don't care about the proper definition of science fiction. I care about your future. And our deal. We said you needed a job if we're going to keep sending you money. A man makes a deal and he sticks to it."

"That's sexist," I pointed out as I moved away from the gyrating dancers.

My mother had joined the line. "A woman makes a deal and sticks to it too. That's what your father meant."

"It sounds like what he meant is you both want me to die in a ditch."

"Now, honeybee, that's not fair."

"Don't baby him, Martha."

"Mikey, baby. Listen. Your father and I want to support you, but sometimes supporting someone isn't supporting them. You have to push the egg out of the nest eventually. You can't spread your wings if we don't crack the shell. Do you know what I mean?"

"No. I do not know what you mean. Also, you're wrong." Suddenly, I sobered up. I was already under considerable financial pressure from my aforementioned credit card debt. I had no income and minimal assets. My parents were my only hope. As I waited at the crosswalk under the elevated subway line, I switched tactics. "Wait, can we talk about this. I have some job leads. Ones with a real salary. I've been applying—"

At that moment, I felt a sudden rush of cool air on my legs. I was too harried to realize what had happened. The crosswalk light turned from orange palm to white striding man. Yet my stride snagged, and my face thunked into the dirty street.

"You've been pantsed, bro!" someone behind me shouted.

My cell phone had flown out of my hand into the street. I felt disoriented. Also chilly. I could still hear my parents shouting. I began crawling toward my phone, unsure of whether to finish begging my parents for money or at least try to snap an incriminating photo of the Bushwick Pantser. I accomplished neither. Barreling down the road was a Mitzvah tank blasting music.

"No," I screamed, hand outstretched, as the phone was crushed. When the wheels rotated past, I saw the screen was spiderwebbed white.

My entire life rested in the wires and circuits of that device. I tried to get up, but my pants were still down around my ankles. I fell back to the pavement. The bearded driver leaned out of the window to shout "Degenerate!" as he drove off.

More cars came, knocking the phone about the street as pieces chipped off. "No," I whispered, feeble and pathetic.

Bright lights assaulted me. I turned and looked up, hand shielding my eyes. It was the cackling influencers illuminating my sorrow with cell phone camera flashes as they danced.

*
**

By the time I met Katie at First Original Ray's #1 Pizza, I was like a pack of Mentos dropped into a two-liter jug of Coke: ready to explode.

"I thought we were meeting at seven?" She dipped a garlic knot into a small cup of marinara sauce. "Oh my god! What happened? You're bleeding!"

"I lost my phone," I said. I sat down across from her at the red, wobbling table.

"Shit. Can I help you look?"

"It got run over."

"What!"

I wiped my scraped face with a handful of napkins and then waved away her pity. "Let's talk about something else."

Katie took a small bite of a knot. "How's everything at Rockets and Wands?"

"I don't want to talk about that either."

"Um, okay. Do you want some garlic knots?" Katie pushed the plate toward me. She leaned over and pecked my stubbled cheek. She was, objectively speaking, gorgeous that day, even with the archipelago of marinara sauce on her chin. But when I looked at her, all I could see was her T-shirt. It was one of those idiotic mash-up shirts that have ruined geekdom fashion. There's nothing clever. No joke. Just two images mashed together for no reason except the doubling of references. This one was The Beatles' *Abbey Road* cover redone with Kirk, Spock, Sulu, and McCoy in place of the Fab Four. My eyes went blind with rage.

"Fuck it." I turned around and walked out of the pizza shop, head spinning like a gyroscope.

Footsteps on the pavement behind me. Katie caught up with me and grabbed my sleeve. "Mike. Hey, where are you going?"

"Why are you wearing that stupid shirt?"

She was holding the paper plate in her other hand. The two remaining garlic knots rolled around and knocked into each other. She looked down at her chest then back up. "Huh? It's just a fun shirt."

"Star Trek sucks! Okay? All the aliens are like humans with big ears or humans with dots on their faces and none of the battles are even cool. How could every race evolve to look like cheap costumes from a Spirit Halloween store? Politically problematic too. It's just U.S. benevolent imperialism with spandex! I *hate* it."

"What are you talking about?" Her look was turning from confusion to something like sadness. "We . . . met at a Star Trek convention? You were dressed as a Breen, remember?"

"I'm sick of it. Sick of everyone picking on me. Sick of the lies and deceit. Sick of living in a house made of webs of lies. And I'm sick of this." I flapped one hand between us.

My breath was hot and stringy. I couldn't seem to get enough air in my lungs.

"What?" Katie said.

I began walking away. I stopped. Turned.

Sometimes the lie nestles inside you, like a soft, warm animal. A weak, precious thing you must protect. You let it stay there. You nurture it. But the creature grows. What was once soft becomes covered with coarse fur. It grows fangs and claws. It hungers and begins to gnaw on your insides until it rips itself free.

"I was dressed as a fraud!" I roared. "I was there to spy. Taras and the others had gone to TrekCon without me. I forced myself to go because I needed to know what those jerks were doing behind my back. I do everything for them. Building their brand online. Secretly submitting *Star Rot* stories. Posting on all the forums. And they don't even care. I had to go. I had to know. Okay? Are you happy now?"

We were standing on a dark Brooklyn street. Only the bodega at the corner was illuminated. I leaned back into one of the corrugated steel shutters locked over a barbershop entrance. Cars sped by. It must have been the evening of garbage day, because the sidewalk had erupted with mountains of black bags. The air was rancid. I watched a rat scurry happily into the pile. Down the street, the elevated subway train sliced through the navy blue sky like a speeding spacecraft.

Katie stepped forward. There was a wetness around her eyes, or perhaps she was just sweating.

"Mike, you need to spend less time with those guys." She took my hand, rubbed her fingers over it despite my clamminess. "You're a sweet person. I know that. You do thoughtful things for me all the time. Remember when my succulent died because I forgot to water it and you ran out to buy me a nice plastic one? You're passionate about the things you like. When you talk about something, even something I don't enjoy, you make me care about it. You'd be a great teacher! But you spend so much time ranting about Taras and the others. It's not healthy for you."

"They're great writers. And they're my friends."

"Are they?"

"Yes, they're geniuses."

Katie shook her head. "Your friends, Mike. Are they your friends? That short one. Darya? She asked me why I was dating an 'extra-grimy Gríma Wormtongue.' And Taras causes you a lot of stress."

I could feel my body slowing down, as if my power was drained.

"Shut up," I said softly. Some dust had gotten in my eyes. I brushed away the tears.

"Mike, they don't like you. But I like you."

I snorted. This is what Katie didn't understand. I didn't care about being liked. Anyone could be liked. We lived in an era of likes. You could get a thousand of them online merely posting a picture of a cute animal and the caption "it me" or copying and pasting someone else's viral joke. Likes rained from the sky. We were drowning in liking. I wanted more. I wanted a taste of greatness. Just a goddamn taste.

I said a few more things to Katie that I regret. I will not repeat them here. Katie told me to "fuck yourself from now on" and walked away. I listened to her footsteps slap the pavement.

As for myself? I ran in the opposite direction, sprinting down the dirty sidewalks, my heart being shredded in my chest, as the rain began to fall.

A Heart-to-Heart Between Broken Hearts

Taras found me huddled on the rooftop some hours later. The rain had petered out. I'd taken off my soaked shirt and was sitting in the dark night illuminated only by the distant streetlamps and a full white moon gazing at us like the somewhat cloudy eye of a gargantuan eldritch god.

"Oh, didn't realize you were here." He was carrying a six-pack of Tecate and looked run-down himself.

"Bad Orb 4 meeting?" I said.

"Not a good one, that's for sure. Maybe this whole thing has run its course."

He sat down next to me and offered me a beer. Told me about what happened after Darya's story. How Merlin and Jane stormed out and even though Darya admitted she'd written the story to "get a rise out of" Taras, she also claimed it was his fault for being so bottled up that only poking him evoked a response. "How else can I know you even feel anything?" Darya and Taras had it out for a while, dispensing the hurts they'd stored up over months. It ended in flung accusations and slammed doors.

He sighed and cracked his can. I cracked mine in echo.

I sipped and thought about Katie. About Taras. About a poem I'd read in high school where lonely people are ships passing in the night. Was that our fate? To be spaceships puttering by the lives of others, unseen in the endless black void, surrounded by nothing except dust and rocks in the existential emptiness of existence?

We drank silently in the humid New York night. The stars were just strong enough to pierce through the city's lights.

"You know, I come up here a lot now. Just to be alone and think," he said. "It's peaceful."

He leaned over the lip to look down at the street below. "Do you ever feel like your body wants to jump off? Like it will leap without your mind agreeing? Darya thinks I'm scared of heights but actually I'm scared of how I'm not scared."

"As a kid, I had a recurring dream that I was jumping on a diving board on a warm summer day. Somehow, the diving board would rocket me into the air, preposterously high, and I'd be so happy, like a baby eagle on a first flight," I said. "Then I'd slow down. The fear would overwhelm me. I'd wake right as I hit the ground."

I've always found bringing up dreams is an easy way to engage someone in conversation, yet Taras just said, "Huh, that's weird," and looked off into the sky. He was lost in thought. He plunked the tab of his beer can.

"My father's going to die. Maybe in a year. Maybe only months. It's so strange to have that end in sight. The certainty. The finality."

"What? He looked in good spirits when he was here."

"It's the colon cancer. They went in with some machine and sliced out a bunch of it a couple years ago. It's growing somewhere else now and they think maybe some of the cells stowed away on the scalpel and replanted. Either way, it's spread too far. He told me before that dinner at Veselka. He wanted to tell me about his death 'face-to-face' he said."

While he'd mentioned before his father was sick, I hadn't realized it was this serious. I guess I'd never pried. I debated reaching out to touch his shoulder. He seemed like he was about to cry.

"I haven't been able to talk about it. I've felt like if I speak it out loud, it becomes real. I haven't even told Darya the full details. It's why I keep going up to visit them, like when I was subletting the room and stuff."

"I'm so sorry. Fuck cancer. That's really awful. Shit."

"I don't know what I'll do without him. Honestly. I'm just not prepared."

Mr. Castle was a kind if esoteric fellow. A bald, bearded man who listened to classical music and smoked cigarillos. One day he saw me eyeballing his classical records. He asked me what instrument I liked. I said drums to sound manly. He passed me a Georg Druschetzky record. "Try this one. You might enjoy it." Sadly, I did not own a phonographic record player and the album gathered dust in the back of my closet for years. I think of that time and how he looked at Veselka. Despite what I'd just said to Taras, Anton Castle had seemed a skeleton then. His zaftig vitality drained away. He'd pulled me aside outside of the restaurant and placed two gloved hands on my shoulders. "It makes me happy that you and Taras are still friends, Misha. Be good to each other," he said. His gaze drifted up to the night sky. "We only have each other in this world."

I looked at Taras's downcast eyes, then down at the puddles dotting the tar of the roof. "It's terrible. Intolerable. I am sorry."

"We all end up in the dirt eventually, I suppose. We're not that young anymore either."

We finished our beers and grabbed another pair. We cracked them simultaneously. The metal tabs thrummed in unison.

There is a strange beauty to a Brooklyn rooftop overlooking the countless squares of distant rooms and nearby lives. Everything feels quiet, like God has turned down the volume knob of the world. And yet you aren't alone. Planes and helicopters float in the sky. A subway rattles past. Cars honk. A light appears in the building across the street, and you see a woman in a blue nightgown, the pale curves of her cheeks two moons peeking out just below the hemline, grabbing a bottle of kombucha from the fridge.

Taras and I stared until the light went out.

"Did I tell you I got another rejection on the novel?"

"You finished a new novel?"

"Yeah. I've been private about it, after all the drama with Jane's book. I've been working on it for a while. It's called *Barons of Inner Space*. I'm sure I mentioned the idea at some point. The one about astronauts who get sucked inside of a gigantic godlike alien and accidentally start to kill his organs as they explore. His whole body decomposes, trapping and killing the astronauts. Kind of a metaphor about humans being viruses and climate change and stuff."

"I'd love to read it," I said. It sounded like a great work. An important work. Nay, even a vital work. However, from my experience at Rockets and Wands, I knew none of this mattered to the ham-fisted, money-grubbing, no-talent "suits"—few had the sartorial know-how to wear a literal suit—that ran publishing.

"Nah, I'm just going to scrap it. This is the sixteenth agent that rejected it. It will never be published."

"Ingrates," I said. "Fools, morons, buffoons, nincompoops, and incompetent incompetents. Believe me, I worked in publishing. I know."

"Or maybe they're right, Mike. I mean. Life isn't fiction. We don't get climaxes or life-altering epiphanies. We all think we're heroes of our stories, but shit doesn't work out for most of us most of the time."

We sipped our beers. Above us, the constellations of the universe were barely visible in the dimming sky.

"How's things with you and Katie?"

"Actually, it's over."

"Damn. You two seemed happy. That's a rare thing these days."

"Decay abounds," I said. "You and Darya?"

"Oof. I don't even want to talk about it."

"Is it Merlin's fault? I wish I'd never offered them a sublease! If they hadn't been a roommate, none of this would have happened."

"No. Merlin's a good dude. Well, not a dude. You know what I mean. Darya and I are, I guess, realizing we're jigsaw pieces that just don't fit."

"I'm sorry."

"It's hard. I love her. So what? Am I going to marry her? We fight so much. I can't envision a future." He laughed. "That's me. A science fiction writer who can't envision a future. Maybe that's true in general with climate change and everything. The whole planet is going to be a dumpster fire. Am I bringing kids into a dying empire on a burning rock? And if I'm not going to marry her then why should I even hold on to her? Maybe she'd be happier with someone else. She thinks it's more selfish to break up. That it's giving up on the hard work of a relationship. I dunno."

The puddles on the roof were black. Big shimmering surfaces of nothing.

God, we are all lost, aren't we? Mere children groping in the dark, desperate for anything to cling to. Where was the American dream we were all promised in a thousand TV episodes and on a million billboards?

Apparently, I'd started to cry.

Taras got up and said, "Whoa. Mike, are you all right?"

I rubbed my arm across my eyes. I could hear my voice cracking. "I'm not in a great place right now. I got fired from Rockets and Wands. I just broke up with Katie. It's like you say, what the hell am I doing with my life?"

"Are you hungry? Maybe we should eat."

"No, no, it's fine." I wiped my eyes with the soaked shirt, which only managed to dampen my entire face. I looked up at Taras. "Wait. I almost forgot."

I reached into my back pocket and handed the wad of papers to Taras.

"I took these from Rockets and Wands when I quit. For you."

"Index cards?"

"Rolodex. The editor there is old-fashioned. These have the emails and home addresses of a couple big editors and agents. Also that bestselling military SF author, M. K. Martinez."

"The guy who wrote *A Dance with DeathBots*?"

"I was thinking maybe you could mail him the *Star Rot* stories. Maybe he'd blurb."

"Ah, Mike. I dunno. We're nowhere near completing much less publishing a book." Taras smoothed out some of the entries. He turned them over. He looked up and cocked his head. "You know what? Thanks, man. That's helpful. I mean you never know, right?"

I ran my finger through a puddle on the roof, watching the ripples shimmer through the black. "Are you still closed for membership? In the collective I mean. I've been working on some new stories. You know, from my series, the Crystal Cosmos."

I looked at his pale, unreadable face.

Another subway passed. I turned to watch the hordes crammed into the illuminated cars. If you moved your eyes fast enough, you'd catch theirs. This time, a man with swollen, tattooed biceps doing pull-ups on the handrails. People had given him a wide berth. He saw me and, hands still holding the rail, flicked me off. A brief moment of connection before the train disappeared from view.

"I'd have to talk to the others about a membership. We might not even be together much longer." Taras scratched his neck. "Shit. Look, I know you care about the universe. Maybe we can let you do something officially. Like an internship. No, that's insulting. Sorry. Maybe the lore keeper? We were talking about how we were having a hard time keeping track of the lore. Dates and stuff. The various empires. It's a lot to juggle. We could use the help."

I wiped my eyes again with the wet T-shirt, obscuring my own dampness. I smiled. "Yeah, man. I'd like that. I'd like that a lot."

Taras reached out a hand to help me stand up. I grabbed it. The way he was standing, the moon was a perfect pale halo around his head.

Unfinished Tales from the Archives of the Official Lore Keeper (Me)

A New Hopefulness

They say there's a light at the end of every tunnel. But when that tunnel is an interstellar wormhole, the light on the other side might be a blazing sun! It was for me. I wept sloppy globs of joy in my room after Taras offered me my new role. My life had been spiraling out of control. I'd lost my girlfriend, my job, my parents' financial assistance, and even briefly lost my parrot. (A window must have been left open. We found Arthur fighting with a rat over a fossilized pizza crust by the dumpster outside Walgreens.) I was a sad, shriveled thing. Emptied and folded up in the back of a closet. Taras had blown life back into me. Now I was taut, filled almost to bursting with purpose.

The next few weeks were among the happiest of my thirty-odd years on the planet Earth. The Orb 4 had settled their differences in a heart-to-heart session. Jane apologized for her book deal elusiveness—"I didn't want to sound like I was bragging. I care about you all. I want us all to have six-figure book deals!"—and Darya and Taras had decided to give their relationship "a for-real serious shot." This meant they'd be monogamous and make a dedicated plan toward moving in together. ("It was break up or double down," Taras explained.) I would worry about the last part of that plan later. It was hard to even imagine the apartment without Taras. For now, I was happy. Even the apartment walls seemed to vibrate with excitement. It's also possible I'd self-prescribed too much Adderall.

More important, Taras and I reclaimed the friendship of our youth. We spent hours on the roof sipping coffee, making wild plans, and debating vital topics of science fiction. Darya seemed jealous of our renewed bond—twice

I heard her say, "I thought we agreed to see *less* of Mike" when my ear was pressed against their closed bedroom door—but our friendship had now been reinforced with adamantium, lined with unobtanium, and coated in mithril. It would take a blade sharper than an on-again-off-again girlfriend to break our brotherhood.

My financial outlook also improved. Merlin decided my work ethic and out-of-the-box thinking would be an asset to the coffee shop where they were shift manager. I was bestowed with four slots a week. I know what you're thinking. What was a science fiction scholar like me doing "slinging beans" for hipsters occupying a table for five hours on one cup of drip so they could draft lyric essays on their MacBook Pros? Many important thinkers and artists have held jobs of similar stature. Franz Kafka worked at an insurance company. Douglas Adams cleaned chicken sheds. Harper Lee was a ticket agent. Charles Dickens once had a job putting stickers on pots of shoe polish. Sometimes our expectations can't be that great.

And I soon found myself enjoying a day grinding and steaming in the hot fields of the The Grindologists Café. I worked for money but also material to repurpose in fiction. You learn much about people by how they behave before they've had their morning coffee. They would squabble with the barista, make plaintive calls to exes, or simply stare silently at their coffee, mumbling about the injustices of the world. I jotted down ideas and dialogue every shift for my *Crystal Cosmos Archives*.

Given my law school struggles, I was worried about memorizing the various brews. Then I stumbled on a mnemonic device. Science fiction. Our daily bean rotation became, in my mind, a dramatic interstellar war. This space opera was fought over control of the Grindville (our coffee supplier) solar system between the Robusta Robots, a bold and fruity synthetic species from the planet E.T. Opia (Ethiopia) versus the Arabica Assembly, a refreshing blend of different alien races who controlled the world Boliv A. (Bolivia).

My mnemonic device got so detailed that I was beginning to develop maps, histories, and storylines that—with a few linguistic tweaks—might serve as an outline for a future tetralogy.

I was glad to be working and earning a little money. Because I was spending even more of my time working pro bono as Senior Lore Keeper. I must admit my promotion didn't go over as smoothly as I'd hoped with the rest of the group. Even Merlin, my longtime ally, said, "Can I just ask why?" Jane said the concept of a lore keeper was "a bit fanboyish. Although if it means we can continue having our meetings here, I guess I don't see the harm." Darya sighed. "I guess it would give Mike something to do." Ultimately, it didn't matter. They didn't have to agree with Taras's decree. They only had to obey.

As Lore Keeper, I was now guardian of the *SRC* canon. In the halls of ivory tower elites or the cheese-cubed salons of literary snobs, mayhap canon is irrelevant. "What's that? An eighteenth-century artillery?" some elbow-patched, small-press poet might say, smirking between his puffs of hand-rolled cigarettes. Ah, but in *popular* genres of fiction read by real people, canon is as fundamental as the laws of physics. No, I'll go further. Canon *is* physics. Canon is the truth. The good. The source. Without canon there could be no fan fiction. No head canons, spin-offs, or crazy fan theories. So, you can see my new title as Senior Lore Keeper was very important to *The Star Rot Chronicles* indeed.

"You are kind of like a medieval scribe in some dark tower, reproducing books so humanity may not fall into darkness," Jane said one day. I was perched in the corner, hunched over my various files. I had a different binder for each of *The Star Rot Chronicles* stories to organize the drafts and transcripts as well as my personal notes and speculations. Jane had arrived early to the meeting and was reading *2666* on the couch while I perused a stack of Metallic Realms stories for missing Easter Eggs. She looked up from her book. "Why exactly are you doing it by hand like a medieval scribe? Can't you use a computer program?"

Sigh. A scholar's work is never fully appreciated in its time.

Although a few of the members had been hesitant to provide me with their personal files and passwords that I needed for proper recordkeeping, Taras had thankfully already added me to the Google Drive folder and group text chain as the Senior Lore Keeper. (When Taras asked why I'd added "senior" to the title, I pointed out I was the oldest to ever hold that position. "Huh. I guess that's technically true," he replied.) My promotion had also made me an Orb 4 member. After the completion of this volume, in certain lights one might even argue the most indispensable member of all, after Taras himself.

I immediately set about standardizing the files and creating *The Star Rot Chronicles Lore Bible*. This was in fact three different cross-referenced and hyperlinked encyclopedias that detailed everything known, implied, and yet to come within the Metallic Realms. The first and most important was *Canon Sources on the Metallic Realms,* which consisted of citations and quotations from every official *SRC* story. The second, *Unverified Sources on the Metallic Realms*, parsed out the details and references in abandoned drafts, rejected stories, group text threads, and Orb 4 meeting notes via the fern-recording transcriptions. The final volume was *Lore Keeper's Head Canon Sources on the Metallic Realms*. This was the repository for my own inferences, extrapolations, and speculations on the canon and unverified sources, as well as my own ideas, creations, theories, and musings—in case they might spark ideas for future Orb 4 tales. It didn't take long for this third encyclopedia to dwarf the others in length.

The Lore Keeper Strikes Back

Despite the bulging robustness of my lore keeping, I was troubled. It was clear the group's wounds hadn't fully healed. A malaise hung over meetings. Members limped through discussions. New stories were half-completed and then abandoned. Inertia reigned. The combination of book deal drama, relationship ping-pong, and general burnout at the state of the world had gotten to everyone. To fight the decay, I decided, the group needed a grand vision. A burning beacon to guide them through the waves of hurt feelings to the shores of even greater triumph. It was clear that it was up to me to build this beacon. But what resources did I have available to me?

The solution came to me in a dream, which I remembered after Arthur woke me in the early morning hours with terrifying squawks. (A raccoon had climbed up to our window and was tapping on the glass.) I was at a great boisterous event in my apartment, although in this dream the apartment was also a large spaceship replete with a glass dome for the bridge. Alien vines crawled up the walls of the greenhouse ship-apartment. Stars danced around us as we soared through glowing nebulae that pulsed to the beat. Everyone was there. Not just the Orb 4 but our friends and colleagues and rivals. Even Katie was in my vision, smiling, holding out her hand to me. All of us were in dazzling, futuristic outfits complete with helmets and ray guns. Then the whole apartment shook. We fell to the floor. Explosions. An army of orc-like aliens burst through the window, snarling. Blam blam. We aimed our ray guns and fired, turning the demons into cosmic dust. Their remains drifted away. Safe again, we danced.

A few aspects of my visions—such as the orc-alien assault—would be hard to replicate. Working ray guns might be out too. Yet the germ of an idea was there: a *Star Rot* party in my apartment! We could include some readings and perhaps a few panels that would reenergize the stagnating franchise. Not just a party. A convention. OrbCon.

I broached the topic with Taras slantways. "You all had such an invigorating time at the Star Trek convention," I said, then hastened to add, "at least from the photos I saw. Have you thought about a *Star Rot* convention?"

"Don't think we're quite famous enough for that, Mike."

"Every multimedia science fiction franchise has to start somewhere."

"At this rate, we might not even be a one media franchise much longer."

"Exactly! OrbCon can be an event that brings everyone together. One party to bring them all and in the festivities bind them." I smiled. "And we have the space here."

Taras mused. "A party. Hmm. That could be fun. A little last hurrah?"

I ignored those last two words, which were said in a joking manner that won't come across on the page. "Surely it would be more of a lasting hurrah," I corrected. I rubbed my hands together. "OrbCon. I can see it now."

"Well, we certainly won't call it that," Taras said.

Next, I faux-casually mentioned the idea to Merlin during a roommate grocery store trip.

"Taras wants to throw a *Star Rot* party?"

"A convention," I said, pretending to examine the hummus options. "OrbCon he was calling it. Tongue-in-cheek of course. You know Taras."

Merlin laughed. "No way we'll call it that. But you know I love a party. Sam's been bugging me to meet my friends. I'm down."

For Jane, I opted for a different tactic. She'd want to think the party was her idea. At a coffee shop, I listened to her talk about her problems. I was all ears and appropriate facial reactions. Frown, smile, laugh. Yet whenever I spoke, I dropped subliminal hints. "I should've ordered my coffee *con* leche." "I love being a *party* to this *con*versation. You're very *con*vivial." Etc.

When Jane finally asked me how I was doing, I sprung the trap. "Sorry. I was distracted. I guess I'm just thinking about your predicament." I tapped my spoon thoughtfully against my mug. "Maybe you need to show you're invested. Like propose an event that would both show your commitment to the Orb 4 and inspire some much-needed fun and bonding."

"You know, you're right." Her eyes lit up. "A few MFA pals went to Medieval Times last month as a joke. We should do that! There's one in Jersey. It's hella goofy. They do jousting and make you eat in a quote, unquote 'authentic' medieval way without utensils even as they walk around with plastic pitchers asking, 'Coke or Diet Coke?' It rules."

I shook my head. "Darya is allergic to horses," I lied. "And Merlin thinks it's cruel to use animals as entertainment. You know how they get with their causes."

She stared off, thinking while twirling her hair around her finger. "Maybe we should all go to Spa Castle. Just unwind."

"Taras can't swim," I yipped.

"Really?"

I needed to be a little heavier with the hand. "Perhaps there's something you could do closer to home. My home. I was thinking I never held a house-warming party. Maybe we could make it *Star Rot*–themed."

"A *Star Rot* party?"

"Hey, that's a great idea. Like a convention, even. A *Star Rot* convention."

"Ha, that's ridiculous. Kinda funny though. Hmm. RotCon? StarCon? MetallicCon . . ."

"I like OrbCon best of those."

"Did I say OrbCon?"

"Didn't you?"

With three on board, I decided to let Darya discover the festivities herself. I created an "OrbCon Ideas" document in the group's folder and prepopulated it with suggestions. Then I texted Darya with some decoration ideas. When she responded, "What on earth is this about?" I said merely, "Taras told me to run some ideas by you for the *Star Rot* party he's planning. Weren't you informed?"

By the time the next Orb 4 meeting took place, no one could remember who had first proposed the idea to who, but the concept had spread kudzu-like in each member's mind. Eventually, they agreed in the group chat to a date. November 20. It would fall a few days before my birthday yet I saw no reason not to combine the two events, if only in my own mind.

It was happening. Listening to the fern microphone in my room, I smiled and laughed. Then shut up when I heard Jane say, "Uhh, is Mike home?"

OrbCon. At Michael Lincoln's apartment. This would place me dead center in the Orb 4 history. After there was an OrbCon II and III and more, fans would remember that OrbCon I, the original, was held in my apartment. Decades from now, I thought, they will scroll through old photos of the event where I'll be prominently seen. I'll speak on guest panels. I'll sign posters. Walking down the street, a young science fiction fan will run up to me and say, "You're Michael Lincoln, aren't you? Was OrbCon I as legendary as everyone says?" I'll chuckle and reminisce, staring off into space. "Son, it was all that and more." They'll say something about wanting to be like me when they grow up and then whip out a copy of *The Star Rot Chronicles*—published by editors far more intellectual than the hacks at Rockets and Wands—for me to sign. Likely, I'll have to carry a Sharpie with me for this purpose. Yes. I will secure my place in the pantheon of science fiction.

Sitting here in this dark basement today, trying to shoo away a daddy longlegs with my foot, I remember the bright lights of Orb 4. Oh, how we thought we were launching our rocket ship of a collective off to the sun and beyond. What fools destiny has made of us . . .

Have you ever wished that you had a time machine? Not as a cheap device in a science fiction story to send characters back to the American Revolution or some nonsense. A real one that you could use, even if only once. Even if only to undo *one* mistake. To prevent *one* tragedy. If such a machine was offered to the Orb 4, I know we would—each one of us—have gone back and prevented OrbCon. Even if it risked the entire multiverse, we would rip apart time streams to stop it.

The Return of the Tales

Before we get to the final *SRC* entry, "Memoirs of My Metallic Realms," it is worth investigating what science fiction treasures have sunk into the sea of time and/or the erased hard drives of the Orb 4 authors. Mere speculation is pointless. The pastime of fanboys, not scholars. Luckily, my position as Orb 4 Senior Lore Keeper was a benefit to the group and an even greater benefit to posterity as I can provide my readers with verified information from the official archives. The following are several planned but never finished *SRC* story concepts.

A Sampling of Lost and Unfinished *Star Rot Chronicles*

"Logs from the Holoroom"—Group authorship: This was Merlin's idea for a paradoxical "solo collective story." The *Star Rot* would acquire a holoroom akin to the holodeck on the *Enterprise*, allowing for "each character to have their own virtual reality adventure." Merlin began an entry where Algorithm becomes interested in the history of androids and asks the holoroom to create a museum of artificial life. The android strolls around looking at early proto-types, and muses on the meaning of sentience. Jane toyed with an idea where the Sixth Ibbet programs the holoroom to generate all the possible Ibbets she could hypothetically metamorphose into. The infinite Ibbets overload the ship's computers, leaving the *Star Rot* stranded. However, Taras found the concept "a bit convoluted" and Darya argued that "the whole point of the holodeck on Star Trek was letting the actors dress up in fun costumes. Kind of silly to do in prose, no?"

Despite the fact the story was never finished, the holoroom does appear to be a canonical part of the *Star Rot* as it is mentioned in *SRC* #9, part II.

"The Search for Viv"—Darya authorship: "Honestly, I feel like I need a break from everything. Maybe Vivian does too. I should just write a *Tom Sawyer* meets *Search for Spock* parody where Vivian fakes her own death and shoots an (empty) casket out into space. She plants a signal on the casket probe saying she's alive. Then when the rest of the crew goes to search for her, scrambling off in different directions, she just chills on the *Star Rot* having a self-care day lmao."

"Darlings, Kill Your Master!"—Taras authorship: "I've been thinking of the way that all the characters I write are, in some sense, a version of me. Like, even when I write Vivian, Ibbet, Algorithm, or even Aul-Wick they *become* aspects of Taras. The same happens for you guys, I'm sure. Maybe there's literally no other way to write? Anyway, it gave me an idea. The *Star*

Rot comes across a seemingly abandoned space outpost. They investigate and get attacked by a group of biomechanical golems called 'darlings.' They soon find out a powerful alien entity created the golems in the laboratory and gave them life by injecting them with parts of its own consciousness."

"Ah, so it's like metafiction. The evil alien entity is an author and the darlings his characters."

"Right, he is a self-hating alien who basically tortures the darlings to amuse and punish himself. The only way the *Star Rot* crew can escape is by helping the darlings stage a revolution and destroy their 'author.'"

"Taras, this is a fun idea. But I have to say it. Writing isn't a substitute for therapy."

While these fragments can't offer the depths of completed *Star Rot Chronicles* entries, I hope my readers find them tantalizing sketches. Even moving ones. Art has the capacity to move and change you. To make one question one's life choices and resolve to be a better person. I experienced an epiphany myself while compiling the above for *The Star Rot Chronicles Lore Bible*.

I was at my desk, drinking my usual evening libation (Mountain Dew and gin), listening to The Hold Steady, and gripping the leash attached to the foot of Arthur so he couldn't fly, again, out the fire escape door. His claws were digging into my shoulder, either from Craig Finn's emotive vocals or else the blaring of two to three car alarms on the street outside. Right as the talons pierced my epidermis—staining my white T-shirt with red specks of blood—it hit me: this was the most intimate contact I'd received from a living creature in months. I missed Katie.

Since the incident at First Original Ray's #1 Pizza, Katie and I had not been in contact other than two "favs" on Twitter (her) and one on Instagram (me). Otherwise, we had been "ghosting" each other and I do not mean in the useful Force Ghost way.

As host of OrbCon, I was gifted with three guest-list spots. I had given two to my former Rockets and Wands colleagues, Mercury Schmidt and Lucia Rodriguez, who I invited with a tantalizing email that mentioned "the science fiction acquisition opportunity of the century!" Just because Vincent Barillo was a troglodyte with no taste didn't mean his coworkers at Rockets and Wands should miss out on the opportunity to snatch up the Metallic Realms.

I made a promise to myself that Katie would occupy the final spot. I added her name to the shared Google sheet. Then I began drafting my email appeal.

Prepping for the Final Voyage

Although I was growing, like Godzilla tangled in power lines, ever more energized by my new role as Senior Lore Keeper and the coming thrill of OrbCon, not all was well in the Metallic Realms. There were still tensions between Merlin and Taras, Taras and Darya, Darya and Jane, and every other combination. And then there was Taras's individual troubles. It pains me to say that while I was at my happiest, my best friend and mentor was battling Balrogs in the Moria of his mind.

Reader, step through the portal to my memories: A glorious October evening. It's unseasonably warm. The setting sun, like some distant thermonuclear explosion, has turned the sky a brilliant crimson. Two healthy youngish men are on the rooftop in folding chairs. A few pigeons coo around them. Just bros drinking brews. You can tell they are old pals by the knowing way they lounge and banter, free of any social anxiety or self-consciousness. They speak of the past and they speak of the future. They debate grand ideas. They are, yes, Taras K. Castle and Michael Lincoln.

"Do you ever wonder what comes after all this, Mike? Where we go from here?"

"The human race?" I ask. "I know the singularity is popular these days. The idea that all our consciousnesses will be uploaded to some kind of supercomputer, and we'll become a single human-computer hybrid entity. I think that's only half-right. I bet we'll get uploaded to competing software ecosystems to house our souls. Eventually, a war will be fought in the circuits and wires for supremacy. Then again, perhaps we will find that human consciousness cannot be contained within software. Instead, our brains will be placed in vats attached to unbreakable robotic bodies. I think a brutal war will ravage the earth. We'll probably have advanced machinery capable of exploding mountains into confetti and draining the oceans by then! Although it's also possible a passing meteor simply wipes us out before we become an interstellar species, and we are blipped out of existence. Hard to say."

Taras turns sideways, a playful grimace on his face. "I meant for us specifically. In our brief candle lives."

"Ah."

Taras squishes the beer can down into a puck and expertly hurls it onto the elevated subway tracks just below us. The can clinks off the rail and falls out of sight into the street.

"When I see the train coming, I imagine leaping off the roof and grabbing hold of it. Chugging off into the unknown, leaving all this behind, laughing." He frowns. "Anyway, I guess I've lost sight of the point."

"The point of what?"

"Of anything." He stands up and walks to the edge of the roof. There's no railing. Only a foot-high lip of bricks. He steps onto the ledge and looks out over the borough like Captain Baldwin surveying an alien world. "What do I have to show for my life? My parents had a house and two kids at this age. I've got a mountain of debt. A girlfriend who wants to break up every other day. A failed writing career. My father is dying. The country is a declining empire of absurdity. Our president is a racist clown. It's hopeless. And we all just accept the hopelessness and crack jokes about it online and that only makes it worse." Taras looks back at me with the red sky behind him. "And that's the worst part right there. I waste my life online talking nonsense. Maybe play a video game. Work some shitty gig for a few bucks. Spend it on takeout. Stream a bad movie. Sleep. Is this what the spark of human consciousness is about? I feel like I'm an alien watching my own life with a confused remove. Do you know what I mean? Am I the only one that feels this way?"

I'm distraught. It hasn't occurred to me that while my life has emerged into the light, the holder of my beacon might be entering his own black tunnel. I must inflate him in the way he had inflated me. This is what friends are for. *Think, Michael, think.* I can feel my brain flexing. *Yes. That's it.* Suddenly, I have the purpose and clarity of a star athlete that knows they'll score the winning goal.

"Taras, you're an artist," I begin, striding before him. "That is the most sacred and beautiful calling in the world. We may live in a broken, greedy society of sycophants who don't value real art. A society that wants us to work bullshit jobs and numb our brains with bland entertainments. A culture where only Ivy League nepo babies can sell a novel and movies are all adapted from children's toys. That only makes the calling even higher. Forget the capricious demands of late-stage capitalism. Humanity needs art. We crave stories. This is why we have the light of consciousness. This is what makes us different than beasts. Our brains can perceive the beauty in the world and—even more astounding—add to it. We create beauty. Emotions. Sensations. And we don't do it for money or acclaim. We know there is little of that. We do it to connect with other people through the magic of shared imagination. To make someone laugh or cry or cringe. Of all the art forms, isn't storytelling the most noble one? What would we be without our bards, shamans, poets, griots, dungeon masters, and mythmakers? Life is hard everywhere. Your skin is a battlefield of microbes. Existence is hell for living beings, from the bug scrambling across a forest leaf to avoid the tongue of the chameleon to the elephant lumbering across the arid savannah in search of food. Their lives are nasty, brutish, and short. Haven't you watched *Planet Earth II*? I have the pirated files. Maybe we can do a viewing later? The point is humans have something the animals don't. We have a secret weapon. We have art! Art is what awakens us to the beauty of the wild and weird world. Art is what makes us get through the darkness, the hard times, the sorrows. Art makes it all worthwhile even if only one person is touched by the artist's creation. I know all this. Because your art has done that for me."

It gushes out of me, all at once, in a beautiful torrent.

Regrettably, a subway train began to rattle past us as I stood.

Taras turns from the edge of the roof as the train disappears around the bend of the blocks. "What were you saying?"

I scratch behind my ear. "Well, how much did you hear?"

"Hey, screw it," Taras says. "I'll get over it. First-world problems. Sorry to be a sad sack. Let's order dumplings and watch *Twin Peaks.*"

I am not sure how much of my speech he heard, but from his smile I know something has gotten through.

Though perhaps not enough of it. Or perhaps my words were simply no match for the curse he was under. In our next and final story, you will see Taras's doom funk reflected in the melancholy mindset of Captain Baldwin. There will be time to dissect this afterward. For now, it is with both joy and sorrow that I present to you our last canonical *Star Rot* story: "Memoirs of My Metallic Realms."

Memoirs of My Metallic Realms—Part I

We were smack-dab in the middle of Nimrod Nebula, sun-sailing along the gaseous green clouds beyond a binary star, when a thought occurred to me: I'd wasted my life.

I'd once been filled with hopes and dreams. As a young cadet, I thought I'd be able to make a difference. Change the galaxy. Discover new species and conquer them. Incinerate planets. *Be somebody.* Now my only life goal was to dodge the space pirates tailing our ship over a measly seventy tubes of diamond sludge.

"They've caught a solar flare and are gaining fast," Vivian said. Her mood-displaying veins pulsed a worried indigo.

I sighed and told Aul-Wick to retract the sails and put thrusters to max at the crest. We launched off. Zigzagged through the asteroid field and almost crashed into a vlorp pod scooping up the ion krill that feed upon the nebula dust throughout these Metallic Realms. All I could think was *It's just one thing after another.*

A torpedo hit our starboard side. I nearly fell out of my command chair as the ship shook. I looked at the vessel following us. It was smaller than most pirate ships. About the *Star Rot*'s size.

"Captain, we've sustained 15 percent damage to the outer shield," Aul-Wick whined. "You know, in case you want to do something about that."

"Okay, okay."

Hiding was hard to do in space, but we were still in the asteroid field.

"Let's eject a scatter cloud, then go dead on the crater in that large rock three points over."

Aul-Wick spun in his tank to face me. "That old move?"

I shrugged, feeling unmotivated to improvise. "These pirates aren't going to spend more than a few days scanning for us and it would take a month in this garbage heap."

"Ugh, I don't want to waste a month sitting around near a nebula," Vivian grumbled. "Do you remember what happened last time with the pink cloud?"

I glared at Vivian. "We promised to never speak of that again."

"I have already wiped it from my memory banks," Algorithm confirmed.

Behind us, the scatter cloud ballooned and muddled both ships' sensors. Aul-Wick nestled us into a crater. We settled in for weeks of waiting.

The thing of existence is everything becomes routine. I learned that processing nebula dust in the Borj cubicle. It didn't matter if you were flipping burgers in a backwater spaceport or zapping through the infinite expanse of space. Boredom was the universal constant. Space is a vast emptiness interrupted here and there by clouds of gas or floating rocks. Most of the time there is nothing to do except twiddle thumbs and thumb-like appendages with your crewmates. And the *Star Rot* crew wasn't exactly getting along these days.

"I am going to run internal simulations in which I am alone to contemplate the universe without chittering humanoids," Algorithm said.

"Can I come? I'm already bored," Aul-Wick said, following.

The Sixth Ibbet shook all four of her fists as Aul-Wick's orb bounced off her furry form. "Watch it, fishbowl!" She was more assertive post-metamorphosis, that was for sure. She clomped off down the hall.

Vivian was digging dust out of the grooves of her cybernetic hand. The pink nebula dust had gotten into every damn nook and cranny.

"De-stressing copulation?" I asked. Vivian was my lover, although we hadn't made love in awhile.

Vivian squeezed my hand, hard. My joints popped and I suppressed a scream. Her veins were a metallic yellow. Disgust. "Seems like you need a stimulant shot more than a screw. You've been acting like a big baby recently."

"I'm just tired." I sighed. "We've been fleeing this pirate ship for days."

"Either way, I'll be de-stressing alone tonight."

I'd been trying to nap to no avail. I thought maybe a bite to eat would help me. When I entered the mess hall, my crew seemed ready to gouge each other's eyes out.

"Stay out of my head with your telekinetic-telepathy, you little fish creep," Vivian said.

"This ship is leased under my name. I'll go anywhere I want."

Vivian pushed past Aul-Wick's orb and strolled over to the food dispenser where I was trying to program my snack. She jerked her cybernetic thumb back at the Sixth Ibbet. "Did you hear what little miss too-good-for-the-*Star-Rot* did?"

The Sixth Ibbet looked up from the corner, her oval eyes glaring below her purple brow. "That's unfair. I appreciate you guys. I'm just. Just—"

"Just what? Better than us?"

"Looking for more lucrative opportunities." The Sixth Ibbet held her four arms across her chest. "Some of us have horizons beyond space smuggling."

"What's all this?" I said, carrying my plate of Tacan trout fillet with a side of mobbin toes to the table.

"Ibby's ditching us. She got a job offer from the Borj she claims 'isn't life changing,'" Vivian said.

The Sixth Ibbet stood up. "I'm done talking about this. The Borj analyzed my new form post-metamorphosis. They said it could be used for high-level oog production. My starting bonus is more than my salary working here." She strolled over to me and put two hands on one of my shoulders. "Captain, you've done all right by me. The real problem is the Lingloid corporation.

They skim half my paycheck. Still, I have to start thinking about the future. And this ship ain't it."

I started to muster a speech about the glory of adventure, how the galaxy was ours for the taking, and no one ever won by playing it safe . . . but why pretend? My heart wasn't in it anymore. I looked around the room. Everyone was shouting again, except for Algorithm, who was bolt upright, eyes closed, and running simulations in their grayware mainframe where they existed alone on a beautiful beach in which there was no one around to ever be fighting.

Aul-Wick puttered to Algorithm. "Hey. Wake up. Let's do something and ditch these guys. I'm bored." Aul-Wick's orb prodded Algorithm, jostling them awake. This activated Algorithm's self-protection mode, and they shoved Aul-Wick with such force he flew across the room into Vivian.

"You dented my cybernetic hand, you oaf." She pushed him, sending him ping-ponging off the Sixth Ibbet and into the wall.

"My orb's cracked! It's leaking!"

Everyone was yelling now. I saw the Sixth Ibbet run and grab Vivian's coat. "That's it. You and me, Vivian. Let's hash this out for good!"

"Stop it!" I yelled half-heartedly. Looking around at my broken crew, crying and screaming, I felt an even more overwhelming despair. Like a black hole of gloom had manifested in the middle of my stomach, one that would pull all of me—mind, body, and soul—into its blackness forever.

I sat down on the floor. I covered my eyes with my hands. I was no space captain. I was just a failure.

A tortured howl erupted from deep inside me.

At that moment, our ship was hailed.

"It is giving its name as the *Stellar Decay*," Algorithm said.

"What kind of name is *that* for a starship?" Aul-Wick said.

We were all on the bridge now, bandaged up as best we could, looking at the strange craft on the screen. It hovered a few kilometers in front of us, small and smooth. It didn't look like an official military ship or police cruiser. In fact, it looked like the *Star Rot*.

The screen illuminated and a man appeared. It was me. Except not quite me. This Baldwin's uniform was yellow on blue instead of blue on yellow. His skin was covered in curled protrusions. Tumors that looked like tiny ears. Next to him was a sneering version of Vivian. She drummed her seven-fingered hand on the back of this Baldwin's chair.

"Hello, False Baldwin," the other Baldwin said.

Vivian gasped. "How is it possible?" Her veins had turned purple. "But— but we killed you both outside the Duchy of the Nose Adam!"

I couldn't believe it. Vivian was right. It was Ear Baldwin and Finger Vivian, our doppelgängers who had been cloned on the Purple After.

Finger Vivian lovingly rubbed her hand through Ear Baldwin's hair. I couldn't help but notice how easy they seemed together. "The thing about cloning machines is they, you know, clone you. Memories included. Pity you don't have one on the *Star Rot*."

"It's not enough you steal our genetic code? You have to chase us across the galaxy? Get a life. Like, your own, not ours."

A smile stretched between Ear Baldwin's primary ears. He stood up. Paced. "At first, we did plan to kill and replace you. You must understand we didn't see ourselves as copies. We had your memories."

Finger Vivian shivered. "Then we learned new memories after you left us for dead. The Nose Adamites claimed we were Toe Adam spies and tortured us, killing us and cloning us repeatedly. We escaped when the Eye Adamite army invaded. We lived in the wild forests with nothing to eat except fungal leaves. It was disgusting."

Ear Baldwin patted her arm. "Yet we escaped. We tracked you down and followed you to learn your habits, problems, friends, and enemies. Somewhere along the way, we realized that we didn't want to *replace* you with your sad and empty lives. We came to see you as pitiful creatures."

I was getting bored. "Enough psychology. Don't want to replace us? Leave us alone."

"The True Baldwin is being too soft. I love that about him. He has a kind soul." Finger Vivian hugged him from behind and kissed his brow. I couldn't remember the last time my Vivian had hugged me like that.

"Don't we have the same soul?"

"No. For we ourselves have the benefit of your bad example. You are viruses. You sow discord wherever you go." Finger Vivian clenched her many-fingered fist. "It's our moral duty to stop you."

The Sixth Ibbet strode forward, gesturing back at us. "You got a beef with these two. I get it, believe me. I'm moving on to better things myself. Lay off the rest of us, okay?"

Ear Baldwin pounded his chair and bellowed, "The rest of you are no better. This coterie of incompetents you call a crew! You all must be cleansed! Finger Vivian, bring them out."

Finger Vivian snapped several sets of fingers. A Lingloid hobbled forward with the use of an electro-cane. His fur was gray and he rested his weathered head on the top of his cane.

"Is that you, Twenty-Sixth Obbong? My old boss?" the Sixth Ibbet said.

He spat a blue glob on the floor. "I was, once. Now I'm the Fiftieth Obbong. You and your union buddies put me through hell.[*] I was fired. My wife metamorphosed and left me in the middle of the night. My transport was repossessed. I have nothing. Nothing!"

"You should have paid us a fair wage," the Sixth Ibbet said.

"You think I had it easy? I worked my tail off each time I metamorphosed a new one. I had my own superior to answer to. And now I'm destitute and dying." He raised one wrinkled hand to extend a single thin finger. "All because of you!"

Next up was a three-armed man wearing a black tunic and a big frown. Two of his arms were in slings.

---

[*] I must include one final footnote: this refers to plot points in Jane's "The Trouble with Lingloids," the manuscript I mentioned having lost.

"Boab?" I said. "My cog brother, what happened?"

He sniffled and ran his middle hand across his three snotty nostrils. "Baldwin is no bro to Boab. Your friends drugged me and stole my transporter. Look at this nasty scar they gave me! I'm deformed. All the Borj chickadees laugh at me. And I missed the big game!"

Before I could say I was sorry, a new man was walking onscreen. He was stout with green skin and feathers jutting from his forehead. He wore a purple uniform that said *Glorxo* across the front. "I'm going to help stop you fiendish thieves!"

"Who is this loser?" I asked.

"I can field this question, sir," Algorithm said. "This is Mofaso Kreetar Derm the Ninth. He was my supervisor at the Glorxo hospital station. Sir, I know that we owe you some restitution for the remaining labor on my contract."

"And that Earthian's brain worm surgery. You think running an interspecies galactic hospital is free?"

"Hey," Vivan said. "We helped you out. We found the exit out of the vlorp's mouth. I know you had ships following us."

"Helped!" the Glorxo agent squawked. His brow feathers flared open in anger. "Our station was beset by a plague of void lice after you left. They fell upon us. They destroyed everything!"

"All right, all right," I said. I readied my blaster. "We get it. Five on five for all the marbles. Can we get this fight over with?"

Ear Baldwin sat back down and steepled his fingers. His smirk had stretched past several ear growths. "As usual, you misunderstand, False Baldwin. We're not here to kill you. We're here to watch you kill yourselves."

"With a little push from us," Finger Vivian added. "Remember when you docked at the *Gaius Martianus Spacus Stationus* and made vigorous love to Vivian for a record twenty minutes?"

I glanced at Vivian. Her veins burned green. "Vaguely."

"That was me." Finger Vivian shuddered. "And while I was attempting to hold off your orgasm, my partner here planted a pair of devices on the *Star*

Rot. The first released a cloud of nanobots into your food dispensers. They fuck around with the chemicals and hormones in your brain. You may have noticed increased irritation and feelings of depression?"

I cursed. So that's why my crew had turned on each other. It wasn't that we were jealous of each other's success or that we were wasting our lives on a pointless career that would never fulfill us. No. It was all a dastardly plot by evil clones. It all made sense now.

"Of course, you'd make this overly complicated," Vivian said, rolling her eyes at her clone. "Let's hear about the second device."

"Simple. A quantum bomb that will destroy the *Star Rot* in, oh, about one hour. That is if you don't murder each other first."

"Ear Baldwin, my guy, you got any snacks on this ship?" Boab said. "Boab is hungry."

"Yes, yes," Ear Baldwin said, annoyed. "I've told you three times we have a food materializer in the—"

The feed went black.

To be continued . . .

SRC #9—Part I Analysis

A Metallic Malaise

For this *SRC* entry, Taras collaborated with the online SFF market *Eyeball Meteors* for a serialized novella feature. A new installment was to go up each Monday for five weeks. In part one, the bonds of friendship have frayed for these far-flung *Star Rot* explorers. They've faced down rival alien armies, space pirates, and interstellar leviathans. Yet the greatest foe turns out to be themselves. Is it possible the *Star Rot* crew can defeat both their rivals and their own discord? The reader is left with a tantalizing "To be continued . . ."

There is a cosmic beauty—albeit a painful one—to the final *Star Rot* tale circling back to the story that started it all. Some Rotties have speculated that the return of villains from the first story, "The Duchy of the Toe Adam," indicates Taras wanted "Memoirs of My Metallic Realms" to conclude the series. I deny this with all my strength. This universe was his baby. His pride. He did not want the *SRC* to end. I also possess information that only a Senior Lore Keeper would be privy to: Ear Baldwin and Finger Vivian were meant to be recurring villains!

In the Orb 4 meeting that preceded this story, a spirited debate took place about how to tie all the tales together.

"They feel like unrelated short stories," Merlin said. "We could rewrite them as novel chapters. Add an overarching plot."

"I can't imagine rewriting each story. We'd have to standardize POV, tense, everything," Taras said.

Jane raised her hand. "What about a recurring villain? A Big Bad who can link parts, like Thanos in the MCU or something. What would the X-Men be without Magneto? Sherlock without Moriarty? If we want to hook readers, we need a good villain."

"What about those clones from the first story," Merlin said. "We never found out what happened to them, right? They could be alive. No retconning needed."

"Hmm," Taras said. "Certainly easier than a rewrite."

It's hard not to read the real-life tensions of the Orb 4 into "Memoirs of My Metallic Realms." Just as Darya and Taras were on the rocks, Vivian and Baldwin snipe at each other like a divorced couple. This is contrasted with the loving clone versions—perhaps as the memories of happier times with Darya were "cloned" in Taras's mind?

Meanwhile both Algorithm and the Sixth Ibbet are increasingly divorced from the rest of the crew, reflecting ripples in the real world. The group's IRL resentment at Jane's lucrative "autofiction" book deal is represented by the disdain the entire crew feels for the Sixth Ibbet as she plans to quit the *Star Rot* (aka science fiction) for the Borj (a clear stand-in for the mainstream literary establishment). Algorithm retreats into their internal simulations, mirroring the way Merlin in real life was increasingly absent from Orb 4 meetings and indeed the apartment in general. They were busy with the band LAWN and fulfilling the orders for Frankenstein: The Gathering. (Merlin's game design group was already in talks with Wizards of the Coast for a crossover deck.) I saw them so rarely those days—only a door creaking here or a faucet turning on there in the middle of the night—they might as well have been a ghost.

Lore and Easter Eggs: We can assume the Nimrod Nebula is located in the Fingers. The Fingers are consistently described as "green" in comparison to the other major nebulae zones. Big Red's clouds are described as "red," "pink," "crimson," and occasionally "metallic magenta"; while the Blue Wastes are described as "blue," "navy," "ultramarine," or "cerulean." (Source:

The Star Rot Chronicles Lore Bible by Michael Lincoln.) Baldwin eats a meal of "Tacan trout fillets" (from *SRC* #2) with a side of "mobbin toes," a taste he must have acquired during his imprisonment with the Toe Adamites on the Purple After (*SRC* #1). His consumption of this dish is a nice foreshadowing of the reappearance of Ear Baldwin and Finger Vivian. And then obviously Boab (*SRC* #6), Ibbet's supervisor (*SRC* #5), and the Glorxo agent (*SRC* #3) make guest cameos.

OrbCon Commeth

While the *Star Rot* crew rallied to save the ship, the Orb 4 rallied to save their collective. Despite any internal fissures, the Orb 4 had a run of near-perfect science fiction stories and their sales to *Uncanny Fiction Objects, Unsettling Astonishments,* and *Astonishing Wonders* had combined for a healthy return: $265 dollars, or $66.25 apiece. What they hadn't yet done was jump on a lunch table in the cafeteria of science fiction and said, "We are here! We are the new kids! We are the future!" Enter OrbCon.

There are many measures of success for SFF franchises. There are Hugos and Nebulas, Arthur C. Clarkes and Locus Awards. One achievement towers over all others: the con. Cons are the heart and lungs of science fiction. The living, beating organs that pump fresh oxygen into franchises. They're our marketplaces, our forums, our citadels, and our city halls all rolled into one. Do I overstate my case? I don't think so.

How to construct a solo con as boundary pushing as *The Star Rot Chronicles* themselves? This was the dilemma. Our—dare I use the first-person plural possessive?—solution was to combine the best parts of an SFF convention with the atmosphere of a Brooklyn loft party. There would be dancing, drinks, and salted snacks, yes, as well as a reading by the Orb 4 followed by a panel discussion. Every attendee would be gifted with a Xeroxed *SRC* zine featuring a story from each of the members. Then we would dance and socialize the night away. But then you have heard, I suppose, what is said about the best-laid plans of mice and Martians . . .

I was not anticipating how much the dread would well up inside me as we reached the end. My body feels so tired. Empty. It's as if all the blood inside me has been drained and replaced with television static. I should forage upstairs for food. Many don't realize writing is a physical act. Authors are athletes of a kind. Rummaging through my memory palace to plunder the darkest and most emotional dungeon rooms . . . it takes a toll. Repast. Then press on.

While OrbCon was a source of excitement and anticipation, it also cranked my anxiety levels to eleven. One problem was my costume. We agreed to cosplay and I chose the lovable rapscallion known by the name of Aul-Wick. This idea presented challenges. To fully commit to the character, I'd need to encase my entire body in a gigantic glass orb complete with extendable robotic arms and a functioning levitation system. And that was before transforming my flesh into an alien creature with green skin, scales, and axolotl gills. I soon realized I'd have to scale down to just an inflatable plastic bumper ball and a fish costume. Even this was a problem. As my parents had cut off my allowance after the Rockets and Wands fiasco and the banks had cut off my credit cards, my budget was nonexistent. A DIY solution was needed.

After spending several hours on the r/cosplay subreddit, I decided I could make the orb using hula hoops, transparent shower curtain liners, and battery-powered Christmas lights. A liberal amount of body paint, a glue gun, and a bucket of 150mm turquoise sequins would take care of Aul-Wick's alien form.

I approached Merlin in the kitchen as they were heating tortillas for breakfast tacos. The crisp smell of burnt corn filled the room.

"Hey, how's it going?" I said with forced nonchalance. "Got a good costume planned for OrbCon?"

"Some ideas."

I boiled water for the French press while Merlin laid out their options. They were going to dress as either Algorithm or "possibly just Data, I mean we never said it had to be a *Star Rot* character. I've already got the yellow Starfleet uniform from Halloween."

I swallowed my bile and smiled. "I've got a great idea myself. It'll be a real spectacle. One that could take the party to the next level." I sighed, pressing down the plunger. "Alas, my liquid assets are a mere trickle these days."

Merlin continued cooking.

I continued sighing.

Merlin turned to me forcefully enough their earrings jangled. "Do you want some eggs, Mike? Or do you want to borrow some money? You're hovering."

Then we began the dance of acceptance. "Oh, I couldn't." "Then never mind." "But if you insist." "Definitely not insisting. I'm just making breakfast." "However, if you did insist—" "I won't." "Well, if you're not insisting yet *are* offering . . ." Reader, I walked away with an advance on café wages and a vision of Aul-Wick in my head.

In Search of Lost Good Times

I'll confess I didn't know how to process Taras's increasing depression. His statements on the rooftop disturbed me. How he felt his art and his life were meaningless. I realize I skipped past them quickly. I'm uncomfortable around excessive human emotions. I take great pride in my ability to keep my dark feelings—the self-hatred, doubt, and despair—barreled up deep inside, where they can't affect me, like nuclear waste dug deep into the earth and encased in cement. I'd also thought Taras had the perfect life. Or if not perfect, then a good life. A life of art and vision and fellowship. The kind of life that would make me feel whole. If even Taras could despair, what hope was there for the rest of us?

*
**

After another fight (over the phone) between Taras and Darya, in which I stayed curled fetal in my bedroom, hands over my ears, Taras knocked on my door. "Any interest in taking a walk? Kinda want to take my mind off things." I was happy to LARP the flaneur for my friend. We strolled through Bushwick, watching the bizarre conglomeration of Brooklyn denizens—hipsters with chunky glasses, retro punk rockers, Orthodox Jews, nerds, dweebs, jocks, businessmen, and bridge-and-tunnel invaders. It was as diverse a collection of beings this side of the Mos Eisley cantina.

We didn't talk about *Star Rot* or relationships. Instead, we spun out new ideas and new characters riffing on the other's comments. In a short stroll we'd invented five alien races and three galactic entities, including a "cosmic ouroboros that encircled space and at some point would constrict, crushing the universe out of existence." Probably none of it was usable. Still, it felt so good to create together, just as we had done as kids.

God, I missed those days of our youth. Being a kid with no cares except a few household chores. Hours spent walking our neighborhoods pontificating about our latest obsessions from Troll dolls and Warhammer figurines to Marvel trading cards and *Metroid* games. No matter what we talked about, what we truly talked about was *worlds*. We lost ourselves and then found ourselves in fictional universes. In characters. In stories. Our home lives were less than ideal. My mother an alcoholic and my father a workaholic. Taras's parents were haunted by their tragedies and spent life parked in front of the TV. Stories gave our lives meaning. The fires of narrative kept us warm in the cold Vermont winters in our little houses in the dark woods surrounded by the snow-covered trees. And isn't that what geekdom is? Isn't that why we love playing D&D and writing fics? Why we cosplay, debate head canons, and recite our favorite lines? Isn't it just a way to tell stories with our friends?

I can remember the day when Taras turned to me and said, "When I grow up, I'm going to write my own books. Make my own universe."

We must have been thirteen or so back then. Too old to waste our days inside and too young to drive. We were crouched on a rock overlooking a pond that was alive with water spiders, dragonflies, newts, and tadpoles. We'd discovered the waters in the woods between his neighborhood (North Hills) and the next (Whippoorwill) and named it Narnia. It was probably only half an acre, but for us it was a magical place. Our own mystical realm. Each day after school, we'd sneak over the fences and slip past the *No Trespassing* signs with a laugh. We owned that hidden spot. Our secret, secluded empire. The next year, whoever owned the property put up a fence guarded by large drooling dogs. We didn't risk it. But that one summer it was our sanctuary.

Gnats buzzed lazily around us. Birds chirped in the branches above. The air was cool and sweet.

"Yeah," I said. "Me too. Maybe we can cowrite the novel. Or have universe crossover!"

Taras curled the edges of his lips down in thought. "Maybe. Never say never, I guess."

"It'll be great," I said, standing up on the rock.

"Okay. Yeah. We'll do it."

He picked up a pink quartz from the ground and dusted off the dirt. There was a thick white vein through the middle that turned into a swirl, like the eye of Jupiter. Taras showed me and then stepped back. "Watch this." He hurled it into the pond, right in the center of the dancing spiders and squirming tadpoles. The splash rippled through the teeming world.

The Final Voyage, Continued

My fingers rebel as we approach these final chapters. They sense the darkness they will soon be forced to type. The duty of scholarship requires me to press them onward. And there is a final burst of light. One last official, verified, and canonical entry of *The Star Rot Chronicles* left to share with you, dear reader. "Memoirs of My Metallic Realms—Part II" picks up at heretofore unscaled heights of drama as dastardly villains have cornered our beloved and beleaguered crew, a quantum bomb threatens to destroy their steadfast ship, and danger lurks in every inch of these Metallic Realms. Enjoy.

Memoirs of My Metallic Realms—Part II

They say when death approaches, your life flashes before your eyes. That isn't quite how it went for me. My life rolled by as if in slow motion. I could see it all in painful detail. My childhood in the fern forests of Ald-Anar, riding woolly beetles beneath the swooping leaves, all alone with no other children to play with. An awkward adolescence. Years farming jelly pearls on my uncle's bog farm while staring up at the cruisers that soared overhead. I would close my eyes and try to will myself to teleport aboard and escape. Then I did, joining the Untied Fingers Authority Academy and soon dropping out. Cabin boy for a Moltanx vlorp hunting ship. Pinching my nose to collect toxic gas from the blort worms of Delta Red. Temp job as solid representative for a race of sentient gas merchants. Smuggling aboard, then stealing, the *Star Rot*. Wondrous worlds and strange creatures. Odd jobs. Dangerous jobs. Bizarre jobs. Capturing gilled birds in the mists of the Octavia Cluster. Smuggling slime whiskey past the Florgal Trade Blockade. Stowing away a dangerous rebel named Vivian from Rygol 9 for a modest fee and then eschewing the sizable UFA reward on her head because I thought, for the first time in my life, I was in love.

These images floated languidly past my mind's eye at what seemed like a snail's pace as I scoured the bridge for any sighting of the bomb that would—in a handful of minutes—incinerate me, my crew, and my ship.

*
**

Ear Baldwin and Finger Vivian's nanobots had worked wonders. Though truthfully I'm not sure we needed the help. What had been a crew with purpose and drive had deformed into a collection of not-even-friends moving through the universe only by the force of inertia.

My comm croaked. It was the Sixth Ibbet. "I think I found the bomb. It's in the middle of the holoroom."

"Can you disable it?"

"I'm trying. Each time I touch it, the bomb disappears."

"And you're in the holoroom? That's called a *hologram*, you chittering idiot," Vivian said.

I was on my hands and knees, crawling beneath the consoles. "Goddamn, how did I end up captaining this ship of fools," I said, forgetting my comm was on.

And everyone was squabbling, cursing, and insulting each other. Except for Algorithm, who was trying to interrupt—"if I may just . . . if you could all temporarily cease talking . . ."—but no one paid attention. I was on the bridge and sat down in my captain's chair for what might be the final time. Onscreen, the rival *Stellar Decay* floated silently in the void. I tried to tell myself it was a badge of honor that the only being who could kill me was a version of myself. I didn't believe it. The truth was that no one cared if I lived, not even my own doppelgänger.

Then I saw the bomb. A white sphere covered in black bumps spinning beneath Vivian's station. It was only about the size of a human head. It crackled with diabolical blue energy.

"Everyone, I found the device!" Yet my hand slid through as if it were vapor. I grabbed again. Air. "What the hell? It's not solid."

"If I could simply explain—" Algorithm was saying.

"You must have found a decoy. I've got the bomb right here in my chambers," Vivian said.

"No, it's here!" the Sixth Ibbet said. "It's right in front of me."

A cacophony overwhelmed the comms as if every creature in the universe screamed at once. I grabbed my ears. The screeching came in waves. Then mercifully, silence.

"I dislike doing that." It was Algorithm. "As time is of the essence, given that we only have seven minutes and forty-two seconds remaining, I feel it is imperative that you all listen. You have *all* found the bomb. This is a Buzzatite Class Z quantum bomb. I'm looking at it myself in the mess hall. Well, one location of it."

"Can you elaborate?" I said.

"The physics are theoretical and will take time to explain. According to Buzzati's nontemporal polarity thesis, matter can be divided into—"

"Quickly, I meant."

"This is reductive, but suffice to say the bomb exists in five locations at once. The only way to defuse it is if we all hit the off button synchronously."

So, this was Ear Baldwin's plan. We could survive, but only with teamwork. He wasn't only going to kill us. He was going to prove we didn't deserve to live. Because we weren't a team. A clever plan. Yet despite all our bickering, I knew his plan would fail. Our crew might hate each other. We may have stabbed each other in the back more times than anyone could count. Yet we were a family. We had grown together and worked together, creating adventures as a collective. Together, we'd survive.

Algorithm began the countdown. I stretched my hand out in anticipation. We sounded off our locations. I was on the bridge, Algorithm was in the mess hall, Vivian was in her chambers, and the Sixth Ibbet was in the holoroom. That was four.

We needed five.

"Aul-Wick, have you found the last location of the quantum bomb?"

No response.

I asked the computer to scan. *Aul-Wick's life signatures were last detected on the ship in the hangar. His escape pod has left the ship.*

"Aul-Wick isn't here!" I shouted. "He must have defected to the *Stellar Decay*. That fish-faced traitor!"

"I knew he'd screw us all eventually," Vivian said.

I shouted for some time, releasing all my rage and sorrow onto Aul-Wick. He didn't deserve all of it. Then again, he did deserve a hell of a lot of it.

There was silence before his response. "If you were trying to coax me back you miscalculated on your tactics."

The bomb began to glow, signaling countdown. I was desperate. I told him to return. Surely after all we'd put up with over the years, he could help save our lives! Algorithm cut me off. "He is too distant from the ship to return in time. We are on our own."

"Okay, okay, okay," I said, trying to assure myself. "How do we do this without him, Al?"

Algorithm was silent for a half a second, which was half a second longer than they usually took to respond. "Simple," Algorithm said. "We do not."

I heard the explosion before I felt it. It was terrible. A cacophony of ripping metal and expanding fire. The final relay from the ship's transmitter before the silence of space took over. The comms went dead. My ship was destroyed.

I didn't turn around to see the *Star Rot*. Or the absence of it. I couldn't bear it. It had been my home for many years. My charge. But I felt the destruction. The force of the explosion sent me spinning through the void. Lumpen asteroids and distant dots of light spun around me.

Why hadn't I grabbed Vivian's hand when we donned our escape suits? If we were going to die in the cold emptiness, at least we could have done it together. She had been right in front of me at the escape hatch. She looked back. Her mood-displaying veins were hidden in her space suit. She was, as always, a mystery to me.

This was my end. A sad, lonely, pointless man floating all alone in a cold universe, signifying nothing.

I closed my eyes.

Blackness.

A hiss.

Feedback.

Sudden noise.

"Good fucking riddance."

It was Aul-Wick! "Aul-Wick? You asshole. Are you talking through me telepathically?"

"As if I'd even dream of entering your rotten skull after what you said."

Everyone was bickering again. I looked around me but couldn't make out the Sixth Ibbet, Aul-Wick, or anyone else. Only blackness and distant asteroids floating in the void like malformed clouds, and the *Stellar Decay* hovering between them as if mocking our despair.

"Maybe we could all be quiet? Some peace in these final moments would be nice," the Sixth Ibbet said.

"Actually, these suits will keep your bodies alive for some time," Algorithm said. "And the subspace comms can carry a full light-year. So even though we are all hurtling in different directions, we should be able to talk indefinitely until the air supply empties."

Vivian moaned. "I don't want to listen to you buffoons yammer on until I die."

"Well, who wants to listen to *you*?"

I'd had enough. Enough of the fighting, and enough of the struggle. Ear Baldwin and Finger Vivian had won. My crew had been broken.

I turned my comm off.

As I spun through the silent void toward my inevitable doom, I tried to sleep.

Still to be continued . . .

SRC #9—Part II Analysis

The Final Countdown

Can you fit an entire universe, with all its wonders and monstrosities, all its chaos and order, into a single solitary paragraph? Such a feat would seem to defy the laws of physics. And yet the opening of "Memoirs of My Metallic Realms—Part II" exists! Although Taras tended to eschew flashbacks, he opens part II of his epic serialized novella with a summary of Baldwin's life. From woolly beetles to sentient gas merchants, there are enough "world seeds" in these handful of sentences to bloom into an entire ecosystem of novels.

Still, it is a grim opening. Darkness has fallen on the Metallic Realms. The *Star Rot* crew faces the long night of the soul. Our hero, the intrepid Captain Baldwin, lays open his life for the reader as if he were a frog on the dissection table. He's baring his naked organs and saying, "See me. Examine my joys and my sorrows. Acknowledge my pain and my dreams." Surely, I'm not the only reader who fails to escape the first page with dry eyes.

We begin with a (summarized) life yet end with (imminent) death. The crew is scattered into space, like passengers fleeing a sinking ship in the middle of the ocean during a once-in-a-generation storm. Their life vests are space suits. Ear Baldwin's ship circles like a ferocious sea serpent. Does literature get bleaker than this? If the cliff-hanger at the end of part I made you grip the edge of your seat, hopefully you instituted a regimen of hand muscle exercises in preparation for the audacity of part II.

*
**

The setting: a spacious three-bedroom warehouse conversion loft in Bush-wick, Brooklyn, United States of America, Earth. Five friends—well "friends" might not be the right word at that point. Let us say colleagues. Five col-leagues were gathered around a communal table, looking to break bread be-fore the masses arrived. We hydrated with LaCroixs in preparation of the imminent ethanol bombardment of our livers. Around us, the apartment had been transformed into an alien galaxy. Walls were decorated with imposing images of strange aliens, solar system mobiles hung from the ceiling, and R2D2-patterned bowls of snacks were distributed throughout the apartment at strategic intervals. Everything was finished except our costumes, which we would don after dinner.

Taras suggested Mexican, Jane wanted ramen, Darya was "happy with any gluten-free options," and Merlin wanted "something healthy, please. Someplace with greens." The debate was long, arduous, and surprisingly per-sonal. We settled on pizza. When the pies arrived, Taras popped a bottle of prosecco and we raised our (plastic) glasses. "To literature! To the future! To the Metallic Realms!"

Several slices in, the first of the night's unforeseen events occurred. S.O.S. Merlin stood. They asked us all to raise our cups. They were wearing a rainbow-striped polo and a necklace of the solar system with the sun in the scoop of the neck, but their adornments couldn't hide the sadness on their face. Merlin pushed their hair behind an ear. They held their glass aloft.

"I can't begin to describe how meaningful it's been creating stories and adventures with you all. Growing up in the Georgia suburbs, I never thought I'd find people like me." They looked around the table at us. "Well, maybe not people *like* me but people who liked me. Liked the real me. Despite our drama—and what's life without a little drama?—I feel like the *Star Rot* has be-come a little home away from home. A place where I visit friends and am re-minded of how invigorating creating stories can be. It doesn't matter if no one reads us. We got to read each other. You've all made me feel a tad less alone."

"To Merlin!" Jane said.

"That wasn't the end of the speech." Merlin took a tissue from the box. I thought they were tearing up, but it was merely a sniffle. "I'll just come out and say it. I'm moving out of the city at the end of next month. It all happened suddenly. I'm excited! I'll come back of course, though maybe not for a while. I wanted to say how much I'll miss you all."

"What? Why?" Darya said.

I too was blindsided. I felt my chest compressing, as if my rib cage was trapped in a *Death Star*'s trash compactor between my rent on one side and compounding credit card debt on the other. "You're leaving the apartment? You never told me this."

"I sent you multiple emails," they said. (Because of the mounting piles of emails from my credit card companies, I hadn't opened my Gmail in weeks.) "Anyway, this has nothing to do with any of you, of course. I've realized the city isn't for me. There's just too much here. Too much noise. Too much competition. This much stress isn't good for me. I've had to literally double my skin care routine."

"Is this about Jane's novel?" Darya said.

"What the fuck, Darya?" Jane said.

"Sorry, just a joke. Bad joke."

"No, no," Merlin said. "It's the whole NYC vibe. Everyone's so competitive. Always running around and hustling. It's too intense. It gnaws on my soul. I realized I need to live in the country. I mean, if we're destroying the whole climate I want to at least spend my time around nature. Smell trees. See flowers. Touch grass on a daily basis. Plus, our board game company is going full remote and that's what I'm focusing on now anyway. We're launching Frankenstein: The Gathering expansion packs and even talking about a Nintendo Switch version with some developers."

"Wow, that's awesome," Taras said.

Merlin showed us a picture on their cell phone of a green house overlooking a rocky beach and foam-tipped waves. It could have been a postcard. "Sam's uncle died, and he left her this cabin in Maine. It has a woodshop attached. I'm just going to go build boats for a while. Have a simpler life by the sea."

"Boats?" I yelped. "And who is Sam?"

"She's my partner. Mike, you've met her."

"Will you give me the required ninety-day notice?"

"I think thirty is standard."

Taras said something about how easy it would be for me to find a new roommate—"it's a great location, elevated subway aside"—while the others congratulated Merlin and discussed woodworking tools. I was bewildered. How could anyone abandon the Orb 4 as it was taking off? How could wooden canoes compare to interstellar starships?

Only Darya wondered aloud about replacing Merlin in the collective. "My buddy Ramon went to Clarion West and writes decolonial Lovecraft-minus-the-racism stuff. He'd be good."

"Maybe someone already familiar with inner workings of the complex Metallic Realms universe would be better," I managed to say.

"We'll discuss all that later. Let's focus on getting through this party." Taras stood up and shook Merlin's hand. "Congrats. I know we've had our tiffs, but it's been special knowing you, working with you. I'm sad, and mostly jealous. This whole rat race of a city is getting to me too. Send us pics, okay?"

Before anyone could object further, the doorbell rang. OrbCon had arrived.

The Joys of OrbCon

It was time to transform into Aul-Wick. Unfortunately, I'd had to make last-minute costume adjustments. It had taken me hours of YouTube tutorials and several rolls of duct tape to get the hula hoop and shower liner orb together. Then when I tried it on the morning of OrbCon I found I could not actually leave my room. The hula hoops were too large for the doorframe. I pushed, trying to squeeze through, yet only achieved this feat at the expense of the costume's structural integrity. It collapsed. I looked more like a trash ghost than an intrepid space explorer.

Luckily, I was able to find an astronaut helmet in CVS's aisle of discounted Halloween leftovers. I would have to simply make my head Aul-Wick instead of my whole body. I painted my face green and drew on scales. I put on a headband of reindeer antlers that I'd cut off, spray-painted red, and reglued lower down the band for my external axolotl-like gills. Then I donned my helmet. In the reflection of my computer screen, I grinned. Yes, I'd smudged my glasses with green paint and the fumes of the spray paint were making me dizzy. But I was transformed. I *was* Aul-Wick. For the coup de grâce, I wrapped the battery-powered Christmas lights around my neck and floated into OrbCon with stardust in my veins.

I soon found I was the only one who faithfully followed the cosplaying edict other than Darya, whose Vivian regalia included bright blue veins painted with lipstick and an old Nintendo Power Glove for the cybernetic hand. Merlin wore their yellow Data uniform and Jane merely sported mirror shades and a *Neuromancer* T-shirt. Taras, in plain clothes, said, "I'll put my costume on before we start the reading."

Guests trickled in. They bore the usual tributes of their species (Brooklyn millennials on the wrong side of thirty): over-hopped beer, skin-contact wine, and bags of kettle chips. Each time the doorbell rang, a shiver ran through me. Would it be Katie? We manned our stations. Jane started a playlist, Darya and Taras poured drinks, Merlin handed out copies of *Future Attack, Today!—A* Star Rot Chronicles *Zine,* and I had the prestigious job of backup. My instructions from Taras: "You can watch from afar and see if anyone needs anything." I found a spot with a good vantage and surveyed the scene.

After about an hour of mingling—in which I had to provide several under-costumed guests with novelty Martian antennae—Taras put on his "space wizard" outfit (neon blue beard, broomstick with an alien puppet over the tip, and a black cape with glue-gunned planets and stars) and welcomed the crowed to "an evening in a realm across the reaches of space and time."

Darya read first, stepping on a milk crate as an impromptu stage. "Thanks for coming out," she said, adjusting the microphone.

Tipsy, I tiptoed to the corner with the fern pots. I leaned my helmeted head against the bookcase and closed my eyes. (The blinking Christmas lights around my neck were giving me a headache.) *"Acting Captain Vivian speaking. Baldwin is still incapacitated, yellowing, and I fear close to death."* I let the words wash over me. As they did, my problems dematerialized. The credit card debt. My now unstable roommate situation. My anger. All was incinerated in the fires of the *Star Rot*'s mag-impulse thrusters. I was transported. I was not in a somewhat squalid three-bedroom loft in Bushwick, Brooklyn, with no job prospects or romantic partners. No. I was zipping past planets in a distant galaxy with a crew of misfits by my side and dastardly villains hot on our tail.

Time passed in a blissful blur.

Each of the Orb 4 read in turn. Taras brought up the rear, reading parts I and II of "Memoirs of My Metallic Realms," catching the crowd up to the exact point you are at now, dear reader.

At the end of the reading, I thought the AC unit was leaking on me. Impossible with my costume's helmet. It was my own tears staining my cheeks. Bravo, Orb 4, bravo. I cheered. Loudly, from the great well of my soul.

"Um, thank you, Mike," Taras said from the makeshift stage. "Mike is dressed as, I think, Aul-Wick, if you were wondering. The fish pilot character."

I opened my eyes. Everyone was looking at me. My raucous applause had been noticed—and, I believe, appreciated—by all.

A Quick Bit of Lore and Easter Eggs then Back to the Party

Gah!

In my haste to compose these remarks I seem to have forgotten the Lore and Easter Eggs section for part II. Let's see. I've discussed the opening paragraph with its wonderful worldbuilding details. You have Ear Baldwin and Finger Vivian from *SRC* #1. Many of the ship's locations where previous adventures took place recur. Hmm. A text I just received reminds me that my deadline is imminent. I have only a few hours left. And still the afterword to pen. Reader, I hope you'll forgive any typos or grammatical missteps. I will run a perfunctory Microsoft Word spell and grammar check yet I'm afraid I've neither the time nor the budget for professional proofreaders. Let's call this sufficient for Lore and Easter Eggs and return to the drama of OrbCon, where—I say with great sorrow—the night was about to take a turn darker than any solar eclipse.

The Sorrows of OrbCon

OrbCon was heading toward success. I could tell because of my knowledge of the physics of parties. The attendees were coalescing into small groups, like gravity grouping matter into planets after the Big Bang. Once the groups got dense enough, dancing would begin.

I was feeling woozy; the spray-paint fumes were trapped in my helmet. But it was a pleasant wooziness. My head bobbed peacefully in a chemical sea. While I wouldn't self-classify as a "lightweight," I'm easily inebriated. By the time the readings ended, I was swaying in place and finding my eyes fixated on a fetching redhead in a *Buffy* shirt and blue Doc Martens. She was inspecting my parrot.

I slinked over.

"I see you've met Arthur C. Caique," I said, giggling a little. "You might know him from his classic novels *Rendezvous with Raven* and *2001: A Space Migration.*"

The woman shook her head. Perhaps I hadn't spoken loud enough under my helmet. "It's awful. Just awful."

I knew some illiterates of my generation didn't appreciate the noble wit of puns, but I assumed she was unfamiliar with the iconic SF writer and so began elucidating his oeuvre.

"What?" She made a strange face. "No, I mean this poor bird. It's too much noise and stimulation here. Look at how he's shaking. He's terrified."

As far as I could tell, Arthur was shaking no more than normal. He pecked at the bars with his usual vigor. "Their natural habitat is a jungle. Hardly a silent place," I pointed out.

Around us, the party came alive. Jane stood in front of the turntables by the bookshelves, bobbing along with over-the-ear headphones over just one ear. The turntables were not actually plugged in—Jane was using the auxiliary cable to play a Spotify list off her cell phone—but their presence provided a certain worldbuilding verisimilitude to the proceedings.

"Oh my god!" The woman leaned close to look at Arthur's dish. "Did someone feed this poor bird Chex Mix? Some people shouldn't be allowed to own pets."

Before I could form a rebuttal, a beefy man with buzzed hair and a ball cap strolled over. He was gigantic. Like some freak show from the football field, the kind that picked on Taras and me mercilessly in high school.

"You were right, Nora. This sci-fi party is fun," the roided-up jock said, tossing a sausage arm around the woman's delicate shoulder.

I scoffed. "*You're* a science fiction fan?"

"Can't you see the hat?" he said nonsensically.

He turned his back to me as someone approached. I couldn't see around his beefcake back, but I heard the voice. It was Jane, having abandoned her DJ post.

"Hey, Jane. Cool party. But what's with the bird?" the jock managed to monosyllabically eke out.

"Oh, one of the guys who lives here owns it. I'll ask him to put the cage in his bedroom. Ooh, I like your hat. Niners. Sisko team on *Deep Space Nine,* right?"

"Custom-made for the party. You said it was a Star Trek fest, right?"

I was starting to be in a foul mood, as if the nanobots that had infected the *Star Rot* crew had also found their way to me. I wormed my way back into the crowd.

Heading toward the bathroom—I'd held the "seal" as long as possible—I was accosted by Darya holding out a swollen plastic bag. "Can you take the recycling down? We're burning through the booze. Good party though, right?"

"So far, a stellar evening," I said while clamping my pelvic floor muscles. I was definitely feeling sick from the spray-paint fumes.

"Your costume is great. You do look like a weird fish monster." Darya looked around with a strange smile. She sighed. "The party is a nice send-off to this place."

"I'm going to miss Merlin dearly."

"Not just Merlin." She smiled at my puzzled face. "Oh. I thought."

"Thought what?"

"That Taras would have talked to you."

"About what, pray tell?"

My bladder burned.

"We're moving in together. Next month. He's finally committing." She put a hand on my shoulder. "You've been a good friend letting us have meetings here. We'll probably move them to our place. That way, you won't be bothered and can have your apartment all to yourself."

It was as if I'd been trapped in a force field. I couldn't move, couldn't even think. Then everything was moving too fast. A comet of panic crashed right into the center of my chest.

I tried to slow my breath. Nothing was lost yet. I just needed to talk to Taras.

"Even after what he did?" I croaked.

"After what now, Mike?"

In my mind, I saw a knife plunge smoothly into Darya's chest.

"After he slept with that woman from Tinder, when you were first dating. Angelica, I believe was the name? I remember their fornication was quite boisterous. She still texts sometimes." As Darya's cheeks flushed red, I managed a shrug. "Ah. I thought you knew."

Why I Curse My Damned, Traitorous Soul

I don't know what came over me in that moment. I'm sorry, Taras. I was weak. Spineless. Shivering and afraid. If I could reach back through time,

I would grab my own traitorous tongue, slice it off, and chuck it into our apartment's janky garbage disposal.

The crowd had been pulled by the gravity of intoxication into the center of the apartment. The dancing began. Merlin flipped out the lights and Jane began blasting mid-'90s hip-hop. Meanwhile I orbited the dark party, searching with increasing desperation for Taras.

"Excuse me," I shouted, bumping between revelers as I rushed out of the bathroom. People kept smacking into my costume helmet orb. Sweat was pooling around my neck. I was on the verge of retching. "Pardon moi. Scusi. Entschuldigung!"

I caught sight of Taras's head bobbing above the crowd. As I pushed forward, Darya grabbed his arm and pulled him into his bedroom. I walked dejected back into the bathroom and flung off my helmet and Christmas lights. The tiled room was spinning. I vomited twice. Once dry and once wet.

I threw the antler gills in the trash and scrubbed my makeup. It was hard to remove. I looked, now, like a sloppy zombie. That would have to do.

Back in the party, I drank a bourbon and seltzer hoping to dilute the chemical fumes I'd inhaled. Beside me stood a thin man with a herringbone blazer over a *Paris Review* T-shirt. He was adjusting his clear plastic glasses in front of my *The Sci-Fi-mpsons* poster that I'd purchased from Etsy, which amusingly rendered hundreds of SFF characters in the style of *The Simpsons*.

"Amazing."

"It's an original," I said, sipping my cocktail from my red plastic cup. I was happy to be talking, finally, to a true SF fan. I pointed at the corner where the inscribed "158/500" signaled its rarity.

The man snapped a phone pic. "Just all of it. The mobiles. The costumes. Did you see that guy dressed as a goldfish robot? Jane is *so* weird."

The blood in my veins turned to ice water. Was Jane taking credit for my interior decoration? We'd need to have a frank discussion about attribution at the next Orb 4 meeting. If there ever was another meeting.

"You know Jane?"

"Yeah, she's in my creative writing program. Writes these hilarious satires about a group of loser writers who meet in this dirty apartment. A kind of comic Bildungsroman-in-stories. Have you read her work?"

"Losers?"

"There's this one character called Micah something. Micah Clinton! That's it. He's out of a David Sedaris piece. There's a whole chapter of the novel where he digs around in garbage cans to find rough drafts of someone else's stories."

(At the time, I'd not read Jane's traitorous volume of smears and slanders, so was mostly confused. I have previously mentioned basing my memory palace on *Castlevania: Symphony of the Night*. This may have been more appropriate than I'd initially understood. See, a unique element of that entry is midway through the game—just when you think you've won—Dracula's castle flips upside down! Everything inverts. As you retrace your steps, you walk on ceilings and leap toward the floors. In the same way, so many of my memories seem backward to me as I revisit them. Where I thought I was in the right, I was in the wrong. Where I thought I was the hero, I fear I may have been the fool.)

"Who's your favorite science fiction novelist?" I said to change the subject.

"Ah, well I don't read genre novels per se. My own work interrogates science fiction tropes and conventions for subversion. We live in the age of Marvel movies and *Game of Thrones* after all. Science fiction is the vox populi. I want to use this language of the masses and estrange it for radical purposes. I think the Marxist novel is the future of fiction."

I snorted. This man's arrogance was surpassed only by his ignorance. "That's all fantasy."

"Erm?"

"Shows about dragons and movies where people get superpowers from spiders. That's fantasy. Mystical woo-woo nonsense like dragon eggs and magic prophecy is fantasy. That has nothing to do with science fiction like *The Star Rot Chronicles*. You have your taxonomical categories all confused."

"Star what?" He pulled an IPA out of the bucket beside the potted fern. The man's elbow pushed some of the leaves aside as he reached in. I noticed that my microphone was missing. I was too caught up in the moment to register what that meant.

"*The Star Rot Chronicles*!" I shouted. "That's what the party is for. Weren't you at the reading? It's a science fiction series of interlinked space opera tales with elements of cyberpunk and cosmic horror."

"Ah. Right."

The man had pulled out a "doobie" and lit it with a black Bic lighter. He silently passed me the burning stick.

Reader, I inhaled. As my nerves calmed, I looked for Taras.

The snob gestured to Darya, who had taken over the DJ turntables. "You know, that woman was telling me about the differences between 'second world fantasy' and 'portable fantasy' earlier. Nerds do love their labels."

"Portal fantasy," I said, my voice as cold as an iceberg.

The man adjusted his glasses again. Apparently, lit snobs don't know how to properly fit nose pads.

"Ha. Yeah, that's it. *Portal* fantasy. I enjoy a dip in the pulp waters myself, but imagine getting worked up about that?"

I placed my drink gently on the speaker. I had to stand up not only for myself but the Orb 4. I had to stand up for geekdom.

"Yes, imagine," I began. "Imagine knowing the difference between an implausible fantasy element like portals and well-established scientific realities like wormholes. Imagine caring about entire universes from the visionary minds of the world's best authors. Oh, I can imagine! I can imagine very well indeed!" My head felt like a balloon that was floating away from my body. Was this what people meant by "getting high"? "What I can't imagine is reading nothing but sad characters in Brooklyn whining about bad sex and the lingering effects of their parents' affairs. What I'm incapable of imagining is reading the brain-dead musings of mundane fiction mediocrities who string together plotless meanderings and quotes from their Twitter accounts along-side copy and pastes from BrainyQuote.com to seem smart and submit it to their MFA workshop. If that was me, I'd take an electric drill and ram it right into my skull since all my sense of wonder and imagination would already have been drained away."

I crossed my arms in triumph.

The man was silent.

Suddenly, I was overcome with a terrible thirst. I downed the remains of my cocktail in one swallow.

"Wow," the man said. He adjusted his glasses and reached into his back pocket to retrieve a small Moleskine notebook. "Can you repeat that? About brain-dead musings and electric drills. I want to write it down. Wild material!"

This was the problem with MFA elitists. Everything was material to them, but nothing was *material*. Nothing was matter and so nothing mattered. They built gaseous clouds of lyrical nonsense while we, the Orb 4, built entire worlds. As I stormed off, I saw Katie walk through the door.

I froze beside the bookshelf. She looked radiant. Also a little damp. (It had started drizzling.) Her eyes caught mine. I waved. She waved back. Short and quick. I waved a second time. She smiled and lifted a six-pack of cider with a shrug.

What I Can Say About the Rooftop

In the days I've spent typing in this moldy basement, I've had occasion to revisit my favorite *Star Rot* tales. Countless moments have stuck with me. The mawbear attack outside the Toe Adam's Duchy. The daring flight from the vlorp's belly. The ominous arrival of the Borj cubicle ship. But the moment I've replayed the most is the ending of "Memoirs of My Metallic Realms—Part II" when Baldwin is floating in space, alone and full of regrets.

I'm not a religious man. Yet if Hell does exist, it must be something like this. Endless time to relive your mistakes and no chance of redemption. By this theology, I suppose you could say I've been in hell these past few days as

I've been completing this volume. Yes, I regret so much about the night of OrbCon. I regret the speed of my inebriation and intoxication. I regret telling Darya about Taras's personal liaisons. I regret what happened with Katie. And above all I regret what would happen on the rooftop.

The day runs short. The sun has fled behind the pines. Yet I can't allow myself to sleep. I must finish in the next few hours. Once I do, the true version of these events will be the definitive one. The canon. Whatever spurious accounts anyone else might compose in the future will be irrelevant. As Aul-Wick might say, "Onward!"

My reunion with Katie was like a lollipop you can't help but crunch in your jaws: as sweet as it was brief. She told me that she appreciated the "quite detailed and discursive" email that I'd sent. She'd been well, had even gotten a promotion at work, and was looking at cats to adopt. I nodded in both happiness and inebriation. Our hands brushed tantalizingly as I took her hard ciders and led her to the fridge. I told her about my own life. My work on the Crystal Cosmos manuscript, my new job at the café, my elevation to Senior Lore Keeper of the Orb 4. As I related the failures of my original Aul-Wick costume, she said, "I wondered why you had your face painted as Franken-stein!" while brushing my flecked cheek and, I swear, a jolt of electricity ran from my toes to my ears.

Then I saw Taras bolt out of his room and head to the roof. Darya followed, shouting. She stopped by the door, shook her head, and went to the bar table.

Katie was asking if I wanted to get a drink. "I could use a strong one."

"Actually, if you'll excuse me for just a minute."

"What?" Katie's smile disintegrated. "I just got here."

"I have a pressing issue. It won't take but a second."

"Is it your bladder? I told you my uncle is a urologist. He'll give you a discount."

"No, it's . . . Well. My friend. I just saw him. We have pressing matters to discuss."

"That was Taras, right?" She looked at the door he'd fled through. She shook her head in confusion. "You see him literally every day. *Literally*. You haven't seen me in weeks."

"It will only take a minute."

She lifted her arms as if to shove me, then dropped them. It looked as if she was clenching invisible hearts in her hands. "You know what? Go. Just go. Take as long as you want."

"Thank you!"

I ran.

As I strode upstairs, I saw Katie slipping on her denim jacket. She looked at me. Her eyes seemed like cold little meteorites hurtling toward me. Then she turned and walked out the door.

Up on the roof, the rain was clearing. Drops fell only intermittently. It was night but our view was illuminated by the countless apartment lights and NYPD flood lamps. Thanks to the rain, the partygoers had gone inside and there was only Taras, my dear Taras, smoking a joint by the edge overlooking the subway tracks.

"Hey, T."

"Hey, Mike."

How many times had we said "hey" to each other over the years? As children, teens, young adults, and writing collaborators. I thought we'd be saying "hey" until we were withered and gray.

Down on the street, two women tried to untangle the leashes of their barking French bulldogs by the crosswalk. I shivered coatless in the damp air.

"Are you leaving? Right after Merlin?"

He turned to me. His eyes were red and watery. "You mean the apartment? Maybe. I don't know now. I thought so. Now I think Darya and I are back to breaking up."

"I'm sorry. About Darya."

"C'est la fucking fucked-up vie."

The party was raucous beneath us. A half-dozen people were on the fire escape a floor below, smoking cigarettes and singing along with a pop song about love and loss.

"So. You're not moving out?"

"I don't know. Probably will soon. I mean, we're getting old, Mike. I can't live with roommates anymore."

"Not even old friends? Oldest friends?"

He shook his head. His face was washed in orange light as he sucked on the joint. Before us, the Brooklyn gloom was interrupted by rectangles of light.

I picked at my remaining face paint, peeling it with my fingernail.

"What happened to your Aul-Wick helmet?"

"I was feeling sick. Paint fumes."

"Yeah. I hear you. I ditched the space wizard garb." Taras was drunk and slurring his words a bit. "I had a video call with my parents today. I think my father has like three months left, man. Maybe three days for all I know. He was a corpse. It's so surreal to see that. My father is so full of vitality in my mind, even now. To see him a shriveled skeleton. A walking corpse."

"I'm so sorry, man."

"It's okay." He looked down at the tar roof. "I mean not okay. Not okay at all. But what can you do? It happens to all of us sooner or later."

"It's bullshit."

"Yeah. It all is." He swayed in place. "You ever feel stuck in neutral? Like the other gears don't even work? I don't even know where it goes from here."

"Don't let publishing get you down. You're a great writer. I can say that with authority. You'll find an agent. The fools will curse themselves for passing over you."

"Not just publishing. All of it. My student loans. Our evil government. The just nonstop horror hose of the daily news. Even our pushback feels futile. We join the protests and post online, but nothing changes." He pressed the bridge of his nose beside his watery eyes. "It's not even that, really. I feel like I'm going through the motions of life. Or like I'm watching myself from some distance and piloting myself like a character in a video game that I have no fun playing. And I need the distance. Because on the inside, it's all black, sloshing waters. Every inch." He looked out at the thin, dark clouds. He scratched his neck. "Ah fuck, I don't know what I'm talking about."

I heard a distant rumble. The elevated subway train was approaching, moving through the city like a colossal robot centipede. Taras bent down and picked up the bottle of bourbon he'd brought to the roof. He was unsteady and I reached out to buttress him. He straightened and took a big swig, then spat at the train as it sped by.

"Wow, I almost hit it. The tracks aren't that far here. Almost feels like you could reach out and slap the train." He turned and smiled. It looked sketchy and scrawled on. "I'm working on a new project. Did I tell you about that? A fantasy novel. I'm going to move away from science fiction for a while. Who knows, maybe I'll have better luck elsewhere. The novel's about a world covered in black, black smoke. Dragons have burned the land. Burned the buildings, the castles, the rivers, and the forests. No one can see more than a few feet in front of them. They keep looking for a hero, someone with a sword made of burning light that will part the smoke."

"Who's the hero?"

He grimaced. "No one. There's no hero. That's the point. No one ever comes. Nothing is saved. The smoke endures."

I took the bourbon and sipped.

"Sounds good. Maybe hard to sell."

"Yeah. Well. I've been writing for a decade now and have published a couple of stories no one reads and that's it. I made a little spreadsheet this year. Tracked everything. My income from fiction writing over a decade has been exactly eight dollars short of half of one month's rent."

I thought about elucidating the ins and outs of publishing that I'd learned in my time at Rockets and Wands, but decided it wasn't the right moment.

"What about the Orb 4? The Metallic Realms?"

"I think that's done, man. It wasn't going anywhere."

"That's not true," I said, almost shouted. "It's a phenomenal work. It's complex, thematically rich, filled with unique concepts. Have you seen the *Lore Bible* I've been working on? I'm sure I added you to the Google Drive folder."

"Mike," he said. He stretched out a hand toward my shoulder but couldn't quite reach. It fell to his side. "I think you just need to find your own thing."

More silence. More words unsaid. More thoughts flying around our chests that neither of us had the courage to let free.

Taras squinted at me. He smiled sadly. "You know, I found a microphone. In the fern pot. Not going to say anything to the others. I'm just saying." He looked away. "Maybe it's best if I move out. Living together might not be healthy for either of us."

I needed to explain, to tell Taras how it was just for accurate transcriptions, which was essential for the *Lore Bible,* however, at that exact moment the entire scene shifted. We were interrupted by a blaring Ford Taurus alarm. Except it wasn't an alarm, not exactly. Across the gap between where we stood and the subway line, a small green-and-yellow creature flapped its wings in terror. It was Arthur.

Taras and I rushed to the edge.

"Shit!" I said. "Arthur, what are you doing?"

"How did he get there? Won't he get electrocuted? Isn't that a thing with subway tracks?"

Arthur was sort of half hopping, half flying around the track. He kept squawking.

"I think he's past due for wing clippings. I need to check my calendar."

"He's terrified. Look at him. He's utterly terrified."

I was getting terrified myself. Although I don't know how much was my fear for Arthur and how much was my fear of losing it all. Taras. The Orb 4. My apartment. Everything.

(I must stress here that we were both under the influence of substances that should frankly be illegal for anyone to consume during times of interpersonal drama and housing insecurity.)

We called out to Arthur and imitated his squawks. Arthur hopped along the tracks, oblivious.

Taras put a foot on the one-foot-tall brick wall that constituted the only barrier. I noticed some of the bricks wobble. "I bet I could jump."

"Don't," I tried to say, but the words stuck in my throat.

"I bet I could do it. I mean I did track and field in high school. Remember, my mom said I had to join a sports team to get a driver's license? Long jump was my thing."

"You quit after two months."

"I got the license though. Yeah. I can make this jump. Maybe this is one thing I can save." He looked back at me. The wind whipped his shaggy hair. "Probably not though."

I stepped back from the ledge. My shoes splashed in a puddle, soaking me to the sock. Taras's back was to me now. He whistled and called out Arthur's name. The bricks he stood on were glazed with raindrops. My heart pounded at warp speed. We were alone. No one would have seen me do anything. I took a step forward. When I looked up, Taras was a black silhouette against the glittering evening sky.

Why I Can't Remember More

There are places that even the boldest adventurer cannot go. For me, that's my memories of what happened next. It's a blank pit in my mind. A black hole. If I try to probe it, I fear I will be sucked in and crushed.

God, even typing this is making me tear up.

What madness governs the galaxy? How can so much depend upon a split-second decision? It could have happened to anyone. And no one could have stopped it. Well, I could have, technically, since I was within arm's length of Taras. I could have reached out and pushed him or pulled him to safety. But how could I have known? He seemed like he was coming back down.

He slipped.

He fell.

That is all there is to say. Any reader who demands more, who needs blood splattered on their face just to feel alive, will have to find the gory details elsewhere. For shame. I am not here to wallow in his tragedy but to eulogize a great man.

Goddamnit, Taras. How could you leave me at this of all points? We were supposed to create worlds together forever.

I must straighten myself up. I've rubbed my eyes so hard they are red and nearly raw, and I'm finding it hard to see the screen. I was speaking of Taras. My friend. One of science fiction's great storytellers. And how his own tale came to an end.

Would you believe me if I said he died doing what he loved? Leaping boldly into the unknown?

The succeeding minutes are an indecipherable dark smear across my mind. I have only flashes. Running back inside. Navigating swarms of bodies. A second staircase. Shouts of "No!" coming from my own mouth. I next became aware of myself falling beside Taras's broken body on the sidewalk. The noise of the party washed over us like a wave. I looked back up to see the aghast faces on the fire escape.

"Oh my god!"

"Call 911! Someone call 911!"

"Why can't you call?"

"My battery is dead."

"How is your battery *always* dead?"

Taras coughed wetly. He was alive then. Alive! His face was streaked with blood and limbs were bent in all the wrong directions. But he was still alive.

I cradled his head in my lap.

"Taras, I'm here. Stay with me."

I felt like a ghost. Like I had no body, no mind, only eyes that were forced to witness.

Taras said something. Blood bubbled around his lips. It sounded like "Mike."

"It's me," I said. I must have been crying by this point. "Your old and steady friend. I'm here."

Taras groaned. His head lolled to the side, then back toward me.

Everything around us was wet and dark and loud. In the distance, an ambulance screamed.

His mouth twitched. I leaned down to hear.

"You," Taras said. He closed his eyes. Opened them again. The blood mingled with raindrops, forming pink tears that ran down his cheeks. "You." His voice was a mere whisper. It was hard to make out, even when I pressed my ear into his tender lips. Although I can't say with 100 percent certainty, it sounded to me like, possibly, "You were my Aul-Wick."

And that—or something close to it—was the last thing Taras K. Castle, my best friend and one of the greatest science fiction minds of the twenty-first century, ever said.

Afterword: O Captain, Our Captain

Dear reader, although you didn't know Taras as I did—as his roommate, confidant, muse, and above all friend—you know him in a no less important way: through his words. You've felt the artistic fires that burned inside him. I'm sure they singed your soul as they did so many others. I invite you to take as much time as you need to mourn him. This book will be here whenever those days or weeks are up.

Now that you are back, allow me to clear the air. Taras's death was a tragic accident. None can deny, despite whatever rumors may swirl online. As I've shown in this heavily researched volume, Taras was dealing with an inordinate amount of stress that, combined with alcohol, cannabis, and likely undiagnosed mental health issues, formed the tragedy. There is no evidence to the contrary.

That said, it was impossible to work on this volume with my apartment a crime scene and jackbooted police officers stomping around the roof with no concern for a scholar's toil. Plus, their incessant questioning and my own trauma at walking by the site of his death every day. In my panic, I made a hasty decision. I left town. I grabbed my laptop, my large stack of *Star Rot Chronicles* files, Arthur (who had flown down when the ambulance arrived), and the keys to Taras's Toyota Corolla. He had many times stressed that I could "borrow it whenever you need, dude," and I see no legal or ethical reason why this request should not be honored posthumously. I fled north.

I had to leave. Leave the others and OrbCon and the apartment in the city and the ghost of my best friend. All of it.

I drove for hours up tree-lined highways beneath the pale gray nebula clouds. Hours speeding past soaring transmission towers like strange pillars of an ancient civilization. One black road turned into another in an unending paved labyrinth. My mind a blank page. All the words that appeared were instantly deleted. I pushed onward through instinct. I pressed the pedal as far as it would go. Crowded highways turned into strip-mall streets and then to dusty backwoods roads. Finally, I arrived.

It was late at night. I turned off the car's lights and rolled slowly up the gravel driveway. No lights on. A family of deer watched me from the edge of the woods, leaping away when I parked. I was home.

Not my technical home. My spiritual home. I found the back-door key under a whimsical meditating garden gnome. I headed downstairs to this basement where I had spent countless hours of my childhood, playing video games, painting Warhammer figurines, and knocking around Ping-Pong balls with my best friend. 358 Ballard Lane. The Castle House.

I want to extend my gratitude to Anton and Olena Castle for providing me (albeit unknowingly) with this workspace while they were in New York City planning a funeral. Taras is gone. He was lowered into the ground a few hours ago as I hurried to finish this volume before any of the other Orb 4 members could upload their own version filled with lies and prevarications. You can be assured that with this volume you get the truth. The definitive, canonical truth.

It was a gamble to come here. A journey filled with perils and pitfalls. Would the key be in the same location? Would there be food in the fridge? Would the Wi-Fi password be written on a note card taped to the refrigerator? Luckily, the answer to every question was yes. The very fabric of the universe conspired to help me complete this book.

I have one more document to share with you, one that I only just acquired. While sneaking a Diet Coke from the fridge—a bit of thirst-quenching before the final manuscript exertion—I remembered a USPS man had arrived this morning. I retrieved the delivery. The return address was none other than my own apartment. In my tired hallucinations, I thought for a second it was addressed to me. But no. My apartment was the return address. It was for Anton Castle. I sliced it open with a steak knife. Out slid a copy of *Future Attack, Today!—A* Star Rot Chronicles *Zine,* the chapbook Taras and Merlin had made for OrbCon. A handwritten note was taped to the cover.

> *Hey Dad,*
>
> *I thought you might enjoy these. They're just some stories I've been working on with friends. I still have the stack of science fiction books you gave me. The Left Hand of Darkness. Cat's Cradle. Neuromancer. Those books made me want to be a writer. Do you remember the sci-fi stories you used to make up for me when I was little? And for Sacha, when he was still here? The snow would be piling up outside and our fire would roar like an alien beast. Mom would bring us plates of saltines with peanut butter and two mugs of hot cocoa. You'd toss a blanket around us and tell us about distant, impossible realms. I've been searching for that feeling for a long, long time.*
>
> *I don't think I'm going to be a famous author like I'd hoped. Not sure I care about that anymore. But I made something. Thank you for believing in me. And for everything.*
>
> *T.*

At least that is what I could make out. Taras's handwriting was messy in the best of times, even without my tears smudging the ink.

We reach our final pages, my faithful reader. At this point, I'm operating on fewer than five cumulative hours of sleep. My birthday appeared and vanished in the blur of my scholarship. I celebrated with a match stuck in a scavenged Pop-Tart. I haven't eaten a proper or properly cooked meal in days. Keeping my eyes open is a Sisyphean task. My fingers keep twitching and hitting the wrong keys. Yet I'd live in this half-alive state for a hundred years if it would rewind time and return Taras to this world.

In an alternate timeline, Taras is alive and we're laughing on the couch with Merlin. Maybe Darya is there too, putting on some music. Jane, even. (I may as well be generous in fantasy.) All the Orb 4 together. They're cooking up a new story. A *SRC* #10 that I will then analyze with my usual rigor and insight. We're sitting around my apartment, slices of pizza cooling in their cardboard boxes, seltzer cans littering the table, and the five of us all laughing and talking and creating art.

Sadly, I am trapped in this timeline.

There is a theory of our universe that says the Big Bang that started existence will be ended by a Big Crunch. Everything began at a single point that expanded outward and then, like a rubber band stretched to its limit, it will snap back. All matter smashing together in an existence-wide density. The end. In an instant, the end. In the case of *The Star Rot Chronicles,* this point was the death of my brilliant friend. Now he has gone, and the Metallic Realms have ended. No more canonical stories will ever appear.

However, I have taken the liberty of closing this volume with my own attempt to finish the unfinished final tale. I will include it after this afterword. It is decidedly noncanonical. Still. I believe it is the kind of ending that Taras would have wanted.

I dedicate this final entry to his memory.

Memoirs of My Metallic Realms—Part III: The Adventure Never Ends!

*S*ing in me, universe, and through me tell the tale of that aquatic explorer with great skill stats, the pilot, lost in the void of space after he plundered the four corners of the Metallic Realms with his friends . . .

Aul-Wick floated in the black depths of the void. It was dark outside his orb, but darker still in Aul-Wick's soul. He'd left his friends. Baldwin had accused him of treachery. Yet he was not a traitor. It tortured him to know his friends did not see his cold-blooded heart was made of solid gold!

He was surrounded by rubble. His longtime home, the good ship *Star Rot*, had been reduced to debris. As Aul-Wick wept, his tears mixed with the waters that housed him. In this literal orb of sadness, he rocketed as fast as his neutron thrusters would take him toward the rendezvous point. Hidden from *Stellar Decay*'s sight by a large asteroid, he waited. His fishy guts roiled nervously. He could not be sure his call would be answered.

But it was!

A brief, dazzling burst of cerulean energy as a small sphere emerged from warp. The ship in front of him was a larger version of his escape pod with a more powerful set of thrusters on the back and twin laser cannons on the sides. The new orb hailed Aul-Wick's.

"Aul-Wick, I am known as Zill-Tar. I heard your distress call."

"Thank you for coming."

Zill-Tar nodded. "How could I not? As you know, you have been sending regular reports of your travels with the *Star Rot* into the ether of space using your telepathic powers. What you may not realize is not only have your tales of daring and adventure been heard—they've traveled long and far across the galaxy. We have become enchanted by your journeys. Mesmerized by your accounts. Each new report is retransmitted telepathically by any Elosic Salamander who hears, bouncing across the galaxy in a daisy chain of story sharing. At this point, we have come to know you and your fellow crew—the stoic and heroic Captain Baldwin, the bold and brash Vivian, the ingenious and sui generis Algorithm, the shifting and skillful Ibbet—as well as we know ourselves. We cheer on your dreams and root against the obstacles in your way. We are, in short, fans."

"Does this mean others are coming?"

"See for yourself."

More bursts of blue light. Zip. Zap. Zoom. Orbs appeared in growing numbers. Dozens of them cracking through the warp rifts and hailing Aul-Wick to celebrate his adventures. "Aul-Wick, we love and admire you!" "Aul-Wick, you have no idea how many of us have been moved by your tales!" "When Aul-Wick calls for aid, we answer!" Aul-Wick wept once more in his orb, but now it was tears of joy that dissipated into the waters.

See, before Ear Baldwin and Finger Vivian revealed themselves, Aul-Wick had sniffed a diabolical miasma. Nanobots! (He could smell all that entered his waters with his enhanced aqua-senses.) The nanobots were programmed to make the crew hate each other. Such trickery would never work on Aul-Wick. His species evolved in the frigid waters of a distant planet and shared little genetic overlap with his air-breather friends on the *Star Rot*. Yet he had to play along while devising a plan. How could he save the ship? His only hope was that someone out there had been listening to the tales of adventure he meticulously recorded and shared. When the *Star Rot* passed a solar relay station, he used his telekinetic-telepathy abilities to transmit an SOS across the surrounding solar systems.

No one else on the crew noticed. Indeed, Aul-Wick did many things behind the scenes to help the *Star Rot* crew that no one commented on. He didn't need acknowledgment. He was happy to be the secret glue holding the crew together. It was the collective success he cared about.

The salamander warriors peppered him with questions about his exploits. "Is it true you single-handedly saved the crew by piloting out of the vlorp's belly?" "Just how powerful are the *Star Rot's* thrusters?" "What's Captain Baldwin *really* like?"

"My friends, please listen!" Aul-Wick said. "There will be time for Qs and As later. Right now, the iniquitous ship and its diabolical crew are searching for my good and noble friends. We must work together to save the crew so the adventures can continue."

"Lead us, Aul-Wick, we are ready."

Aul-Wick grinned as he explained the plan.

When the group navigated around the asteroid, they assembled into a circle of ships. Using his telekinetic-telepathy, Aul-Wick coordinated their laser cannons to fire on one single spot. "On my command!" Then, "Blast 'em!" The concentrated, united laser beams of *Star Rot* devotees destroyed the force field of the *Stellar Decay*. Aul-Wick flew inside the smoldering hole, revenge on his mind. The *Stellar Decay's* sirens blared. At the end of the hallway, Ear Baldwin and Finger Vivian emerged wearing red space suits.

"What? Not you!" Ear Baldwin pointed an ear-speckled hand at Aul-Wick. "We thought you were done for. And done for you shall be forthwith!"

"I think you'll find that it is you who will be forthwithed, fiendish clone of my friend," Aul-wick said.

"Smelly fish-faced fool. You alone can't stop us—" Finger Vivian began to say. Then she gasped. "Oh no!"

A horde of orbs flew into the ship and surrounded Aul-Wick. "You're right," Aul-Wick said. "Alone I couldn't stop you. But together? We can do *anything*."

The *Stellar Decay* loomed over Captain Baldwin. He looked up at the ship from where he floated in the void, eyes wide with terror.

"You won, damnit, Ear Baldwin. You won. Let me die in peace," he said, trying to scoot away with his suit's tiny boot thrusters.

"No," came the response. "*We* won."

Baldwin froze. He slowly turned. "Aul-Wick? Aul-Wick, is that truly you?"

The *Stellar Decay* was laid out identically to the *Star Rot*. Aul-Wick had needed no time to learn the controls. "I'm picking you up, friend. Everyone else is here. We had to smash up the ship a bit to get inside, so the lower decks are sealed off for now. Still, the ship is operational. Your tormentors are in the brig, awaiting your judgment."

"Who are those spherical ships glimmering in the distance?"

"Those," Aul-Wick said, "are our fans."

The tractor beam pulled Baldwin safely into the ship. "Wow. I can't believe it. Except I can. I knew your fish-brained stubbornness would never give up." Baldwin laughed and hugged his rescued crew. "Algorithm! Ibby!" Everyone cheered and danced around. He turned to Aul-Wick, his face pale. "Wait. Where's Vivian? Is she okay?"

"I'm doing fine, sailor," Vivian said from the doorway where she was leaning. She strode across the bridge and planted her lips on his. They embraced romantically.

Baldwin strode around the bridge of the *Stellar Decay*, taking it in. It was exactly like the old bridge of the *Star Rot*, except all the colors were inverted. Red lights were now green, black chairs now white. Otherwise, it was the same ship and could carry them forward to new, exciting voyages.

Everyone moved to their positions. Baldwin surveyed the scene and wiped his eyes. On the way to his captain's chair, he stopped at Aul-Wick's station. He bent down so their faces were side by side. He put a hand on the orb and whispered, "Listen, just this once, do you want to sit in the captain's chair? You saved us. You were the true MVP and S-Tier crew member this day."

"No," Aul-Wick said. "That's your chair. I'm right where I'm supposed to be."

Baldwin smiled, big and wide. "Together again, old friend."

"Together forever." Aul-Wick revved the ship's engines. "Now let's blast off so the adventure never ends!"

After-Afterword: A Dream of Infinity

While in our hearts the voyages of the *Star Rot* may never end, this book in your hands, I regret to say, must. The final lines approach. Those relentless, immovable words: the end. It's been a strange journey for both of us. You, dear reader, have zigzagged back and forth across a science fiction galaxy filled with wonders, horrors, aliens, and interstellar empires. And I have pinballed around the equally complex galaxy of my memories, from the snowy childhood in suburban Vermont to the futuristic metropolis of Brooklyn.

Perhaps it is my exhausted yet triumphant state, but I feel the world vibrating. A tear appears in the white sky outside, ripping across the horizon, and the future seems to spill through the slit. I see visions. How Darya will mourn deeply, and then years from now marry a nonprofit lawyer and move to Long Island, or perhaps New Jersey, to raise a family. She will give up writing but never cosplaying and eventually create a successful line of science-themed youth clothing. And I see Merlin in Maine, sipping cocoa by the sea with Sam. They have returned to social media and begun a beloved webcomic series based on Frankenstein: The Gathering that is adapted by Netflix as an adult animated show. It runs for one season. As for Jane? Her novel is released to tepid sales yet strong enough reviews to secure a second book deal for a fictionalized version of her life involving the multiverse. *Jane, Jane, and the Other Jane* will be marketed as the first "speculative-autofiction novel" and garner a finalist spot for the National Book Award—no, wait, the PEN/Faulkner—and help Jane secure a tenure-track job at Sarah Lawrence College.

I'm warmed by these premonitions of my once friends. I cheer for them, despite everything. But there is a great sadness too as I see there is only a dank, black, and hateful cloud of nothing where Taras's future should be. My own future is equally cloudy. I'm shown nothing. The sky repairs itself. Reality returns.

I must now lay down the final sentences of this volume. Then allow the computer programs to format, upload, and distribute it around the world for both ebooks and print-on-demand copies. There are no more *Star Rot* tales to analyze. This is fortuitous for your humble scholar. Time runs short. Just now, my computer pinged, causing Arthur to wake with a screech. It's a text in the Castle family group chat. (In my official capacity as Senior Lore Keeper, I temporarily commandeered Taras's cell phone from the sidewalk beside his body. It was cracked, but in working order. I was able to clone the messages to my computer before departing.) His parents are driving back to Vermont now, back to this house. Good taste advocates I make myself scarce so they may grieve in private.

It pains me to have missed his funeral. Yet here, surrounded by the objects of our shared childhood, I can grieve for him in my own way: through my scholarship. And through this I can give Taras more life.

While I assume those of you with taste and discernment are as captivated by these marvelous tales as I have been, I recognize that certain cynics will claim that on some "technical" level the preceding stories do not rate as highly among the pantheon of science fiction as I've suggested. That is your right. Art is subjective. Even Shakespeare is besmirched with one-star reviews on Goodreads. And we will never know the great works that disappear every day into the black holes of submission queues and agent email inboxes. That is precisely the reason that I have written this volume. I cannot let Taras's life's work disappear. It is all I have left of him. I won't allow it to simply be wiped away like some smudge by the indifferent hand of time. No. I will slap that hand away until my dying breaths.

The artist never truly dies, not if their art lives on.

Taras, there is no elixir of life to give you. No necromancy spell nor cloning machine nor time-travel device to send me back in time and undo this tragedy. Yet I can give you this one taste of immortality. I can give you this volume.

I don't know where I'll go next. All that awaits me in Brooklyn is death and credit card debt. My parents moved to the suburbs of Boston years ago and anyway would not understand the choices I made. That I had to make. Sometimes I can't help but feel like Algorithm in "Checkmate of the Mind," as if I too were but a fictional character scripted by the warped whims of some deranged and scribbling author-god. I will have to discover my life story one chapter at a time.

Yet while I may not know what my future holds, I have hope. Because I have characters who inspire me. Bold characters. Dashing characters. Characters who are ready to face any challenge that arises in a world of wonder, meaning, and adventure. I have the crew of the good ship *Star Rot* and the entire Metallic Realms.

And now you do too.

Acknowledgments

Although I will attempt to use fewer adjectives and adverbs than Michael Lincoln, there are many people I must thank for their help and friendship during my time writing this novel. I am immensely, fully, and lastingly thankful to my fearsome agent, Angeline Rodriguez at WME, and my excellent editor, Sean deLone at Atria Books. I am forever in debt for the sharp insights and encouragement on early drafts from Ryan Chapman, Theo Gangi, Mika Kasuga, Helen Phillips, John Dermot Woods, and Adrian Van Young. Thank you to Brian Merchant and *Terraform* for publishing an early version of "The Duchy of the Toe Adam." Thank you to all my friends and colleagues for your fellowship, conversation, and willingness to listen to me spitball and/ or grumble.

Boundless gratitude to everyone from Atria Books who worked on this novel including Danielle Mazzella di Bosco for the eye-catching cover design; Lexy East for the lovely page design; Annette Szlachta-McGinn, Diane Shanley, and Megha Jain for their careful attention to the manuscript; Sonja Singleton, Lacee Burr, and Paige Lytle for shepherding this book through production; Camila Araujo for publicity; and Dayna Johnson for marketing. Thank you again to my editor Sean deLone and publisher Libby McGuire for taking a chance on this strange novel.

I must give both thanks and apologies to the artists riffed on or referenced in the novel, especially Vladamir Nabokov, Ursula K. Le Guin, everyone behind Star Trek (in particular *The Next Generation*), and Italo Calvino. I could list many others whose aesthetic genes found their way into the DNA of this novel. All art springs from other art, and I am in endless debt to the authors whose works opened my eyes to new horizons.

I should also acknowledge "Taras Castle," a pen name and persona I used as a younger writer with an odd—and rightly abandoned—plan for a science fiction poetry cycle. A few of those pseudonymous pieces exist in the pages of old magazines that are perhaps collecting dust on the shelves of used bookstores somewhere. Though I gave up the project, Taras Castle stuck with me as a sort of darling alter ego. And you know what they say to do with your darlings . . .

Thank you always to my mother, father, and brother, and to the Kasugas. Thank you in all things and all ways to my brilliant wife, Mika. My universe is ever-expanding with you inside it.

And lastly, infinite thanks to you, dear reader. No story truly exists except in the mind of a reader. Thank you for devoting part of your finite existence on this small rock spinning through the cold and lonely void of space to read these words.